SHE LOVES [image_ref] ...T, SHE LOVES [image_ref] ...!!!

Eight large ships ....darkness between the s.... that was their sea, and began to move about the planet Noorhut in a carefully timed pattern of orbits. They stayed much too far out to permit any instrument of space-detection to suspect that the Noorhut might be their common center of interest. Though the men who crewed the eight ships bore the people of Noorhut no ill will, hardly anything could have looked less promising for Noorhut than the cargo they had on board.

Seven of them were armed with a gas which was not often used any more. A highly volatile lethal catalyst, it sank to the solid surface of a world over which it was freed and spread out swiftly there to the point where its presence could no longer be detected by any chemical means. However its effect of drawing the final breath almost imperceptibly out of all things that were oxygen-breathing was not noticeably reduced by diffusion.

The eighth ship was equipped with a brace of torpedoes, which were normally released some hours after the gas-carriers dispersed their invisible death. They were quite small torpedoes, since the only task remaining for them would be to ignite the surface of the planet that had been treated with the catalyst.

All those things might presently happen to Noorhut. But they would happen only if a specific message was flashed from it to the circling squadron—the message that Noorhut already was lost to a deadly foe who must, at any cost now, be prevented from spreading out from it to other inhabited worlds.

AGENT OF VEGA
& Other Stories

JAMES H. SCHMITZ

EDITED BY ERIC FLINT & GUY GORDON

Agent of Vega & Other Stories

"Agent of Vega" was first published in *Astounding Science Fiction*, July 1949. "The Illusionists" was first published in *Astounding Science Fiction*, in March 1951, under the title "Space Fear." "The Second Night of Summer" was first published in *Galaxy*, December 1950. "The Truth About Cushgar" was first published in *Astounding Science Fiction*, November 1950. (The four Agent of Vega stories were first collected and issued in book form under that title by Gnome Press in 1960.) "The Custodians" was first published in *Astounding Science Fiction*, December 1968. "Gone Fishing" was first published in *Astounding Science Fiction*, May 1961. "The Beacon to Elsewhere" was first published in *Amazing*, April 1963. "The End of the Line" was first published in *Astounding Science Fiction*, July 1951. "Watch the Sky" was first published in *Astounding Science Fiction*, August 1962. "Greenface" was first published in *Unknown*, August 1943. "Rogue Psi" was first published in *Amazing*, August 1962.

A Baen Books Original

Baen Publishing Enterprises
P.O. Box 1403
Riverdale, NY 10471
www.baen.com

ISBN: 0-671-31847-0

Cover art by Bob Eggleton

First printing, November 2001

Distributed by Simon & Schuster
1230 Avenue of the Americas
New York, NY 10020

Production by Windhaven Press, Auburn, NH
Printed in the United States of America

CONTENTS

"*That* was an epiphany. . . ."

Mercedes Lackey

There's a commercial on cable stations lately that talks about moments of epiphany—moments when you understand something that changes your life.

I've had at least one of those moments—and when it was over, my life had been changed forever.

It was when, when I was eleven or thereabouts, I went looking in the living room for something to read.

Now, in my house, books were everywhere and there was very little my brother and I were forbidden to read. We both had library cards as soon as we got past "Run, Spot, run," and by the time I was nine I was coming home with armloads of books every week and still running out of things to read before the week was over.

By the time I was ten, I had special permission to take books out of the adult section—yes, in those dark days, you needed a permission slip from your parents to read things that weren't in the children's section.

Now, the peculiar thing here is that although I read anything that looked like a fairy-tale and every piece of historical fiction I could find, I hadn't discovered classic juvenile science fiction. I can't think *why*—unless it was because my library didn't have any. It was a very small branch library, and I hadn't yet learned that you could request anything that was in the card-catalog for the whole county-wide system. It might also have been because my branch library had helpfully segregated the juvenile section into "Boys" and "Girls," and I wasn't brave enough to cross the invisible line-of-death dividing the two. I do recall reading two little books called *Space Cat* and *Space Cat Meets Mars* and loving them—and also something called *City Under the Back Steps* about a kid who gets shrunk and joins an ant colony—but that was in a different library, before we moved, and perhaps the books hadn't been so helpfully segregated there. Be that as it may, although I was knee-deep in the historical novels of Anya Seton and Rosemary Sutcliff by then, I hadn't ventured into the adult Science Fiction section. I hadn't fallen headfirst into Andre Norton's myriad worlds, I hadn't joined Heinlein's resourceful heroes, I hadn't discovered Anderson, Asimov, Clarke, Nourse, Simak. . . .

All that was about to change. Because my father *had*.

My father was a science fiction reader; in our house, where library books were everywhere, it was my father who bought the paperbacks. They were divided pretty equally in thirds—suspense (including spy-novels), war, and science fiction.

It was the start of summer vacation, I had already bored through my stack of nine books, and we weren't going back to the library for another two days. I was desperate. I ventured into the living room, and picked up James Schmidt's *Agent of Vega*.

I'm not sure why. It certainly wasn't the cover—in those days, science fiction books were sporting rather odd abstract paintings—possibly trying to divorce themselves from the Bug Eyed Monsters of the pulp covers so that they could be taken Seriously. That wasn't going to happen, not in the Sixties, but you couldn't fault the editors for trying. It wasn't the title—I hadn't a clue what, or who, Vega was, and I wasn't interested in the James Bond books (yet) that featured the only other "agent" I knew of. Perhaps it was just desperation. I asked politely if I could read it, was granted permission, and trotted away to my room with my prize.

Five minutes later, it was true love.

It was an epiphany.

Here was everything I had been looking for—exotic settings, thrills, adventure, *heroines* who were just as resourceful and brave as the heroes, and something more. There was a magic in the words, but there was more than that. It was *imagination*.

No one, *no one*, since my fairy-tales, had written like this. This James Schmitz fellow seemed as familiar with androids and alien planets as I was with the ice-cream man and the streets of my home town.

And here, for the first time, I encountered *psionics*.

Psi! There was even an abbreviation for it! Telepathy! Telekinesis! Teleportation! Empathy! Precognition!

Oh, these were words to conjure with! Better than the magic of the fairy-tales, these were *scientific* which meant that someone, somewhere (oh let it be me! Me!) might find a way to get one of these powers for himself!

Much has been made of the "sense of wonder" that

science fiction evokes, and believe me, there was
nothing to evoke that sense quite like the worlds of
James Schmitz. *Especially* for someone who had never
read anything like this before. The man had the right
stuff; no doubt of it. By the time that I was done with
that book, I was well and truly hooked.

And my life had just taken that irrevocable,
epiphanal change.

There was no going back; when we got to the library,
I flew to the science fiction section, and (once I had
cleaned out the Schmitz) proceeded to work my way
down the alphabet. I did the same in the school library
(earning some peculiar looks from the librarian, I can
tell you, since girls weren't supposed to like science
fiction). Shortly after that, I discovered that there were
whole stores devoted *just to books*—I had always lived
in suburbs, and back in those days, there weren't Malls.
There were a few—a very few—strip-malls, few of
which devoted any space to anything other than stores
with "Boutique" in the name, and there were no real
chain bookstores. But we went to Chicago for dental
and optometrist appointments, and there in Chicago
were *bookstores*.

And after *that*, thanks to the helpful little bits in
the back of the books (oh, Ace Doubles! *two* books—
all right, novellas—for the price of one!) I learned that
you could actually *order books from the company*.

Bliss limited only by my allowance!

But my allowance didn't allow me to buy all the
books I craved, nor did the librarian oblige by ordering nothing but science fiction with the meager bud-
get allocated to her. So, there was nothing for it.

I had to write my own.

Now, I never would have come to *this* moment, if
not (again) for James Schmitz. The novels arranged in
their imposing hard covers on the library shelves could

not possibly have been written by mere human beings, right? I couldn't aspire to *that*. (Even if the dust jackets had actually featured any information about the authors, thus removing them to the realms of mortals, the librarian had helpfully taken them off because "they always got torn and dirty.") But there was lots of information on the paperback covers—and more, *much* more about those authors in the science fiction *magazines* I had discovered in the local drugstore! Why, they even argued with each other in the letter columns, sounding exactly like myself and my little brother in the midst of a squabble! Yes indeed, these books were written by human beings just like me. If they could write books, so could I.

So, thanks to James Schmitz, I became an author—first an under-the-bed author (who hid my notebooks full of illustrated stories under the bed where my brother wouldn't find them), then turning in my stories to high-school literary contests, then writing as a hobby in college—*then* writing fanfic and actually getting published (!!!).

And then, finally, actually, making the big leap into Professional Status.

Through it all, the memory of that book, that moment, has stayed with me. The sense of wonder and excitement has never faded, and never will.

Thank you, James Schmitz, wherever you are.

And thank *you*, Eric Flint and Jim Baen, for bringing his Right Stuff back again. Maybe some other kid, desperate for something to read, will have an epiphany of his or her own.

THE CONFEDERACY
OF VEGA

Agent of Vega

❧

"It just happens," the Third Co-ordinator of the Vegan Confederacy explained patiently, "that the local Agent—it's Zone Seventeen Eighty-two—isn't available at the moment. In fact, he isn't expected to contact this HQ for at least another week. And since the matter really needs prompt attention, and you happened to be passing within convenient range of the spot, I thought of you."

"I like these little extra jobs I get whenever you think of me," commented the figure in the telepath transmitter before him. It was that of a small, wiry man with rather cold yellow eyes—sitting against an undefined dark background, he might have been a minor criminal or the skipper of an aging space-tramp.

"After the last two of them, as I recall it," he continued pointedly, "I turned in my final mission report from the emergency treatment tank of my ship—And if you'll remember, I'd have been back in my own Zone by now if you hadn't sent me chasing a wild-eyed rumor in this direction!"

He leaned forward with an obviously false air of hopeful anticipation. "Now this wouldn't just possibly be another hot lead on U-1, would it?"

"No, no! Nothing like that!" the Co-ordinator said soothingly. In his mental file the little man was listed as "Zone Agent Iliff, Zone Thirty-six Oh-six; unrestricted utility; try not to irritate—" There was a good deal more of it, including the notation:

"U-1: The Agent's failure-shock regarding this subject has been developed over the past twelve-year period into a settled fear-fix of prime-motive proportions. The Agent may now be entrusted with the conclusion of this case, whenever the opportunity is presented."

That was no paradox to the Co-ordinator who, as Chief of the Department of Galactic Zones, was Iliff's immediate superior. He knew the peculiar qualities of his agents—and how to make the most economical use of them, while they lasted.

"It's my own opinion," he offered cheerily, "that U-1 has been dead for years. Though I'll admit Correlation doesn't agree with me there."

"Correlation's often right," Iliff remarked, still watchfully. He added, "U-1 appeared excessively healthy the last time I got near him."

"Well, that was twelve standard years ago," the Co-ordinator murmured. "If he were still around, he'd have taken a bite out of us before this—a big bite! Just to tell us he doesn't think the Galaxy is quite wide enough for him and the Confederacy both. He's not the type to lie low longer than he has to." He paused. "Or do you think you might have shaken some of his supremacy ideas out of him that last time?"

"Not likely," said Iliff. The voice that came from the transmitter, the thought that carried it, were equally impassive. "He booby-trapped me good. To him it wouldn't even have seemed like a fight."

The Co-ordinator shrugged. "Well, there you are! Anyway, this isn't that kind of job at all. It's actually a rather simple assignment."

Iliff winced.

"No, I mean it! What this job takes is mostly tact— always one of your strongest points, Iliff."

The statement was not entirely true; but the Agent ignored it and the Co-ordinator went on serenely:

". . . so I've homed you full information on the case. Your ship should pick it up in an hour, but you might have questions; so here it is, in brief:

"Two weeks ago, the Bureau of Interstellar Crime sends an operative to a planet called Gull in Seventeen Eighty-two—that's a mono-planet system near Lycanno, just a bit off your present route. You been through that neighborhood before?"

Iliff blinked yellow eyes and produced a memory. "We went through Lycanno once. Seventeen or eighteen Habitables; population A-Class Human; Class D politics—How far is Gull from there?"

"Eighteen hours' cruising speed, or a little less—but you're closer to it than that right now. This operative was to make positive identification of some ex-spacer called Tahmey, who'd been reported there, and dispose of him. Routine interstellar stuff, *but*—twenty-four hours ago, the operative sends back a message that she finds positive identification impossible . . . and that she wants a Zone Agent."

He looked expectantly at Iliff. Both of them knew perfectly well that the execution of a retired piratical spacer was no part of a Zone Agent's job—furthermore, that every Interstellar operative was aware of the fact; and finally, that such a request should have induced the Bureau to recall its operative for an immediate

mental overhaul and several months' vacation before
he or she could be risked on another job.

"Give," Iliff suggested patiently.

"The difference," the Co-ordinator explained, "is that
the operative is one of our Lannai trainees."

"I see," said the Agent.

He did. The Lannai were high type humanoids and
the first people of their classification to be invited to
join the Vegan Confederacy—till then open only to
Homo sapiens and the interesting variety of mutant
branches of that old Terrestrial stock.

The invitation had been sponsored, against formidable opposition, by the Department of Galactic Zones,
with the obvious intention of having the same privilege extended later to as many humanoids and other
nonhuman races as could meet the Confederacy's
general standards.

As usual, the Department's motive was practical
enough. Its king-sized job was to keep the eighteen
thousand individual civilizations so far registered in its
Zones out of as much dangerous trouble as it could,
while nudging them unobtrusively, whenever the occasion was offered, just a little farther into the path of
righteousness and order.

It was slow, dangerous, carefully unspectacular
work, since it violated, in fact and in spirit, every
galactic treaty of nonintervention the Confederacy
had ever signed. Worst of all, it was work for which
the Department was, of necessity, monstrously under-
staffed.

The more political systems, races and civilizations
it could draw directly into the Confederacy, the
fewer it would have to keep under that desperately
sketchy kind of supervision. Regulations of
membership in Vega's super-system were interpreted

broadly, but even so they pretty well precluded any dangerous degree of deviation from the ideals that Vega championed.

And if, as a further consequence, Galactic Zones could then draw freely on the often startling abilities and talents of nonhuman peoples to aid in its titanic project—

The Department figuratively licked its chops.

The opposition was sufficiently rooted in old racial emotions to be extremely bitter and strong. The Traditionalists, working chiefly through the Confederacy's Department of Cultures, wanted no dealings with any race which could not trace its lineage back through the long centuries to Terra itself. Nonhumans had played a significant part in the century-long savage struggles that weakened and finally shattered the first human Galactic Empire.

That mankind, as usual, had asked for it and that its grimmest and most powerful enemies were to be found nowadays among those who could and did claim the same distant Earth-parentage did not noticeably weaken the old argument, which to date had automatically excluded any other stock from membership. In the High Council of the Confederacy, the Department of Cultures, backed by a conservative majority of the Confederacy's members, had, naturally enough, tremendous influence.

Galactic Zones, however—though not one citizen in fifty thousand knew of its existence, and though its arguments could not be openly advanced—had a trifle more.

So the Lannai were in—on probation.

"As you may have surmised," the Third Co-ordinator said glumly, "the Lannai haven't exactly been breaking their necks trying to get in with us, either. In fact, *their* government's had to work for the alliance against almost the same degree of popular disapproval; though on the whole they seem to be a rather more reasonable sort of people than we are. Highly developed natural telepaths, you know—that always seems to make folks a little easier to get along with."

"What's this one doing in Interstellar?" Iliff inquired.

"We've placed a few Lannai in almost every department of the government by now—not, of course, in Galactic Zones! The idea is to prove, to our people and theirs, that Lannai and humans can work for the same goal, share responsibilities, and so on. To prove generally that we're natural allies."

"Has it been proved?"

"Too early to say. They're bright enough and, of course, the ones they sent us were hand-picked and anxious to make good. This Interstellar operative looked like one of the best. She's a kind of relative of the fifth ranking Lannai ruler. That's what would make it bad if it turned out she'd blown up under stress. For one thing, their pride could be hurt enough to make them bolt the alliance. But our Traditionalists certainly would be bound to hear about it, and," the Co-ordinator concluded heatedly, "the Co-ordinator of Cultures would be rising to his big feet again on the subject in Council!"

"An awkward situation, sir," Iliff sympathized, "demanding a great deal of tact. But then you have that."

"I've got it," agreed the Co-ordinator, "but I'd prefer not to have to use it so much. So if you can find some way of handling that little affair on Gull discreetly— Incidentally, since you'll be just a short run then from Lycanno, there's an undesirable political trend reported building up there. They've dropped from D to H-Class politics inside of a decade. You'll find the local Agent's notes on the matter waiting for you on Gull. Perhaps you might as well skip over and fix it."

"All right," said Iliff coldly. "I won't be needed back in my own Zone for another hundred hours. Not urgently."

"Lab's got a new mind-lock for you to test," the Co-ordinator went on briskly. "You'll find that on Gull, too."

There was a slight pause.

"You remember, don't you," the Agent inquired gently then, as if speaking to an erring child, "what happened the last time I gave one of those gadgets a field test on a highpowered brain?"

"Yes, of course! But if this one *works*," the Co-ordinator pointed out, almost wistfully, "we've got something we really do need. And until I know it does work, under ultimate stresses, I can't give it general distribution. I've picked a hundred of you to try it out." He sighed. "Theoretically, it will hold a mind of any conceivable potential within that mind's own shields, under any conceivable stress, and still permit almost normal investigation. It's been checked to the limit," he concluded encouragingly, "under lab conditions—"

"They all were," Iliff recollected, without noticeable enthusiasm. "Well, I'll see what turns up."

"That's fine!" The Co-ordinator brightened visibly. He added, "We wouldn't, of course, want you to take any *unnecessary* risks—"

For perhaps half a minute after the visualization tank of his telepath transmitter had faded back to its normal translucent and faintly luminous green, Iliff continued to stare into it.

Back on Jeltad, the capitol planet of the Confederacy, fourteen thousand light-years away, the Co-ordinator's attention was turning to some other infinitesimal-seeming but significant crisis in the

Department's monstrous periphery. The chances were he would not think of Iliff again, or of Zone Seventeen Eighty-two, until Iliff's final mission report came in—or failed to come in within the period already allotted it by the Department's automatic monitors.

In either event, the brain screened by the Coordinator's conversational inanities would revert once more to that specific problem then, for as many unhurried seconds, minutes or, it might be, hours as it required. It was one of the three or four human brains in the galaxy for which Zone Agent Iliff had ever felt anything remotely approaching genuine respect.

"How far are we from Gull now?" he said without turning his head.

A voice seemed to form itself in the air a trifle above and behind him.

"A little over eight hours, cruising speed—"

"As soon as I get the reports off the pigeon from Jeltad, step it up so we get there in four," Iliff said. "I think I'll be ready about that time."

"The pigeon just arrived," the voice replied. It was not loud, but it was a curiously *big* voice with something of the overtones of an enormous bronze gong in it. It was also oddly like a cavernous amplification of Iliff's own type of speech.

The agent turned to a screen on his left, in which a torpedo-like twenty-foot tube of metal had appeared, seemingly suspended in space and spinning slowly about its axis. Actually, it was some five miles from the ship—which was as close as it was healthy to get to a homing pigeon at the end of its voyage—and following it at the ship's exact rate of speed, though it was driven by nothing except an irresistible urge to get to its "roost," the pattern of which had been stamped in its molecules. The roost was on Iliff's ship, but the pigeon would never get there. No one knew just what sort of subdimensions it flashed through on its way to its objective or what changes were wrought on it before it reappeared, but early experiments with the gadget had involved some highly destructive explosions at its first contact with any solid matter in normal space.

So now it was held by barrier at a safe distance while its contents were duplicated within the ship. Then something lethal flickered from the ship to the pigeon and touched it; and it vanished with no outward indication of violence.

For a time, Iliff became immersed in the dossiers provided both by Interstellar and his own department. The ship approached and presently drove through the boundaries of Zone Seventeen Eighty-two, and the big voice murmured:

"Three hours to Gull."

"All right," Iliff said, still absently. "Let's eat."

Nearly another hour passed before he spoke again. "Send her this. Narrow-beam telepath—Gull itself should be close enough, I think. If you can get it through—"

He stood up, yawned, stretched and bent, and straightened again.

"You know," he remarked suddenly, "I wouldn't be a bit surprised if the old girl wasn't so wacky, after all. What I mean is," he explained, "she really might *need* a Zone Agent."

"Is it going to be another unpredictable mission?" the voice inquired.

"Aren't they always—when the man picks them for us? What was *that?*"

There was a moment's silence. Then the voice told him, "She's got your message. She'll be expecting you."

"Fast!" Iliff said approvingly. "Now listen. On Gull, we shall be old Trader Casselmath with his stock of exotic and expensive perfumes. So get yourself messed up for the part—but don't spill any of the stuff, this time."

The suspect's name was Deel. For the past ten years he had been a respected—and respectable—citizen and merchant of the mono-planet System of Gull. He was supposed to have come there from his birthplace, Number Four of the neighboring System of Lycanno.

But the microstructural plates the operative made of him *proved* he was the pirate Tahmey who, very probably, had once been a middling big shot among the ill-famed Ghant Spacers. The Bureau of Interstellar Crime had him on record; and it was a dogma of criminology that microstructural identification was final and absolute—that the telltale patterns could not be duplicated, concealed, or altered to any major degree without killing the organism.

The operative's people, however, were telepaths, and she was an adept, trained in the widest and most intensive use of the faculty. For a Lannai it was natural to check skeptically, in her own manner, the mechanical devices of another race.

If she had not been an expert she would have been caught then, on her first approach. The mind she attempted to tap was guarded.

By whom or what was a question she did not attempt to answer immediately. There were several of these watch-dogs, of varying degrees of ability. Her thought faded away from the edge of their watchfulness before their attention was drawn to it. It slid past them and insinuated itself deftly through the crude electronic thought-shields used by Tahmey. Such shields were a popular commercial article, designed to protect men with only an average degree of mental training against the ordinary telepathic prowler and entirely effective for that purpose. Against her manner of intrusion they were of no use at all.

But it was a shock to discover then that she was in no way within the mind of Tahmey! This was, in literal fact, the mind of the man named Deel—for the past ten years a citizen of Gull, before that of the neighboring System of Lycanno.

The fact was, to her at least, quite as indisputable as the microstructural evidence that contradicted it. This was not some clumsily linked mass of artificial memory tracts and habit traces, but a living, matured mental personality. It showed few signs of even as much psychosurgery as would be normal in a man of Deel's age and circumstances.

But if it *was* Deel, why should anyone keep a prosperous, reasonably honest and totally insignificant planeteer under telepathic surveillance? She considered investigating the unknown watchers, but the aura of cold, implacable alertness she had sensed in her accidental near-contact with them warned her not to force her luck too far.

"After all," she explained apologetically, "I had no way of estimating their potential."

"No," Iliff agreed, "you hadn't. But I don't think that was what stopped you."

The Lannai operative looked at him steadily for a moment. Her name was Pagadan and, though no more human than a jellyfish, she was to human eyes an exquisitely designed creature. It was rather startling to realize that her Interstellar dossier described her as a combat-type mind—which implied a certain ruthlessness, at the very least—and also that she had been sent to Gull to act, among other things, as an executioner.

"Now what did you mean by that?" she inquired, on a note of friendly wonder.

"I meant," Iliff said carefully, "that I'd now like to

hear all the little details you didn't choose to tell
Interstellar. Let's start with your trip to Lycanno."

"Oh, I see!" Pagadan said. "Yes, I went to Lycanno,
of course—" She smiled suddenly and became with
that, he thought, extraordinarily beautiful, though the
huge silvery eyes with their squared black irises, which
widened or narrowed flickeringly with every change of
mood or shift of light, did not conform exactly to any
standard human ideal. No more did her hair, a silver-
shimmering fluffy crest of something like feathers—
but the general effect, Iliff decided, remained somehow
that of a remarkably attractive human woman in permanent fancy dress. According to the reports he'd
studied recently, it had pleased much more conservative tastes than his own.

"You're a clever little man, Zone Agent," she said
thoughtfully. "I believe I might as well be frank with
you. If I'd reported everything I know about this case—
though for reasons I shall tell you I really found out
very little—the Bureau would almost certainly have
recalled me. They show a maddening determination to
see that I shall come to no harm while working for
them." She looked at him doubtfully. "You understand
that, simply because I'm a Lannai, I'm an object of
political importance just now?"

Iliff nodded.

"Very well. I discovered in Lycanno that the case
was a little more than I could handle alone." She
shivered slightly, the black irises flaring wide with what
was probably reminiscent fright.

"But I did not want to be recalled. My people," she
said a little coldly, "will accept the proposed alliance
only if they are to share in your enterprises and responsibilities. They do not wish to be shielded or protected,
and it would have a poor effect on them if they learned
that we, their first representatives among you, had been

relieved of our duties whenever they threatened to involve us in personal danger."

"I see," Iliff said seriously, remembering that she was royalty of a sort, or the Lannai equivalent of it. He shook his head. "The Bureau," he said, "must have quite a time with you."

Pagadan stared and laughed. "No doubt they find me a little difficult at times. Still, I *do* know how to take orders. But in this case it seemed more important to make sure I was not going to be protected again than to appear reasonable and co-operative. So I made use, for the first time, of my special status in the Bureau and insisted that a Zone Agent be sent here. However, I can assure you that the case has developed into an undertaking that actually will require a Zone Agent's peculiar abilities and equipment."

"Well," Iliff shrugged, "it worked and here I am, abilities, equipment and all. What was it you found on Lycanno?"

There was considerable evidence to show that, during the years Tahmey was on record as having been about his criminal activities in space, the man named Deel was living quietly on the fourth planet of the Lycanno System, rarely even venturing beyond its atmospheric limits because of a pronounced and distressing liability to the psychosis of space-fear.

Pagadan gathered this evidence partly from official records, partly and in much greater detail from the unconscious memories of some two hundred people who had been more or less intimately connected with Deel. The investigation appeared to establish his previous existence in Lycanno beyond all reasonable doubt. It did nothing to explain why it should have become merged fantastically with the physical appearance of the pirate Tahmey.

This Deel was remembered as a big, blond, healthy

man, good-natured and shrewd, the various details of his features and personality blurred or exaggerated by the untrained perceptions of those who remembered him. The description, particularly after this lapse of time, could have fitted Tahmey just as well—or just as loosely.

It was as far as she could go along that line. Officialdom was lax in Lycanno, and the precise identification of individual citizens by microstructural images or the like was not practiced. Deel had been born there, matured there, become reasonably successful. Then his business was destroyed by an offended competitor, and it was indicated to him that he would not be permitted to re-establish himself in the System.

He had business connections on Gull; and after undergoing a lengthy and expensive conditioning period against the effects of space-fear, he ventured to make the short trip, and was presently working himself back to a position comfortably near the top on Gull.

That was all. Except that—somewhere along the line—his overall physical resemblance to Tahmey had shifted into absolute physical identity. . . .

"I realize, of course, that the duplication of a living personality in another body is considered almost as impossible as the existence of a microstructural double. But it does seem that Tahmey-Deel has to be one or the other."

"Or," Iliff grunted, "something we haven't thought of yet. This is beginning to look more and more like one of those cases I'd like to forget. Well, what did you do?"

"If there was a biopsychologist in the Lycanno System who had secretly developed a method of personality transfer in some form or other, he was very probably a man of considerable eminence in that line

of work. I began to screen the minds of persons likely
to know of such a man."

"Did you find him?"

She shook her head and grimaced uncomfortably.
"*He* found *me*—at least, I think we can assume it was
he. I assembled some promising leads, a half dozen
names in all, and then—I find this difficult to
describe—from one moment to another I knew I was
being . . . sought . . . by another mind. By a mind of
quite extraordinary power, which seemed fully aware
of my purpose, of the means I was employing—in fact,
of everything except my exact whereabouts at the
moment. It was intended to shock me into revealing
that—simply by showing me, with that jolting abruptness, how very close I stood to being caught."

"And you didn't reveal yourself?"

"No," she laughed nervously. "But I went 'akaba'
instead. I was under it for three days and well on my
way back to Gull when I came out of it—as a passenger
on a commercial ship! Apparently, I had abandoned my
own ship on Lycanno and conducted my escape fault-
lessly and without hesitation. Successfully, at any rate—
But I remember nothing, of course."

"That was quite a brain chasing you then." Iliff
nodded slowly. The akaba condition was a disconcerting
defensive trick which had been played on him on
occasion by members of other telepathic races. The
faculty was common to most of them, completely involuntary, and affected the pursuer more or less as if he
had been closing in on a glow of mental light and
suddenly saw that light vanish without a trace.

The Departmental Lab's theory was that under the
stress of a psychic attack which was about to overwhelm
the individual telepath, a kind of racial Overmind took
over automatically and conducted its member-mind's
escape from the emergency, if that was at all possible,

with complete mechanical efficiency before restoring it to awareness of itself. It was only a theory since the Overmind, if it existed, left no slightest traces of its work—except the brief void of one of the very few forms of complete and irreparable amnesia known. For some reason, as mysterious as the rest of it, the Overmind never intervened if the threatened telepath had been physically located by the pursuer.

They stared at each other thoughtfully for a moment, then smiled at the same instant.

"Do you believe now," Pagadan challenged, "that this task is worthy of the efforts of a Vegan Zone Agent and his shipload of specialists?"

"I've been afraid of that right along," Iliff said without enthusiasm. "But look, you seem to know a lot more about Galactic Zones than you're really supposed to. Like that business about our shipload of specialists—that kind of information is to be distributed only 'at or above Zone Agent levels.' Where did you pick it up?"

"On Jeltad—above Zone Agent levels," Pagadan replied undisturbed. "Quite a bit above, as a matter of fact! The occasion was social. And now that I've put you in your place, when do you intend to investigate Deel? I've become casually acquainted with him and could arrange a meeting at almost any time."

Iliff rubbed his chin. "Well, as to that," he said, "Trader Casselmath dropped in to see a few of Deel's business associates immediately after landing today. They were quite fascinated by the samples of perfume he offered them—he does carry an excellent line of the stuff, you know, though rather high-priced. So Deel turned up too, finally. You'll be interested to hear he's using a new kind of mind-shield now."

She was not surprised. "They were warned, naturally,

from Lycanno. The mentality there knew I had been investigating Deel."

"Well, it shows the Brain wasn't able to identify you too closely, because they're waiting for you to pick up your research at this end again. The shield was hair-triggered to give off some kind of alarm. Old Casselmath couldn't be expected to recognize that, of course. He took a poke at it, innocently enough—just trying to find out how far Deel and company could be swindled."

She leaned forward, eyes gleaming black with excitement. "What happened?"

Iliff shrugged. "Nothing at all obvious. But somebody did come around almost immediately to look Casselmath over. In fact, they pulled his simple mind pretty well wide open, though the old boy never noticed it. Then they knew he was harmless and went away."

Pagadan frowned faintly.

"No," Iliff said, "it wasn't the Brain. These were stooges, though clever ones—probably the same that were on guard when you probed Tahmey-Deel the first time. But they've been alerted now, and I don't think we could do any more investigating around Deel without being spotted. After your experience on Lycanno, it seems pretty likely that the answers are all there, anyway."

She nodded slowly. "That's what I think. So we go to Lycanno!"

Iliff shook his head. "Just one of us goes," he corrected her. And before her flash of resentment could be voiced he added smoothly, "That's for my own safety as much as for yours. The Brain must have worked out a fairly exact pattern of your surface mentality by now. You couldn't get anywhere near him without being discovered. If we're together, that means I'm discovered, too."

She thought it over, shrugged very humanly and admitted, "I suppose you're right. What am I to do?"

"You're to keep a discreet watch—a very discreet watch—on Deel and his guardians. How Deel manages to be Tahmey, or part of him, at the same time is something the Brain's going to have to explain to us; and if he has a guilty conscience, as he probably has, he may decide to let the evidence disappear. In that case, try to keep a line on where they take Deel—but don't, under any circumstances, take any direct action until I get back from Lycanno."

The black-and-silver eyes studied him curiously. "Isn't that likely to be quite a while?" Pagadan inquired—with such nice control that he almost overlooked the fact that this politically important non-human hothead was getting angry again.

"From what we know now of the Brain, he sounds like one of our tougher citizens," he admitted. "Well, yes . . . I might be gone all of two days."

There was a moment of rather tense silence. Then Iliff murmured approvingly:

"See now! I just *knew* you could brake down on that little old temperament."

The Lannai released her breath. "I only hope you're half as good as you think," she said weakly. "But I am almost ready to believe you will do it in two days."

"Oh, I will," Iliff assured her, "with my shipload of specialists." He stood up and looked down at her unsmiling. "So now if you'll give me the information you gathered on those top biopsychologists in Lycanno, I'll be starting."

She nodded amiably. "There are two things I should like to ask you though, before you go. The one is—

why have you been trying to probe through my mind-shields all evening?"

"It's a good thing to find out as much as you can about the people you meet in this business," Iliff said without embarrassment. "So many of them aren't really nice. But your shields are remarkably tough. I got hardly any information at all."

"You got nothing!" she said flatly, startled into contradiction.

"Oh, yes. Just a little—when you were giving me that lecture about the Lannai being a proud people and not willing to be protected, and all that. For a moment there you were off guard—"

He brought the captured thought slowly from his mind: the picture of a quiet, dawnlit city—seas of sloping, ivory-tinted roofs, and towers slender against a flaming sky.

"That is Lar-Sancaya the Beautiful—my city, my home-planet," Pagadan said. "Yes, that was my thought. I remember it now!" She laughed. "You *are* a clever little man, Zone Agent! What information was in that for you?"

Iliff shrugged. He still showed the form of old Casselmath, the fat, unscrupulous little Terran trader whose wanderings through the galaxy coincided so often with the disappearance of undesirable but hitherto invulnerable citizens, with the inexplicable diversion of belligerent political trends, and the quiet toppling of venal governments. A space-wise, cynical, greedy but somehow ridiculous figure. Very few people ever took Casselmath seriously.

"Well, for one thing that the Lannai are patriots," he said gloomily. "That makes them potentially dangerous, of course. On the whole, I'm rather glad you're on our side."

She grinned cheerfully. "So am I—on the whole. But

now, if you'll forgive a touch of malice, which you've quite definitely earned, I'd like the answer to my second question. And that is—what sent that little shock through your nerves when I referred to Tahmey's probable connection with the Ghant Spacers a while ago?"

Old Casselmath rubbed the side of his misformed nose reflectively.

"It's a long, sad story," he said. "But if you want to know—some years back, I set out to nail down the boss of that outfit, the great U-1, no less. That was just after the Confederacy managed to break up the Ghant fleet, you remember—Well, I finally thought I'd got close enough to him to try a delicate probe at his mind— ugh!"

"I gather you bounced."

"Not nearly fast enough to suit me. The big jerk knew I was after him all the time, and he'd set up a mind-trap for me. Mechanical and highly powered. I had to be helped out of it, and then I was psychoed for six months before I was fit to go back to work.

"That was a long time ago," Casselmath concluded sadly. "But when it comes to U-1, or the Ghant Spacers, or anything at all connected with them, I've just never been the same since."

Pagadan studied her shining nails and smiled sweetly.

"Zone Agent Iliff, I shall bring you the records you want—and you may then run along. From now on, of course, I know exactly what to do to make you *jump*."

He sat bulky and expressionless at his desk, raking bejeweled fingers slowly through his beard—a magnificent, fan-shaped beard, black, glossy and modishly curled. His eyes were as black as the beard but so curiously lusterless he was often thought to be blind.

For the first time in a long, long span of years, he was remembering the meaning of fear.

But the alien thought had not followed him into the Dome—at least, he could trust his protective devices here. He reached into a section of the flowing black outer garments he wore, and produced a silvery, cone-shaped device. Placing the little amplifier carefully on the desk before him, he settled back in his chair, crossed his hands on his large stomach and half closed his eyes.

Almost immediately the recorded nondirectional thought impulses began. So faint, so impersonal, that even now when he could study their modified traces at leisure, when they did not fade away the instant his attention turned to them, they defied analysis except of the most general kind. And yet the unshielded part of his mind had responded to them, automatically and stupidly, for almost an hour before he realized—

Long enough to have revealed—almost anything!

The gems on his hand flashed furious fire as he whipped the amplifier off the desk and sent it smashing against the wall of the room. It shattered with a tinny crackle and dropped to the floor where a spray of purple sparks popped hissing from its crumpled surfaces and subsided again. The thought-impulses were stilled.

The black-bearded man glared down at the broken amplifier. Then, by almost imperceptible degrees, his expression began to change. Presently, he was laughing silently.

No matter how he had modified and adapted this human brain for his purpose, it remained basically what it had been when he first possessed himself of it. Whenever he relaxed his guidance, it reverted automatically to the old levels of emotional reaction.

He had forced it to develop its every rudimentary faculty until its powers were vastly superior to those of any normal member of its race. No ordinary human being, no matter how highly gifted, could be the equal of one who had had the advantage of becoming host-organism to a parasitizing Ceetal. Not even he, the Ceetal himself, was in any ordinary way the equal of this hypertrophied human intellect—he only controlled it. As a man controls a machine he has designed to be enormously more efficient than himself.

But if he had known the human breed better, he would have selected a more suitable host from it, to begin with. At its best, this one had been a malicious mediocrity; and its malice only expanded with its powers so that, within the limits he permitted, it now used the mental equipment of a titan to pamper the urges of an ape. A scowling moron who, on the invisible master's demand, would work miracles! Now, at the first suggestion that its omnipotence might be threatened, it turned guilt-ridden and panicky, vacillating between brute fright and brute rages.

Too late to alter that—he was linked to his slave for this phase of his life-cycle. For his purposes, the brute was at any rate adequate, and it often amused him to observe its whims. But for the new Ceetals—for those who would appear after his next Change—he could and would provide more suitable havens.

One of them might well be the spy who had so alarmed his human partner. The shadowy perfection of his mental attack in itself seemed to recommend him for the role.

Meanwhile, however, the spy still had to be caught.

In swift waves of relaxation, the Ceetal's influence spread through the black-bearded man's body and back into the calming brain. His plan was roughly ready, the trap for the spy outlined, but his human thought-machine was infinitely better qualified for such work. Controlled now, its personal fears and even the memory of them neutralized, it took up the problem *as* a problem—swept through it, clarifying, developing, concluding:

It was quite simple. The trap for this spy would be baited with the precise information he sought. On Gull, meanwhile, Tahmey remained as physical bait for the other spy, the first one—the nonhuman mind which had escaped by dint of the instantaneous shock-reflex that plucked it from his grasp as he prepared to close in. That the two were collaborating was virtually certain, that both were emissaries of the Confederacy of Vega was a not too unreasonable conjecture. No other organization suspected of utilizing combat-type minds of such efficiency was also likely to be interested in the person of Tahmey.

He was not, of course, ready to defy the Confederacy as yet—would not be for some time. A new form of concealment for Tahmey might therefore be necessary. But with the two spies under control, with the information extracted from them, any such difficulties could easily be met.

The black-bearded man's hands began to move heavily and unhurriedly over the surface of the desk, activating communicators and recorders.

The plan took shape in a pattern of swift, orderly arrangements.

Four visitors were waiting for him when he transferred himself to the principal room of the Dome—three men and a woman of the tall handsome Lycannese breed. The four faces turning to him wore the same expression, variously modified, of arrogant impatience.

These and a few others, to all of whom the black-bearded man was known simply as the Psychologist, had considered themselves for a number of years to be the actual, if unknown, rulers of the Lycannese System. They were very nearly right.

At his appearance, two of them began to speak almost simultaneously.

But they made no intelligible sound.

Outwardly, the black-bearded man had done nothing at all. But the bodies of the four jerked upright in the same instant, as if caught by a current of invisible power. They froze into that attitude, their faces twisted in grotesque terror, while his heavy-lidded, sardonic eyes shifted from one to the other of them.

"Must it always affect you like *that*," he said in friendly reproach, "to realize what I actually am? Or do you feel guilty for having planned to dispose of me, as a once-useful inferior who can no longer further your ambitions?" He paused and studied them again in turn, and the pleasantness went out of his expression.

"Yes, I knew about that little plot," he announced, settling his bulk comfortably on a low couch against the wall. He looked critically at his fingernails. "Normally, I should simply have made its achievement impossible, without letting you find out what had gone wrong. But as things stand, I'm afraid I shall be obliged to dispense with you entirely. I regret it, in a way. Our association has been a useful and amusing one—to me, at least. But, well—"

He shook his head.

"Even I make mistakes," he admitted frankly. "And recent events have made it clear that it was a mistake to involve somewhat ordinary human beings as deeply in my experiments and plans as I involved you—and also that companion of yours, whose absence here may have caused you to speculate. He," the Psychologist explained good-naturedly, "will outlive you by a day or so." He smiled. "Oddly enough, his brief continued usefulness to me is due to the fact that he is by far the least intelligent of you—so that I had really debated the advisability of dropping him from our little circle before this."

His smile broadened invitingly, but he showed no resentment when none of the chalk-faced, staring puppets before him joined in his amusement.

"Well," he beamed, "enough of this! There are minds on our track who seem capable of reaching you through any defense I can devise. Obviously, I cannot take that risk. Your friend, however, will live long enough to introduce me to one of these minds—another one of your ever-surprising species—who should eventually be of far greater value to me than any of you could hope to be. Perhaps even as valuable as the person you know as Tahmey. Let that thought console you in your last moments—which," he concluded, glancing at a pearly oblong that was acquiring a shimmering visibility in the wall behind the four Lycannese, "are now at hand."

Two solidly built men came into the room through the oblong, saluted, and waited.

The black-bearded one gave them a genial nod and jerked his thumb in the general direction of the motionless little group of his disposed associates.

"Strangle those four," he said, "in turn—"

He looked on for a few moments but then grew bored. Rising from the couch, he walked slowly toward one of the six walls of the room. It began to turn transparent as he approached, and when he stood before it the port-city of Lycanno IV, the greatest city in the Lycannese System, was clearly visible a few thousand feet below.

He gazed down at the scene almost affectionately, savoring a mood of rich self-assurance. For he was, as he had just now proved once more, the city's absolute master—master of the eight million human beings who lived there; of the two billion on the planet; of the sixteen billion in the System. Not for years had his mastery been seriously challenged.

His lusterless black eyes shifted slowly to Lycanno's two suns, moving now toward their evening horizon. Scattered strategically through the galaxy, nearly a thousand such suns lighted as many planetary systems, each of which was being gathered slowly into a Ceetal's grasp. The black-bearded man did not entertain the delusion that Lycanno by itself was an important conquest—no more than each of those other fractional human civilizations. But when the time came finally—

He permitted himself to lapse into a reverie of galactic conquest. But curiously, it was now the human brain and mind which indulged itself in this manner. The parasite remained lightly detached, following the imaginings without being affected by them, alert for some new human foible which it might turn some day to Ceetal profit.

It was, the Ceetal realized again, an oddly complicated organism, the human one. His host fully understood the relationship between them, and his own subordinate part in the Ceetal's plans. Yet he never let himself become conscious of the situation and frequently appeared to feel an actual identity with the parasite. It was strange such a near-maniac species could have gained so dominant a position in this galaxy.

There was a sudden minor commotion in the center of the room, harsh snoring sounds and then a brief, frenzied drumming of heels on the carpeted floor.

"You are getting careless," the Psychologist said coldly, without turning his head. "Such things can be done quietly."

The small yellow-faced man with the deep-set amber eyes drew a good number of amused and curious stares during the two days he was registered at the Old Lycannese Hotel.

He expected nothing else. Even in such sophisticated and galactic-minded surroundings, his appearance was fantastic to a rather indecent degree. The hairless dome of his head sloped down comically into a rounded snout. He was noseless and apparently earless, and in animated moments his naked yellow scalp would twitch vigorously like the flanks of some vermin-bitten beast.

However, the Old Lycannese harbored a fair selection of similarly freakish varieties of humanity within its many-storied walls—mutant humanity from worlds that were, more often than not, only nameless symbols on any civilized star-map. Side by side with them, indistinguishable to the average observer, representatives of the rarer humanoid species also came and went—on the same quest of profitable trade with Lycanno.

The yellow-faced man's grotesqueness, therefore, served simply to classify him. It satisfied curiosity almost as quickly as it drew attention; and no one felt urged to get too sociable with such a freak. Whether mutant human or humanoid, he was, at any rate, solvent and had shown a taste for quiet luxury. The hotel saw that he got what he wanted, pocketed his money and bothered its managerial head no further about him.

This curiosity-distracting effect, the yellow-faced man considered, as he strolled across the ground-floor lobby, was almost as satisfactory when it was applied to those who had reason to take a much sharper practical interest in any stranger! Two members of the Psychologist's bodyguard, behind whom he was heading toward an open elevator which led to the roof-terraces, had scrutinized him swiftly in passing a moment before—but only long enough to re-establish his identity beyond any doubt. They had checked that in detail the previous day—a Talpu, Humanoid, from a system of the Twenty-eighth Median Cluster, dealing in five varieties of gems—three of them previously unknown to Lycanno. Queer-looking little duck, but quite harmless.

The Psychologist's bodyguards took few chances, but they were not conditioned to look for danger in so blatantly obvious a shape.

The Psychologist himself, whose dome-shaped dwelling topped one section of the Old Lycannese Hotel, was taking no chances at all these days.

From the center of the moving cluster of his henchmen he gave the trailing humanoid's mind a flicking probe and encountered a mind-shield no different than was to be expected in a traveler with highly valuable commercial secrets to preserve—a shield he could have dissolved in an instant with hardly any effort at all.

However, so sudden an operation would have entailed leaving a small yellow maniac gibbering in agony on the floor of the lobby behind him—a complication he preferred to avoid in public. He dropped the matter from his thoughts, contemptuously. He knew of the Talpu—a base, timid race, unfit even for slavery.

A secondary and very different shield, which the more obvious first one had concealed from the Psychologist's probe, eased cautiously again in the yellow-faced man's mind, while the Talpu surface thoughts continued their vague quick traceries over both shields, unaffected either by the probe or by the deeper reaction it had aroused.

As the Psychologist's group reached the automatic elevator, the humanoid was almost side by side with its rearmost members and only a few steps behind the dignitary himself. There the party paused briefly while one of the leading guards scanned the empty compartment, and then stood aside to let the Psychologist enter. That momentary hesitation was routine procedure. The yellow-faced man had calculated with it, and he did not pause with the rest—though it was almost another half-second before any of the Psychologist's watch-dogs realized that *something* had just passed with a shadowy unobtrusiveness through their ranks.

By then, it was much too late. The great man had just stepped ponderously into the elevator; and the freakish little humanoid, now somehow directly behind him, was entering on his heels.

Simultaneously, he performed two other motions, almost casually.

As his left hand touched the switch that started the elevator on its way to the roof, a wall of impalpable force swung up and outwards from the floor-sill behind him, checking the foremost to hurl themselves at this impossible intruder—much more gently than if they had run into a large feather cushion but also quite irresistibly. The hotel took no chances of having its patrons injured on its premises; so the shocked bodyguards simply found themselves standing outside the elevator again before they realized it had flashed upward into its silvery shaft.

As it began to rise, the yellow-faced man completed his second motion. This was to slip a tiny hypodermic needle into the back of the Psychologist's neck and depress its plunger.

One could not, of course, openly abduct the system's most influential citizen without arousing a good deal of hostile excitement. But he had, Iliff calculated, when the elevator stopped opposite his apartments near the top of the huge hotel, a margin of nearly thirty seconds left to complete his getaway before any possible counterattack could be launched. There was no need to hurry.

A half dozen steps took him from the elevator into

his rooms, the Psychologist walking behind him with a look of vague surprise on his bearded face. Another dozen steps brought the two out to an open-air platform where a rented fast planecar was waiting.

At sixty thousand feet altitude, Iliff checked the spurt of their vertical ascent and turned north. The land was darkening with evening about the jewel-like sparkle of clustered seaboard cities, but up here the light of Lycanno's primary sun still glittered greenly from the car's silver walls. The speeding vehicle was shielded for privacy from all but official spy-rays, and for several more minutes he would have no reason to fear those. Meanwhile, any aerial pursuer who could single him out from among the myriad similar cars streaming into and out of the port city at that hour would be very good indeed.

Stripping the vivo-gel masks carefully from his head and hands, he dropped the frenziedly twitching half-alive stuff into the depository beside his seat where the car's jets would destroy it.

The Psychologist sat, hunched forward and docile, beside him—dull black eyes staring straight ahead. So far, the new Vegan mind-lock was conforming to the Third Co-ordinator's expectations.

Interrogation of the prisoner took place in a small valley off the coast of an uninhabited island, in the subpolar regions. A dozen big snake-necked carnivores scattered from the carcass of a still larger thing on which they had been feeding as the planecar settled down; and their snuffing and baffled howls provided a background for the further proceedings which Iliff found grimly fitting. He had sent out a fear-impulse adjusted to the beast-pack's primitive sensation-level, which kept them prowling helplessly along the rim of a hundred-yard circle.

In the center of this circle Iliff sat cross-legged on the ground, watching the Quizzer go about its business.

The Quizzer was an unbeautiful two-foot cube of machine. Easing itself with delicate ruthlessness through the Psychologist's mental defenses, it droned its findings step by step into Iliff's mind. He could have done the work without its aid, since the shield had never been developed that could block a really capable investigator if he was otherwise unhampered. But it would have taken a great deal longer; and at best he did not expect to have more time than he needed to extract the most vital points of information. Besides, he lacked the Quizzer's sensitivity; if he was hurried, there was a definite risk of doing irreparable injury to the mind under investigation—at that stage, he hadn't been able to decide whether or not it would be necessary to kill the Psychologist.

The second time the Quizzer contacted the Ceetal, he knew. The little robot reported an alien form of awareness which came and went through the Quizzer's lines of search as it chose and was impossible to localize.

"It is the dominant consciousness in this subject. But it is connected with the organism only through the other one."

The Quizzer halted again. It was incapable of surprise or confusion, but when it could not classify what it found it stopped reporting. It was bothered, too, by the effects of the mind-lock—an innovation to which it was not adjusted. The chemical acted directly on the shields, freezing those normally flexible defensive patterns into interlocked nets of force which isolated the energy centers of the nervous system that produced them.

"Give me anything you get on it!" Iliff urged.

The machine still hesitated. And then:

"It thinks that if it could break the force you call the mind-lock and energize the organism it could kill you instantly. But it is afraid that it would cause serious injury to the organism in doing so. Therefore it is willing to wait until its friends arrive and destroy you. It is certain that this will happen very quickly now."

Iliff grunted. That was no news to him, but it gave him an ugly thrill nevertheless. He'd found it necessary to cut his usual hit-and-run tactics very fine for this job; and so far he had got nothing he could use out of it.

"Does this primary consciousness," he inquired, "know what you're trying to do and what you're telling me?"

"It knows what I'm trying to do," the machine responded promptly. "It does not know that I'm telling you anything. It is aware of your presence and purpose but it can receive no sense impression of any kind. It can only think."

"Good enough," Iliff nodded. "It can't interfere with your activity then?"

"Not while the mind-lock keeps it from arousing its energy sources."

"What of the other one—the human consciousness?"

"That one is somnolent and completely helpless. It is barely aware of what is occurring and has made no attempt to interfere. It is only the mind-lock that blocks my approach to the information you require. If you could dissolve that force, there would be no difficulty."

Iliff wasted a baleful look on his squat assistant. "Except," he pointed out, "that I'd get killed!"

"Undoubtedly," the machine agreed with idiotic unconcern. "The energy centers of this organism are overdeveloped to an extent which, theoretically, should have drained it of its life-forces many years ago. It appears that the alien consciousness is responsible both for the neural hypertrophy and for the fact that the organism as a whole has been successfully adapted to meet the resultant unnatural stresses."

Towards the end of the next half-hour, the pattern of information finally began to take definite shape—a shape that made Iliff increasingly anxious to get done with the job. But which showed also that the Third Coordinator's hunch had been better than he knew!

Lycanno was long overdue for a Zone Agent's attentions.

He should, he supposed, have been elated; instead, he was sweating and shivering, keyed to nightmarish tensions. Theoretically, the mind-lock might be unbreakable, but the Ceetal, for one, did not believe it. It did fear that to shatter lock and shields violently might destroy its host and thereby itself; so far, that had kept it from making the attempt. That, and the knowledge it shared with its captor—that they could not remain undiscovered much longer.

But at each new contact, the Quizzer unemotionally reported an increase in the gathering fury and alarm with which the parasite observed the progress of the investigation. It had been coldly contemptuous at first; then the realization came slowly that vital secrets *were* being drawn, piece by piece, from the drugged human mind to which it was linked—and that it could do nothing to check the process.

By now, it was dangerously close to utter frenzy, and for many minutes Iliff's wrist-gun had been trained on the hunched and motionless shape of the Psychologist. Man and Ceetal would die on the spot if necessary. But even in its death-spasms, he did not want to be in the immediate neighborhood of that mind and the powers it could unleash if it broke loose. Time and again, he drew the Quizzer back from a line of investigation that seemed too likely to provide the suicidal impulse. Other parts of the pattern had been gained piecemeal, very circumstantially.

It was tight, carefully balanced work. However, there were only a few more really important points left now. There might be just time enough—

Iliff jerked upright as a warning blared from an automatic detector he had installed in the planecar the day before, raising a chorus of furious carnivore yells from the rim of the hundred-yard fear-circle.

"Two planetary craft approaching at low cruising speeds," it detailed. "Sector fourteen, distance eighty-five miles, altitude nineteen miles. Surface and psyche scanners are being used."

And, an instant later:

"You have been discovered!"

The rescuers were several minutes earlier than he'd actually expected. But the warning gave him the exact margin required for his next action, and the uncertainty and tension vanished from his mind.

He snapped a command to the Quizzer:

"Release the subject—then destroy yourself!"

Freed from invisible tentacles, the Psychologist's body rolled clumsily forward to the turf, and at once came stumbling to its feet. Behind it, the Quizzer flared up briefly in a shower of hissing sparks, collapsed, liquefied, and fused again into metallic formlessness.

Seconds later, Iliff had lifted the planecar over the valley's tree-top level. The vehicle's visiglobe was focused locally—every section of the dark little valley appeared as distinct in it as if flooded with brilliant daylight. Near its center, the figure of the Psychologist was groping through what, to him, was near-complete blackness down into the open ground. Whether the alien mind understood that its men had arrived and was attempting to attract their attention, Iliff would never know.

It did not matter, now. The planecar's concealed guns were trained on that figure; and his finger was on the trigger-stud.

But he did not fire. Gliding out from under the trees, the lean, mottled shapes of the carnivore-pack had appeared in the field of the globe. Forgetting the intangible barrier of fear as quickly as it ceased to exist, they scuttled back towards their recently abandoned feast—and swerved, in a sudden new awareness, to converge upon the man-form that stumbled blindly about near it.

Iliff grimaced faintly, spun the visiglobe to wide-range focus and sent the planecar hurtling over the shoreline into the sea. The maneuver would shield him from the surface scanners of the nearest pursuers and give him a new and now urgently needed headstart.

It would please his scientific colleagues back on Jeltad, he knew, to hear that the Ceetal had been mistaken about the strength of their mind-lock. For the brief seconds it survived in the center of the raven-ing mottled pack, that malevolent intellect must have put forth every effort to break free and destroy its attackers.

It had been quite unsuccessful.

Near dawn, in the fifth-largest city of Lycanno IV, a smallish military gentleman proceeded along the docks of a minor space port towards a large, slow-looking, but apparently expensive craft he had regis-tered there two days before. Under one arm he carried a bulging brief case of the openly spy-proof type employed by officials of the Terran embassy.

The burden did not detract in the least from his air of almost belligerent dignity—an attitude which still characterized most citizens of ancient Earth in the afterglow of her glory. The ship he approached was surrounded by a wavering, globular sheen of light, like a cluster of multiple orange halos, warning dock attendants and the idly curious from coming within two hundred feet of it.

Earthmen were notoriously jealous of their right to privacy.

The military gentleman, whose size was his only general point of resemblance to either Iliff or the yellow-faced man who had been a guest of the Old Lycannese Hotel not many hours earlier, walked into the area of orange fire without hesitation. From the ship, a brazen, inhuman voice boomed instantly at him, both audibly and in mental shock-waves that would have rocked the average intruder back like a blow in the face:

"Withdraw at once! This vessel is shielded from investigation in accordance with existing regulations. Further unauthorized advance into the area defined by the light-barrier—"

The voice went silent suddenly. Then it continued, subvocally:

"You are being observed from a strato-station. Nothing else to report. We can leave immediately."

In the strato-station, eighty miles above, a very young, sharp-faced fleet lieutenant was turning to his captain:

"Couldn't that be—?"

The captain gave him a sardonic, worldly-wise smile.

"No, Junior," he said mildly, "that could not be. That, as you should recall, is Colonel Perritaph, recently attached to the Terran Military Commission. We checked him through this port yesterday morning. But," he added, "we're going to have a little fun with the colonel. As soon as he's ready to take off, he'll drop that light-barrier. When he does, spear him with a tractor and tell him he's being held for investigation, because there's a General Emergency out."

"Why not do it now? Oh!"

"You catch on, Junior—you do catch on," his superior approved tolerantly. "No light-barrier is to be monkeyed with, ever! Poking a tractor-beam into one *may* do no harm. On the other hand, it may blow up the ship, the docks, or, just possibly, our cozy little station up here—all depending on what stuff happens to be set how. But once the colonel's inside and has the crate under control, he's not going to blow up anything, even if we do hurt his tender Terran feelings a bit."

"That way we find out what he's got in the ship, diplomatic immunity or not," the lieutenant nodded, trying to match the captain's air of weary omniscience.

"We're not interested in what's in the ship," the captain said softly, abashing him anew. "Terra's a couple of hundred years behind us in construction and armaments—always was." This was not strictly true; but the notion was a popular one in Lycanno, which had got itself into a brief, thunderous argument with the aging Mother of Galactic Mankind five hundred years before and limped for a century and a half thereafter. The unforeseen outcome had, of course, long since been explained—rotten luck and Terran treachery—and the whole regrettable incident was not often mentioned nowadays.

But, for a moment, the captain glowered down in the direction of the distant spaceport, unaware of what moved him to malice.

"We'll just let him squirm around a bit and howl for his rights," he murmured. "They're so beautifully sensitive about those precious privileges!"

There was a brief pause while both stared at the bulky-looking ship in their globe.

"Wonder what that G.E. really went out for," the lieutenant ventured presently.

"To catch one humanoid ape—as described," the captain grinned. Then he relented. "I'll tell you one thing—it's big enough that they've put out the Fleet to blast anyone who tries to sneak off without being identified."

The lieutenant tried to look as if that explained it, but failed. Then he brightened and announced briskly: "The guy's barrier just went off!"

"All right. Give him the tractor!"

"It's—"

Up from the dock area then, clearly audible through their instruments, there rose a sound: a soft but tremendous *WHOOSH!* The cradle in which the slow-looking ship had rested appeared to quiver violently. Nothing else changed. But the ship was no longer there.

In white-faced surprise, the lieutenant goggled at the captain. "Did . . . did it blow up?" he whispered.

The captain did not answer. The captain had turned purple, and seemed to be having the worst kind of trouble getting his breath.

"Took off—*under space-drive!*" he gasped suddenly. "How'd he do that without wrecking— With a tractor on him!"

He whirled belatedly, and flung himself at the communicators. Gone was his aplomb, gone every trace of worldly-wise weariness.

"Station 1222 calling Fleet!" he yelped. "Station 1222 calling—"

While Lycanno's suns shrank away in the general-view tank before him, Iliff rapidly sorted the contents of his brief case into a small multiple-recorder. It had been a busy night—to those equipped to read the signs the Fourth Planet must have seemed boiling like a hive of furious bees before it was over! But he'd done most of what had seemed necessary, and the pursuit never really got within minutes of catching up with him again.

When the excitement died down, Lycanno would presently discover it had become a somewhat cleaner place overnight. For a moment, Iliff wished he could be around when the real Colonel Perritaph began to express his views on the sort of police inefficiency which had permitted an impostor to make use of his name and position in the System.

Terra's embassies were always ready to give a representative of the Confederacy a helping hand, and no questions asked; just as, in any all-out war, its tiny, savage fleet was regularly found fighting side by side with the ships of Vega—though never exactly together with them. Terra was no member of the Confederacy; it was having no foreigners determine its policies. On the whole, the Old Planet had not changed so very much.

When Iliff set down the empty brief case, the voice that had addressed him on his approach to the ship spoke again. As usual, it was impossible to say from just where it came; but it seemed to boom out of the empty air a little above Iliff's head. In spite of its curious resemblance to his own voice, most people would have identified it now as the voice of a robot.

Which it was—for its size the most complicated robot-type the science of Vega and her allies had yet developed.

"Two armed space-craft, Lycannese destroyer-type, attempting interception!" it announced. After the barest possible pause, it added: "Instructions?"

Iliff grinned a little without raising his head. No one

else would have noticed anything unusual in the ste-
reotyped warning, but he had been living with that
voice for some fifteen years.

"Evasion, of course, you big ape!" he said softly.
"You'll have had all the fighting you want before you're
scrapped."

His grin widened then, at a very convincing illusion
that the ship had shrugged its sloping and monstrously
armored shoulders in annoyed response. That, however,
was due simply to the little leap with which the suns
of Lycanno vanished from the tank in the abruptness
of full forward acceleration.

In effect, the whole ship was the robot—a highly
modified version of the deadly one-man strike-ships of
the Vegan battle fleet, but even more heavily armed
and thus more than qualified to take on a pair of
Lycannese destroyers for the split-second maneuverings
and decisions, the whole slashing frenzy of a deep-space
fight. Its five central brains were constructed to produce, as closely as possible, replicas of Iliff's own basic
mental patterns, which made for a nearly perfect rap-
port. Beyond that, of course, the machine was super-
sensed and energized into a truly titanic extension of
the man.

Iliff did not bother to observe the whiplash evasion
tactics which almost left the destroyers' commanders
wondering whether there had been any unidentified
spaceship recorded on their plates in the first place.
That order was being carried out much more competently than if he had been directing the details himself; and meanwhile there was other business on
hand—the part of his job he enjoyed perhaps least of
all. A transmitter was driving the preliminary reports
of his actions on Lycanno Four across nearly half the
galaxy to G.Z. Headquarters Central on the planet of
Jeltad.

There, clerks were feeding it, in series with a few thousand other current intermission reports, into more complex multiple-recorders, from which various sections were almost instantaneously disgorged, somewhat cut and edited.

"She has not responded to her personal beam," the robot announced for the second time.

"Sure she just wasn't able to get back at us?"

"There is no indication of that."

"Keep it open then—until she does answer," Iliff said. Personal telepathy at interstellar ranges was always something of an experiment, unless backed at both ends by mechanical amplifiers of much greater magnitude than were at Pagadan's disposal.

"But I do wish," he grumbled, "I'd been able to find out what made the Ceetal so particularly interested in Tahmey! Saving him up, as host, for the next generation, of course. If he hadn't been so touchy on that point—" He scowled at the idly clicking transmitter before him. Deep down in his mind, just on the wrong side of comprehension, something stirred slowly and uneasily and sank out of his awareness again.

"Correlation ought to call in pretty soon," he reassured himself. "With the fresh data we've fed them, they'll have worked out a new line on the guy."

"Departmental Lab is now attempting to get back on transmitter," the robot informed him. "Shall I blank them out till you've talked with Correlation?"

"Let them through," Iliff sighed. "If we have to, we'll cut them off—"

A staccato series of clicks conveying an impression of agitated inquiry, rose suddenly from the transmitter. Still frowning, he adjusted light-scales, twisted knobs, and a diminutive voice came gushing in mid-speech from the instrument. Iliff listened a while; then he broke in impatiently.

"Look," he explained, "I've homed you the full recorded particulars of the process they used. You'll have the stuff any minute now, and you'll get a lot more out of that than I could tell you. The man I got it from was the only one still alive of the group that did the job; but he was the one that handled the important part—the actual personality transfer.

"I cleared his mind of all he knew of the matter and recorded it, but all I understood myself was the principle involved—if that."

The voice interjected a squeaky, rapid-fire protest. Iliff cut in again quickly:

"Well, if you need it now—You're right about there not having been any subjective switching of personalities involved, and I'm not arguing about whether it's impossible. These people just did a pretty complete job of shifting everything that's supposed to make up a conscious individual from one human body to another. From any objective point of view, it *looks* like a personality transfer.

"No, they didn't use psychosurgery," he went on. "Except to fill in a six-months' sequence of memory tracts to cover the interval they had Tahmey under treatment. What they used was a modification of the electronic method of planting living reflex patterns in robot brains. First, they blanked out Tahmey's mind completely—neutralized all established neural connections and so on, right down to the primary automatic reflexes."

"The 'no-mind' stage?" Lab piped.

"That's right. Then they put the Lycannese Deel in a state of mental stasis. They'd picked him because of his strong physical resemblance to Tahmey."

"That," Lab instructed him sharply, "could have no

effect on the experiment as such. Did they use a chemical paralyzing agent to produce the stasis?"

"I think so. It's in the report—"

"You—Zone Agents! How long did they keep the two nerve systems linked?"

"About six months."

"I see. Then they broke the flow and had a *complete* copy of the second subject's neural impulse paths stamped into the first subject's nervous system. Re-energized, the artificial personality would pick up at the exact point it entered mental stasis and continue to develop normally from there on. I see, I see, I see . . . but what happened to the second subject— Deel?"

"He died in convulsions a few seconds after they returned him to consciousness."

Lab clicked regretfully. "Usual result of a prolonged state of mental stasis—and rather likely to limit the usefulness of the process, you know. Now, there are a few important points—"

"Correlation!" the robot said sharply into Iliff's mind.

The squeaky voice thinned into an abrupt high whistle and was gone.

"I'm here, Iliff! Your friend and guide, Captain Rashallan of Correlation, himself. You haven't started to close in on that Tahmey bird yet, have you? You aren't anywhere near him yet?"

"No," Iliff said. He squinted down at the transmitter and was surprised by a sudden sense of constriction in his throat. "Why?"

The Correlation man took about three minutes to tell him. He ended with:

"We've just had a buzz from Lab—they were trying to get back to you, but couldn't—and what they want us to tell you fits right in—"

"The neutralization of a nervous system that produces the no-mind stage is an effect that wears off completely within two years. Normally, the result is the gradual re-establishment of the original personality; but, in this case, there can be no such result because all energy centers are channeling constantly into the Deel personality.

"*However*, there's no reason to doubt that 'Tahmey' is now also present in the system—though unconscious and untraceable because unenergized. Obviously, the Ceetal could have no reason to be interested in a commonplace mentality such as Deel's.

"Now you see how it ties in! Whether it was the Ceetal's intention or not—and it's extremely probable, a virtual certainty, that it was—the whole artificial creation remains stable only so long as the Deel personality continues to function.

"The instant it lapses, the original personality will be energized. You see what's likely to happen to any probing outsider then?"

"Yes," Iliff said, "I see."

"Assuming it's been arranged like that," said Captain Rashallan, "the trigger that sets off the change is, almost certainly, a situational one—and there will be a sufficient number of such triggered situations provided so that any foreseeable emergency pattern is bound to develop one or more of them.

"The Ceetal's purpose with such last-resort measures would be, of course, to virtually insure the destruction of any investigator who had managed to overcome his other defenses, and who was now at the point of getting a direct line on *him* and his little pals.

"So you'll have to watch . . . well, Zones wants to get through to you now, and they're getting impatient. Good luck, Iliff!"

Iliff leaned forward then and shut off the transmitter.

For a moment or so after that, he sat motionless, his yellow eyes staring with a hard, flat expression at something unseen. Then he inquired:

"Did you get Pagadan?"

"There've been several blurred responses in the past few minutes," the robot answered. "Apparently, she's unable to get anything beyond the fact that you *are* trying to contact her—and she is also unable to amplify her reply to the extent required just now. Do you have any definite message?"

"Yes," Iliff said briskly. "As long as you get any response from her at all, keep sending her this: 'Kill Tahmey! Get off Gull!' Make it verbal and strong. Even if the beam doesn't clear, that much might get through."

"There's a very good chance of it," the robot agreed. It added, after a moment, "But the Interstellar operative is not very likely to be successful in either undertaking, Iliff."

There was another pause before Iliff replied.

"No," he said then. "I'm afraid not. But she's a capable being—she does have a chance."

FOR DISTRIBUTION AT AND
ABOVE ZONE AGENT LEVELS

Description: ... mind-parasite of extragalactic origin, accidentally introduced into our Zones and now widely scattered there ... In its free state a nonmaterial but coherent form of conscious energy, characterized by high spatial motility.

... basic I.Q. slightly above A-type human being. Behavior ... largely on reflex-intuition levels. The basic procedures underlying its life-cycle are not consciously comprehended by the parasite and have not, at present, been explained.

Cycle: . . . the free state, normally forming only a fraction of the Ceetal life-cycle, may be extended indefinitely until the parasite contacts a suitable host-organism. Oxygen-breathing life-forms with neural mechanisms in the general class of the human nervous system and its energy areas serve this purpose.

On contacting a host, the Ceetal undergoes changes in itself enabling it to control the basic energizing drives of the host-organism. It then develops the host's neural carriers to a constant point *five times* beyond the previous absolute emergency overload.

In type-case Ceetal-Homo-Lycanno S-4, 1782—a drastic localized hypertrophy of the central nerve tissue masses was observed, indicating protective measures against the overload induced in the organism.

The advantages to the parasite of developing a host-organism of such abnormal potency and efficiency in its environment are obvious, as it is indissolubly linked to its host for the major part of its long parasitic stage and cannot survive the host's death. Barring accidents or superior force, it is, however, capable of prolonging the host's biological life-span almost indefinitely.

At the natural end of this stage, the Ceetal reproduces, the individual parasite dividing into eight free-stage forms. The host is killed in the process of division, and each Ceetal is freed thereby to initiate a new cycle.

CHIEF G.Z.: FROM CORRELATION

F. The numerical strength of the original swarm of free-stage Ceetals can thus be set at

approximately forty-nine thousand. The swarm
first contacted the Toeller Planet and, with the
exception of less than a thousand individuals,
entered symbiosis with the highest life-form
evolved there.

The resultant emergence of the "Toeller-
Worm," previously regarded as the most
remarkable example known of spontaneous
mental evolution in a species, is thereby
explained. The malignant nature of the Super-
Toeller mirrors the essentially predatory characteristics of the Ceetal. Its complete
extermination by our forces involved the
destruction of the entire Ceetal swarm, except-
ing the individuals which had deferred adopting
a host.

G. Practical chances of a similar second
swarm of these parasites contacting our galaxy
are too low to permit evaluation.

H. The threat from the comparatively few
remaining Ceetals derives from the survivors'
decision to select their hosts only from civilized species with a high basic I.Q., capable of
developing and maintaining a dominating influence throughout entire cultural systems.

In the type-case reported, the Ceetal not
only secured a complete political dominance
of the Class-Twelve System of Lycanno but
extended its influence into three neighboring
systems.

Since all surviving Ceetals maintain contact
with each other and the identity and location
of one hundred and eighteen of these survivors was given in the Agent's report, it should
not be too difficult to dispose of them before
their next period of reproduction—which

would, of course, permit the parasite to dis-
perse itself to a dangerous extent throughout
the galaxy.

The operation cannot be delayed, however,
as the time of reproduction for the first Ceetals
to adopt hosts of human-level I.Q. following
the destruction of the Toeller-Worms can now
be no more than between two and five years—
standard—in the future. The danger is significantly increased, of course, by their more
recent policy of selecting and conserving hosts
of *abnormally* high I.Q. rating well in advance
of the "change."

The menace to civilization from such beings,
following their mental hypertrophy and under
Ceetal influence, can hardly be overstated.

The problem of disposing of all surviving
Ceetals—or, failing that, of all such prospective super-hosts—must therefore be considered
one of utmost urgency.

"They're telling me!" the Third Co-ordinator said
distractedly. He rubbed his long chin, and reached for
a switch.

"Psych-tester?" he said. "You heard them? What are
the chances of some other Ceetal picking up U-1?"

"It must be assumed," a mechanical voice replied,
"that the attempt will be made promptly. The strike
you have initiated against those who were revealed
by the Agent's report cannot prevent some unknown
survivor from ordering U-1's removal to another place
of concealment, where he could be picked up at will.
Since you are counting on a lapse of two days before
the strike now under way will have yielded sufficient
information to permit you to conclude the operation against the Ceetals, several of them may

succeed in organizing their escape—and even a single Ceetal in possession of such a host as U-1 would indicate the eventual dominance of the species. Galactic Zones has no record of any other mentality who would be even approximately so well suited to their purposes."

"Yes," said the Co-ordinator. "Their purposes—you think then if U-1 got their treatment, being what he is, he could take us?"

"Yes," the voice said. "He could."

The Co-ordinator nodded thoughtfully. His face looked perhaps a little harsher, a little grayer than usual.

"Well, we've done what we can from here," he said presently. "The first *other* Agent will get to Gull in eleven hours, more or less. There'll be six of them there tomorrow. And a fleet of destroyers within call range—none of them in time to do much good, I'm afraid!"

"That is the probability," the voice agreed.

"Zone Agent Iliff has cut communication with us," the Co-ordinator went on. "Correlation informed him they had identified Tahmey as U-1. He would be, I suppose, proceeding at top velocities to Gull?"

"Yes, naturally."

"Interstellar reports they have not been able to contact their operative on Gull. It appears," the Co-ordinator concluded, rather bleakly, "that Zone Agent Iliff understands the requirements of the situation."

"Yes," the voice said, "he does."

"G.Z. Headquarters is still trying to get through," the robot said. After a moment, it added, "Iliff, this is no longer a one-agent mission."

"You're right about that! Half the Department's probably blowing its jets trying to converge on Gull right now. They'll get there a little late, though.

Meanwhile they know what we know, or as much of it as is good for them. How long since you got the last sign from Pagadan?"

"Over two hours."

Iliff was silent a moment. "You might as well quit working her beam," he said finally. "But keep it open, just in case. And pour on that power till we get to Gull!"

It did not take long after his landing on that planet to establish with a reasonable degree of certainty that if Pagadan was still present, she was in no condition to respond to any kind of telepathic message. It was only a very little later—since he was working on the assumption that caution was not a primary requirement just now—before he disclosed the much more significant fact that the same held true of the personage who had been known as Deel.

The next hour, however—until he tapped the right three or four minds—was a dragging nightmare. Then he had the additional information that the two he sought had departed from the planet, together, but otherwise unaccompanied, not too long after he had sent Pagadan his original message.

He flashed the information back to the docked ship, adding:

"It's a question, of course, of who took whom along. My own guess is Pagadan hadn't tripped any triggers yet and was still in charge—and U-1 was still Deel—when they left here. The ship's a single-pilot yacht, shop-new, fueled for a fifty-day trip. No crew; no destination recorded."

"Pass it on to Headquarters right away! They still won't be able to do anything about it; but anyway, it's an improvement."

"That's done," the robot returned impassively. "And now?"

"I'm getting back to you at speed—we're going after them, of course."

"She must have got the message," the robot said after a moment, "but not clearly enough to realize exactly what you wanted. How did she do it?"

"Nobody here seems to know—she blasted those watch-dogs in one sweep, and Gull's been doing flip-flops quietly ever since. The Ceetal's gang is in charge of the planet, of course, and they think Deel and his kidnapers are still somewhere around. They've just been alerted from Lycanno that something went wrong *there* in a big way; but again they don't know what."

"And now they've also begun to suspect somebody's been poking around in their minds pretty freely this last hour or so."

The two men in the corridor outside the Port Offices were using mind-shields of a simple but effective type. It was the motor tension in their nerves and muscles that warned him first, surging up as he approached, relaxing slightly—but only slightly—when he was past.

He drove the warning to the ship.

"Keep an open line of communication between us, and look out for yourself. The hunt's started up at this end!"

"The docks are clear of anything big enough to matter," the robot returned instantly. "I'm checking upstairs. How bad does it look? I can be with you in three seconds from here."

"You'd kill a few thousand bystanders doing it, big boy! This section's built up. Just stay where you are. There are two men following me, a bunch more waiting behind the next turn of this corridor. All wearing mind-shields—looks like government police."

A second later: "They're set to use paralyzers, so

there's no real danger. The Ceetal's outfit wants me alive, for questioning."

"What will you do?"

"Let them take me. It's you they're interested in! Lycanno's been complaining about us, and they think we might be here to get Deel and the Lannai off the planet. How does it look around you now?"

"Quiet, but not good! There're some warships at extreme vision range where they can't do much harm; but too many groups of men within two hundred miles of us are wearing mind-shields and waiting for something. I'd say they're ready to use fixed-mount space guns now, in case we try to leave without asking again."

"That would be it—Well, here go the paralyzers!"

He stepped briskly around the corridor corner and stopped short, rigid and transfixed in flickering white fountains of light that spouted at him from the nozzles of paralyzer guns in the hands of three of the eight men waiting there.

After a fifth of a second, the beams snapped off automatically. The stiffness left Iliff's body more slowly; he slumped then against the wall and slid to the floor, sagging jaw drawing his face down into an expression of foolish surprise.

One of the gunmen stepped towards him, raised his head and pried up an eyelid.

"He's safe!" he announced with satisfaction. "He'll stay out as long as you want him that way."

Another man spoke into a wristphone.

"Got him! Orders?"

"Get him into the ambulance waiting at the main entrance of the building!" a voice crackled back. "Take him to Dock 709. We've got to investigate that ship, and we'll need him to get inside."

"Thought it would be that," Iliff's murmur reached the ship. "They'll claim I was in an accident or something and ask to bring me in." The thought trailed off, started up again a moment later: "They might as well be using sieves as those government-issue mind-shields! These boys here don't know another thing except that I'm wanted, but we can't afford to wait any longer. We'll have to take them along. Get set to leave as soon as we're inside!"

The eight men who brought him through the ship's ground lock—six handling his stretcher, two following helpfully—were of Gull's toughest; an alert, well-trained and well-armed group, prepared for almost any kind of trouble. However, they never had a chance.

The lock closed soundlessly, but instantaneously, on the heels of the last of them. From the waiting ambulance and a number of other camouflaged vehicles outside concealed semi-portables splashed wild gusts of fire along the ship's flanks—then they were variously spun around or rolled over in the backwash of the take-off. A single monstrous thunderclap seemed to draw an almost visible line from the docks towards the horizon; the docks groaned and shook, and the ship had once more vanished.

A number of seconds later, the spaceport area was shaken again—this time by the crash of a single fixed-mount space gun some eighty miles away. It was the only major weapon to go into action against the fugitive on that side of the planet.

Before its sound reached the docks, two guns on the opposite side of Gull also spewed their stupendous charges of energy into space, but very briefly. Near the pole, the ship had left the planet's screaming atmosphere in an apparent head-on plunge for Gull's single moon, which was the system's main fortress. This cut off all fire until, halfway to the satellite, the robot veered off at right angles and flashed out of range on the first half-turn of a swiftly widening evasion spiral.

The big guns of the moon forts continued to snarl into space a full minute after the target had faded beyond the ultimate reach of their instruments.

Things *could* have been much worse, Iliff admitted. And presently found himself wondering just what he had meant by that.

He was neither conscious nor unconscious. Floating in a little Nirvana of first-aid treatment, he was a disembodied mind vaguely aware of being hauled back once more—and more roughly than usual—to the world of reality. And as usual, he was expected to be doing something there—something disagreeable.

Then he realized the robot was dutifully droning a report of recent events into his mind while it continued its efforts to rouse him.

It really wasn't so bad! They weren't actually crippled; they could still outrun almost anything in space they couldn't outfight—as the pursuit had learned by now. No doubt, he might have foreseen the approximate manner in which the robot would conduct their escape under the guns of an alerted planet and a sizable section of that planet's war fleet—while its human master and the eight men from Gull hung insensible to everything in the webs of the force-field that had closed on them with the closing of the ground lock.

A clean-edged sixteen-foot gap scooped out of the compartment immediately below the lock was, of course, nobody's fault. Through the wildest of accidents, they'd been touched there, briefly and terribly, by the outer fringe of a bolt of energy hurled after them by one of Gull's giant moon-based guns.

The rest of the damage—though consisting of comparatively minor rips and dents—could not be so simply dismissed. It was the result, pure and simple, of slashing headlong through clusters of quick-firing fighting ships, which could just as easily have been avoided.

Dreamily, Iliff debated taking a run to Jeltad and having the insubordinate electronic mentality put through an emotional overhaul there. It wasn't the first time the notion had come to him, but he'd always relented. Now he would see it was attended to. And at once—

With that, he was suddenly awake and aware of the job much more immediately at hand. Only a slight sick fuzziness remained from the measures used to jolt him out of the force-field sleep and counteract the dose of paralysis rays he'd stopped. And that was going, as he bent and stretched, grimacing at the burning tingle of the stuff that danced like frothy acid through his arteries. Meanwhile, the robot's steel tentacles were lifting his erstwhile captors, still peacefully asleep, into a lifeboat which was then launched into space, came round in a hesitant half-circle and started resolutely back towards Gull.

"Here's our next move," Iliff announced as the complaining hum of the lifeboat's "pick-me-up" signals began to fade from their instruments. "They didn't get much of a start on us—and in an ordinary stellar-type yacht, at that. If they're going where I think they are, we might catch up with them almost any moment. But we've got to be sure, so start laying a global interception pattern at full emergency speeds—centered on Gull, of course. Keep detectors full on and telepath broadcast at ultimate nondirectional range. Call me if you get the faintest indication of a pick-up on either line."

The muted brazen voice stated:

"That's done."

"Fine. The detectors should be our best bet. About the telepath: we're not going to call Pagadan directly, but we'll try for a subconscious response. U-1's got to be in charge by now, unless Correlation's quit being omniscient, but he might not spot that—at least, not right away. Give her this—"

Events had been a little too crowded lately to make the memory immediately accessible. But, after a moment's groping, he brought it from his mind: the picture of a quiet, dawnlit city—seas of sloping, ivory-tinted roofs and slender towers against a flaming sky.

The pickup came on the telepath an hour later.

"They're less than half a light-year out. Shall I slide in and put a tractor on them?"

"Keep sliding in, but no tractors! Not yet." Iliff chewed his lower lip thoughtfully. "Sure she didn't respond again?"

"Not after that first subconscious reply. But the yacht may have been blanked against telepathy immediately afterwards."

"Well, anyway, she was still alive then," Iliff said resignedly. "Give Headquarters the yacht's location, and tell them to quit mopping their brows because U-1's on his own now—and any Ceetal that gets within detection range of him will go free-stage the hard way. Then drop a field of freezers over that crate. I want her stopped dead. I guess I'll have to board—"

He grimaced uncomfortably and added, "Get in there fast, fella, but watch the approach! There *couldn't* be any heavy armament on that yacht, but U-1's come up with little miracles before this. Maybe that Ceetal was lucky the guy never got back to Lycanno to talk to him. It's where he was pointed, all right."

"Headquarters is now babbling emotional congratulations," the robot reported, rather coldly. "They also say two Vegan destroyers will be able to reach the yacht within six hours."

"That's nice!" Iliff nodded. "Get just a few more holes punched in you, and we could use those to tow you in."

Enclosed in a steel bubble of suit-armor, he presently propelled himself to the lock. The strange ship, still some five minutes' flight away in fact, appeared to be lying motionless at point-blank range in the portscreens—bow and flanks sparkling with the multiple pinpoint glitter of the freezer field which had wrapped itself around her like a blanket of ravenous, fiery leeches. Any ripple or thrust of power of which she was capable would be instantly absorbed now and dissipated into space; she was effectively immobilized and would remain so for hours.

"But the field's not flaring," Iliff said. He ran his tongue gently over his lips. "That guy does know his stuff! He's managed to insulate his power sources and he's sitting there betting we won't blast the ship but come over and try to pry him out. The trouble is, he's right."

The robot spoke then, for the first time since it had scattered the freezer field in the yacht's path. "Iliff," it stated impersonally and somewhat formally, "regulations do not permit you to attempt the boarding of a hostile spaceship under such suicidal conditions. I am therefore authorized—"

The voice broke off, on a note of almost human surprise. Iliff had not shifted his eyes from the portscreen below him. After a while, he said dryly:

"It was against regulations when I tinkered with your impulses till I found the set that would let you interfere with me for my own good. You've been without that set for years, big boy—except when you were being overhauled."

"It was a foolish thing to do," the robot answered. "I was given no power to act against your decisions,

even when they included suicide, if they were justified in the circumstances that formed them. That is
not the case here. You should either wait for the
destroyers to come up or else let me blast U-1 and
the yacht together, without any further regard for the
fate of the Interstellar operative—though she is
undoubtedly of some importance to civilization."

"Galactic Zones thinks so," Iliff nodded. "They'd
much rather she stays alive."

"Obviously, that cannot compare with the importance
of destroying U-1 the instant the chance is offered. As
chief of the Ghant Spacers, his murders were counted,
literally, by planetary systems. If you permit his escape
now, you give him the opportunity to resume that
career."

"I haven't the slightest intention of permitting his
escape," Iliff objected mildly.

"My responses are limited," the robot reminded him.
"Within those limits I surpass you, of course, but
beyond them I need your guidance. If you force an
entry for yourself into that ship, you may logically
expect to die, and because of the telepathic block
around it I shall not be aware of your death. You
cannot be certain then that I shall be able to prevent
a mind such as that of U-1 from effecting his escape
before the destroyers get here."

Iliff snarled, suddenly white and shaking. He
checked himself with difficulty, drew a long, slow
breath. "I'm scared of the guy!" he complained, somewhat startled himself by his reaction. "And you're not
making me feel any better. Now quit giving good
advice, and just listen for a change!"

He went on carefully:

"The Lannai's quite possibly dead. But if she isn't,
U-1 isn't likely to kill her now until he finds out what
we're after. Even for him, it's a pretty desperate mess—

he'll figure we're Vegan, so he won't even try to dicker. But he'll also figure that as long as we think she's alive, we'll be just a little more cautious about how we strike at him.

"So it's worth taking a chance on trying to get her out of there. And here's what you do. In the first place, don't under any circumstances get any closer than medium beaming range to that crate. Then, just before I reach the yacht, you're to put a tractor on its forward spacelock and haul it open. That will let me in close to the control room, and that's where U-1's got to be.

"Once I'm inside, the telepath block will, of course, keep me from communicating. If the block goes down suddenly and I start giving you orders from in there, ignore them! The chances are I'll be talking for U-1. You understand that—I'm giving you an order now to ignore any subsequent orders until you've taken me back aboard again?"

"I understand."

"Good. Whatever happens, you're to circle that yacht for twenty minutes after I enter, and at the exact end of that time you're to blast it. If Pagadan or I, or both of us, get out before the time is up, that's fine. But don't pick us up, or let us come aboard, or pay any attention to any instructions we give you until you've burned the yacht. If U-1 is able to control us, it's not going to do him any good. If he comes out himself— with or without us, in a lifeboat or armor—you blast him instantly, of course. Lab would like to study that brain all right, but this is one time I can't oblige them. You've got all that?"

"I've got it, yes."

"Then can you think of any other trick he might pull to get out of the squeeze?"

The robot was silent a moment. "No," it said then. "I can't. But U-1 probably could."

"Yes, he probably could," Iliff admitted thoughtfully. "But not in twenty minutes—and it will be less than that, because he's going to be a terribly occupied little pirate part of the time, and a pretty shaky one, if nothing else, the rest of it. I may not be able to take him, but I'm sure going to make his head swim!"

It was going wrong before it started—but it was better not to think of that.

Actually, of course, he had never listed the entering of a hostile ship held by an experienced and desperate spacer among his favorite games. The powers that hurled a sliver of sub-steel alloys among the stars at dizzying multiples of the speed of light could be only too easily rearranged into a variety of appalling traps for any intruder.

U-1, naturally, knew every trick in the book and how to improve on it. On the other hand, he'd been given no particular reason to expect interception until he caught and blocked their telepath-beam—unless he had managed, in that space of time, to break down the Lannai's mind-shields without killing her, which seemed a next to impossible feat even for him.

The chances were, then, that the spacer had been aware of pursuit for considerably less than an hour, and that wasn't time enough to become really well prepared to receive a boarding party—or so Iliff hoped.

The bad part of it was that it was taking a full four minutes in his armor to bridge the gap between the motionless, glittering yacht and the robot, which had now begun circling it at medium range. That was a quite unavoidable safety measure for the operation as a whole—and actually U-1 should not be able to strike at him by any conceivable means before he was inside the yacht itself. But his brief outburst on the ship was the clearest possible warning that his emotional control had dropped suddenly, and inexplicably, to a point just this side of sanity.

He'd lived with normal fear for years—that was another thing; but only once before had he known a sensation comparable to this awareness of swirling, white-hot pools of unholy terror—held back from his mind now by the thinnest of brittle crusts. That had been long ago, in Lab-controlled training tests.

He knew better, however, than to try to probe into that sort of phenomenon just now. If he did, the probability was that it would spill full over him at about the moment he was getting his attack under way—which would be, rather definitely, fatal.

But there were other methods of emotional control, simple but generally effective, which might help steady him over the seconds remaining:

There was, for example, the undeniably satisfying reflection that not only had the major disaster of a Ceetal-dominated galaxy been practically averted almost as soon as it was recognized, but that in the same operation—a bonus from Lady Luck!—the long, long hunt for one of civilization's most ruthless enemies was coming to an unexpectedly sudden end. Like the avenging power of Vega personified was the deadly machine behind him, guided by a mind which was both more and less than his own, as it traced its graceful geometrical paths about the doomed yacht. Each completed circle would presently indicate that exactly one more minute had passed of the twenty which were the utmost remaining of U-1's life.

Just as undeniable, of course, was the probability that Pagadan's lease on life would run out even sooner than that—if she still lived.

But there wasn't much he could do about it. If he waited for the Vegan destroyers to arrive, the Lannai would have no chance at all. No normal being could survive another six hours under the kind of deliberately measured mental pressure U-1 would be exerting on her now to drain every possible scrap of information through her disintegrating protective patterns.

By acting as he was, he was giving her the best chance she could get after he had sent her in to spring the trap about U-1 on Gull. In the circumstances, that, too, had been unavoidable. Ironically, the only alternative to killing U-1 outright, as she no doubt had tried to do, was to blunder into one of the situational traps indicated by Correlation, and so restore that grim spacer to his own savage personality—which could then be counted on to cope with any Ceetal attempt to subordinate him once more to their purposes.

Waiting the few hours until he could get there to do the job himself might have made the difference between the survival or collapse of civilization not many decades away. If he had hesitated, the Department would have sent the Interstellar operative in, as a matter of course—officially, and at the risk of compromising the whole Lannai alliance as a consequence.

No, there hadn't been any real choice—the black thoughts rushed on—but just the same it was almost a relief to turn from that fact to the other one that his own chances of survival, just now, were practically as bad. Actually, there was no particular novelty in knowing he was outmatched. Only by being careful to remain the aggressor always, consciously and in fact, by selecting time and place and method of attack, was he able regularly to meet the superiority of the monstrous mentalities that were an Agent's most specific game. And back of him had been always the matchless resources of the Confederacy, to be drawn on as and when he needed them.

Now that familiar situational pattern was almost

completely reversed. U-1, doomed himself as surely as human efforts could doom him, had still been able to determine the form of the preliminary attack and force his enemy to adopt it.

So, as usual, the encounter would develop by plan, but the plan would not be Iliff's. His, for once, was to be the other role, that of the blundering, bewildered quarry, tricked into assault, then rushed through it to be struck down at the instant most favorable to the hunter.

Almost frantically, he tore his mind back from the trap. But it was just a little late—the swirling terror had touched him, briefly, and he knew his chances of success were down by that further unnecessary fraction.

Then the two-hundred-foot fire-studded bulk of the yacht came flashing toward him, blotting out space; and as he braked his jets for the approach he had time to remind himself that the quarry's rush did, after all, sometimes carry it through to the hunter. And that, in any event, he'd thought it all out and decided he still disliked an unfinished job—and that he *had* liked Pagadan.

Swinging himself up to the yacht's forward spacelock, every weapon at the ready, he caught the robot's brief thought:

"He's waiting for you! All locks have been released from inside."

Iliff's "Hm-m-m!" was a preoccupied salute to his opponent's logic. The lock had swung gently open before him—there was, of course, no point in attempting to hold it closed against a more powerful ship's sucking tractors; it would, simply, have been destroyed. Gingerly, he floated up to and through the opening, rather like a small balloon of greenish steel-alloy in his bulky armor.

No force-field gripped at his defenses, no devastating

bolts of radiant energy crashed at him from the inner walls. That spectral, abnormal terror of a moment ago became a dim sensation which stirred somewhere far down in his mind—and was gone.

He was on the job.

He drove through the inner transmitter, and felt the telepathic barrier that had blanked out the yacht dissolve and reform again behind him. In that instant, he dropped his shields and sent his mind racing full-open through the ship's interior.

There was the briefest of flickering, distorted thought-images from Pagadan. No message, no awareness of his presence—only the unconscious revelation of mind, still alive but strained to the utmost, already marked by the incoherence of ultimate exhaustion. As he sensed it, it vanished. Something had driven smoothly, powerfully, and impenetrably between— something that covered the Lannai's mind like a smothering fog.

Iliff's shields went up just in time. Then he himself was swaying, physically, under as stunning a mental attack as he had ever sustained.

Like the edge of a heavy knife, the impalpable but destructive force sheared at him—slashed once, twice, and was flicked away before he could grip it, leaving his vision momentarily blurred, his nerve-centers writhing.

A wash of corrosive atomic fire splashed blindingly off the front of his armor as he appeared in the control-room door—through it twin narrow-beam tractor rays came ramming in reversed, brain-jarring thrusts at his face-piece. He drove quickly into the room and let the tractors slam him back against the wall. They could not harm him. They were meant to startle and confuse, to destroy calculation before the critical assault.

The fire was different. For perhaps a minute, his

armor could continue to absorb it, but no longer. He was being hurried into the attack from every side. There had been no serious attempt to keep him from getting to the control room—he was meant to come to it.

He saw Pagadan first then, as he was meant to see her. Halfway down the narrow room, she sat facing him, only a few feet from the raised control platform against the wall, across which the projector fire came flashing in bluish twelve-inch jets. She was in an ordinary space-suit—no armor. She sat rigid and motionless, blocking his advance down that side of the room because the suit she wore would have burst into incandescence at the first splash of the hellish energies pouring dangerously past her.

U-1 made the point obvious—since he was here to get his ally out of the trap, he could not kill her.

He accepted the logic of that by flicking himself farther along the opposite wall, drawing the fire behind him. As he did so, something like a giant beetle shifted position beyond the massive steel desk on the control platform and dipped from sight again, and he knew then that U-1 was in armor almost as massive as his own—armor that had been a part of Pagadan's Interstellar equipment. To the end, that was the only glimpse he had of the spacer.

There remained then only the obvious frontal attack with mind-shields locked—across the platform to bring his own powerful projectors to bear directly on his opponent's armor.

If he *could* do that, he would very likely win almost instantly, and without injuring Pagadan. Therefore, whatever was to happen to him would happen in the instant of time he was crossing the room to reach the spacer.

And his gamble must be that his armor would carry him through it.

Some eight seconds had passed since he entered the room. A stubby tentacle on the front of his chest armor now raised a shielded projectile gun and sprayed the top of the desk beyond which U-1 crouched with a mushrooming, adhesive blanket of incendiaries. The tractor rays, their controls smothered in that liquid flaring, ceased to be a distraction; and Iliff launched himself.

The furious glare of U-1's projectors winked out abruptly.

The force that slammed Iliff down on the surface of the platform was literally bone-shattering.

For an endless, agonizing instant of time he was in the grip of the giant power that seemed to be wrenching him down into the solid hull of the ship. Then, suddenly released, he was off the edge of the platform and on the floor beside it. Momentarily, at least, it took him out of the spacer's line of fire.

But that was about all. He felt bones in his shattered right arm grinding on each other like jagged pebbles as he tried to reach for the studs that would drive him upward again. Throughout his body, torn muscles and crushed nerve-fibers were straining to the dictates of a brain long used to interpret physical pain as a danger signal only; but to activate any of the instruments of the miniature floating tank that encased him was utterly impossible.

He was doubly imprisoned then—in that two and a half ton coffin, and in ruined flesh that jerked aimlessly in animal agonies or had gone flaccid and unfeeling. But his brain, under its multiple separate protective devices, retained partial control; while the mind that was himself was still taut as a coiled snake, bleakly unaffected by the physical disaster.

He knew well enough what had happened. In one titanic jolt, the control platform's gravity field had received the full flow of the projector's energies. It had burned out almost instantaneously under that incalculable overload—but not quite fast enough to save him.

And now U-1's mind came driving in, probing for the extent of his enemy's helplessness, then coldly eager for the kill. At contact range, it would be only a matter of seconds to burn through that massive but no longer dangerous armor and blast out the life that lingered within.

Dimly, Iliff felt him rise and start forward. He felt the probing thoughts flick about him again, cautious still, and then the mind-shields relaxing and opening out triumphantly as the spacer approached. He dropped his own shields, and struck.

Never before had he dared risk the sustained concentration of destructive energy he hurled into U-1's mind—for, in its way, it was an overload as unstable as that which had wrecked the gravity field. Instantly, the flaring lights before his face-piece spun into blackness. The hot taste of gushing blood in his mouth, the last sensation of straining lungs and pain-rocked twitching nerves vanished together. Blocked suddenly and completely from every outward awareness, he had become a bodiless force bulleting with deadly resolution upon another.

The attack must have shaken even U-1's battle-hardened soul to its core. Physically, it stopped him in mid-stride, held him rigid and immobilized with nearly the effect of a paralysis gun. But after the first near-fatal moment of shock, while he attempted automatically and unsuccessfully to restore his shields before that rush of destruction, he was fighting back— and not with a similar suicidal fury but with a grim cold weight of vast mental power which yielded further ground only slowly if at all.

With that, the struggle became so nearly a stalemate that it still meant certain victory for the spacer. Both knew the last trace of physical life would drain out of Iliff in minutes, though perhaps only Iliff realized that his mind must destroy itself even more swiftly.

Something tore through his consciousness then like jagged bolts of lightning. He thought it was death. But it came again and again—until a slow, tremendous surprise welled up in him:

It was the *other* mind which was being torn! Dissolving now, crumbling into flashing thought-convulsions like tortured shrieks, though it still struggled on against him—and against something else, something which was by then completely beyond Iliff's comprehension.

The surprise dimmed out, together with his last awareness of himself—still driving relentlessly in upon a hated foe who would not die.

The voice paused briefly, then added: "Get that part to Lab. They'll be happy to know they hit it pretty close, for once."

It stopped again. After a moment the bright-looking young man in the Jeltad Headquarters office inquired, not too deferentially:

"Is there anything else, sir?"

He'd glanced up curiously once or twice at the vision tank of the extreme-range communicator before him, while he deftly distributed Iliff's after-mission report through the multiple-recorders. However, it wasn't the first time he'd seen a Zone Agent check in from the Emergency Treatment Chamber of his ship, completely enclosed in a block of semisolid protective gel, through which he was being molded, rayed, dosed, drenched, shocked, nourished and psychoed back to health and sanity.

With the irreverence of youth, the headquarters man considered that these near-legendary heroes of the Department bore on such occasions, when their robots even took care of heartbeat and breathing for them, a striking resemblance to damaged and bad-tempered embryos. He hoped suddenly no one happened to be reading his mind.

"Connect me," Iliff's voice said, though the lips of the figure in the vision tank did not move, "with Three for a personal report."

"I've been listening," came the deep, pleasantly modulated reply from an invisible source. "Switch off, Lallebeth—you've got all you need. All clear now, Iliff—and once more, congratulations!" And the picture of the tall, gray-haired, leanfaced man, who was the Third Co-ordinator of the Vegan Confederacy, grew slowly through the telepath transmitter into the mind of the small, wiry shape—half restored and covered with irregular patches of new pink skin—in the ship's Emergency Treatment Chamber.

"Back in the tank again, eh?" the Co-ordinator observed critically. "For the second day after a mission, you don't look too bad." He paused, considering Iliff closely. "Gravity?" he inquired.

"Gravity!" admitted the embryo.

"That will mess a fellow up!" The Co-ordinator was nodding sympathetically, but it seemed to Iliff that his superior's mind was on other matters, and more pleasing ones.

"Lab's just going to have to design me a suit," Three ran on with his usual chattiness, "which will be nonreactive to any type of synthetigravs, including tractors. Theoretically impossible, they say, of course! But I'm sure the right approach—"

He interrupted himself:

"I imagine you'll want to know what happened after

she got you back to your ship and contacted the destroyers?"

"She left word she was going to get in touch with you on her way back to Jeltad," Iliff said.

"Well, she did that. A remarkably energetic sort of person in a quiet way, Iliff. Fully aware, too, as I discovered, of the political possibilities in the situation. I persuaded her, of course, to take official credit for the death of U-1, and the termination of that part of the Ceetal menace—and, incidentally, for saving the life of one of our Department Agents."

"That wasn't so incidental," Iliff remarked.

"Only in comparison with the other, of course. She really did it then?"

"Oh, she did it all right! I was on my way out fast when she burned him down. Must have been a bad shock to U-1. I understand he hadn't released her mind for more than three or four seconds before she was reaching for his projector."

The Co-ordinator nodded. "The mental resiliency of these highly developed telepathic races must be really extraordinary! Any human being would have remained paralyzed for minutes after such pressures—perhaps for hours. Well, he wasn't omniscient, after all. He thought he could just let her lie there until he was finished with you."

"How long had he been pouring it on her?"

"About four hours! Practically ever since they hit space, coming out from Gull."

"She didn't crack at all?" Iliff asked curiously.

"No, but she thinks she couldn't have lasted more than another hour. However, she seemed to have had no doubt that *you* would arrive and get her out of the mess in time. Rather flattering, eh?"

The agent considered. "No," he said then. "Not necessarily."

His superior chuckled. "At any rate, she was reluctant to take credit for U-1. She thought if she accepted, you might feel she didn't fully appreciate your plunging in to the rescue."

"Well, you seem to have reassured her. And now, just what are the political results going to be?"

"It's too early to say definitely, but even without any help from us they'd be pretty satisfactory. The Ceetal business isn't for public consumption, of course—the boys made a clean sweep of that bunch a few hours back, by the way—but there've always been plenty of idiots building U-1 up into a glamorous figure. The Mysterious Great Bandit of the Spaceways and that sickening kind of stuff. They'll whoop it up just as happily now for the Champion of Vegan Justice who sent the old monster on his way, to wit—the Lannai Pagadan! It won't hurt either that she's really beautiful.

"And through her, of course, the glamor reflects back on her people, our nonhuman allies."

Iliff said thoughtfully: "Think they'll stay fashionable long enough to cinch the alliance?"

The Co-ordinator looked rather smug. "I believe that part of it can be safely left to me! Especially," he added deliberately, "since most of the organized resistance to said alliance has already collapsed."

Iliff waited and made no comment, because when the old boy got as confidential as all that, he was certainly leading up to something. And he did not usually bother to lead up to things without some good reason—which almost always spelled a lot of trouble for somebody else.

There was nobody else around at all, except Iliff.

"I had an unexpected visit three days ago," the Co-ordinator continued, "from my colleague, the Sixteenth

Co-ordinator, Department of Cultures. He'd been conducting, he said, a personal investigation of Lannai culture and psychology—and had found himself forced to the conclusion there was no reasonable objection to having them join us as full members of the Confederacy. 'A people of extraordinary refinement . . . high moral standards—' Hinted we'd have no further trouble with the Traditionalists either. Remarkable change of heart, eh?"

"Remarkable!" Iliff agreed, watchfully.

"But can you imagine," inquired the Co-ordinator, "what brought Sixteen—between us, mind you, Iliff, as pig-headed and hidebound an obstructionist as the Council has been hampered by in centuries—to this state of uncharacteristic enlightenment?"

"No," Iliff said, "I can't."

"Wait till you hear this then! After we'd congratulated each other and so on, he brought the subject back to various Lannai with whom he'd become acquainted. It developed presently he was interested in the whereabouts of one particular Lannai he'd met in a social way right here on Jeltad a few weeks before. He understood she was doing work—"

"All right," Iliff interrupted. "It was Pagadan."

The Co-ordinator appeared disappointed. "Yes, it was. She told you she'd met him, did she?"

"She admitted to some circulating in our upper social levels," Iliff said. "What did you tell him?"

"That she was engaged in highly confidential work for the Department at present, but that we expected to hear from her within a few days—I had my fingers crossed there!—and that I'd see to it she heard he'd been inquiring about her. Afterwards, after he'd gone, I sat down and sweated blood until I got her message from the destroyer."

"You don't suspect, I suppose, that she might have psychoed him?"

"Nonsense, Iliff!" the Co-ordinator smiled blandly. "If I had the *slightest* suspicion of that, it would be my duty to investigate immediately. Wouldn't it? But now, there's one point—your robot, of course, made every effort to keep Pagadan from realizing there was no human crew manning the ship. However, she told me frankly she'd caught on to our little Department secret and suggested that the best way to keep it there would be to have her transferred from Interstellar to Galactic. As a manner of fact, she's requested Zone Agent training! Think she'd qualify?"

"Oh, she'll qualify!" Iliff said dryly. "At that, it might be a good idea to get her into the Department, where we can try to keep an eye on her. It would be too bad if we found out, ten years from now, that a few million Lannai were running the Confederacy."

For an instant, the Co-ordinator looked startled. "Hm-m-m," he said reflectively. "Well, that's hardly likely. However, I think I'll take your advice. I might send her over to your Zone in a week or so, and—"

"Oh, no," Iliff said quietly. "Oh, no, you don't! I've been waiting right along for the catch, and this is one job Headquarters is going to swing without me."

"Now, Iliff—"

"It's never happened before," Iliff added, "but right now the Department is very close to its first case of Zone Agent mutiny."

"Now, Iliff, take it easy!" The Co-ordinator paused. "I must disapprove of your attitude, of course, but frankly I admire your common sense. Well, forget the suggestion—I'll find some other sucker."

He became pleasantly official.

"I suppose you're on your way back to your Zone at present?"

"I am. In fact, we're almost exactly in the position we'd reached when you buzzed me the last time. Now, there wouldn't happen to be some little job I could knock off for you on the way?"

"Well—" the Co-ordinator began, off guard. For the shortest fraction of a second, he had the air of a man consulting an over-stuffed mental file.

Then he started and blinked.

"In your condition? Nonsense, Iliff! It's out of the question!"

On the last word, Iliff's thought and image flickered out of his mind. But the Third Co-ordinator sat motionless for another moment or so before he turned off the telepath transmitter. There was a look of mild surprise on his face.

Of course, there had been no change of expression possible in that immobilized and anaesthetized embryonic figure—not so much as the twitch of an eyelid! But in that instant, while he was hesitating, there *had* seemed to flash from it a blast of such cold and ferocious malignity that he was almost startled into flipping up his shields.

"Better lay off the little devil for a while!" he decided. "Let him just stick to his routine. I'll swear, for a moment there I saw smoke pour out of his ears."

He reached out and tapped a switch.

"Psych-tester? What do you think?"

"The Agent requires no deconditioning," the Psych-tester's mechanical voice stated promptly. "As I predicted at the time, his decision to board U-1's ship was in itself sufficient to dissolve both the original failure-shock and the artificial conditioning later connected with it. The difficulties he experienced, between the decision and his actual entry of the ship, were merely symptoms of that process and have had no further effect on his mental health."

The Co-ordinator rubbed his chin reflectively.

"Well, that sounds all right. Does he realize I . . . uh . . . had anything to do—?"

"The Agent is strongly of the opinion that you suspected Tahmey of being U-1 when you were first informed of the Interstellar operative's unusual report, and further, that you assigned him to the mission for this reason. While approving of the choice as such, he shows traces of a sub-level reflection that your tendency towards secretiveness will lead you to . . . outfox . . . yourself so badly some day that he may not be able to help you."

"Why—"

"He has also begun to suspect," the Psych-tester continued, undisturbed, "that he was fear-conditioned over a period of years to the effect that any crisis involving U-1 would automatically create the highest degree of defensive tensions compatible with his type of mentality."

The Co-ordinator whistled softly.

"He's caught on to that, eh?" He reflected. "Well, after all," he pointed out, almost apologetically, "it wasn't such a bad idea in itself! The boy does have this tendency to bull his way through, on some short-cut or other, to a rather dangerous degree. And there was no way of foreseeing the complications introduced by the Ceetal threat and his sense of responsibility towards the Lannai, which made it impossible for him to obey that urgent mental pressure to be careful in whatever he did about U-1."

He paused invitingly, but the Psych-tester made no comment.

"It's hard to guess right every time!" the Co-ordinator concluded defensively.

He shook his head and sighed, but then forgot Iliff entirely as he turned to the next problem.

The Illusionists

The three Bjanta scouts were within an hour's flight of the yellow dwarf star of Ulphi when the *Viper's* needle-shape drove into their detection range, high up but on a course that promised almost to intersect their own.

It didn't exactly come to that point, though the unwary newcomer continued to approach for several minutes more. But then, with an abruptness which implied considerable shock on board at discovering Bjanta ahead, she veered off sharply and shot away at a very respectable speed.

The scout disks swung about unhurriedly, opened out in pursuit formation and were presently closing in again, with leisurely caution, on the fugitive. Everything about that beautifully designed, blue-gleaming yacht suggested the most valuable sort of catch. Some very wealthy individual's plaything it might have been, out of one of the major centers of civilization, though adventuring now far from the beaten path of commercial spaceways. In which case, she would be very competently piloted and crewed and somewhat better armed than the average freighter. Which should make her capable of resisting their combined attack for a maximum of four or five minutes—or, if she preferred energy-devouring top velocity, of keeping ahead of them for even one or two minutes longer than that.

But no Bjanta was ever found guilty of impulsive recklessness. And, just possibly, this yacht could also turn out to be another variation of those hellish engines of destruction which Galactic humanity and its allies had been developing with ever-increasing skill during the past few thousand years, against just such marauders as they.

As it happened, that described the *Viper* exactly. A Vegan G.Z. Agent-Ship, and one of the last fifty or so of her type to be completed, she was, compared with anything else up to five times her three-hundred-foot length, the peak, the top, the absolute culmination of space-splitting sudden death. And, furthermore, she knew it.

"They're maintaining pattern and keeping up with no sign of effort," her electronic brain reported to her pilot. "Should we show them a little more speed?"

"The fifteen percent increase was plenty," the pilot returned in a pleasant soprano voice. Her eyes, the elongated silver eyes and squared black pupils of a Lannai humanoid, studied the Bjantas' positions in the vision tank of the long, wide control desk at which she sat. "If they edge in too far, you can start weaving, but remember they're sensitive little apes! Anything fancy before we get within range of our cruiser is bound to scare them off."

There was silence for a moment. Then the ship's robot voice came into the control room again.

"Pagadan, the disk low in Sector Twelve is almost at contact beaming range. We could take any two of them at any moment now, and save the third for the test run!"

"I know it, little *Viper*," Pagadan said patiently. "But this whole job's based on the assumption that the Bjantas are operating true to form. In that case, the Mother Disk should be somewhere within three light-years behind us, and the cruiser wants to run two of these scouts back far enough to show just where it's lying. We need only the one for ourselves."

Which was something the *Viper* already knew. But it had been designed to be a hunting machine more nearly than anything else, and at times its hunting impulses had to be diverted. Pagadan did that as automatically as she would have checked a similar impulse in her own mind—in effect, whenever she was on board, there was actually no very definite boundary between her own thoughts and those that pulsed through the *Viper*. Often the Lannai would have found it difficult to say immediately whether it was her organic brain or its various electronic extensions in the ship which was attending to some specific bit of business. Just now, as an example, it was the *Viper* who had been watching the communicators.

"The Agent-Trainee on the O-Ship off Ulphi is trying to talk to you, Pagadan," the robot-voice came into the room. "Will you adjust to his range?"

The Lannai's silver-nailed hand shot out and spun a tiny dial on the desk before her. From a communicator to her left a deep voice inquired, a little anxiously:

"Pag? Do you hear me? This is Hallerock. Pag?"

"Go ahead, chum!" she invited. "I was off beam for a moment there. The planet still look all right?"

"No worse than it ever did," said Hallerock. "But this is about your Fleet operation. The six destroyers are spread out behind you in interception positions by now, and the cruiser should be coming into detection dead ahead at any moment. You still want them to communicate with you through the Observation Ship here?"

"Better keep it that way," Pagadan ordered. "The Bjantas might spot Fleet signals, as close to me as they are, but it's a cinch they can't tap *this* beam! I won't slip up again. Anything from the Department?"

"Correlation is sending some new stuff out on the Ulphi business, but nothing important. At any rate, they didn't want to break into your maneuver with the Bjantas. I told them to home it here to the O-Ship. Right?"

"Right," Pagadan approved. "You'll make a Zone Agent yet, my friend! In time."

"I doubt it," Hallerock grunted. "There's no real future in it anyway. Here's the cruiser calling again, Pag! I'll be standing by—"

Pagadan pursed her lips thoughtfully as a barely audible click indicated her aide had gone off communication. She'd been a full-fledged Zone Agent of the Vegan Confederacy for exactly four months now—the first member of any nonhuman race to attain that rank in the super-secretive Department of Galactic Zones. Hallerock, human, was an advanced Trainee. Just how advanced was a question she'd have to decide, and very soon.

The surface reflections vanished from her mind at the *Viper's* sub-vocal warning:

"Cruiser—dead ahead!"

"The disk on your left!" Pagadan snapped. "Cut it off from the others as soon as they begin to turn. Give it a *good* start then—and be sure you're crowding the last bit of speed out of it before you even think of closing in. We may not be able to get what we're after—probably won't—but Lab can use every scrap of information we collect on those babies!"

"We'll get what we're after, too," the *Viper* almost purred. And, a bare instant later:

"They've spotted the cruiser. *Now!*"

In the vision tank, the fleeing disk grew and grew. During the first few minutes, it had appeared there only as a comet-tailed spark, a dozen radiant streamers of different colors fanning out behind it—not an image of the disk itself but the tank's visual representation of any remote moving object on which the ship's detectors were held. The shifting lengths and brightness of the streamers announced at a glance to those trained to read them the object's distance, direction, comparative and absolute speeds and other matters of interest to a curious observer.

But as the *Viper* began to reduce the headstart the Bjanta had been permitted to get, at the exact rate calculated to incite it to the most intensive efforts to hold that lead, a shadowy outline of the disk's true shape began to grow about the spark. A bare quarter million miles away finally, the disk itself appeared to be moving at a visual range of two hundred yards ahead of the ship, while the spark still flickered its varied information from the center of the image.

Pagadan's hands, meanwhile, played continuously over the control desk's panels, racing the ship's recording instruments through every sequence of descriptive analysis of which they were capable.

"We're still getting nothing really new, I'm afraid," she said at last, matter-of-factly. She had never been within sight of a Bjanta before; but Vega's Department of Galactic Zones had copies of every available record ever made of them, and she had studied the records. The information was largely repetitious and not conclusive enough to have ever permitted a really decisive thrust against the marauders. Bjantas no longer constituted a major threat to civilization, but they had never stopped being a dangerous nuisance along its fringes—space-vermin of a particularly elusive and obnoxious sort.

"They've made no attempt to change direction at all?" she inquired.

"Not since they first broke out of their escape-curve," the *Viper* replied. "Shall I close in now?"

"Might as well, I suppose." Pagadan was still gazing, almost wistfully, into the tank. The disk was tilted slightly sideways, dipping and quivering in the familiar motion-pattern of Bjanta vessels; a faint glimmer of radiation ran and vanished and ran again continuously around its yard-thick edge. The Bjantas were conservatives; the first known recordings made of them in the early centuries of the First Empire had shown space-machines of virtually the same appearance as the one now racing ahead of the *Viper*.

"The cruiser seems satisfied we check with its own line on the Mother Disk," she went on. She sighed, tapping the tank anxiously. "Well, nudge them a bit—and be ready to jump!"

The *Viper's* nudging was on the emphatic side. A greenish, transparent halo appeared instantly about the disk; a rainbow-hued one flashed into visibility just beyond it immediately after. Then the disk's dual barrier vanished again; and the disk itself veered crazily off its course, flipping over and over like a crippled bat, showing at every turn the deep, white-hot gash the *Viper's* touch had seared across its top.

It was on the fifth turn, some four-tenths of a second later, that it split halfway around its rim. Out of that yawning mouth a few score minute duplicates of itself were spewed into space and flashed away in all directions—individual Bjantas in their equivalent of a combined spacesuit and lifeboat. As they dispersed the stricken scout gaped wider; a blinding glare burst out of it; and the disk had vanished in the traditional Bjanta style of self-destruction when trapped by superior force.

Fast as the reaction had been, the *Viper's* forward surge at full acceleration following her first jabbing beam was barely slower. She stopped close enough to the explosion to feel its radiations activate her own barriers; and even before she stopped, every one of her grappling devices was fully extended and combing space about her.

Within another two seconds, therefore, each of the fleeing Bjantas was caught—and at the instant of contact, all but two had followed the scout into explosive and practically traceless suicide. Those two, however, were wrenched open by paired tractors which gripped and simultaneously twisted as they gripped—an innovation with which the *Viper* had been outfitted for this specific job.

Pagadan, taut and watching, went white and was on her feet with a shriek of inarticulate triumph.

"You *did* it, you sweetheart!" she yelped then. "First ones picked up intact in five hundred years!"

"They're not intact," the *Viper* corrected, less excitedly. "But I have all the pieces, I think!"

"The bodies are hardly damaged," gloated Pagadan, staring into the tank. "It doesn't matter much about the shells. Just bring it all in easy now! The lovely things! Wait till Lab hears we got them."

She hovered around nervously while the flat, brown, soft-shelled—and really not badly dented—bodies of the two Bjantas were being drawn in through one of the *Viper's* locks and deposited gently in a preservative tank, where they floated against the top, their twenty-two angular legs folded up tightly against their undersides. Most of the bunched neural extensions that made them a unit with the mechanisms of their detachable space-shells had been sheared off, of course; but the *Viper* had saved everything.

"Nice work, Pag!" Hallerock's voice came from the communicator as she returned exultantly to the control room. "No chance of any life being left in those things, I suppose?"

"Not after that treatment!" Pagadan said regretfully. "But I'm really not complaining. You heard me then?"

"I did," acknowledged Hallerock. "Paralyzing sort of war whoop you've got! Want to see the recording the cruiser shot back to me on the Mother Disk? That run just went off, too, as per schedule."

"Put it on!" Pagadan said, curling herself comfortably and happily into her desk chair. "So they found Mommy, eh? Never had such fun before I started slumming around with humans. What were the destructive results?"

"They did all right. An estimated forty-five percent of the scouts right on the strike—and they figure it will be over eighty before the survivors get out of pursuit range. One of the destroyers and a couple of the cruiser's strike-ships were slightly damaged when the core blew up. Nothing serious."

The visual recording appeared on the communication screen a moment later. It was very brief, as seen from the cruiser—following its hornet-swarm of released strike-ships in on the great, flat, scaly-looking pancake bulk of the Mother Disk, while a trio of destroyers closed down on either side. As a fight, Pagadan decided critically, it was also the worst flop she'd seen in years, considering that the trapped quarry was actually a layered composite of several thousand well-armed scouts! For a brief instant, the barriers of every charging Vegan ship blazed a warning white; then the screen filled momentarily with a rainbow-hued sparkle of scouts scattering under the lethal fire of the attackers—and the brighter flashing of those that failed.

As both darkened out and the hunters swirled off in pursuit of the fugitive swarms, an ellipsoid crystal-line core, several hundred yards in diameter, appeared where the Disk had lain in space. The Bjanta breeding center. It seemed to expand slightly.

An instant later, it was a miniature nova.

Pagadan blinked and nodded approvingly as the screen went blank.

"Tidy habit! Saves us a lot of trouble. But *we* made the only real haul of the day, *Viper*, old girl!" She grimaced. "So now we've still got to worry about that sleepwalking silly little planet of Ulphi, and the one guy on it who isn't . . . isn't sleepwalking, anyway. And a couple of other—" She straightened up suddenly. "Who's that working your communicators now?"

"That's the robot-tracker you put on the Department of Cultures investigator on Ulphi," the *Viper* informed her. "He wants to come in to tell you the lady's got herself into some kind of jam with the population down there. Shall I switch him to the O-Ship and have the Agent-Trainee check and take over, if necessary?"

"Hold it!" Pagadan's hands flew out towards the section of instrument panel controlling the communicators. "Not if it's the D.C. girl! That would mess up all my plans. The tracker's ready and equipped to see nothing happens to her before I get there. Just put that line through to me, fast!"

Some while later, she summoned Hallerock to the O-Ship's communicator.

" . . . So I'm picking you up in a few minutes and

taking you on board the *Viper*. Central Lab wants a set of structural recordings of these pickled Bjantas right away—and you'll have to do it, because I won't have the time."

"What happened?" her aide inquired, startled.

"Nothing very serious," Pagadan said soothingly. "But it's likely to keep me busy for the next few hours. Our D.C. investigator on Ulphi may have got an accidental whiff of what's rancid on the planet—anyway, somebody's trying to get her under mental control right now! I've got her covered by a tracker, of course, so she's in no real danger; but I'll take the *Viper's* skiff and go on down as soon as I get you on board. By the way, how soon can you have the hospital ship prepared for its job?"

Hallerock hesitated a moment. "I suppose it's ready to start any time. I finished treating the last of the personnel four hours ago."

"Good boy," Pagadan applauded. "I've got something in mind—not sure yet whether it will work. But that attack on the D.C. might make it possible for us to wind up the whole Ulphi operation inside the next twenty-four hours!"

It had started out, three weeks before, looking like such a nice little mission. Since it was her fifth assignment in four months, and since there had been nothing even remotely nice about any of the others, Pagadan could appreciate that.

Nothing much to do for about three or four weeks now, she'd thought gratefully as she hauled out her skiff for a brief first survey of the planet of Ulphi. She had landed as an ostensible passenger on a Vegan destroyer, the skiff tucked away in one of the destroyer's gun locks, while the *Viper* went on orbit at a safe distance overhead. That gleaming deep-space machine looked a trifle too impressive to be a suitable vehicle for Pelial, the minor official of Galactic Zones, which was Pagadan's local alias. And as Ulphi's entire population was planet-bound by congenital space-fear, the skiff would provide any required amount of transportation, while serving principally as living quarters and a work-office.

But there would be really nothing to do. Except, of course, to keep a casual eye on the safety of the other Vegans newly arrived on the planet and cooperate with the Fleet in its unhurried preparations to receive the Bjantas, who were due to appear in about a month for the ninth of their series of raids on Ulphi. Those obliging creatures conducted their operations in cycles of such unvarying regularity that it was a pleasure to go to work on them, once you'd detected their traces and could muster superior force to intercept their next return.

On Ulphi Bjantas had been reaping their harvest of life and what they could use of civilization's treasures and tools at periods which lay just a fraction over three standard years apart. It had done no very significant damage as yet, since it had taken eight such raids to frighten the population into revealing its plight by applying for membership in the far-off Confederacy of Vega and the protection that would bring them. The same cosmic clockwork which first set the great Disk on this course would be returning it now, predictably, to the trap Vega had prepared.

Nothing for Pagadan to worry about. Nobody, actually, seemed to have much confidence that the new shell-cracker beams installed on the *Viper* to pick up a couple of Bjantas in an unexploded condition would work as they should, but that problem was Lab's and not hers. And, feeling no doubt that she'd earned a little vacation, they were presenting her meanwhile with these next three weeks on Ulphi. The reports of the officials of other Confederacy government branches who had preceded Pagadan here had described it as a uniquely charming little backwater world of humanity, cut off by the development of planetary space-fear from the major streams of civilization for nearly four hundred years. Left to itself in its amiable climate, Ulphi had flowered gradually into a state of quaint and leisurely prettiness.

So went the reports!

Jauntily, then, Pagadan set forth in her skiff to make an aerial survey of this miniature jewel of civilization and pick out a few of the very best spots for some solid, drowsy loafing.

Two days later, her silver hair curled flat to her skull with outraged shock, she came back on board the *Viper*. The activated telepath transmitter hummed with the ship's full power, as it hurled her wrathful message to G.Z. Headquarters Central on the planet of Jeltad— in Vega's system, eight thousand light-years away.

At Central on Jeltad, a headquarters clerk, on his way out to lunch, paused presently behind the desk of another. His manner was nervous.

"What's the Pyramid Effect?" he inquired.

"You ought to know," his friend replied. "If you don't, go punch it from Restricted Psych-Library under that heading. I've got a final mission report coming through." He glanced around. "How come the sudden urge for knowledge, Linky?"

Linky jerked a thumb back towards his desk transmitter. "I got that new Lannai Z.A. on just before the end of my stretch. She was blowing her silver top about things in general—had me lining up interviews with everybody from Snoops to the Old Man for her! The Pyramid Effect seems to be part of it."

The other clerk snickered. "She's just diving into a mission then. I had her on a few times while she was in Zonal Training. She'll swear like a Terran till she hits her stride. After that, the rougher things get the sweeter she grows. You want to wait a little? If I get this beam through, I'll turn it over to a recorder and join you for lunch."

"All right." Linky hesitated a moment and then drifted back towards his desk. At a point well outside the vision range of its transmitter screen, he stopped and listened.

" . . . Well, *why* didn't anybody know?" Pagadan's voice came, muted but crackling. "That Department of Cultures investigator has been on Ulphi for over a month now, and others just as long! You get copies of their reports, don't you? You couldn't put any two of them together without seeing that another Telep-Two thinks he's invented the Pyramid Effect out here—there isn't a thing on the crummy little planet that doesn't show it! And I'll be the daughter of a C-Class human," she added bitterly, "if it isn't a type-case in full flower, with all the trimmings! Including immortalization and the Siva Psychosis. No, I do *not* want Lab to home any of their findings out to me! Tell them I'm staying right here on telepath till they've sorted out what I gave them. Where's Snoops, that evil little man? Or can somebody locate that fuddle-headed, skinny, blond clerk I had on a few minutes—"

Linky tiptoed gently back out of hearing.

"She's talking to Correlation now," he reported to his friend. "Not at the sweetness stage yet. I think I'll put in a little time checking the Library at that."

The other clerk nodded without looking up. "You could use the Head's information cabinet. He just went out."

"Pyramid Effect," Psych-Library Information

instructed Linky gently a minute later. "Restricted, Galactic Zones. Result of the use of an expanding series of psychimpulse-multipliers, organic or otherwise, by Telepaths of the Orders Two to Four, for the transference of directional patterns, compulsions, illusions, et cetera, to large numbers of subjects.

"The significant feature of the Pyramid Effect is its elimination of excessive drain on the directing mentality, achieved by utilizing the neural or neural-type energies of the multipliers themselves in transferring the directed impulses from one stage to the next.

"Techniques required to establish the first and second stages of multipliers are classified as Undesirable General Knowledge. Though not infrequently developed independently by Telepaths above the primary level, their employment in any form is prohibited throughout the Confederacy of Vega and variously discouraged by responsible governments elsewhere.

"Establishment of the third stage, and subsequent stages, of impulse-multipliers involves a technique-variant rarely developed by uninstructed Telepaths below the Order of Five. It is classified, under all circumstances, as Prohibited General Knowledge and is subject to deletion under the regulations pertaining to that classification.

"Methodology of the Pyramid Effect may be obtained in detail under the heading 'Techniques: Pyramid Effect'—"

The gentle voice subsided.

"Hm-m-m!" said Linky. He glanced about but there was nobody else in immediate range of the information cabinet. He tapped out "Techniques: Pyramid Effect," and punched.

"The information applied for," another voice stated tunelessly, "is restricted to Zone Agent levels and above. Your identification?"

Linky scowled, punched "Cancellation" quickly, murmured "Nuts!" and tapped another set of keys.

"Psychimpulse-multiplier," the gentle voice came back. "Restricted, Galactic Zones. Any person, organic entity, energy form, or mentalized instrument employed in distributing the various types of telepathic impulses to subjects beyond the scope of the directing mentality in range or number—Refer to 'Pyramid Effect'—"

That seemed to be that. What else was the Z.A. crying about? Oh, yes!

"Siva Psychosis," the gentle voice resumed obligingly. "Symptom of the intermediate to concluding stages of the Autocrat Circuit in human-type mentalities—Refer to 'Multiple Murder: Causes'—"

Linky grimaced.

"Got what you wanted?" The other clerk was standing behind him.

Linky got up. "No," he said. "Let's go anyhow. Your Final Mission came through?"

His friend shook his head.

"The guy got it. Ship and all. The automatic death signals just started coming in. That *bong-bong . . . bong-bong* stuff always gets on my nerves!" He motioned Linky into an elevator ahead of him. "They ought to work out a different sort of signal."

"Understand you've been having some trouble with Department of Cultures personnel," Snoops told the transmitter genially.

"Just one of them," Pagadan replied, regarding him with disfavor. Probably, he wasn't really evil but he certainly looked it—aged in evil, and wizened with it. Also, he had been, just now, very hard to find. "That particular one," she added, "is worse than any dozen others I've run into, so far!"

"DC-COIF 1227, eh?" Snoops nodded. "Don't have to make up a dossier for you on her. Got it all ready."

"We've had trouble with her before, then?"

"Oh, sure! Lots of times. System Chief Jasse—beautiful big thing, isn't she?" Snoops chuckled. "I've got any number of three-dimensionals of her."

"You would have," said Pagadan sourly. "For a flagpole, she's not so bad looking, at that. Must be eight feet if she's an inch!"

"Eight foot two," Snoops corrected. "What's she up to now, that place you're at—Ulphi?"

"Minding other people's business like any D.C. Mostly mine, though she doesn't know that. I'm objecting particularly to her practice of pestering the Fleet for information they either don't have or aren't allowed to give for reasons of plain standard operational security. There's a destroyer commander stationed here who says every time she looks at him now, he gets a feeling he'd better watch his step or he'll get turned over and whacked."

"She wouldn't do that," Snoops said earnestly. "She's a good girl, that Jasse. Terribly conscientious, that's all. You want that dossier homed out to you or right now, vocally?"

"Both. Right now I want mostly background stuff, so I'll know how to work her. I'd psycho it out of her myself, but she's using a pretty good mind-shield and I can't spend too much mission-time on the Department of Cultures."

Snoops nodded, cleared his throat, rolled his eyes up reflectively, closed them and began.

"Age twenty-five, or near enough to make no difference. Type A-Class Human, unknown racial variant. Citizen of the Confederacy; home-planet Jeltad. Birthplace unknown—parentage, ditto; presumably spacer stock."

"Details on that!" interrupted Pagadan.

He'd intended to, Snoops said, looking patient.

Subject, at about the age of three, had been picked up in space, literally, and in a rather improbable section—high in the northern latitudes where the suns thinned out into the figurative Rim. A Vegan scout, pausing to inspect an area littered with the battle-torn wreckage of four ships, found her drifting about there unconscious and half-alive, in a spacesuit designed for a very tall adult—the kind of adult she eventually became.

Investigation indicated she was the only survivor of what must have been an almost insanely savage and probably very brief engagement. There was some messy evidence that one of the ships had been crewed by either five or six of her kind. The other three had been manned by Lartessians, a branch of human space marauders with whom Vega's patrol forces were more familiar than they particularly wanted to be.

So was Pagadan. "They fight just like that, the crazy apes! And they're no slouches—our little pet's people must be a rugged lot to break even with them at three-to-one odds. But we've got no record at all of that breed?"

He'd checked pretty closely but without results, Snoops shrugged. And so, naturally enough, had Jasse herself later on. She'd grown up in the family of the scout's second pilot. They were earnest Traditionalists, so it wasn't surprising that at sixteen she entered the Traditionalist College on Jeltad. She was a brilliant student and a spectacular athlete—twice a winner in Vega's System Games.

"Doing what?" inquired Pagadan curiously.

Javelin, and one of those swimming events; Snoops wasn't sure just which— She still attended the College intermittently; but at nineteen she'd started to work as a field investigator for the Department of Cultures. Which wasn't surprising either, since Cultures was practically the political extension of the powerful Traditionalist Creed—

They had made her a System Chief only three years later.

"About that time," Snoops concluded, "was when we started having trouble with Jasse. She's smart enough to suspect that whatever Galactic Zones is doing doesn't jibe entirely with our official purpose in life." He looked mildly amused. "Seems to think we might be some kind of secret police—you know how Traditionalists feel about anything like *that!*"

Pagadan nodded. "Everything open and aboveboard. They mean well, bless them!"

She went silent then, reflecting; while the alien black-and-silver eyes continued to look at Snoops, or through him possibly, at something else.

He heard himself saying uneasily, "You're not going to do her any harm, Zone Agent?"

"Now why should I be doing System Chief Jasse any harm?" Pagadan inquired, much too innocently. "A good girl, like you say. And so lovely looking, too—in spite of that eight-foot altitude."

"Eight foot two," Snoops corrected mechanically. He didn't feel at all reassured.

The assistant to the Chief of G.Z. Office of Correlation entered the room to which his superior had summoned him and found the general gazing pensively upon a freshly assembled illumined case-chart.

The assistant glanced at the chart number and shrugged sympathetically.

"I understand she wants to speak to you personally," he remarked. "Is it as bad as she indicates?"

"Colonel Dubois," the general said, without turning his head, "I'm glad you're here. Yes, it's just about as bad!" He nodded at the upper right region of the chart where a massed group of symbols flickered uncertainly. "That's the bulk of the information we got from the Zone Agent concerning the planet of Ulphi just now. Most of the rest of it has been available to this office for weeks."

Both men studied the chart silently for a moment.

"It's a mess, certainly," the colonel admitted then. "But I'm sure the Agent understands that, when an emergency is not indicated in advance, all incoming information is necessarily handled here in a routine manner, which frequently involves a considerable time-lag in correlation."

"No doubt she does," agreed the general. "However, we keep running into her socially when she's around the System, my wife and I. Particularly my wife. You understand that I should like our summation of this case to be as nearly perfect as we can make it?"

"I understand, sir."

"I'm going to read it," the general sighed. "I want you to check me closely. If you're doubtful on any point of interpretation at all, kindly interrupt me at once."

They bent over the chart together.

"The over-all pattern on Ulphi," the general stated, "is obviously that produced by an immortalized A-Class human intellect, Sub-Class Twelve, variant Telep-Two—as developed in planetary or small-system isolation, over a period of between three and five centuries."

He'd lapsed promptly, Colonel Dubois noted with a trace of amusement, into a lecturer's tone and style. Being one of the two men primarily responsible for devising the psychomathematics of correlation and making it understandable to others, the general had found plenty of opportunity to acquire such mannerisms.

"In that time," he went on, "the system of general controls has, of course, become almost completely automatic. There is, however, continuing and fairly intensive activity on the part of the directing mentality. Development of the Siva Psychosis is at a phase typical for the elapsed period—concealed and formalized killings cloaked in sacrificial symbolism. Quantitatively, they have not begun as yet to affect the population level. The open and indiscriminate slaughter preceding the sudden final decline presumably would not appear, then, for at least another century.

"Of primary significance for the identification of the controlling mentality is this central grouping of formulae. Within the historical period which must have seen the early stages of the mentality's dominance, the science of Ulphi—then practically at Galactic par—was channeled for thirty-eight years into a research connected with the various problems of personal organic immortality. Obviously, under such conditions, only the wildest sort of bad luck could prevent discovery and co-ordination of the three basic requirements for any of the forms of individual perpetuation presently developed.

"We note, however, that within the next two years the investigation became completely discredited, was dropped and has not been resumed since.

"The critical date, finally, corresponds roughly to the announced death of the planet's outstanding psychic leader of the time—an historical figure even on present-day Ulphi, known as Moyuscane the Immortal Illusionist.

"Corroborative evidence—"

The reading took some fifteen minutes in all.

"Well, that's it, I think," the general remarked at last. "How the old explorers used to wonder at the frequency with which such little lost side-branches of civilization appeared to have simply and suddenly ceased to exist!"

He became aware of the colonel's sidelong glance. "You agree with my interpretation, colonel?"

"Entirely, sir."

The general hesitated. "The population on Ulphi hasn't been too badly debased as yet," he pointed out. "Various reports indicate an I.Q. average of around eleven points below A-Class—not too bad, considering the early elimination of the strains least acceptable to the controlling mentality, and the stultifying effect of life-long general compulsions on the others.

"They're still eligible for limited membership—capable of self-government and, with help, of self-defense. It will be almost a century, of course, before they grow back to a point where they can be of any real use to us. Meanwhile, the location of the planet itself presents certain strategic advantages—"

He paused again. "I'm afraid, colonel," he admitted, "that I'm evading the issue! The fact remains that a case of this kind simply does not permit of solution by this office. The identification of Moyuscane the Immortal as the controlling mentality is safe enough, of course. Beyond that we cannot take the responsibility for anything but the most general kind of recommendation. But now, colonel—since I'm an old man, a cowardly old man who really hates an argument—I'm going on vacation for the next hour or so.

"Would you kindly confront the Zone Agent with our findings? I understand she is still waiting on telepath for them."

Zone Agent Pagadan, however, received the information with a degree of good nature which Colonel Dubois found almost disquieting.

"Well, if you can't, you can't," she shrugged. "I rather

expected it. The difficulty is to identify our Telep-Two physically without arousing his suspicions? And the danger is that no one knows how to block things like a planet-wide wave of suicidal impulses, if he happens to realize that's a good method of self-defense?"

"That's about it," acknowledged the colonel. "It's very easy to startle mentalities of his class into some unpredictable aggressive reaction. That makes it a simple matter to flush them into sight, which helps to keep them from becoming more than a temporary nuisance, except in such unsophisticated surroundings as on Ulphi. But in the situation that exists there—when the mentality has established itself and set up a widespread system of controls—it does demand the most cautious handling on the part of an operator. This particular case is now further aggravated by the various psychotic disturbances of Immortalization."

Pagadan nodded. "You're suggesting, I suppose, that the whole affair should be turned over to Interstellar Crime for space-scooping or some careful sort of long-range detection like that?"

"It's the method most generally adopted," the colonel said. "Very slow, of course—I recall a somewhat similar case which took thirty-two years to solve. But once the directing mentality has been physically identified without becoming aware of the fact, it can be destroyed safely enough."

"I can't quite believe in the necessity of leaving Moyuscane in control of that sad little planet of his for another thirty-two years, or anything like it," the Lannai said slowly. "I imagine he'll be willing to put up with our presence until the Bjanta raids have been deflected?"

"That seems to be correct. If you decide to dig him out yourself, you have about eight weeks to do it. If the Bjantas haven't returned to Ulphi by then, he'll understand that they've either quit coming of their own accord, as they sometimes do—or that they've been chased off secretly. And he could hardly help hitting on the reason for that! In either case, the Senate of Ulphi will simply withdraw its application for membership in the Confederacy. It's no secret that we're too completely tied up in treaties of nonintervention to do anything but pull our officials out again, if that's what they want."

"The old boy has it all figured out, hasn't he?" Pagadan paused. "Well—we'll see. Incidentally, I notice your summation incorporated Lab's report on the space-fear compulsion Moyuscane's clamped on Ulphi. Do you have that with you in detail—Lab's report, I mean? I'd like to hear it."

"It's here, yes—" A muted alto voice addressed Pagadan a moment later:

"In fourteen percent of the neuroplates submitted with the Agent's report, space-fear traces were found to extend into the subanalytical levels normally involved in this psychosis. In all others, the symptoms of the psychosis were readily identifiable as an artificially induced compulsion.

"Such a compulsion would maintain itself under reality-stresses to the point required to initiate space-fear death in the organism but would yield normally to standard treatment."

"Good enough," Pagadan nodded. "Fourteen percent space-fear susceptibility is about normal for that type of planetary population, isn't it? But what about Moyuscane himself? Is there anything to show, anywhere, that he suffered from the genuine brand of the psychosis—that he is one of that fourteen percent?"

"Well—yes, there is!" Colonel Dubois looked a little startled. "That wasn't mentioned, was it? Actually, it shows up quite clearly in the historical note that none of his reported illusion performances had any but planetary backgrounds, and usually interior ones, at that. It's an exceptional Illusionist, you know, who won't play around with deep-space effects in every conceivable variation. But Moyuscane never touched them—"

"Telepath is now cleared for Zone Agent 131.71," the Third Co-ordinator of the Vegan Confederacy murmured into the transmitter before him.

Alone in his office as usual, he settled back into his chair to relax for the few seconds the visualization tank would require to pick up and re-structure Zone Agent Pagadan's personal beam for him.

The office of the Chief of Galactic Zones was as spacious as the control room of a first-line battleship, and quite as compactly equipped with strange and wonderful gadgetry. As the master cell of one of the half dozen or so directing nerve-centers of Confederacy government, it needed it all. The Third Co-ordinator was one of Jeltad's busier citizens, and it was generally understood that no one intruded on his time except for some extremely good and sufficient reason.

However, he was undisturbed by the reflection that there was no obvious reason of any kind for Zone Agent Pagadan's request for an interview. The Lannai was one of the Third Co-ordinator's unofficial group of special Agents, his trouble-shooters de luxe, whom he could and regularly did unleash in the pits of space against virtually any kind of opponent—with a reasonable expectation of being informed presently of the Agent's survival and success. And whenever one of that fast-moving pack demanded his attention, he took it for granted they had a reason and that it was valid enough. Frequently, though not always, they would let him know then what it was.

The transmitter's visualization tank cleared suddenly from a smokily glowing green into a three-dimensional view of the *Viper's* control room; and the Co-ordinator gazed with approval on the silver-eyed, spacesuited, slender figure beyond the ship's massive control desk. Human or not, Pagadan was nice to look at.

"And what do you want now?" he inquired.

"Agent-Trainee Hallerock," the Lannai informed him, "6972.41, fourth year."

"Hm-m-m. Yes, I know *him!*" The Co-ordinator tapped the side of his long jaw reflectively. "Rather striking chap, isn't he?"

"He's beautiful!" Pagadan agreed enthusiastically. "How soon can you get him out here?"

"Even by Ranger," the Co-ordinator said doubtfully, "it would be ten days. There's an Agent in the nearest cluster I could route out to you in just under four."

She shook her head. "Hallerock's the boy—gloomy Hallerock. I met him a few months ago, back on Jeltad," she added, as if that made it clear. "What are his present estimated chances for graduation?"

The inquiry was strictly counter-regulation, but the Co-ordinator did not raise an eyebrow. He nudged a switch on his desk.

"I'll let the psych-tester answer that."

"If the Agent-Trainee were admitted for graduation," a deep mechanical voice came immediately from the wall to his left, "the percentage of probability of his passing all formal tests would be ninety-eight point seven. But because of a background conditioned lack of emotional adjustment to Vegan civilization, graduation has been indefinitely postponed."

"What I thought," Pagadan nodded. "Well, just shoot him out to me then—by Ranger, please!—and I'll do him some good. That's all, and thanks a lot for the interview!"

"It was a pleasure," said the Co-ordinator. Then, seeing her hand move towards her transmitter switch, he added hastily, "I understand you've run into a secondary mission problem out there, and that Correlation foresees difficulties in finding a satisfactory solution."

The Lannai paused, her hand on the switch. She looked a little surprised. "That Ulphian illusionist? Shouldn't be too much trouble. If you're in a hurry for results though, please get behind Lab Supply on the stuff I requisitioned just now—the Hospital ship, the Kynoleen and the special types of medics I need. Push out that, and Hallerock, to me and you'll have my final mission report in three weeks, more or less."

She waved a cheerful farewell and switched off, and the view of the *Viper's* control room vanished from the transmitter.

The Co-ordinator chewed his upper lip thoughtfully.

"Psych-tester," he said then, "just what is the little hellcat cooking up now?"

"I must remind you," the psych-tester's voice returned, "that Zone Agent 131.71 is one of the thirty-two individuals who have been able to discern my primary purpose here, and who have established temporary blocks against my investigations. She is, furthermore, the first to have established a block so nearly complete that I can offer no significant answer to your question. With that understood, do you wish an estimate?"

"No!" grunted the Co-ordinator. "I'd forgotten. I can make a few wild guesses myself." He ran his hand gently through his graying hair. "Let's see—this Hallerock's trouble is a background conditioned lack of adjustment to our type of civilization, you say?"

"He comes," the psych-tester reminded him, "of the

highly clannish and emotionally planet-bound strain of Mark Wieri VI."

The Co-ordinator nodded. "I remember now. Twenty-two thousand light-years out. They've been isolated there almost since the First Stellar Migrations—were rediscovered only a dozen years or so ago. Extra good people! But Hallerock was the only one of them we could talk into going to work for us."

"He appears to be unique among them in being galactic-minded in the Vegan sense," the psych-tester agreed. "Subconsciously, however, he remains so strongly drawn to his own kind that a satisfactory adjustment to permanent separation from them has not been achieved. Outwardly, the fact is expressed only in a lack of confidence in himself and in those with whom he happens to be engaged in any significant work; but the tendency is so pronounced that it has been considered unsafe to release him for Zonal duty."

"Ninety-eight point seven!" the Co-ordinator said. He swore mildly. "That means he's way the best of the current batch—and I could use a couple like that so beautifully right now! Psychoing won't do it?"

"Nothing short of complete mind-control for a period of several weeks."

The Co-ordinator shook his head. "It would settle his personal difficulties, but he'd be spoiled for us." He considered again, briefly, sighed and decided: "Pagadan's claimed him, anyway. She may wreck him completely; but she knows her therapy at that. Better let her give it a try."

He added, as if in apology:

"I'm sure that if we could consult Trainee Hallerock on the question, he'd agree with us—"

He was reaching out to punch down a desk stud with the last words and continued without a noticeable break:

"Central Communicator clear for Lab report on the rate of spread of the Olleeka plagues—"

His mind clearing also with that of any other matter, he settled back quietly and waited for Lab to come in.

System Chief Jasse, D.C. Cultural Field Investigator, listened attentively till her study recorder had clicked out "Report Dispatched." Then she sat frowning at the gadget for a moment.

The home office would like that report! A brisk, competent review of a hitherto obscure section of Ulphi's long-past rough and ready colonial period, pointing out and explaining the contrast between those days and the present quaintly perfect Ulphian civilization. It was strictly in line with the Department of Cultures' view of what any group of A-Class human beings, left to themselves, could achieve and it had sounded plausible enough when she played it back. But somehow it left her dissatisfied. Somehow Ulphi itself left her dissatisfied.

Perhaps she just needed a vacation! As usual, when a new case was keeping her busy, she had been dosing herself with insomniates for the past two weeks. But in her six years of work with Cultures she had never felt the need for a vacation before.

Patting back a yawn in the process of formation, Jasse shook her head, shut off the recorder and stepped out before the study mirror. Almost time for another appointment—some more historical research.

Turning once slowly before the tall mirror, she checked the details of her uniform and its accessories— the Traditionalist Greens which had been taken over with all their symbolic implications by the Department of Cultures. Everything in order, including the concealed gravmoc batteries in belt and boots and the electronic mind-shield switch in her wrist bracelet. No weapons to check; as a matter of policy they weren't carried by D.C. officials.

She pulled a bejeweled cap down on her shoulder-length wave of glossy black hair, grimaced at the face that, at twenty-five or thereabouts, still wore an habitual expression of intent, childish seriousness, and left the study.

By the lake shore, fifty feet from the D.C. mobile-unit's door, the little-people were waiting. Six of them today—middle-aged historians in the long silver-gray garments of their guild, standing beside a beautifully shaped vehicle with a suggestion of breath-taking speed about its lines. The suggestion didn't fool Jasse, who knew by experience that its looks were the only breath-taking thing about an Ulphian flow-car. The best it would produce in action was an air-borne amble, at so leisurely a pace that throughout her first trip in one of the things she had felt like getting out and pushing.

One mustn't, of course, she reminded herself conscientiously, settling back in the flow-car, judge any human culture by the achievements of another! Granted that Ulphi had long since lost the driving power of Vega's humming technologies, who was to say that it hadn't found a better thing in its place?

A fair enough question, but Jasse doubtfully continued to weigh the answer while the lengthy little Ulphian ritual of greetings and expressions of mutual esteem ran its course and came to an end in the flow-car. Then her escort of historical specialists settled down to shop talk in their flowery derivative of one of the twelve basic human dialects, and she began automatically to contribute her visiting dignitary's share to the conversation—just enough to show she was deeply interested but no more. Her attention, however, remained on the city below.

They were gliding only five hundred feet above the lake's shoreline, but all roofs were low enough to permit a wide view—and everything, everywhere, was in superbly perfect symmetry and balance. The car's motion did not change that impression. As it drove on, the gleaming white and softly tinted buildings about and below it flowed steadily into new and always immaculate patterns of sweeping line and blended color, merging in and out of the lake front with a rightness that trembled and stopped at the exact point of becoming too much so.

And that was only a direct visual expression of the essence of Ulphi's culture. Every social aspect of the planet showed the same easy order, the same minute perfectionist precision of graceful living—achieved without apparent effort in cycle on cycle of detail.

Jasse smiled pleasantly at her companions. The puzzling fact remained that this planetary batch of little-people just wasn't particularly bright! And any population with the gumption of a flock of rabbits should have sent a marauding Mother Disk of Bjantas on its way in a panicky hurry, without having to ask for help to solve *that* sort of problem!

She really must need a vacation, Jasse sighed, disturbed by such unorthodox reflections. A-Class humans just didn't go off on the wrong track, however gracefully, unless they were pushed there—so her doubts about Ulphi meant simply that she hadn't found the key to it yet.

Possibly she could do with a few weeks of re-indoctrination in basic Traditionalism.

"The Tomb of Moyuscane the Immortal—the last of our Great Illusionists!"

Jasse regarded the tomb with an air of respectful appreciation. Tombs, on the whole, she could do without; but this one undoubtedly was something special. She and Requada-Attan, Historian and Hereditary Custodian of the Tomb, had come together out of one of the main halls of the enormous building complex which housed the Historical Institute of Ulphi's Central City into a small, transparently over-roofed park. The remainder of her escort had shown her what they had to show and then withdrawn respectfully to their various duties; but Requada-Attan, probably not averse to having a wider audience benefit by the informative lecture he was giving the distinguished visitor, had left the gate to the park open behind them. A small crowd of sightseeing Ulphians had drifted in and was grouped about them by now.

"A fitting resting place for the Immortal One!" Jasse commented piously.

That brought a murmur of general appreciation from the local citizens. She suspected wryly that she, with her towering height and functional Vegan uniform, was the real center of interest in this colorfully robed group of little-people—few of them came up to a point much above the level of her elbows. But otherwise, the Tomb of Moyuscane must seem well worth a visit to a people as culturally self-centered as the Ulphians. Set against the rather conventional background of a green grove and whispering fountains, it was a translucently white monument, combining stateliness and exquisite grace with the early sweeping style which the last four centuries had preserved and expanded over the planet.

"The common people have many interesting superstitions about the Tomb," Requada-Attan confided loudly. "They say that Moyuscane's illusions are still to be seen within this park occasionally. Especially at night."

His round, pink face smiled wisely up at her. It was obvious that he, a historical scientist, did not share such superstitions.

Illusion performances, Jasse thought, nodding. She'd seen a few of those of a minor sort herself, but the records indicated that some centuries ago on Ulphi they had been cultivated to an extent which no major civilization would tolerate nowadays. The Illusionists of Ulphi had been priest-entertainers and political leaders; their mental symphonies—final culmination and monstrous flowering of all the tribal dances and varied body-and-mind shaking communal frenzies of history—had swayed the thinking and the emotional life of the planetary race. And Moyuscane the Immortal had wound up that line of psychic near-rulers as the greatest of them all.

It was rather fascinating at that, she decided, to go adventuring mentally back over the centuries into the realm of a human power which, without word or gesture, could sweep up and blend the emotions of thousands of other human beings into a single mighty current that flowed and ebbed and thundered at the impulses of one will through the channels its imagination projected.

Fascinating—but a little disturbing, too!

"I think—" she began, and stopped.

Words and phrases which had been no previous part of her thoughts suddenly were floating up in her mind—and now, quite without her volition, she was beginning to utter them!

"But that explains it!" her voice was saying, with a note of pleased, friendly surprise. "I've been wondering about you, Requada-Attan, you and your mysterious, beautiful world! I should have known all along that it was simply the dream-creation of an artist—that one of your Great Illusionists was still alive—"

The last words seemed to drop one by one into a curiously leaden silence, and then they stopped. Jasse was still only completely, incredulously astonished. Then something began to stir in that heavy silence about her; and her head came sharply around.

It was their faces that warned her—once before, she'd seen the expression of a mob that was acting under mental compulsion; and so she knew at once and exactly what she'd have to do next. Not stop to figure out what had happened, or try to reason with them, argue, threaten, or waste time yelling for help. Just get out of the immediate neighborhood, fast!

There weren't, of course, really enough Ulphians around to be called a mob—hardly more than twenty adults in all. That they had been directed against her was obvious enough, in the eyes that saw only her now, and in the synchronized motion with which they were converging quietly on the spot where she stood.

They stopped moving as if at a command Jasse could not hear, as she swung about, unconsciously with a very similar quietness, to face them.

Requada-Attan was under it, too! He still stood nearest her, about four steps to her left. Straight ahead, between Jasse and the gate, was the next closest group: two husky-looking young men with the shaved heads and yellow robes of professionals from the School of Athletes; and immediately behind them another silver-robed historian whom she had noticed previously—an elderly man, very thin and tall. No weapons in sight anywhere—

The three ahead were the ones to pass then! Jasse took two quick steps in their direction; and gravel scattered instantly under their sandaled feet, as they came to meet her in a rush. All about was the same sudden noise and swirl of motion.

But it was Requada-Attan who reached her first, with a quickness she hadn't counted on in a man of his plump build. Abruptly his weight was dragging at her arm, both hands gripped about her wrist, and jerking sideways to throw her off balance. Jasse twisted free sharply—that wrist carried her mind-shield bracelet and had to be guarded!—hauled the Hereditary Custodian off his feet with her right hand, sent him rolling before the knees of the charging yellow-robes.

They went down in a satisfactorily sprawling confusion, the thin historian turning a complete clumsy somersault with flapping garments across them a moment later. But the others had arrived by then, and Jasse became temporarily the center of a clawing, grappling, hard-breathing but voiceless cluster of humanity. What sent the first shock of real fright through her was that most of them seemed to be trying to get at her shield-bracelet! Because that indicated a mental attack was impending—mental attacks and mass compulsions on present-day Ulphi!

The jolt of that realization—the implication that hidden powers had been roused into action against her on this innocuous-looking world—might have resulted in a rash of snapping necks and other fatal incidents all around Jasse. Though Cultures frowned on weapons for its officials, the ancient Terran Art of the Holds was highly regarded among Traditionalists everywhere and had been developed by them to a polished new perfection. But she hauled herself back promptly from the verge of slipping into that well-drilled routine, which she never yet had put to its devastating practical use. The situation, so far, certainly wasn't as bad as all that—if she just kept her head! Slapping, shoving, shaking and turning, she twisted her way through this temporarily demented group of little-people, intent primarily on staying on her feet and keeping her left wrist out of reach.

Then the yellow-robed athletes were up again, and Jasse bumped the two shaven heads together with measured violence, stepped with great caution across an overturned but viciously kicking little boy—found herself suddenly free, and tripped up the last of the lot to come plunging in, a youngish, heavy-set woman.

The brief and practically bloodless melee had circled to within a dozen strides of the gateway of the park. She darted through it, slammed the high bronze gate behind her, saw Requada-Attan's key still in the lock and had her assailants shut in an instant later.

She could spare a moment then to look back at them. Most of them were still on the ground or clambering awkwardly to their feet. With one exception, all stared after her with those chillingly focused and expressionless eyes. The exception was a white-robed, dark-skinned man of middle age with a neatly trimmed fringe of brown beard around his chin, who stood on a tiled walk a little apart from the others. He was watching them, and Jasse could not recall having noticed him before.

Then their eyes met for an instant as she was turning away, and there was conscious intelligence in his look, mingled with something that might have been fright or anger.

At least, she thought, loping worriedly down one of the corridors towards the main halls of the Institute from which she had come, she wasn't the only one who had got a surprise out of the affair! She would have time to think about that later. The immediate problem was how to get out of this mess, and it would be stupid to assume that she had succeeded in that.

There were plenty of other people in those buildings ahead, and she had no way at all of knowing what their attitude would be.

She came with swift caution out of the corridor, into a long, sunbright and apparently deserted hall.

The opposite wall was formed of vertical blue slabs of some marble-like mineral with wide window embrasures between. The tops of feathery trees and the upper parts of buildings, a good distance off, were visible beyond the windows. Several hundred feet away in either direction a high doorway led out of the hall.

Both exits were blocked just now by a wedged, immobile mass of little-people. Robes of all colors— citizens of all types and classes, hastily assembled to stop her again. Even at this distance their faces sickened her. Apparently they had been directed simply to prevent her from leaving this hall, until—

It clamped down then about her skull—and tightened!

Mental attack!

Jasse's hands leaped to her temples in a convulsive, involuntary motion, though she knew there was nothing tangible there to seize. It was inside her, an enormous massing of tiny, hard pressures which were not quite pain, driving upon an equal number of critical linkages within her brain. In her first flash of panicky reaction, it seemed the burst of an overwhelming, irresistible force. A moment later, she realized it was quite bearable.

She should have known, of course with her mindshield activated as it was, it would take some while before that sort of thing could have much effect. The only immediately dangerous part of it was that it cut down the time she could afford to spend on conducting her escape.

She glanced again at the nearer of the two doorways, and knew instantly she wasn't even going to consider fighting her way through another mindless welter of grappling human bodies like that! The nearest window was a dozen steps away.

A full hundred yards beneath her, the building's walls dropped sheer into a big, blue-paved courtyard, with a high-walled park on the opposite side and open to the left on a city street, a block or more away. The street carried a multicolored, murmuring stream of traffic, too far off to make any immediate difference. A few brightly dressed people were walking across the courtyard below—they made no difference either. The important thing was the row of flow-cars parked against the wall down there, hardly eighty feet to her right.

Her hand dropped to her belt and adjusted the gravmoc unit. She felt almost weightless as she swung over the sill and pushed away from the building; but she touched the pavement in something less than eighteen seconds, rolled over twice and came up running.

There was scattered shouting then. Two young women, about to step out of one of the cars, stared in open-mouthed surprise as she came towards them. But neither they nor anyone else made any attempt to check her departure.

She had one of the vehicles airborne, and headed in the general direction of the lake-front section which was being used as a spaceport by the one Vegan destroyer stationed on Ulphi, before she was reminded suddenly that Central City had police ships for emergency use, which could fly rings around any flow-car— and that long, silvery, dirigible-like shapes seemed to be riding on guard directly over the area to which she wanted to go!

A few minutes later, she realized the ship might also be several miles to either side of the spaceport. At this distance and altitude she couldn't tell, and the flow-car refused to be urged any higher.

She had kept the clumsy conveyance on its course, because she hadn't really much choice of direction. There was no way of contacting or locating any of the other Vegan officials currently operating on Ulphi except through the destroyer itself or through the communicators in her own study; and her mobile-unit was also in the spaceport area. There were enough similar cars moving about by themselves to keep her from being conspicuous, though traffic, on the whole, was moderate over the city and most of it was confined to fairly definite streams between the more important points.

A second police ship became briefly visible far to her right, gliding close to the building tops and showing hardly more than its silhouette through a light haze which veiled that sector. If they knew where she was, either of the two could intercept her within minutes.

Very probably though, Jasse reassured herself, nobody did know just where she was. The mental force still assailing her shield was non-directional in any spatial sense; and her departure from the Historical Institute must have been much more sudden and swift than had been anticipated by her concealed attackers. In spite of her size, strangers were quite likely to underestimate her because of her slender build and rather childlike features, and on occasions like this that could be very useful. But—

Jasse bit her lip gently, conscious of a small flurry of panic bubbling up inside her and subsiding again, temporarily.

Because they needed only to ring off the spaceport, far enough away from the destroyer to avoid arousing its interest, and then wait for her arrival. She would have to come to them then—and soon! Her shield was still absorbing the punishment it was getting, but secondary effects of that unrelenting pressure had begun to show up. The barest touch of a dozen different, slowly spreading sensations within her brain—burning, tingling, constricting, dully throbbing sensations. Within the last few minutes, the first flickering traces of visual and auditory disturbances had appeared. Effects like that could build up for an indeterminate time without doing any real damage. But in the end they would merge suddenly into an advanced stage of blurred confusion—technically, her shield might still maintain its function; but she would no longer know or be able to control what she did.

A curiously detached feeling overcame Jasse then as the flow-car carried her steadily forward into whatever lay ahead. What she had to do was clear enough: go on until she was discovered and then ground the flow-car and try her luck on foot. But meanwhile, who or what had stirred up this mess about her? What were they after?

She sat quietly behind the flow-car's simple controls, leaning forward a trifle to conceal herself, while her mind ran over the implications of the odd little speech she had made in the park before Moyuscane's tomb. Those hadn't been her thoughts; if they had been, she wouldn't have uttered them voluntarily—so, shielded or not, somebody must have been tampering with her mind before this! Were there opposing groups of mental adepts on Ulphi, and was one of them trying to use her, and Vega, against the other in some struggle for control of this planetary civilization?

Once more then, System Chief Jasse surprised herself completely—this time by a flash of furious exasperation with the lofty D.C. policies which had put her in a spot like this unarmed. To trust in the innate rightness of A-Class humanity was all very well. But, mysterious superior mentalities or not, a good, ordinary, old-fashioned blaster in her hand would have been *so* satisfactory just now!

"Oh, Suns and Planets!" Jasse muttered aloud, shocked into a half-forgotten Traditionalist invocation acquired during her childhood. "They've got me fighting mad!"

And at that moment, a clean-edged shadow, which was not the shadow of any cloud, came sliding soundlessly over the flow-car and stayed there.

Jasse, heart pounding wildly, was still trying to twist around far enough to look up without pitching herself out of the car or releasing its controls when a voice, some twenty feet above her, remarked conversationally:

"Say—I thought it was you!"

She stared up speechlessly.

The words had been Vegan—and nothing like that dull-green, seamless, thirty-foot sliver of space-alloy floating overhead had ever been dreamed up on Ulphi! While the pert, huge-eyed face that peered down at her out of the craft's open lock—she remembered suddenly the last time she'd met that member of a nonhuman race in a G.Z. space-duty uniform and the polite effort she'd made to mask the antipathy and suspicions which were bound to arise in a Traditionalist when confronted by any such half-and-half creature.

But—safe!

A shaking began in her knees. She sat down quietly.

And Zone Agent Pagadan, for whom any kind of thought-shield on which she really directed her attention became as sheerest summer gossamer—unless, of course, it was backed by a mind that approximated her own degree of nerve-energy control—smiled amiably and chalked one up to her flair for dramatic timing.

"Remember me, eh?" she nodded. "Pelial, of Galactic Zones, at your service! I was scoping the area from ten miles above and spotted you drifting along by yourself. What occurs, my tall colleague? Are you just going sightseeing in that piece of primitive craftsmanship, or did your pilot fall out?"

"Ulp—!" began Jasse, nodding and shaking her head at the same time. Pagadan's contemplative eyes became a little bigger.

"Skip it!" she said apprehensively. "From close up, you look both chewed on and distraught, my girl! What happ— Hey, hang on a moment and I'll slide in close and take you aboard. Maybe you ought to be home in bed, or something."

The head withdrew; and Jasse took a deep, sighing breath, raked a snarled strand of black hair out of her forehead and dabbed tentatively at a deep scratch on the back of her hand.

She did look a mess, now that she noticed it—the Greens were badly ripped and streaked with the blue chalk of the pavement over which she had rolled; and her jeweled cap was gone. A moment passed before she realized suddenly that the clinging constrictions of the mental attack were gone, too!

She was still wondering about that as she swung over into the space-skiff, steadied by Pagadan's gloved hand.

Then, as the skiff's lock slammed shut behind her, she made another discovery:

Her shield-bracelet hung free, attached to her wrist now only by its safety chain. The shield switch flickered, warningly red, on "Open"—

"Your mind-shield?" The Lannai Agent, measuring a rose-colored liquid carefully from a fat little jug into a cup, absently repeated Jasse's stunned exclamation.

"Probably snagged the bracelet while you were climbing in from the car. It happens." She glanced around and her eyes caught the light with a wicked crystalline glitter. "Why? Could it matter? Was someone pressuring you?"

"They were before," Jasse whispered; and suddenly there wasn't any question about her being frightened! Panic hammered into her brain and stayed; a dizzy shimmering grew before her eyes. Mixed with that came a queer, growing feeling as if something were surging and pulsing within her skull—a wildly expectant feeling of *something* about to happen.

She realized the Lannai was holding the filled cup to her lips.

"Drink that!" the cool voice ordered. "Whatever you've got it's good for. Then just settle back, relax, and let's hear what you know!"

The liquid she had gulped, Jasse noticed, wasn't really rose-colored as she had thought, but a deep, dim, ruby red, almost black—an enormously *quiet* color—and with a highly curious slowing-down effect on things, too! For instance, you might realize perfectly well that somewhere, out around the edges of you, you were still horribly upset, with fear-thoughts racing about everywhere at a dizzy speed. Every so often, one of them would turn inwards and come shooting right at you, flashing like a freezing arrow into the deep-red dusk where you were. But just as you started to shrink away from it, you noticed it was getting slower and slower, the farther it came; until finally it just stayed where it was, and then gradually melted away.

They never could get through to reach you. It was rather comical!

It appeared she had asked some question about it, because the big-eyed little humanoid was saying:

"You like the effect, eh? That's just antishock, little chum! Thought you knew the stuff . . . don't they teach you anything at Cultures?"

That was funny, too! Cultures, of course, taught you everything there was to know! But wait—hadn't there been . . . what had there been that she—? Jasse decided to examine that point about Cultures very carefully, some other time.

By and large there seemed to be a good deal of quiet conversation going on around her. Perhaps she was doing some of it, but it was hard to tell; since, frankly, she wasn't much interested in those outside events any more. And then, for a while, the two tall shapes, the man and the woman, came up again to the barrier in her past and tried to talk to her, as they always did when she was feeling anxious and alone. A little puzzled, because she didn't feel that way now, Jasse watched them from her side of the barrier, which was where the explosions and shrieking lights were, that had brought terror and hurt and the sudden forgetting which none of Culture's therapists had been able to lift. Dimly, she could sense the world behind them, to which they wanted her to go—the star-glittering cold and the great silent flows of snow, and the peace and enchantment that were there. But she could make no real effort to reach it now, and in the end the tall shapes seemed to realize that and went away.

Or else, they merely faded out of her sight as the color about her deepened ever more from ruby redness into the ultimate, velvety, all-quieting, all-slowing-down *black*—

"Wonderful—" Jasse murmured contentedly, asleep.

"Hallerock?"

"Linked in, Pag! I'm back on the Observation Ship again. Go ahead."

"Just keep this thought-line down tight! Everything's working like a charm, so far. I tripped the D.C.'s shield open when I took her aboard, and our good friend Moyuscane came right in, all set to take control and find out whether we actually knew something about him and his setup here or not. Then he discovered I was around, and he's been lying quiet and just listening through her ever since."

"What makes him shy of you?" Hallerock inquired.

"He tried a long-range probe at my shields a couple of weeks ago. I slapped him on the beak—some perfectly natural startled-reaction stuff by another telepath, you understand. But he certainly didn't like it! He went out fast, that time—"

"I don't blame him," Hallerock said thoughtfully. "Sometimes you don't realize your own strength. Does the D.C. really have anything on him?"

"No. It's about as we suspected. She made some sort of innocent remark—I couldn't take the chance of digging around in her mind long enough to find out just what—and Moyuscane jumped to the wrong conclusions."

"I was wondering, you know," Hallerock admitted, "whether you mightn't have done some work on the Cultures girl in advance—something that would get her to drop a few bricks at some appropriate occasion."

"Well, you're just naturally a suspicious little squirt!" Pagadan replied amiably. "To use Confederacy personnel against their will and knowledge for any such skulduggery is strictly counter-regulation. I advise you to make a note of the fact! However, it was the luckiest sort of coincidence. It should save us a week or two of waiting, especially since you have the hospital ship and staff all prepared. Moyuscane's got himself a listening-post right in our ranks now, and that's all he needs to stay reasonably safe—he thinks!"

Hallerock appeared to be digesting this information for a moment. Then his thought came again:

"Where are you at present?"

"Down at the Central City spaceport, still in the *Viper's* skiff. The D.C.'s under antishock and asleep on the bunk here."

"Oh," said Hallerock, "you're all ready to start the drive then?"

"Wake up, little brother!" Pagadan advised him. "It started ten minutes ago! The last thing I told the girl before she went down deep was that a Vegan Fleet Hospital Ship was approaching Ulphi with a brand-new, top-secret drug against space-fear, called Kynoleen—a free gift from the Confederacy to the afflicted population of this planet."

"Well . . . I suppose I'd better set the H-Ship down at the spaceport about an hour from now, then?"

"One hour would be about right. Moyuscane must be in a considerable stew at the prospect of having the Kynoleen disclose the fact that most of the local population is suffering from an artificially imposed space-fear psychosis, but it won't take him long to see to it that the drug won't actually be used around here for quite some time. When that's settled, we'll let him breathe easier for about three hours. Then I'll wake up the D.C., make sure he's listening through her and feed him the *big* jolt. So see I get that message we've prepared half an hour beforehand—three hours and thirty minutes from now! And send it as a straight coded communication, to make it look authentic."

"All right," Hallerock said doubtfully. "But wouldn't it be better to check over the entire schedule once more—just to be sure nothing can go wrong?"

"There's no need for that!" the Lannai said, surprised. "We've got Moyuscane analyzed down to the length of his immortal whiskers, and we've worked out the circumstances required to produce the exact effects we want. It's just a matter of timing it now. You're not letting yourself get rattled by a Telepath of the Second Order, are you? If he didn't happen to have the planet under control, this wouldn't be a job for Galactic Zones at all."

"Possibly not," said Hallerock reasonably, "but then he does have it under control. Enough to hash it up from one pole to the other if he panics. That's what keeps putting this dew on my brow."

"Agent-Trainee Hallerock," Pagadan replied impatiently, "I love you like a son or something, but at times you talk like a dope. Even a Telep-Two doesn't panic, unless you let him get the idea he's cornered. All we've got to do is keep Moyuscane's nose pointed towards the one way out and give him time enough to use it when we switch on the pressure—but not quite time enough to change his mind again. If it makes you feel any better, you could put trackers on any unprotected Vegans for the next eight hours."

Hallerock laughed uneasily. "I just finished doing that," he admitted.

Pagadan shrugged. Gloomy old Hallerock! From here on out, he'd be waiting for the worst to happen, though this kind of a job, as anyone who had studied his training records would know, was right up his alley. And it had been a pleasure, at that, to observe the swift accuracy with which he'd planned and worked out the schedule and details of this operation, in spite of head-shakings and forebodings. The only thing he couldn't possibly have done was to take the responsibility for it himself.

She smiled faintly, and came over to sit down for a while beside the bunk on which Jasse was lying.

❖   ❖   ❖

Two hours later, when her aide contacted her again, he seemed comparatively optimistic.

"Reaction as predicted," he reported laconically. "I'm beginning to believe you might know what you're doing."

"Moyuscane's got the Kynoleen space-tests stalled?"

"Yes. The whole affair was hushed up rather neatly. The H-Ship is down now at some big biochemical center five hundred miles from Central City, and the staff was routed through to top officials immediately. The question was raised then whether Ulphian body chemistry mightn't have varied just far enough from standard A-Class to make it advisable to conduct a series of local lab experiments with the drug before putting it to use. Our medics agreed and were asked, as between scientists, to keep the matter quiet meanwhile, to avoid exciting the population unduly. There also was the expected vagueness as to how long the experiments might take."

"It makes it so much easier," Pagadan said gratefully, "when the opposition is using its brains! Was anyone shown around the ship?"

"A few dozen types of specialists are still prowling all over it. They've been introduced to our personnel. It seems a pretty safe bet," Hallerock acknowledged hesitantly, "that Moyuscane has discovered there isn't a shielded mind among them, and that he can take control of the crate and its crew whenever he wants." He paused. "So now we just wait a while?"

"And let him toy around with the right kind of ideas," agreed Pagadan. "He should be worried just enough by now to let them come floating up naturally."

Night had fallen over Central City when the message she was expecting was rattled suddenly from the skiff's communicator. She decoded it, produced evidence of considerable emotional shock, shook Jasse awake and, in a few dozen suitably excited sentences, handed Moyuscane his jolt. After that, though, there were some anxious moments before she got her patient quieted down enough to let the antishock resume its over-all effect.

"She kept wanting to get up and do something about it!" Pagadan reported to Hallerock, rubbing a slightly sprained wrist. "But I finally got it across that it wasn't Cultures' job to investigate undercover mass homicide on a foreign planet, and that one of our own Zone Agents, no less, was landing secretly tomorrow to take charge of the case."

"And that," said Hallerock darkly, "really *is* switching on the pressure!"

"Just pressure enough for our purpose. It's still a big, hidden organization that's suspected of those fancy murder rituals, and not just one little telepath who's played at being planetary god for the past few centuries. Of course, if we'd pointed a finger straight at Moyuscane himself, he would have cracked right there."

She passed a small handkerchief once, quickly, over her forehead. "This kind of thing is likely to be a bit nerve-wracking until you get used to it," she added reassuringly. "I can remember when I've felt just about as jumpy as you're feeling now. But all we have to do is to settle down and let Moyuscane work out his little problem by himself. He can't help seeing the answer—"

But a full two hours passed then, and the better part of a third, while Pelial, the minor official of Galactic Zones, continued to work quietly at her files of reports and recordings, and received and dispatched various coded communications connected with the impending arrival of her superior—the hypothetical avenging Zone Agent.

By now, she conceded at last, she might be

beginning to feel a little disturbed, though, naturally, she had prepared alternative measures, in case—

Hallerock's thought flashed questioningly into her mind then. For a moment, Pagadan stopped breathing.

"Linked!" she told him crisply. "Go ahead!"

"The leading biochemists of Ulphi," Hallerock informed her, "have just come up with a scientific achievement that would be regarded as noteworthy almost anywhere—"

"You subhuman comic!" snapped Pagadan. "*Tell* me!"

" . . . Inasmuch as they were able to complete— analyze, summarize and correlate—all tests required to establish the complete harmlessness of the new space-fear drug Kynoleen for all type variations of Ulphian body-chemistry. They admit that, to some extent, they are relying—"

"Hallerock," Pagadan interrupted, in cold sincerity now, "you drag in one more unnecessary detail, and the very next time I meet you, you're going to be a great, big, ugly-looking dead body!"

"That's not like you, Pag!" Hallerock complained. "Well, they rushed fifty volunteers over to the H-Ship anyway, to have Kynoleen given a final check in space right away—all Ulphi is now to have the benefit of it as soon as possible. But nobody seemed particularly upset when our medics reminded them they had been informed that the ship was equipped to conduct tests on only *one* subject at a time—"

Pagadan drew a shivery breath and sat suffused for a moment by a pure, bright glow of self-admiration.

"When will they take off with him?" she inquired with quiet triumph.

"They took off ten minutes ago," her aide returned innocently, "and headed straight out. As a matter of fact, just before I beamed you, the test-subject had discovered that ten minutes in space will get you a whole lot farther than any Telep-Two can drive a directing thought. It seemed to disturb him to lose contact with Ulphi—WOW! Watch it, Pag! Supposing I hadn't been shielded when that lethal stunner of yours landed!"

"That's a beautiful supposition!" hissed Pagadan. "Some day, you won't be! But the planet's safe, anyway—I guess I can forgive you. And now, my friend, you may start worrying about the ship!"

"I've got to compliment you," she admitted a while later, "on the job you did when you installed those PT-cells. What I call perfect coverage! Half the time I don't know myself from just what point of the ship I'm watching the show."

She was curled up now in a large chair, next to the bunk on which Jasse still slumbered quietly; and she appeared almost as completely relaxed as her guest. The upper part of her head was covered by something like a very large and thick-walled but apparently light helmet, which came down over her forehead to a line almost with her eyes, and her eyes were closed.

"Just at the moment"—Hallerock hesitated—"I think you're using the Peeping Tommy in the top left corner of the visitank Moyuscane's looking into. He still doesn't really like the idea of being out in deep space, does he?"

"No, but he's got his dislike of it under control," Pagadan said lazily. "He's the one," she added presently, "who directed the attack on our D.C. today at the Historical Institute. She has a short but very sharp memory-picture of him. So it *is* Moyuscane, all right!"

"You mean," Hallerock asked, stunned, "you weren't really sure of it?"

"Well—you can't ever be *sure* till everything's all

over," Pagadan informed him cheerfully. "And then you sometimes wonder." She opened her eyes, changed her position in the chair and settled back carefully again. "Don't you pass out on me, Hallerock!" she warned. "You're supposed to be recording every single thing that happens on the H-Ship for Lab!"

There hadn't been, Hallerock remarked, apparently still somewhat disturbed, very much to record as yet. The dark-skinned, trimly bearded Ulphian volunteer was, of course, indulging in a remarkable degree of activity, considering he'd been taken on board solely as an object of scientific investigation. But no one about him appeared to find anything odd in that. Wherever he went, padding around swiftly on bare feet and dressed in a set of white hospital pajamas, the three doctors who made up the ship's experimental staff followed him earnestly, with a variety of instruments at the ready, rather like a trio of mother hens trailing an agitated chicken. Occasionally, they interrupted whatever he was doing and carried out some swift examination or other, to which he submitted indifferently.

But he spoke neither to them nor to any of the ship's officers he passed. And they, submerged in their various duties with an intentness which alone might have indicated that this was no routine flight, appeared unaware of his presence.

"The old boy's an organizer," Pagadan conceded critically. "He's put a flock of experts to work for him, and he's smart enough to leave them alone. They've got the ship on her new course by now, haven't they? Can you make out where they think they're going?"

Hallerock told her.

"An eighty-three day trip!" she said thoughtfully. "Looks like he didn't want to have anything at all to do with us any more! Someone on board must know what's in that region—or was able to get information on it."

Up to the end, that was almost all there was to see. At a velocity barely below the cruising speed of a Vegan destroyer, the H-Ship moved away from Ulphi. Like a harried executive, too involved in weighty responsibilities to bother about his informal attire, the solitary Ulphian continued to roam about within the ship, disregarded by all but his attendant physicians. But finally—he was back in the ship's big control room by then and had just cast another distasteful glance at the expanse of star-glittering blackness within the visitank between the two pilots—Moyuscane began to speak.

It became startlingly clear in that instant how completely alone he actually was among the H-Ship's control crew. Like a man who knows he need not act with restraint in a dream peopled by phantoms, the ex-ruler of Ulphi poured forth what was in his mind, in a single screaming spurt of frustrated fury and fears and hopes that should have swung the startled attention of everybody within hearing range upon him, like the sudden ravings of a madman.

The pilots became involved with the chief navigator and his two assistants in a brisk five-cornered discussion of a stack of hitherto unused star-plates. The three doctors gathered about the couch on which Moyuscane sat—exchanged occasional comments with the calm unhurriedness of men observing the gradual development of a test, the satisfactory conclusion of which already is assured.

As suddenly as the outburst had begun, it was over. The Ulphian wiped his mouth with the back of his hand, and sat scowling quietly at the floor.

"I think," said Pagadan, "you could start the destroyers out after them now, Hallerock!"

"I just did," Hallerock said. "I clocked the end of 'minimum effective period' right in the middle of that little speech."

"So did I," she replied. "And I hope it won't be too long now. I've got work to do here, and it shouldn't wait."

There were sufficiently deadly gadgets of various types installed throughout the fugitive ship, which they could have operated through the PT-cells. But since all of them involved some degree of risk to the ship's personnel they were intended for emergency use only— in case Moyuscane attempted to vent his annoyance with the change in his worldly fortunes on one of his new subjects. Pagadan, however, had not believed that the recent lord of all Ulphi would be capable of wasting any part of his reduced human resources for any motive so impractical as spite.

Convinced by now that she was right in that, she waited, more patiently on the whole than Hallerock, for something safer than gun or gas to conclude Moyuscane's career.

It caught up with him some twenty minutes later— something that touched him and went through him in a hardly perceptible fashion, like the twitching of a minor electric shock.

The reaction of the two watchers was so nearly simultaneous that neither knew afterwards which of them actually tripped the thought-operated mechanism which filled the H-Ship briefly with a flicker of cold radiation near the upper limit of visibility for that particular crew.

To that signal, the ship's personnel reacted in turn, though in a far more leisurely manner. They blinked about doubtfully for a few seconds as if trying to remember something; and then—wherever they were and whatever they happened to be doing—they settled down deliberately on chairs, bunks, beds, and the floor, stretched out, and went to sleep.

Moyuscane alone remained active, since his nerve centers had not been drenched several days before with a catalyst held there in suspense until that flare of radiance should touch it off. Almost within seconds though, he was plucked out of his appalled comprehension of the fact that there was no longer a single mind within his reach that would respond to control. For Kynoleen gave complete immunity to space-fear within the time limit determined by the size of the dose and the type of organism affected, but none at all thereafter. And whatever the nature of the shattering terrors the hidden mechanisms of the mind flung up when gripped in mid-space by that dreaded psychosis, their secondary effects on body and brain were utterly devastating.

Swiftly and violently, then, Moyuscane the Immortal died, some four centuries after his time, bones and muscles snapping in the mounting fury of the Fear's paroxysms. Hallerock, still conscientiously observing and recording for G.Z. Lab's omnivorous files, felt somewhat sick. But Pagadan appeared undisturbed.

"I'd have let him out an easier way if it could have been done safely," her thought came indifferently. "But he would, after all, have considered this barely up to his own standards of dispatch. Turn the ship back now and let the destroyers pick it up, will you, Hallerock? I'll be along to see you after a while—"

The *Viper* came slamming up behind the Observation Ship some five hours later, kicked it negligently out of its orbit around Ulphi, slapped on a set of tractors fore and aft, and hauled it in, lock to lock.

"Just thirty-five seconds ago," Hallerock informed Pagadan coldly as she trotted into the O-Ship's control room, "every highly condemned instrument on this unusually condemned crate got knocked clean out of alignment! Any suggestions as to what might have caused it?"

"Your language, my pet!" Pagadan admonished, for his actual phrasing had been more crisp. She flipped a small package across his desk into his hands. "To be studied with care immediately after my departure! But you might open it now."

A five-inch cube of translucence made up half the package. It contained the full-length image of a slender girl with shining black hair, who carried a javelin in one hand and wore the short golden skirt of a contestant in the planetary games of Jeltad.

"Cute kid!" Hallerock acknowledged. "Vegan, eh? The rest of it's a stack of her equation-plates? Who is she and what do I do about it?"

"That's our Department of Cultures investigator," Pagadan explained.

"The System Chief?" Hallerock said surprised. He glanced at the image again, which was a copy of one of Snoops' three-dimensionals, and looked curiously up at the Lannai. "Didn't you just finish doing a mental job on her?"

"In a way. Mostly a little hypno-information to bring her up to date on what's been going on around Ulphi— including her part in it. She was asleep in that D.C. perambulator she's camping in here when I left her."

"As I understand it," Hallerock remarked thoughtfully, "the recent events on Ulphi would be classified as information very much restricted to Galactic Zones! So you wouldn't have spotted the makings of a G.Z. parapsychic mind in a D.C. System Chief, would you?"

"Bright boy! I'll admit it's an unlikely place to look for one, but she is a type we can use. I'm releasing her now for G.Z. information, on Agent authority. Her equation-plates will tell you how to handle her in case she runs into emotional snags while absorbing it. You're to be stationed on Ulphi another four months anyway, and you're to consider that a high-priority part of your job."

"I will? Another four months?" Hallerock repeated incredulously. "I was winding up things on the O-Ship to start back to Jeltad. You don't need me around here any more, do you?"

"I don't, no!" Pagadan appeared to be quietly enjoying herself. "The point is, though, I'm the one who's leaving. Got word from Central two hours ago to report back at speed, just as soon as we'd mopped up Old Man Moyuscane."

"What for?" Hallerock began to look bewildered. "The Agent work isn't finished here."

She shook her head. "Don't know myself yet! But it's got to do with the recordings on those pickled Bjantas you homed back to Lab. Central sounded rather excited." The silver eyes were sparkling with unconcealed delight now. "It's to be a Five-Agent Mission, Hallerock!" she fairly sang. "Beyond Galactic Rim!"

"Beyond the Rim? For Bjanta? They've got something really new on them then!" Hallerock had come to his feet.

Pagadan nodded and smacked her lips lightly. "Sounds like it, doesn't it? New and conclusive—and we delivered it to them! But now look what a face it's making," she added maliciously, "just because it doesn't get to go along!"

Hallerock scowled and laughed. "Well, I've been wondering all this time about those Bjantas. Now you take out after them—and I can hang around Ulphi dishing out a little therapy to a D.C. neurotic."

"We all start out small," said the Lannai. "Look at

me—would you believe that a few short years ago I was nothing but the High Queen of Lar-Sancaya? Not," she added loyally, "that there's a sweeter planet anywhere, from the Center to the Clouds or beyond!"

"And that stretch distinctly includes Ulphi," Hallerock stated, unreconciled to his fate. "When's the new Agent coming out to this hive of morons?"

Pagadan slid to her feet off the edge of the desk and surveyed him pityingly. "You poor chump! What I gave you just now was Advance Mission Information, wasn't it? Ever hear of a time that wasn't restricted to Zone Agent levels? Or do I have to tell you officially that you've just finished putting in a week as a Z.A. under orders?"

Hallerock stared at her. His mouth opened and shut and opened again. "Here, wait a—" he began.

She waved him into silence with both fists.

"Close it kindly, and listen to the last instructions I'm giving you! Ulphi's being taken in as a Class 18 System-outpost garrison. I imagine even you don't have to be told that the only thing not strictly routine about the procedure will be the elimination of every traceable connection between its present culture and Moyuscane's personal influence on it—and our recent corrective operation?"

"Well, of course!" Hallerock said hoarsely. "But look here, Pag—"

"Considerable amount of detail work in that, naturally—it's why the monitors at Central have assigned you four whole months for the job. When you're done here, report back to Jeltad. They've already started roughing out your robot, but they'll need you around to transfer basic impulse patterns and so on. A couple of months more, and you'll be equipped for any dirty work they can think up—and I gather the Chief's already thought up some sweet ones especially for you! So God help you—and now I'm off. Unless you've got some more questions?"

Hallerock looked at her, his face impassive now. If she had been human he couldn't have told her. But, unlike most of the men of Pagadan's acquaintance, Hallerock never forgot that the Lannai were of another kind. It was one of the things she liked about him.

"No, I haven't any questions just now," he said. "But if I'm put to work by myself on even a job like this, I'm going to feel lost and alone. I just don't have the feeling that I can be trusted with Z.A. responsibility."

Pagadan waved him off again, impatiently.

"The feeling will grow on you," she assured him.

And then she was gone.

As motion and velocity were normally understood, the *Viper's* method of homeward progress was something else again. But since the only exact definition of it was to be found in a highly complex grouping of mathematical concepts, such terms would have to do.

She was going home, then, at approximately half her normal speed, her automatic receptors full out. Pagadan sat at her desk, blinking reflectively into the big vision tank, while she waited for a call that had to be coming along any moment now.

She felt no particular concern about it. In fact, she could have stated to the minute how long it would take Hallerock to recover far enough from the state of slight shock she'd left him in to reach out for the set of dossier-plates lying on his desk. A brief section of System Chief Jasse's recent behavior-history, with the motivation patterns underlying it, was revealed in those plates, in the telepathic shorthand which turned any normally active hour of an individual's life into as complete a basis for analysis as ordinary understanding required.

She'd stressed that job just enough to make sure he'd attend to it before turning to any other duties. And Hallerock was a quick worker. It should take him only three or four minutes to go through the plates, the first time.

But then he'd just sit there for about a minute, frowning down at them, looking a little baffled and more than a little worried. Poor old Hallerock! Now he couldn't even handle a simple character-analysis any more unaided!

Grimly he'd rearrange the dossier-plates, tap them together into a neat little pile, and start all over again. He'd go through each one very slowly and carefully now, determined to catch the mistake that *had* to be there!

Pagadan grinned faintly.

Almost to the calculated second, his search-thought came flickering after her down the curving line to Jeltad. As the *Viper's* receptors caught it and brought it in, she flipped over the transmitter switch:

"Linked, Hallerock—nice reach you've got! What gives, my friend?"

There was a short pause; then:

"Pag, what's wrong with her—the D.C., I mean?"

"Wrong with her?" Pagadan returned, on a note of mild surprise.

"In the plates," Hallerock explained carefully. "She's an undeveloped parapsychic, all right—a Telep-Three, at the least. But she's also under a master-delusion—thinks she's a physical monster of some kind! Which she obviously isn't."

The Lannai hesitated, letting a trickle of uncertainty through to him to indicate a doubtful mental search. There wasn't, after all, anything that took quite such ticklish, sensitive handling as a parapsychic mind that had gone thoroughly off the beam.

"Oh, that!" she said, suddenly and obviously relieved. "That's no delusion, Hallerock—just one of those typical sub-level exaggerations. No doubt I overemphasized it a little. There's nothing wrong with her really—she's A-Class plus. Very considerably plus, as you say. But she's not a Vegan."

"Not a Vegan? Well, why should—"

"And, of course, she's always been quite sensitive about that physical peculiarity!" Pagadan resumed, with an air of happy discovery. "Even as a child. But with the Traditionalist training she was getting, she couldn't consciously admit any awareness of isolation from other human beings. It's just that our D.C.'s a foundling, Hallerock. I should have mentioned it, I suppose. They picked her up in space, and she's of some unidentified human breed that grows around eight foot tall—"

Back in the study of her mobile-unit, System Chief Jasse wiped her eyes, blew her nose, and pocketed her handkerchief decisively.

She'd blubbered for an hour after she first woke up. The Universe of the Traditionalists had been such a nice, tidy, easy-to-understand place to live in, even if she'd never felt *completely* at her ease there! It had its problems to be met and solved, of course; and there were the lesser, nonhuman races, to be coolly pitied for their imperfections and kept under control for their own good, and everybody else's. But that A-Class humanity could work itself into such a dismally gruesome mess as it had done on Ulphi—that just wasn't any part of the Traditionalist picture! They didn't want any such information there. They could live more happily without it.

Well, let them live happily then! She was still Jasse, the spaceborn, and in return for knocking down the mental house of cards she'd been living in, the tricky little humanoid at any rate had made her aware of some unsuspected possibilities of her own which she could now develop.

She began to re-examine those discoveries about herself with a sort of new, cool, speculating interest. There were two chains of possibilities really—that silent, cold, whitely enchanted world of her childhood dreams came floating up in her mind again, clear and distinct under its glittering night-sky now that the barriers that had blurred it in her memory had been dissolved. The home-world of her distant race! She could go to it if she chose, straight and unerringly, and find the warm human strength and companionship that waited there. That knowledge had been returned to her, too.

But was that what she wanted most?

There was another sort of companionship, the Lannai had implied, and a different sort of satisfaction she could gain, beyond that of placidly living out her life among her own kind on even the most beautiful of frozen worlds. They were constructing a civilized galaxy just now, and they would welcome her on the job.

She'd bathed, put on a fresh uniform and was pensively waiting for her breakfast to present itself from the wall-butler in the study, when the unit's automatic announcer addressed her:

"Galactic Zones Agent Hallerock requesting an interview."

Jasse started and half turned in her chair to look at the closed door. Now what did that mean? She didn't want to see any of *them* just yet! She intended to make up her own mind on the matter.

She said, a little resentfully:

"Well . . . let him right in, please!"

The study door opened as she flipped the lock-switch on her desk. A moment later, Hallerock was bowing to her from the entrance hall just beyond it.

Jasse began to rise, glanced up at him; and then sat back suddenly and gave him another look.

"Hello, Jasse!" Hallerock said, in a voice that sounded amiable but remarkably self-assured.

Even when not set off as now by his immaculate blue and white G.Z. dress uniform, Zone Agent Hallerock undoubtedly was something almost any young woman would look at twice. However, it wasn't so much that he was strikingly handsome with his short-cropped dark-red hair and the clear, black-green eyes with their suggestion of some icy midnight ocean. The immediate point was that you didn't have to look twice to know that he came from no ordinary planet of civilization.

Jasse got up slowly from behind her desk and came around it and stood before Hallerock.

Basically, that was it perhaps—the world he came from! Mark Wieri VI, a frontier-type planet, so infernally deserving of its classification that only hare-brained first-stage Terrans would have settled there in the first place. Where the equatorial belt was a riot of throbbing colors, a maddened rainbow flowering and ripening, for two months of a thirty-eight month year—and then, like the rest of that bleak world forever, sheet-ice and darkness and the soundless, star-glittering cold.

Even back on Terra, two paths had been open to life that faced the Great Cold as its chosen environment. To grow squalidly tough, devoted to survival in merciless single-mindedness—or to flourish into a triumphant excess of strength that no future challenge could more than half engage.

On Mark Wieri's world, human life had adapted, inevitably, to its relentlessly crushing environment. In

the two hundred and eighty-odd generations between
the last centuries of the First Stellar Migrations and
the day an exploring Giant-Ranger of the Confederacy
turned in that direction, it had become as much a part
of its background as the trout is of its pool. And no
more than the trout could it see any purpose in leaving so good a place again.

But it had not, in any sense, grown squalid.

So Jasse stood before Hallerock, and she was still
looking up at him. There were nine foot three inches
of him to look up to, shaped into four hundred and
sixty-five lean pounds of tigerish symmetry.

The dress uniform on a duty call was a clue she
didn't miss or need. The ice of his home-planet was
in Hallerock's eyes; but so was the warm, loyal human
strength that had triumphed over it and carelessly paid
in then the full, final price of conquest. This son of
the conquerors alone had been able to sense that the
galaxy itself was now just wide and deep and long
enough for man; and so he'd joined the civilization that
was of a like spirit.

But he, too, had been a giant among little-people
then. If his conscious thoughts wouldn't admit it, every
cell of his body knew he'd lost his own kind.

Jasse, all her mind groping carefully, questioningly
out towards this phenomenon, this monster-slayer of
Galactic Zones—beginning to understand all that and
a good deal more—slowly relaxed again.

A kinsman of hers! Her own eyes began to smile,
finally.

"Hello, Hallerock!" Jasse said.

And that was, Pagadan decided, about the right
moment to dissolve the PT-cell she'd spent an hour
installing in the wall just above the upper right-hand
corner of Jasse's study mirror.

Those two baby giants might be all full of emotional flutters just now at having met someone from the old home town; but they were going to start thinking of their good friend Pagadan almost immediately! And one of the very first things that would leap to Hallerock's suspicious mind would be the possible presence of a Peeping Tommy.

Good thing those tiny units left no detectable trace!

She pulled off the PT-helmet, yawned delicately and sat relaxed for a minute, smirking reminiscently into the vision-tank.

"What I call a really profitable mission!" she informed the vision-tank. "Not a slip anywhere either—and just think how tame it all started out!"

She thought about that for a moment. The silver eyes closed slowly; and opened again.

"It's no particular wonder," she remarked, "that Central's picked me for a Five-Agent job—after only five missions! When you get right down to it, you can't beat a Lannai brain!"

The hundred thousand friendly points of light in the vision-tank applauded her silently. Pagadan smiled at them. In the middle of the smile her eyes closed once more—and this time, they stayed closed. Her head began to droop forward.

Then she sat up with a start.

"Hey," she said in drowsy indignation, "what's all this?"

"Sleepy gas," the *Viper's* voice returned. "If you're headed for another job, you're going to sleep all the way to Jeltad. You need your rest."

"That's a whole week!" Pagadan protested. But though she could not remember being transported there, she was in her somno-cabin by then, and flat on her back. Pillows were just being shoved under her head; and lights were going out all over the ship.

"You big, tricky bum!" she muttered. "I'll dismantle your reflexes yet!"

There was no answer to that grim threat; but she couldn't have heard it anyway. A week was due to pass before Zone Agent Pagadan would be permitted to become aware of her surroundings again.

Meanwhile, a dim hum had begun to grow throughout the *Viper's* giant body. Simultaneously, in the darkened and deserted control room, a bright blue spark started climbing steadily up the velocity indicator.

The humming rose suddenly to a howl, thinned out and became inaudible.

The spark stood gleaming steadily then at a point just below the line marked "Emergency."

Space had flattened out before the *Viper*—she was homeward-bound with another mission accomplished.

She began to travel—

The Second Night
of Summer

~~~

On the night after the day that brought summer officially to the land of Wend, on the planet of Noorhut,
the shining lights were seen again in the big hollow
at the east end of Grimp's father's farm.

Grimp watched them for more than an hour from
his upstairs room. The house was dark, but an occasional murmur of voices floated up to him through the
windows below. Everyone in the farmhouse was looking
at the lights.

On the other farms around and in the village, which
was over a hill and another two miles up the valley,
every living soul who could get within view of the
hollow was probably doing the same. For a time, the
agitated yelling of the Village Guardian's big pank-
hound had sounded clearly over the hill, but he had
quieted down then very suddenly—or had *been* quieted down, more likely, Grimp suspected. The Guardian

was dead-set against anyone making a fuss about the lights—and that included the pank-hound, too.

There was some excuse for the pank-hound's excitement, though. From the window, Grimp could see there were a lot more lights tonight than had turned up in previous years—big, brilliant-blue bubbles, drifting and rising and falling silently all about the hollow. Sometimes one would lift straight up for several hundred feet, or move off over the edge of the hollow for about the same distance, and hang there suspended for a few minutes, before floating back to the others. That was as far as they ever went away from the hollow.

There was, in fact, no need for the Halpa detector-globes to go any farther than that to get the information wanted by those who had sent them out, and who were listening now to the steady flow of brief reports, in some Halpa equivalent of human speech-thought, coming back to them through the globes:

"No signs of hostile activity in the vicinity of the breakthrough point. No weapons or engines of power within range of detection. The area shows no significant alterations since the last investigation. Sharp curiosity among those who observe us consciously— traces of alarm and suspicion. But no overt hostility."

The reports streamed on without interruption, repeating the same bits of information automatically and incessantly, while the globes floated and dipped soundlessly above and about the hollow.

Grimp continued to watch them, blinking sleepily now and then, until a spreading glow over the edge of the valley announced that Noorhut's Big Moon was coming up slowly, like a Planetary Guardian, to make its own inspection of the lights. The globes began to dim out then, just as they always had done at moonrise in the preceding summers; and even before the top rim of the Big Moon's yellow disk edged over the hills, the hollow was completely dark.

Grimp heard his mother starting up the stairs. He got hurriedly into bed. The show was over for the night and he had a lot of pleasant things to think about before he went to sleep.

Now that the lights had showed up, his good friend Grandma Erisa Wannattel and her patent-medicine trailer were sure to arrive, too. Sometime late tomorrow afternoon, the big draft-trailer would come rolling up the valley road from the city. For that was what Grandma Wannattel had done the past four summers— ever since the lights first started appearing above the hollow for the few nights they were to be seen there each year. And since four years were exactly half of Grimp's whole life, that made Grandma's return a mathematical certainty for him.

Other people, of course, like the Village Guardian, might have a poor opinion of Grandma, but just hanging around her and the trailer and the gigantic, exotic-looking rhinocerine pony that pulled it was, in Grimp's opinion, a lot better even than going to the circus.

And vacations started the day after tomorrow! The whole future just now, in fact, looked like one good thing after another, extending through a vista of summery infinities.

Grimp went to sleep happily.

At about the same hour, though at a distance greater than Grimp's imagination had stretched as yet, eight large ships came individually out of the darkness between the stars that was their sea, and began to move about Noorhut in a carefully timed pattern of orbits. They stayed much too far out to permit any instrument of space-detection to suspect that Noorhut might be their common center of interest.

But that was what it was. Though the men who crewed the eight ships bore the people of Noorhut no ill will, hardly anything could have looked less promising for Noorhut than the cargo they had on board.

Seven of them were armed with a gas which was not often used any more. A highly volatile lethal catalyst, it sank to the solid surface of a world over which it was freed and spread out swiftly there to the point where its presence could no longer be detected by any chemical means. However, its effect of drawing the final breath almost imperceptibly out of all things that were oxygen-breathing was not noticeably reduced by diffusion.

The eighth ship was equipped with a brace of torpedoes, which were normally released some hours after the gas-carriers dispersed their invisible death. They were quite small torpedoes, since the only task remaining for them would be to ignite the surface of the planet that had been treated with the catalyst.

All those things might presently happen to Noorhut. But they would happen only if a specific message was flashed from it to the circling squadron—the message that Noorhut already was lost to a deadly foe who must, at any cost now, be prevented from spreading out from it to other inhabited worlds.

Next afternoon, right after school, as Grimp came expectantly around the bend of the road at the edge of the farm, he found the village policeman sitting there on a rock, gazing tearfully down the road.

"Hello, Runny," said Grimp, disturbed. Considered in the light of gossip he'd overheard in the village that morning, this didn't look so good for Grandma. It just didn't look good.

The policeman blew his nose on a handkerchief he

carried tucked into the front of his uniform, wiped his eyes, and gave Grimp an annoyed glance.

"Don't *you* call me Runny, Grimp!" he said, replacing the handkerchief. Like Grimp himself and most of the people on Noorhut, the policeman was brown-skinned and dark-eyed, normally a rather good looking young fellow. But his eyes were swollen and red-rimmed now; and his nose, which was a bit larger than average, anyway, was also red and swollen and undeniably runny. He had hay-fever bad.

Grimp apologized and sat down thoughtfully on the rock beside the policeman, who was one of his numerous cousins. He was about to mention that he had overheard Vellit using the expression when she and the policeman came through the big Leeth-flower orchard above the farm the other evening—at a much less leisurely rate than was their custom there. But he thought better of it. Vellit was the policeman's girl for most of the year, but she broke their engagement regularly during hay-fever season and called him cousin instead of dearest.

"What are you doing here?" Grimp asked bluntly instead.

"Waiting," said the policeman.

"For what?" said Grimp, with a sinking heart.

"Same individual you are, I guess," the policeman told him, hauling out the handkerchief again. He blew. "This year she's going to go right back where she came from or get pinched."

"Who says so?" scowled Grimp.

"The Guardian, that's who," said the policeman. "That good enough for you?"

"He can't do it!" Grimp said hotly. "It's our farm, and she's got all her licenses."

"He's had a whole year to think up a new list she's got to have," the policeman informed him. He fished in the breast-pocket of his uniform, pulled out a folded paper, and opened it. "He put thirty-four items down here I got to check—she's bound to miss on one of them."

"It's a dirty trick!" said Grimp, rapidly scanning as much as he could see of the list.

"Let's us have more respect for the Village Guardian, Grimp!" the policeman said warningly.

"Uh-huh," muttered Grimp. "Sure . . ." If Runny would just move his big thumb out of the way. But what a list! Trailer; rhinocerine pony (beast, heavy draft, imported); patent medicines; household utensils; fortunetelling; pets; herbs; miracle-healing—

The policeman looked down, saw what Grimp was doing, and raised the paper out of his line of vision. "That's an official document," he said, warding Grimp off with one hand and tucking the paper away with the other. "Let's us not get our dirty hands on it."

Grimp was thinking fast. Grandma Wannattel did have framed licenses for some of the items he'd read hanging around inside the trailer, but certainly not thirty-four of them.

"Remember that big skinless werret I caught last season?" he asked.

The policeman gave him a quick glance, looked away again, and wiped his eyes thoughtfully. The season on werrets would open the following week and he was as ardent a fisherman as anyone in the village—and last summer Grimp's monster werret had broken a twelve-year record in the valley.

"Some people," Grimp said idly, staring down the valley road to the point where it turned into the woods, "would sneak after a person for days who's caught a big werret, hoping he'd be dumb enough to go back to that pool."

The policeman flushed and dabbed the handkerchief gingerly at his nose.

"Some people would even sit in a haystack and use spyglasses, even when the hay made them sneeze like crazy," continued Grimp quietly.

The policeman's flush deepened. He sneezed.

"But a person isn't that dumb," said Grimp. "Not when he knows there's anyway two werrets there six inches bigger than the one he caught."

"*Six inches?*" the policeman repeated a bit incredulously—eagerly.

"Easy," nodded Grimp. "I had a look at them again last week."

It was the policeman's turn to think. Grimp idly hauled out his slingshot, fished a pebble out of his small-pebble pocket, and knocked the head off a flower twenty feet away. He yawned negligently.

"You're pretty good with that slingshot," the policeman remarked. "You must be just about as good as the culprit that used a slingshot to ring the fire-alarm signal on the defense unit bell from the top of the schoolhouse last week."

"That'd take a pretty good shot," Grimp admitted.

"And who then," continued the policeman, "dropped pepper in his trail, so the pank-hound near coughed off his head when we started to track him. The Guardian," he added significantly, "would like to have a clue about that culprit, all right."

"Sure, sure," said Grimp, bored. The policeman, the Guardian, and probably even the pank-hound, knew exactly who the culprit was; but they wouldn't be able to prove it in twenty thousand years. Runny just had to realize first that threats weren't going to get him anywhere near a record werret.

Apparently, he had; he was settling back for another bout of thinking. Grimp, interested in what he would produce next, decided just to leave him to it. . . .

Then Grimp jumped up suddenly from the rock.

"There they are!" he yelled, waving the slingshot.

A half-mile down the road, Grandma Wannattel's big, silvery trailer had come swaying out of the woods behind the rhinocerine pony and turned up toward the farm. The pony saw Grimp, lifted its head, which was as long as a tall man, and bawled a thunderous greeting. Grandma Wannattel stood up on the driver's seat and waved a green silk handkerchief.

Grimp started sprinting down the road.

The werrets should turn the trick—but he'd better get Grandma informed, just the same, about recent developments here, before she ran into Runny.

Grandma Wannattel flicked the pony's horny rear with the reins just before they reached the policeman, who was waiting at the side of the road with the Guardian's check-list unfolded in his hand.

The pony broke into a lumbering trot, and the trailer swept past Runny and up around the bend of the road, where it stopped well within the boundaries of the farm. They climbed down and Grandma quickly unhitched the pony. It waddled, grunting, off the road and down into the long, marshy meadow above the hollow. It stood still there, cooling its feet.

Grimp felt a little better. Getting the trailer off community property gave Grandma a technical advantage. Grimp's people had a favorable opinion of her, and they were a sturdy lot who enjoyed telling off the Guardian any time he didn't actually have a law to back up his orders. But on the way to the farm, she had confessed to Grimp that, just as he'd feared, she didn't have anything like thirty-four licenses. And now the policeman was coming up around the bend of the road after them, blowing his nose and frowning.

"Just let me handle him alone," Grandma told Grimp out of the corner of her mouth.

He nodded and strolled off into the meadow to pass the time with the pony. She'd had a lot of experience in handling policemen.

"Well, well, young man," he heard her greeting his cousin behind him. "That looks like a bad cold you've got."

The policeman sneezed.

"Wish it were a cold," he said resignedly. "It's hay-fever. Can't do a thing with it. Now I've got a list here—"

"Hay-fever?" said Grandma. "Step up into the trailer a moment. We'll fix that."

"About this list—" began Runny, and stopped. "You think you got something that would fix it?" he asked skeptically. "I've been to I don't know how many doctors and they didn't help any."

"Doctors!" said Grandma. Grimp heard her heels click up the metal steps that led into the back of the trailer. "Come right in, won't take a moment."

"Well—" said Runny doubtfully, but he followed her inside.

Grimp winked at the pony. The first round went to Grandma.

"Hello, pony," he said.

His worries couldn't reduce his appreciation of Grandma's fabulous draft-animal. Partly, of course, it was just that it was such an enormous beast. The long, round barrel of its body rested on short legs with wide, flat feet which were settled deep in the meadow's mud by now. At one end was a spiky tail and at the other a very big, wedge-shaped head, with a blunt, badly chipped horn set between nose and eyes. From nose to tail and all around, it was covered with thick, rect-angular, horny plates, a mottled green-brown in color.

Grimp patted its rocky side affectionately. He loved the pony most for being the ugliest thing that had ever showed up on Noorhut. According to Grandma, she had bought it from a bankrupt circus which had imported it from a planet called Treebel; and Treebel was supposed to be a world full of hot swamps, inexhaustibly explosive volcanoes, and sulphurous stenches.

One might have thought that after wandering around melting lava and under rainfalls of glowing ashes for most of its life, the pony would have considered Noorhut pretty tame. But though there wasn't much room for expression around the solid slab of bone supporting the horn, which was the front of its face, Grimp thought it looked thoroughly contented with its feet sunk out of sight in Noorhut's cool mud.

"You're a big fat pig!" he told it fondly.

The pony slobbered out a long, purple tongue and carefully parted his hair.

"Cut it out!" said Grimp. "Ugh!"

The pony snorted, pleased, curled its tongue about a huge clump of weeds, pulled them up, and flipped them into its mouth, roots, mud, and all. It began to chew.

Grimp glanced at the sun and turned anxiously to study the trailer. If she didn't get rid of Runny soon, they'd be calling him back to the house for supper before he and Grandma got around to having a good talk. And they weren't letting him out of doors these evenings, while the shining lights were here.

He gave the pony a parting whack, returned quietly to the road, and sat down out of sight near the back door of the trailer, where he could hear what was going on.

" . . . so about the only thing the Guardian could tack on you now," the policeman was saying, "would be a Public Menace charge. If there's any trouble about the lights this year, he's likely to try that. He's not a bad Guardian, you know, but he's got himself talked into

thinking you're sort of to blame for the lights showing up here every year."

Grandma chuckled. "Well, I try to get here in time
to see them every summer," she admitted. "I can see
how that might give him the idea."

"And of course," said the policeman, "we're all trying
to keep it quiet about them. If the news got out, we'd
be having a lot of people coming here from the city,
just to look. No one but the Guardian minds you being
here, only you don't want a lot of city people tramping around your farms."

"Of course not," agreed Grandma. "And I certainly
haven't told anyone about them myself."

"Last night," the policeman added, "everyone was
saying there were twice as many lights this year as
last summer. That's what got the Guardian so
excited."

Chafing more every minute, Grimp had to listen
then to an extended polite argument about how much
Runny wanted to pay Grandma for her hay-fever
medicines, while she insisted he didn't owe her anything at all. In the end, Grandma lost and the policeman paid up—much too much to take from any friend
of Grimp's folks, Grandma protested to the last. And
then, finally, that righteous minion of the law came
climbing down the trailer steps again, with Grandma
following him to the door.

"How do I look, Grimp?" he beamed cheerfully as
Grimp stood up.

"Like you ought to wash your face sometime,"
Grimp said tactlessly, for he was fast losing patience
with Runny. But then his eyes widened in surprise.

Under a coating of yellowish grease, Runny's nose
seemed to have returned almost to the shape it had
out of hay-fever season, and his eyelids were hardly
puffed at all! Instead of flaming red, those features,

furthermore, now were only a delicate pink in shade. Runny, in short, was almost handsome again.

"Pretty good, eh?" he said. "Just one shot did it. And I've only got to keep the salve on another hour. Isn't that right, Grandma?"

"That's right," smiled Grandma from the door, clinking Runny's money gently out of one hand into the other. "You'll be as good as new then."

"Permanent cure, too," said Runny. He patted Grimp benevolently on the head. "And next week we go werret-fishing, eh, Grimp?" he added greedily.

"I guess so," Grimp said, with a trace of coldness. It was his opinion that Runny could have been satisfied with the hay-fever cure and forgotten about the werrets.

"It's a date!" nodded Runny happily and took his greasy face whistling down the road. Grimp scowled after him, half-minded to reach for the slingshot then and there and let go with a medium stone at the lower rear of the uniform. But probably he'd better not.

"Well, that's that," Grandma said softly.

At that moment, up at the farmhouse, a cow horn went "Whoop-whoop!" across the valley.

"Darn," said Grimp. "I knew it was getting late, with him doing all that talking! Now they're calling me to supper." There were tears of disappointment in his eyes.

"Don't let it fuss you, Grimp," Grandma said consolingly. "Just jump up in here a moment and close your eyes."

Grimp jumped up into the trailer and closed his eyes expectantly.

"Put out your hands," Grandma's voice told him.

He put out his hands, and she pushed them together to form a cup.

Then something small and light and furry dropped

into them, caught hold of one of Grimp's thumbs, with tiny, cool fingers, and chittered.

Grimp's eyes popped open.

"It's a lortel!" he whispered, overwhelmed.

"It's for you!" Grandma beamed.

Grimp couldn't speak. The lortel looked at him from a tiny, black, human face with large blue eyes set in it, wrapped a long, furry tail twice around his wrist, clung to his thumb with its fingers, and grinned and squeaked.

"It's wonderful!" gasped Grimp. "Can you really teach them to talk?"

"Hello," said the lortel.

"That's all it can say so far," Grandma said. "But if you're patient with it, it'll learn more."

"I'll be patient," Grimp promised, dazed. "I saw one at the circus this winter, down the valley at Laggand. They said it could talk, but it never said anything while I was there."

"Hello!" said the lortel.

"Hello!" gulped Grimp.

The cow horn whoop-whooped again.

"I guess you'd better run along to supper, or they might get mad," said Grandma.

"I know," said Grimp. "What does it eat?"

"Bugs and flowers and honey and fruit and eggs, when it's wild. But you just feed it whatever you eat yourself."

"Well, good-by," said Grimp. "And golly—thanks, Grandma."

He jumped out of the trailer. The lortel climbed out of his hand, ran up his arm, and sat on his shoulder, wrapping its tail around his neck.

"It knows you already," Grandma said. "It won't run away."

Grimp reached up carefully with his other hand and patted the lortel.

"I'll be back early tomorrow," he said. "No school . . . They won't let me out after supper as long as those lights keep coming around."

The cow horn whooped for the third time, very loudly. This time it meant business.

"Well, good-by," Grimp repeated hastily. He ran off, the lortel hanging on to his shirt collar and squeaking.

Grandma looked after him and then at the sun, which had just touched the tops of the hills with its lower rim.

"Might as well have some supper myself," she remarked, apparently to no one in particular. "But after that I'll have to run out the go-buggy and create a diversion."

Lying on its armor-plated belly down in the meadow, the pony swung its big head around toward her. Its small yellow eyes blinked questioningly.

"What makes you think a diversion will be required?" its voice asked into her ear. The ability to produce such ventriloquial effects was one of the talents that made the pony well worth its considerable keep to Grandma.

"Weren't you listening?" she scolded. "That policeman told me the Guardian's planning to march the village's defense unit up to the hollow after supper, and start them shooting at the Halpa detector-globes as soon as they show up."

The pony swore an oath meaningless to anyone who hadn't been raised on the planet Treebel. It stood up, braced itself, and began pulling its feet out of the mud in a succession of loud, sucking noises.

"I haven't had an hour's straight rest since you talked me into tramping around with you eight years ago!" it complained.

"But you've certainly been seeing life, like I promised," Grandma smiled.

The pony slopped in a last, enormous tongueful of wet weeds. "That I have!" it said, with emphasis.

It came chewing up to the road.

"I'll keep a watch on things while you're having your supper," it told her.

As the uniformed twelve-man defense unit marched in good order out of the village, on its way to assume a strategic position around the hollow on Grimp's father's farm, there was a sudden, small explosion not very far off.

The Guardian, who was marching in the lead with a gun over his shoulder and the slavering pank-hound on a leash, stopped short. The unit broke ranks and crowded up behind him.

"What was that?" the Guardian inquired.

Everybody glanced questioningly around the rolling green slopes of the valley, already darkened with evening shadows. The pank-hound sat down before the Guardian, pointed its nose at the even darker shadows in the woods ahead of them, and growled.

"Look!" a man said, pointing in the same direction.

A spark of bright green light had appeared on their path, just where it entered the woods. The spark grew rapidly in size, became as big as a human head—then bigger! Smoky green streamers seemed to be pouring out of it . . .

"I'm going home right now," someone announced at that point, sensibly enough.

"Stand your ground!" the Guardian ordered, conscious of the beginnings of a general withdrawal movement behind him. He was an old soldier. He unslung his gun, cocked it, and pointed it. The pank-hound got up on his six feet and bristled.

"Stop!" the Guardian shouted at the green light.

It expanded promptly to the size of a barrel, new streamers shooting out from it and fanning about like hungry tentacles.

He fired.

"*Run!*" everybody yelled then. The pank-hound slammed backward against the Guardian's legs, upsetting him, and streaked off after the retreating unit. The green light had spread outward jerkily into the shape of something like a many-armed, writhing starfish, almost the size of the trees about it. Deep, hooting sounds came out of it as it started drifting down the path toward the Guardian.

He got up on one knee and, in a single drumroll of sound, emptied all thirteen charges remaining in his gun into the middle of the starfish. It hooted more loudly, waved its arms more wildly, and continued to advance.

He stood up quickly then, slung the gun over his shoulder, and joined the retreat. By the time the unit reached the first houses of the village, he was well up in the front ranks again. And a few minutes later, he was breathlessly organizing the local defenses, employing the tactics that had shown their worth in the raids of the Laggand Bandits nine years before.

The starfish, however, was making no attempt to follow up the valley people's rout. It was still on the path at the point where the Guardian had seen it last, waving its arms about and hooting menacingly at the silent trees.

"That should do it, I guess," Grandma Wannattel said. "Before the first projection fizzles out, the next one in the chain will start up where they can see it from the village. It ought to be past midnight before anyone starts bothering about the globes again. Particularly since there aren't going to be any globes around tonight—that is, if the Halpa attack-schedule has been correctly estimated."

"I wish we were safely past midnight right now," the rhinocerine pony worriedly informed her. Its dark shape stood a little up the road from the trailer, outlined motionlessly like a ponderous statue against the red evening sky. Its head was up; it looked as if it were listening. Which it was, in its own way—listening for any signs of activity from the hollow.

"No sense getting anxious about it," Grandma remarked. She was perched on a rock at the side of the road, a short distance from the pony, with a small black bag slung over her shoulder. "We'll wait here another hour till it's good and dark and then go down to the hollow. The breakthrough might begin a couple of hours after that."

"It *would* have to be us again!" grumbled the pony. In spite of its size, its temperament was on the nervous side. And while any companion of Zone Agent Wannattel was bound to run regularly into situations that were far from soothing, the pony couldn't recall any previous experience that had looked as extremely un-soothing as the prospects of the night-hours ahead. On far-off Vega's world of Jeltad, in the planning offices of the Department of Galactic Zones, the decision to put Noorhut at stake to win one round in mankind's grim war with the alien and mysterious Halpa might have seemed as distressing as it was unavoidable. But the pony couldn't help feeling that the distress would have become a little more acute if Grandma's distant employers had happened to be standing right here with the two of them while the critical hours approached.

"I'd feel a lot better myself if Headquarters hadn't picked us for this particular operation," Grandma admitted. "Us and Noorhut . . ."

Because, by what was a rather singular coincidence,

considering how things stood there tonight, the valley was also Grandma's home. She had been born, quite some while before, a hundred and eighty miles farther inland, at the foot of the dam of the great river Wend, which had given its name to the land, and nowadays supplied it with almost all its required power.

Erisa Wannattel had done a great deal of traveling since she first became aware of the fact that her varied abilities and adventuresome nature needed a different sort of task to absorb them than could be found on Noorhut, which was progressing placidly up into the final stages of a rounded and balanced planetary civilization. But she still liked to consider the Valley of the Wend as her home and headquarters, to which she returned as often as her work would permit. Her exact understanding of the way people there thought about things and did things also made them easy for her to manipulate; and on occasion that could be very useful.

In most other places, the means she had employed to turn the Guardian and his troop back from the hollow probably would have started a panic or brought armed ships and radiation guns zooming up for the kill within minutes. But the valley people had considered it just another local emergency. The bronze alarm bell in the village had pronounced a state of siege, and cow horns passed the word up to the outlying farms. Within minutes, the farmers were pelting down the roads to the village with their families and guns; and, very soon afterward, everything quieted down again. Guard lines had been set up by then, with the women and children quartered in the central buildings, while the armed men had settled down to watching Grandma's illusion projections—directional video narrow beams—from the discreet distance marked by the village boundaries.

If nothing else happened, the people would just stay there till morning and then start a cautious investigation. After seeing mysterious blue lights dancing harmlessly over Grimp's farm for four summers, this section of Wend was pretty well conditioned to fiery apparitions. But even if they got too adventurous, they couldn't hurt themselves on the projections, which were designed to be nothing but very effective visual displays.

What it all came to was that Grandma had everybody in the neighborhood rounded up and immobilized where she wanted them.

In every other respect, the valley presented an exceptionally peaceful twilight scene to the eye. There was nothing to show that it was the only present point of contact between forces engaged in what was probably a war of intergalactic proportions—a war made wraith-like but doubly deadly by the circumstance that, in over a thousand years, neither side had found out much more about the other than the merciless and devastating finality of its forms of attack. There never had been any actual battles between Mankind and the Halpa, only alternate and very thorough massacres— all of them, from Mankind's point of view, on the wrong side of the fence.

The Halpa alone had the knowledge that enabled them to reach their human adversary. That was the trouble. But, apparently, they could launch their attacks only by a supreme effort, under conditions that existed for periods of less than a score of years, and about three hundred years apart as Mankind measured time.

It was hard to find any good in them, other than the virtue of persistence. Every three hundred years, they punctually utilized that brief period to execute one more thrust, carefully prepared and placed, and carried out with a dreadfully complete abruptness, against some new point of human civilization—and this time the attack was going to come through on Noorhut.

"Something's starting to move around in that hollow!" the pony announced suddenly. "It's not one of their globe-detectors."

"I know," murmured Grandma. "That's the first of the Halpa themselves. They're going to be right on schedule, it seems. But don't get nervous. They can't hurt anything until their transmitter comes through and revives them. We've got to be particularly careful now not to frighten them off. They seem to be even more sensitive to emotional tensions in their immediate surroundings than the globes."

The pony made no reply. It knew what was at stake and why eight big ships were circling Noorhut somewhere beyond space-detection tonight. It knew, too, that the ships would act only if it was discovered that Grandma had failed. But—

The pony shook its head uneasily. The people on Treebel had never become civilized to the point of considering the possibility of taking calculated risks on a planetary scale—not to mention the fact that the lives of the pony and of Grandma were included in the present calculation. In the eight years it had been accompanying her on her travels, it had developed a tremendous respect for Erisa Wannattel's judgment and prowess. But, just the same, frightening the Halpa off, if it still could be done, seemed like a very sound idea right now to the pony.

As a matter of fact, as Grandma well knew, it probably could have been done at this stage by tossing a small firecracker into the hollow. Until they had established their planetary foothold, the Halpa took extreme precautions. They could spot things in the class of radiation weapons a hundred miles away, and either that or any suggestion of local aggressiveness or of long-range observation would check the invasion attempt on Noorhut then and there.

But one of the principal reasons she was here tonight was to see that nothing *did* happen to stop it. For this assault would only be diverted against some other world then, and quite probably against one where the significance of the spying detector-globes wouldn't be understood before it was too late. The best information system in the Galaxy couldn't keep more than an insignificant fraction of its populations on the alert for dangers like that—

She bounced suddenly to her feet and, at the same instant, the pony swung away from the hollow toward which it been staring. They both stood for a moment then, turning their heads about, like baffled hounds trying to fix a scent on the wind.

"It's Grimp!" Grandma exclaimed.

The rhinocerine pony snorted faintly. "Those are his thought images, all right," it agreed. "He seems to feel you need protection. Can you locate him?"

"Not yet," said Grandma anxiously. "Yes, I can. He's coming up through the woods on the other side of the hollow, off to the left. The little devil!" She was hustling back to the trailer. "Come on, I'll have to ride you there. I can't even dare use the go-buggy this late in the day."

The pony crouched beside the trailer while she quickly snapped on its saddle from the top of the back steps. Six metal rings had been welded into the horny plates of its back for this purpose, so it was a simple job. Grandma clambered aloft, hanging onto the saddle's hand-rails.

"Swing wide of the hollow!" she warned. "This could spoil everything. But make all the noise you want. The

Halpa don't care about noise as such—it has to have emotional content before they get interested—and the quicker Grimp spots us, the easier it will be to find him."

The pony already was rushing down into the meadow at an amazing rate of speed—it took a lot of very efficient muscle to drive as heavy a body as that through the gluey swamps of Treebel. It swung wide of the hollow and of what it contained, crossed a shallow bog farther down the meadow with a sound like a charging torpedo-boat, and reached the woods.

It had to slow down then, to avoid brushing off Grandma.

"Grimp's down that slope somewhere," Grandma said. "He's heard us."

"They're making a lot of noise!" Grimp's thought reached them suddenly and clearly. He seemed to be talking to someone. "But we're not scared of them, are we?"

"Bang-bang!" another thought-voice came excitedly.

"It's the lortel," Grandma and the pony said together.

"That's the stuff!" Grimp resumed approvingly. "We'll slingshot them all if they don't watch out. But we'd better find Grandma soon."

"Grimp!" shouted Grandma. The pony backed her up with a roaring call.

"Hello?" came the lortel's thought.

"Wasn't that the pony?" asked Grimp. "All right— let's go that way."

"Here we come, Grimp!" Grandma shouted as the pony descended the steep side of a ravine with the straightforward technique of a rockslide.

"That's Grandma!" thought Grimp. "Grandma!" he yelled. "Look out! There's monsters all around!"

❖   ❖   ❖

"What you missed!" yelled Grimp, dancing around the pony as Grandma Wannattel scrambled down from the saddle. "There's monsters all around the village and the Guardian killed one and I slingshot another till he fizzled out and I was coming to find you—"

"Your mother will be worried!" began Grandma as they rushed into each other's arms.

"No," grinned Grimp. "All the kids are supposed to be sleeping in the school house, and she won't look there till morning, and the schoolteacher said the monsters were all"—he slowed down cautiously— "ho-lucy-nations. But he wouldn't go look when the Guardian said they'd show him one. He stayed right in bed! But the Guardian's all right—he killed one and I slingshot another and the lortel learned a new word. Say 'bang-bang', lortel!" he invited.

"Hello!" squeaked the lortel.

"Aw," said Grimp disappointedly. "He can say it, though. And I've come to take you to the village so the monsters don't get you. Hello, pony!"

"Bang-bang," said the lortel distinctly.

"See?" cried Grimp. "He isn't scared at all—he's a real brave lortel! If we see some monsters don't you get scared either, because I've got my slingshot," he said, waving it bloodthirstily, "and two back pockets still full of medium stones. The way to do it is to kill them all!"

"It sounds like a pretty good idea, Grimp," Grandma agreed. "But you're awfully tired now."

"No, I'm not!" Grimp said, surprised. His right eye sagged shut and then his left and he opened them both with an effort and looked at Grandma.

"That's right," he admitted. "I am . . ."

"In fact," said Grandma, "you're asleep!"

"No, I'm n—" objected Grimp. Then he sagged toward the ground, and Grandma caught him.

"In a way I hate to do it," she panted, wrestling him aboard the pony, which had lain down and flattened itself as much as it could to make it easier. "He'd probably enjoy it. But we can't take a chance. He's a husky little devil, too," she groaned, giving a final boost, "and those ammunition pockets don't make him any lighter!" She clambered up again herself and noticed that the lortel had transferred itself to her coat collar.

The pony stood up cautiously.

"Now what?" it said.

"Might as well go straight to the hollow," said Grandma, breathing hard. "We'll probably have to wait around there a few hours, but if we're careful it won't do any harm."

"Did you find a good deep pond?" Grandma asked the pony a little later, as it came squishing up softly through the meadow behind her to join her at the edge of the hollow.

"Yes," said the pony. "About a hundred yards back. That should be close enough. How much more waiting do you think we'll have to do?"

Grandma shrugged carefully. She was sitting in the grass with what, by daylight, would have been a good view of the hollow below. Grimp was asleep with his head on her knees; and the lortel, after catching a few bugs in the grass and eating them, had settled down on her shoulder and dozed off too.

"I don't know," she said. "It's still three hours till Big Moonrise, and it's bound to be some time before then. Now you've found a waterhole, we'll just stay here together and wait. The one thing to remember is not to let yourself start getting excited about them."

The pony stood huge and chunky beside her, its forefeet on the edge of the hollow, staring down.

Muddy water trickled from its knobby flanks. It had brought the warm mud-smells of a summer pond back with it to hang in a cloud about them.

There was vague, dark, continuous motion at the bottom of the hollow. A barely noticeable stirring in the single big pool of darkness that filled it.

"If I were alone," the pony said, "I'd get out of here! I know when I ought to be scared. But you've taken psychological control of my reactions, haven't you?"

"Yes," said Grandma. "It'll be easier for me, though, if you help along as much as you can. There's really no danger until their transmitter has come through."

"Unless," said the pony, "they've worked out some brand-new tricks in the past few hundred years."

"There's that," Grandma admitted. "But they've never tried changing their tricks on us yet. If it were us doing the attacking, we'd vary our methods each time, as much as we could. But the Halpa don't seem to think just like we do about anything. They wouldn't still be so careful if they didn't realize they were very vulnerable at this point."

"I hope they're right about that!" the pony said briefly.

Its head moved then, following the motion of something that sailed flutteringly out of the depths of the hollow, circled along its far rim, and descended again. The inhabitants of Treebel had a much deeper range of dark-vision than Grandma Wannattel, but she was also aware of that shape.

"They're not much to look at," the pony remarked. "Like a big, dark rag of leather, mostly."

"Their physical structure is believed to be quite simple," Grandma agreed slowly. The pony was tensing up again, and it was best to go on talking to it, about almost anything at all. That always helped, even though the pony knew her much too well by now to be really fooled by such tricks.

"Many very efficient life-forms aren't physically complicated, you know," she went on, letting the sound of her voice ripple steadily into its mind. "Parasitical types, particularly. It's pretty certain, too, that the Halpa have the hive-mind class of intelligence, so what goes for the nerve-systems of most of the ones they send through to us might be nothing much more than secondary reflex-transmitters. . . ."

Grimp stirred in his sleep at that point and grumbled. Grandma looked down at him. "You're sound asleep!" she told him severely, and he was again.

"You've got plans for that boy, haven't you?" the pony said, without shifting its gaze from the hollow.

"I've had my eye on him," Grandma admitted, "and I've already recommended him to Headquarters for observation. But I'm not going to make up my mind about Grimp till next summer, when we've had more time to study him. Meanwhile, we'll see what he picks up naturally from the lortel in the way of telepathic communication and sensory extensions. I think Grimp's the kind we can use."

"He's all right," the pony agreed absently. "A bit murderous, though, like most of you . . ."

"He'll grow out of it!" Grandma said, a little annoyedly, for the subject of human aggressiveness was one she and the pony argued about frequently. "You can't hurry developments like that along too much. All of Noorhut should grow out of that stage, as a people, in another few hundred years. They're about at the turning-point right now—"

Their heads came up together, then, as something very much like a big, dark rag of leather came fluttering up from the hollow and hung in the dark air above them. The representatives of the opposing powers that were meeting on Noorhut that night took quiet stock of one another for a moment.

The Halpa was about six feet long and two wide, and considerably less than an inch thick. It held its position in the air with a steady, rippling motion, like a bat the size of a man. Then, suddenly, it extended itself with a snap, growing taut as a curved sail.

The pony snorted involuntarily. The apparently featureless shape in the air turned towards it and drifted a few inches closer. When nothing more happened, it turned again and fluttered quietly back down into the hollow.

"Could it tell I was scared?" the pony asked uneasily.

"You reacted just right," Grandma said soothingly. "Startled suspicion at first, and then just curiosity, and then another start when it made that jump. It's about what they'd expect from creatures that would be hanging around the hollow now. We're like cows to them. They can't tell what things are by their looks, like we do—"

But her tone was thoughtful, and she was more shaken than she would have cared to let the pony notice. There had been something indescribably menacing and self-assured in the Halpa's gesture. Almost certainly, it had only been trying to draw a reaction of hostile intelligence from them, probing, perhaps, for the presence of weapons that might be dangerous to its kind.

But there was a chance—a tiny but appalling chance—that the things *had* developed some drastically new form of attack since their last breakthrough, and that they already were in control of the situation . . .

In which case, neither Grimp nor anyone else on Noorhut would be doing any more growing-up after tomorrow.

Each of the eleven hundred and seventeen planets

that had been lost to the Halpa so far still traced a fiery, forbidding orbit through space—torn back from the invaders only at the cost of depriving it, by humanity's own weapons, of the conditions any known form of life could tolerate.

The possibility that this might also be Noorhut's future had loomed as an ugly enormity before her for the past four years. But of the nearly half a hundred worlds which the Halpa were found to be investigating through their detector-globes as possible invasion points for this period, Noorhut finally had been selected by Headquarters as the one where local conditions were most suited to meet them successfully. And that meant in a manner which must include the destruction of their only real invasion weapon, the fabulous and mysterious Halpa transmitter. Capable as they undoubtedly were, they had shown in the past that they were able or willing to employ only one of those instruments for each period of attack. Destroying the transmitter meant therefore that humanity would gain a few more centuries to figure out a way to get back at the Halpa before a new attempt was made.

So on all planets but Noorhut the detector-globes had been encouraged carefully to send back reports of a dangerously alert and well-armed population. On Noorhut, however, they had been soothed along . . . and just as her home-planet had been chosen as the most favorable point of encounter, so was Erisa Wannattel herself selected as the agent most suited to represent humanity's forces under the conditions that existed there.

Grandma sighed gently and reminded herself again that Headquarters was as unlikely to miscalculate the overall probability of success as it was to select the wrong person to achieve it. There was only the tiniest, the most theoretical, of chances that something might go wrong and that she would end her long career with the blundering murder of her own homeworld.

But there was that chance.

"There seem to be more down there every minute!" the pony was saying.

Grandma drew a deep breath.

"Must be several thousand by now," she acknowledged. "It's getting near breakthrough time, all right, but those are only the advance forces." She added, "Do you notice anything like a glow of light down there, towards the center?"

The pony stared a moment. "Yes," it said. "But I would have thought that was way under the red for you. Can you see it?"

"No," said Grandma. "I get a kind of a feeling, like heat. That's the transmitter beginning to come through. I think we've got them!"

The pony shifted its bulk slowly from side to side. "Yes," it said resignedly, "or they've got us."

"Don't think about that," Grandma ordered sharply and clamped one more mental lock shut on the foggy, dark terrors that were curling and writhing under her conscious thoughts, threatening to emerge at the last moment and paralyze her actions.

She had opened her black bag and was unhurriedly fitting together something composed of a few pieces of wood and wire, and a rather heavy, stiff spring . . .

"Just be ready," she added.

"I've been ready for an hour," said the pony, shuffling its feet unhappily.

They did no more talking after that. All the valley had become quiet about them. But slowly the hollow below was filling up with a black, stirring, slithering tide. Bits of it fluttered up now and then like strips of black smoke, hovered a few yards above the mass, and settled again.

Suddenly, down in the center of the hollow, there was something else.

The pony had seen it first, Grandma Wannattel realized. It was staring in that direction for almost a minute before she grew able to distinguish something that might have been a group of graceful miniature spires. Semi-transparent in the darkness, four small domes showed at the corners, with a larger one in the center. The central one was about twenty feet high and very slender.

The whole structure began to solidify swiftly . . .

The Halpa Transmitter's appearance of crystalline slightness was perhaps the most mind-chilling thing about it. For it brought instantly a jarring sense of what must be black distance beyond all distances, reaching back unimaginably to its place of origin. In that unknown somewhere, a prodigiously talented and determined race of beings had labored for human centuries to prepare and point some stupendous gun . . . and were able then to bridge the vast interval with nothing more substantial than this dark sliver of glass that had come to rest suddenly in the valley of the Wend.

But, of course, the Transmitter was all that was needed; its deadly poison lay in a sluggish, almost inert mass about it. Within minutes from now, it would waken to life, as similar transmitters had wakened on other nights on those lost and burning worlds. And in much less than minutes after that, the Halpa invaders would be hurled by their slender machine to every surface section of Noorhut—no longer inert, but quickened into a ravening, almost indestructible form of vampiric life, dividing and subdividing in its incredibly swift cycle of reproduction, fastening to feed anew, growing and dividing again—

Spreading, at that stage, much more swiftly than it could be exterminated by anything but the ultimate weapons!

The pony stirred suddenly, and she felt the wave of panic roll up in it.

"It's the Transmitter, all right," Grandma's thought reached it quickly. "We've had two descriptions of it before. But we can't be sure it's *here* until it begins to charge itself. Then it lights up—first at the edges, and then at the center. Five seconds after the central spire lights up, it will be energized too much to let them pull it back again. At least they couldn't pull it back after that, the last time they were observed. And then we'd better be ready—"

The pony had been told all that before. But as it listened it was quieting down again.

"And you're going to go on sleeping!" Grandma Wannattel's thought told Grimp next. "No matter what you hear or what happens, you'll sleep on and know nothing at all any more until I wake you up . . ."

Light surged up suddenly in the Transmitter—first into the four outer spires, and an instant later into the big central one, in a sullen red glow. It lit the hollow with a smoky glare. The pony took two startled steps backwards.

"Five seconds to go!" whispered Grandma's thought. She reached into her black bag again and took out a small plastic ball. It reflected the light from the hollow in dull crimson gleamings. She let it slip down carefully inside the shaftlike frame of the gadget she had put together of wood and wire. It clicked into place there against one end of the compressed spring.

Down below, they lay now in a blanket fifteen feet thick over the wet ground, like big, black, water-sogged leaves swept up in circular piles about the edges of the hollow. The tops and sides of the piles were stirring and shivering and beginning to slide down toward the Transmitter.

" . . . five, and go!" Grandma said aloud. She raised the wooden catapult to her shoulder.

The pony shook its blunt-horned head violently from side to side, made a strangled, bawling sound, surged forward, and plunged down the steep side of the hollow in a thundering rush.

Grandma aimed carefully and let go.

The blanket of dead-leaf things was lifting into the air ahead of the pony's ground-shaking approach in a weightless, silent swirl of darkness, which instantly blotted both the glowing Transmitter and the pony's shape from sight. The pony roared once as the blackness closed over it. A second later, there was a crash like the shattering of a hundred-foot mirror—and at approximately the same moment, Grandma's plastic ball exploded somewhere in the center of the swirling swarm.

Cascading fountains of white fire filled the whole of the hollow. Within the fire, a dense mass of shapes fluttered and writhed frenziedly like burning rags. From down where the fire boiled fiercest rose continued sounds of brittle substances suffering enormous violence. The pony was trampling the ruined Transmitter, making sure of its destruction.

"Better get out of it!" Grandma shouted anxiously. "What's left of that will all melt now anyway!"

She didn't know whether it heard her or not. But a few seconds later, it came pounding up the side of the hollow again. Blazing from nose to rump, it tramped past Grandma, plunged through the meadow behind her, shedding white sheets of fire that exploded the marsh grass in its tracks, and hurled itself headlong into the pond it had selected previously. There was a great splash accompanied by sharp hissing noises. Pond and pony vanished together under billowing clouds of steam.

"That was pretty hot!" its thought came to Grandma. She drew a deep breath.

"Hot as anything that ever came out of a volcano!" she affirmed. "If you'd played around in it much longer, you'd have fixed up the village with roasts for a year."

"I'll just stay here for a while, till I've cooled off a bit," said the pony.

Grandma found something strangling her then, and discovered it was the lortel's tail. She unwound it carefully. But the lortel promptly re-anchored itself with all four hands in her hair. She decided to leave it there. It seemed badly upset.

Grimp, however, slept on. It was going to take a little maneuvering to get him back into the village undetected before morning, but she would figure that out by and by. A steady flow of cool night air was being drawn past them into the hollow now and rising out of it again in boiling, vertical columns of invisible heat. At the bottom of the deluxe blaze she'd lit down there, things still seemed to be moving about—but very slowly. The Halpa were tough organisms, all right, though not nearly so tough, when you heated them up with a really good incendiary, as were the natives of Treebel.

She would have to make a final check of the hollow around dawn, of course, when the ground should have cooled off enough to permit it—but her century's phase of the Halpa War did seem to be over. The defensive part of it, at any rate—

Wet, munching sounds from the pond indicated the pony felt comfortable enough by now to take an interest in the parboiled vegetation it found floating around it. Everything had turned out all right.

So she settled down carefully on her back in the long marsh grass without disturbing Grimp's position too much, and just let herself faint for a while.

By sunrise, Grandma Wannattel's patent-medicine trailer was nine miles from the village and rolling steadily southwards up the valley road through the woods. As usual, she was departing under a cloud.

Grimp and the policeman had showed up early to warn her. The Guardian was making use of the night's various unprecedented disturbances to press through a vote on a Public Menace charge against Grandma in the village; and since everybody still felt rather excited and upset, he had a good chance just now of getting a majority.

Grimp had accompanied her far enough to explain that this state of affairs wasn't going to be permanent. He had it all worked out.

Runny's new immunity to hay-fever had brought him and the pretty Vellit to a fresh understanding overnight; they were going to get married five weeks from now. As a married man, Runny would then be eligible for the post of Village Guardian at the harvest elections— and between Grimp's cousins and Vellit's cousins, Runny's backers would just about control the vote. So when Grandma got around to visiting the valley again next summer, she needn't worry any more about police interference or official disapproval. . . .

Grandma had nodded approvingly. That was about the kind of neighborhood politics she'd begun to play herself at Grimp's age. She was pretty sure by now that Grimp was the one who eventually would become her successor, and the guardian not only of Noorhut and the star-system to which Noorhut belonged, but of a good many other star-systems besides. With careful schooling, he ought to be just about ready for the job by the time she was willing, finally, to retire.

An hour after he had started back to the farm, looking suddenly a little forlorn, the trailer swung off the valley road into a narrow forest path. Here the pony lengthened its stride, and less than five minutes later they entered a curving ravine, at the far end of which lay something that Grimp would have recognized instantly, from his one visit to the nearest port city, as a small spaceship.

A large round lock opened soundlessly in its side as they approached. The pony came to a stop. Grandma got down from the driver's seat and unhitched it. The pony walked into the lock, and the trailer picked its wheels off the ground and floated in after it. Grandma Wannattel walked in last, and the lock closed quietly on her heels.

The ship lay still a moment longer. Then it was suddenly gone. Dead leaves went dancing for a while about the ravine, disturbed by the breeze of its departure.

In a place very faraway—so far that neither Grimp nor his parents nor anyone in the village except the schoolteacher had ever heard of it—a set of instruments began signalling for attention. Somebody answered them.

Grandma's voice announced distinctly:

"This is Zone Agent Wannattel's report on the successful conclusion of the Halpa operation on Noorhut—"

High above Noorhut's skies, eight great ships swung instantly out of their watchful orbits about the planet and flashed off again into the blackness of the boundless space that was their sea and their home.

The Truth about Cushgar

∽◈∾

There was, for a time, a good deal of puzzled and uneasy speculation about the methods that had been employed by the Confederacy of Vega in the taming of Cushgar. The disturbing part of it was that nothing really seemed to have happened!

First, the rumor was simply that the Confederacy was preparing to move into Cushgar—and then, suddenly, that it *had* moved in. This aroused surprised but pleased interest in a number of areas bordering the Confederacy. The Thousand Nations and a half-dozen similar organizations quietly flexed their military muscles, and prepared to land in the middle of the Confederacy's back as soon as it became fairly engaged in its ambitious new project. For Cushgar and the Confederacy seemed about as evenly matched as any two powers could possibly be.

But there was no engagement, then. There was not even anything resembling an official surrender. Star system by system, mighty Cushgar was accepting the governors installed by the Confederacy. Meekly, it coughed up what was left of the captive peoples and the loot it had pirated for the past seven centuries. And, very simply and quietly then, under the eyes of a dumfounded galaxy, it settled down and began mending its manners.

Then the rumors began. The wildest of them appeared to have originated in Cushgar itself, among its grim but superstitious inhabitants.

The Thousand Nations and the other rival combines gradually relaxed their various preparations and settled back disappointedly. This certainly wasn't the time to jump! The Confederacy had sneaked something over again; it was all done with by now.

But *what* had they done to Cushgar—and how?

In the Confederacy's Council of Co-ordinators on Vega's planet of Jeltad, the Third Co-ordinator, Chief of the Department of Galactic Zones, was being freely raked over the coals by his eminent colleagues.

They, too, wanted to know about Cushgar; and he wasn't telling.

"Of course, we're not actually accusing you of anything," the Fifth Co-ordinator—Strategics—pointed out. "But you didn't expect to advance the Council's plans by sixty years or thereabouts without arousing a certain amount of curiosity, did you?"

"No, I didn't expect to do that," the Third Co-ordinator admitted.

"Come clean, Train!" said the First. Train was the name by which the Third Co-ordinator was known in this circle. "How did you do it?" Usually they were allies in these little arguments, but the First's curiosity was also rampant.

"Can't tell you!" the Third Co-ordinator said flatly. "I made a report to the College, and they'll dish out to your various departments whatever they ought to get."

He was within his rights in guarding his own department's secrets, and they knew it. As for the College—that was the College of the Pleiades, a metaphysically inclined body which was linked into the affairs of Confederacy government in a manner the College itself presumably could have defined exactly. Nobody else could. However, they were the final arbiters in a case of this kind.

The Council meeting broke up a little later. The Third Co-ordinator left with Bropha, a handsome youngish man who had been listening in, in a liaison capacity for the College.

"Let's go off and have a drink somewhere," Bropha suggested. "I'm curious myself."

The Co-ordinator growled softly. His gray hair was rumpled, and he looked exhausted.

"All right," he said. "I'll tell *you*—"

Bropha's title was President of the College of the Pleiades. That was a good deal less important than it sounded, since he was only the executive scientist in charge of the College's mundane affairs. However, he was also the Third Co-ordinator's close personal friend and had been cleared for secrets of state of any kind whatsoever.

They went off and had their drink.

"You can't blame them too much," Bropha said soothingly. "After all, the conquest of Cushgar has been regarded pretty generally as the Confederacy's principal and most dangerous undertaking in the century immediately ahead. When the Department of Galactic Zones pulls it off suddenly—apparently without preparation or losses—"

"It wasn't without losses," the Co-ordinator said glumly.

"Wasn't it?" said Bropha.

"It cost me," said the Co-ordinator, "the best Zone Agent I ever had—or ever hope to have. Remember Zamm?"

Bropha's handsome face darkened.

Yes, he remembered Zamm! There were even times when he wished he didn't remember her quite so vividly.

But two years would have been much too short an interval in any case to forget the name of the person who had saved his life—

At the time, the discovery that His Excellency the Illustrious Bropha was lost in space had sent a well-concealed ripple of dismay throughout the government of the Confederacy. For Bropha was destined in the Confederacy's plans to become a political figure of the highest possible importance.

Even the Third Co-ordinator's habitual placidity vanished when the information first reached him. But he realized promptly that while a man lost in deep space was almost always lost for good, there were any number of mitigating factors involved in this particular case. The last report on Bropha had been received from his personal yacht, captained by his half brother Greemshard; and that ship was equipped with devices which would have tripped automatic alarms in monitor-stations thousands of light-years apart if it had been suddenly destroyed or incapacitated by any unforeseen accident or space attack.

Since no such alarm was received, the yacht was still functioning undisturbed somewhere, though somebody on board her was keeping her where-abouts a secret.

It all pointed, pretty definitely, at Greemshard!

For its own reasons, the Department of Galactic

Zones had assembled a dossier on Bropha's half brother which was hardly less detailed than the information it had available concerning the illustrious scientist himself. It was no secret to its researchers that Greemshard was an ambitious, hard-driving man, who for years had chafed under the fact that the goal of his ambitions was always being reached first and without apparent effort by Bropha. The study of his personality had been quietly extended then to a point where it could be predicted with reasonable accuracy what he would do in any given set of circumstances; and with the department's psychologists busily dissecting the circumstances which surrounded the disappearance of Bropha, it soon became apparent what Greemshard had done and what he intended to do next.

A prompt check by local Zone Agents indicated that none of the powers who would be interested in getting Bropha into their hands had done so as yet, and insured, furthermore, that they could not do so now without leading the Confederacy's searchers directly to him. Which left, as the most important remaining difficulty, the fact that the number of places where the vanished yacht could be kept unobtrusively concealed was enormously large.

The number was a limited one, nevertheless—unless the ship was simply drifting about space somewhere, which was a risk no navigator of Greemshard's experience would be willing to take. And through the facilities of its home offices and laboratories and its roving army of Agents, the Third Department was equipped, as perhaps no other human organization ever had been, to produce an exact chart of all those possible points of concealment and then to check them off in the shortest possible time.

So the Co-ordinator was not in the least surprised when, on the eighth day of the search instigated by

the department, a message from Zone Agent Zamman
Tarradang-Pok was transferred to him, stating that
Bropha had been found, alive and in reasonably good
condition, and would be back in his home on Jeltad
in another two weeks.

"In a way, though, it's too bad it had to be that
space-pixy Zamm who found him!" one of the Co-
ordinator's aides remarked.

And to that, after a moment's reflection, the Chief
of Galactic Zones agreed.

The moon where Bropha's yacht lay concealed was
one of three approximately Earth-sized, ice-encrusted
satellites swinging about the sullen glow of a fiery giant-
planet.

The robot-ship of Zone Agent Zamman Tarradang-
Pok, working along its allotted section of the general
search-pattern, flashed in at the moon on a tangent to
its orbit, quartered its surface in two sweeping turns
and vanished again toward the nearer of the two other
satellites.

All in all, that operation was completed in a matter of seconds; but before the ship left, Zone Agent
Zamm had disembarked from it in a thirty-foot space-
duty skiff—crammed to its skin just now with the kind
of equipment required to pull off a miniature invasion-
in-force. Whatever sort of camouflaged power station
was down there had been shut off the instant it
detected her ship's approach. While that didn't necessarily reveal a bad conscience, the momentary pattern of radiations Zamm's instruments had picked up
suggested an exact duplicate of the type of engines
which powered Bropha's yacht.

So it probably was the yacht, Zamm decided—and
it would be hidden just below the moon's frozen surface. She had pin-pointed the spot; and on the

opposite side of the big satellite the skiff came streaking down into a thin, icy atmosphere.

"You can start hoping that ship was one of those I've been waiting for," Greemshard was remarking meanwhile. "Or else just somebody who isn't interested in us."

He stood in the center of the yacht's control room, staring at Bropha with intense dislike and a touch of fear. A suspicion had begun to grow on Greemshard that with all his cleverness and planning he might have worked himself at last into an impossible situation. None of the dozens of coded messages he had sent out during the past few days had been answered or perhaps even received. It was a little uncanny.

"Whatever happens," he concluded, "they're not getting you back alive!"

Bropha, flattened by gravity shackles to one wall of the room, saw no reason to reply. For the greater part of the past week, he had been floating mentally in some far-off place, from where he detachedly controlled the ceaseless complaints of various abused nerve-endings of his body. His half brother's voice hardly registered. He had begun to review instead, for perhaps the thousandth futile time, the possibilities of the trap into which he had let Greemshard maneuver him. The chances were he would have to pay the usual penalty of stupidity, but it was unlikely that either Greemshard or his confederates would get any benefit out of that.

Bropha was quite familiar—though Greemshard was not—with the peculiar efficiency of the organization headed by his friend, the Third Co-ordinator.

"Do not move, Captain Greemshard!"

That was all that tinkling, brittle voice really said. But it was a moment or so before Bropha grasped the meaning of the words.

He had, he realized, been literally shocked into full

consciousness by something that might have been the thin cry of a mindless death as it rose before its victim—a sound that ripped the clogging pain-veils from his thoughts and triggered off an explosion of sheer animal fright. Bropha's brain was a curiously sensitive tool in many ways; it chose to ignore the explicit substance of Zamm's curt warning and, instead, to read in it things like an insatiable hunger, and that ultimate threat. And also, oddly enough, a wailing, bleak despair.

Later on, he would admit readily that in his wracked condition he might have put a good deal more into the voice than was actually there. He would point out, however, that Greemshard, who was not an imaginative man and recklessly brave, seemed to be similarly affected. His half brother, he saw, stood facing him some twenty feet away, with his back to the door that led from the control room into the main body of the yacht; and the expression on his face was one Bropha could never remember afterwards without a feeling of discomfort. There was an assortment of weapons about Greemshard's person and on a desk to one side and within easy reach of him; but for that moment at least he did not move.

Then Bropha's startled gaze shifted beyond Greemshard.

The passage door had disappeared, and a pale-green fire was trickling swiftly from about its frame. He saw Zone Agent Zamm next, standing just beyond the door with a gun in her hand, and several squat, glittering shapes looming up behind her. The shock of almost superstitious fear that had roused him left Bropha in that instant, because he knew at once who and what Zamm was.

At about the same moment, Greemshard made his bid—desperately and with the flashing speed of a big, strong animal in perfect condition.

He flung himself sideways to reach the floor behind the desk, one hand plucking at a gun in his belt; but he was still in mid-leap when some soundless force spun him about and hurled him across the room, almost to Bropha's feet. What was left of Greemshard lay twitching there violently for a few seconds more, and was still. A faint smell of ozone began to spread through the room.

Bropha looked down at the headless body and winced. As children and half-grown boys, he and Greemshard had been the best of friends; and later, he had understood his half brother better than Greemshard ever knew. For a moment at least, the events of the last few days seemed much less important than those years that were past.

Then he looked back at the figure behind the coldly flaming door frame across the room and stammered: "Thank you, Zone Agent!"

His first glance at Zamm had showed him that she was a Daya-Bal; and up to that moment he would have thought that no branch of humanity was emotionally less suited than they to perform the duties of an Agent of Galactic Zones. But under the circumstances, the person who had effected an entry into that room, in the spectacularly quiet and apparently instantaneous fashion which alone could have saved his life, was not likely to be anything else.

Like a trio of goblin hounds, three different pieces of robotic equipment came variously gliding and floating through the glowing door frame on Zamm's heels, and began to busy themselves gently about a now rather shock-dazed Bropha. His rescuer, he found himself thinking presently, seemed really more bizarre in these surroundings than her mechanical assistants!

Zamm was not in armor but in a fitted spacesuit,

so her racial characteristics were unmistakable. By ordinary human standards, the rather small Daya-Bal body was excessively thin and narrow; but Zamm's white face with its pale eyes and thin, straight nose matched it perfectly, and every motion showed the swift, unconscious grace which accounted for some of the fascination her people exerted on their more normally constructed cousins. Bropha, who had spent over a year among the Daya-Bal planets in the Betelgeuse region, and during that time had also come under the spell of what was perhaps the youngest true branch of *Genus Homo*, addressed Zamm, by and by, in her own language.

He noted her smile of quick pleasure and the flash of interest in her eyes, and listened carefully to her reply, which began as an apology for causing irreparable damage to his ship in the process of boarding it. Such responses all seemed disarmingly normal; and he felt unable to recapture the sensations which had awakened him so suddenly when he heard her challenge to Greemshard.

Greemshard's death, too—however he might feel about it personally—was, after all, simply the fate of a criminal who had been misguided enough to resist certain arrest. As it happened, Bropha never did learn the exact circumstances under which the four members of Greemshard's little gang, who were acting as the yacht's crew, had departed this life just before Zamm appeared at the control room; but it could be assumed that the situation there had been a somewhat similar one.

His explanations, however, completely failed to satisfy him—because he knew the Daya-Bals.

He spent most of the two weeks required for the return trip to Jeltad in a bed under robotic treatment.

The physical damage his misadventure had cost him wasn't too serious, but it had to be repaired promptly; and such first-aid patchwork usually involved keeping a human brain anaesthetized to the point of complete unconsciousness. But Bropha's level of mind-training permitted him to by-pass that particular effect, and to remain as aware of his surroundings as he chose to be; and he remained much more aware of them than Zamman Tarradang-Pok or her robots appeared to realize.

To the average bedridden traveler, that endless drive on a silent ship through the unreal-seeming voids of the overspeed might have seemed monotonous to the point of dreary boredom. Bropha—alert, wondering and reflecting—soon gained a different impression of it. Little enough was actually happening; but even the slightest events here seemed weighted to him with some abnormal dark significance of their own. It was almost, he thought, as if he were catching an occasional whispered line or two of some grim drama—the actors of which moved constantly all about him but were very careful to stay out of his sight!

One day, finally, his watching was briefly rewarded; though what he observed left him, if anything, more puzzled than before. But afterwards, he found that a faint echo of the chill Zamm's voice first aroused in him had returned. In his mind, it now accompanied the slight shape which came occasionally through the shadowed passage before his cabin and, much more rarely, paused there quietly to look in on him.

Simultaneously, he discovered that a sense of something depressing and frightening had crept into his concept of this stupendously powered ship of Zamm's, with its electronic mentality through which sensations and reflexes flashed in a ceaseless billionfold shift of balances, over circuits and with meanings to which nothing remotely like a parallel existed in any human brain. Its racing drive through apparent nothingness, at speeds which no longer could be related mentally to actual motion, was like the expression of some fixed, nightmarish purpose which Bropha's presence had not changed in any way. For the moment, he was merely being carried along in the fringe of the nightmare— soon he would be expelled from it.

And then that somehow terrible unit, the woman of a race which mankind had long regarded as if they were creatures of some galactic Elfland—beings a little wiser, gentler, a little farther from the brute than their human brothers—and her train of attendant robots, of which there seemed to be a multi-shaped, grotesque insect-swarm about the ship, and finally the titanic, man-made monster that carried them all, would go rushing off again on their ceaseless, frightening search.

For what?

Without being able to give himself a really good reason for it even now, Bropha was, in brief, profoundly disturbed.

But one day he came walking up into the control room, completely healed again, though still a little uncertain in his stride and more than a little dissatis-fied in his thoughts. Vega was now some twenty-five light-years away in space; but in the foreshortening magic of the ship's vision tank, its dazzling, blue-white brilliance floated like a three-inch fire-jewel before them. A few hours later, great Jeltad itself swam sud-denly below with its wind-swept blues and greens and snowy poles—to the eyes of the two watchers on the ship much more like the historical Earth-home of both their races than the functional, tunneled hornet-hive that Terra was nowadays.

So Bropha came home. Being Bropha, his return was celebrated as a planetary event that night, centered about a flamboyant festival at his fine house overlooking the tall, gray towers of Government Center. Being also the Bropha who could not leave any human problem unsettled, once it came to his attention, he tried to make sure that the festival would be attended both by his rescuer and by her boss—his old friend, the Third Co-ordinator of the Vegan Confederacy.

However, only one of them appeared.

"To tell you the truth," Bropha remarked, "I didn't expect her to show up. And to tell you the truth again, I feel almost relieved, now that she didn't." He nodded down at the thronged and musical garden stretches below the gallery in which they sat. "I can't imagine Zamm in a setting like that!"

The Co-ordinator looked. "No," he agreed thoughtfully; "Zamm wouldn't fit in."

"It would be," said Bropha, rather more dramatically than was customary for him, "like seeing some fever-dream moving about in your everyday life—it wouldn't do!"

"So you want to talk about her," the Co-ordinator said; and Bropha realized suddenly that his friend looked soberly amused.

"I do," he admitted. "In fact, it's necessary! That Agent of yours made me extremely uneasy."

The Co-ordinator nodded.

"It hasn't anything to do," Bropha went on, "with the fact of her immense personal attractiveness. After all, that's an almost uniform quality of her race. I've sometimes thought that racial quality of the Daya-Bals might be strong enough to have diverted our sufficiently confused standards of such abstractions as beauty and perfection into entirely new channels—if their people happened to be spread out among our A-Class civilizations."

The Co-ordinator laughed. "It just might be, at that! Perhaps it's fortunate for us they've lost the urges of migrating and dominating the widest possible range of surroundings."

Bropha didn't agree.

"If they hadn't lost them," he said, "they'd be something other than they are—probably something a good deal less formidable. As it is, they've concentrated on themselves. I've heard them described as metaphysicists and artists. But those are our terms. Personally I think the Daya-Bals understand such terms in a way we don't. While I was living among them, anyway, I had a constant suspicion that they moved habitually in dimensions of mental reality I didn't know of as yet—"

He stopped and hauled himself back.

"You were going to speak of Zamm," his friend reminded him.

"Well, in a way I *am* speaking of her!" Bropha said slowly. "Obviously, the mere fact that a Daya-Bal is working for you, for the Department of Galactic Zones—and operating one of those really hellish robot ships of yours—is a flat contradiction to everything we know about them. Or think we know! A fallen angel would seem much less of a paradox. And there was the manner in which she killed Greemshard—"

The Co-ordinator raised a bushy gray eyebrow.

"Naturally," Bropha assured him, "I'm not blaming her for Greemshard's death. Under the circumstances, that had become unavoidable, in any case. But Zamm killed him"—he was selecting his words carefully now—"as if she were under some inescapable compulsion to do it. I don't know how else to describe the action."

He waited, but Zamm's boss offered no comment.

"There were two other incidents," Bropha continued, "on our way back here. The first was on the same day that we took off from that chunk of ice of a moon. We chased something. I didn't see what it was and I didn't ask her. There was a little maneuvering and a fairly long, straight run, about two minutes. We got hit by something heavy enough to slow us; and then the ship's automatics went off. That was all. Whatever it was, it was finished."

"It was finished, all right!" the Co-ordinator stated. "That was a Shaggar ship. They seem to be migrating through that section. Zamm reported the incident, and as I was following your return with interest, I heard of it directly."

"I'm not questioning the ethics of your Agent's work, you know," Bropha said after a pause. "Having seen something of what the Shaggar will do to anybody who can't outfight them, I also realize that killing them, in particular, is in a class with destroying a plague virus. No, the point is simply that I saw Zamm's face immediately afterwards. She came past my cabin and looked in at me for a moment. I don't believe she actually saw me! Her eyes looked blind. And her face had no more expression than a white stone—"

He added doubtfully, "And that's not right either! Because at the same time I had the very clear impression that she was staring past me at something. I remember thinking that she hated whatever she saw there with an intensity no sane being should feel against anything." He paused again. "You know now what I'm trying to say?"

"It's fairly obvious," the Co-ordinator replied judicially, "that you believe one of my Agents, at least, is a maniac."

"It sounds thoroughly ungrateful of me," Bropha nodded, "but that's about it—except, of course, that I don't actually believe it! However, for the sake of my own peace of mind, I'd be obliged if you'd take the trouble to look up the facts on Zone Agent Zamm and let me know what the correct explanation is."

It was the Co-ordinator who hesitated now.

"She's a killer, certainly," he said at last. He smiled faintly. "In fact, Bropha, you've been granted the distinction of being rescued by what is quite probably the grand champion killer of the department. Zamm's a Peripheral Agent—roving commission you might call it. No fixed zone of operations. When she runs out of work, she calls in to Central and has them lay out a pattern of whatever foci of disturbance there are in the areas she's headed for. She checks in here at Jeltad about once a year to have her ship equipped with any worthwhile innovations Lab's cooked up in the interval."

He reflected a moment. "I don't know," he said, "whether you were in a condition to notice much about that ship of hers?"

"Not much," Bropha admitted. "I remember, when she called it back to pick us up, it seemed bulkier than most Agent ships I'd seen—a big, dull-black spheroid mostly. I saw very little of its interior. Why?"

"As an Agent ship, it's our ultimate development in self-containment," the Co-ordinator said. "In that particular type, camouflage and inconspicuousness are largely sacrificed to other advantages. Self-repair's one of them; it could very nearly duplicate itself in case of need. Those are the peripheral ships—almost perpetual travelers. The Agents who direct them prowl along the fringes of our civilizations and deal with whatever needs to be dealt with there before it gets close enough to cause serious trouble."

"I understand the need for such Agents," Bropha said slowly. "I should think, however, that they would be selected for such work with particular care."

"They are," said the Co-ordinator.

"Then supposing," said Bropha, "that another people, like the Daya-Bals—who are experts in other branches of robotics—came into possession of such a ship. They could duplicate it eventually?"

"After some fifty years of study, they could," the Co-ordinator agreed. "It wouldn't worry us much since we expect to be studying hard ourselves throughout any given fifty years of history. Actually, of course, we have a theory that our Agents are psychologically incapable of giving away departmental secrets in a manner that could cause us harm."

"I know," said Bropha. "That's why I was surprised to discover that there are . . . or were . . . two other Daya-Bals on Zamm's ship."

For the first time, the Co-ordinator looked a little startled.

"What made you think so?"

"I heard them talking," Bropha said, "on various occasions, though I didn't make out what they said. And finally I saw them—they came past my door, following Zamm." He paused. "I was under drugs at the time," he admitted, "and under treatment generally. But I can assure you that those incidents were not hallucinations."

"I didn't think they were," said the Co-ordinator. "Is that why you're trying to check on Zamm's motivations?"

Bropha hesitated. "It's one of the reasons."

The Co-ordinator nodded. "Fifteen years ago, Zamm lost her husband and child in a space attack on a Daya-Bal liner. There were three survivors—Zamm was one—but they'd been unconscious through most of the action and could give no description of the attackers. The bodies of most of the other passengers and of the crew were identified, but about fifty remained unaccounted for. Zamm's husband and child were among that number. She believes they were taken along alive by the unknown beings that wrecked and looted the ship."

"That's not so unreasonable!" Bropha said. But he looked rather shaken, suddenly.

"No," agreed the Co-ordinator. "Under the circumstances, though, it's extremely unreasonable of her to expect to find them again. You might say that Zamm is under a delusion in that she believes she will be able to beat probability at such outrageous odds. But that's the extent of her 'insanity'—according to our psychologists."

Bropha started to speak, but then shook his head.

"So it's not too hard to understand that Zamm hates the things she hunts," the Co-ordinator pointed out. "In her eyes, they must be much the same as the things that took her family from her—they might even, by coincidence, be those very things themselves!"

"But that doesn't—" Bropha began again.

"And her delusion appears to have blinded her neither to the difficulties of the task nor to the methods most likely to overcome them," the Co-ordinator continued blandly. "A few years after her loss, she reduced the odds against her at one stroke to the lowest practical level by coming to work for us. In effect, that put the Department of Galactic Zones permanently on the job of helping her in her search! For the past dozen years, any trace of a Daya-Bal any of our operatives has discovered outside of the Betelgeuse Zone has been reported to Zamm in a matter of hours. Now, those two you saw on her ship—can you describe them?"

"It was dark in the passage," Bropha said hesitantly. He was a little pale now. "However, I couldn't be mistaken! It was a man and a boy."

The Co-ordinator was silent for a moment.

"I thought it would be that," he admitted. "Well, it's

an unpleasant notion to our way of thinking, I grant you—even a somewhat nightmarish one. There's a flavor of necromancy. However, you can see it's obviously not a matter that involves any question of Zamm's loyalty. As you say, the Daya-Bals are very clever in robotics. And she was a neurosurgeon before she came to us. Those were just two marionettes, Bropha!"

He stood up. "Shall we rejoin your party, now?"

Bropha had come to his feet, too. "And you still say she isn't insane?" he cried.

The Co-ordinator spread his hands. "So far as I can see, your experience offers no contradictory proof. So I shall simply continue to rely on the department's psychologists. You know their verdict: that whatever our Agents may do, their judgment will be almost as nearly infallible as it is possible for highly-trained human-type intelligences to become. And, further, that no matter how widely their motivations may vary, they will not vary ever to the extent of being unacceptable to the department."

Three days out in space by now, Zone Agent Zamm was rapidly approaching the point at which she had first swerved aside to join the search for Bropha.

She was traveling fast—a great deal faster than she had done while taking her damaged and politically valuable passenger home. With him on board she'd felt obliged to loiter, since the department did not recommend top velocities when some immediate emergency wasn't impending. Only vessels of the truly titanic bulk of Vega's Giant Rangers could navigate with apparent safety at such speeds; while to smaller ships things were likely to happen—resulting usually in sudden and traceless disappearances which had been the subject of much unsatisfactory theorizing in Department Lab and similar scientific centers throughout civilization. But

Zamm was impatient both with the numbing, sense-less vastness of space and with its less open dangers. Let it snap at her from ambush if it liked! It always missed.

"Want a hot-spot chart on this line I'm following, for a week's cruising range," she informed the ship's telepath transmitter; and her request was repeated promptly in Galactic Zones Central on the now faraway planet of Jeltad.

Almost as promptly, a three-dimensional star-map swam into view on the transmitter-screen before Zamm. She studied it thoughtfully.

The green dot in the center indicated her position. Visually, it coincided with the fringe of a group of short crimson dashes denoting the estimated present posi-tion of the migrating Shaggar ships she had contacted briefly and reported on her run to Jeltad. A cloud of white light far ahead was a civilized star cluster. Here and there within that cluster, and scattered also around the periphery of the chart, some dozens of near-microscopic sun-systems stood circled in lines of deep red. Enclosing the red circles appeared others: orange, purple, green—indicating the more specific nature of the emergency.

Zamm stabbed a pointer at three systems marked thus as focal points of trouble inviting a Zone Agent's attention, near the far left of the chart.

"Going to try to pick up the Shaggar drift again," she announced. "If we find it, we ought to be some-where up in that area before we're done with them. Get me the particulars on what's wrong around there, and home it out to me. That's all—"

She switched off the transmitter. The star-map vanished and a soft, clear light filled the room. Zamm rubbed a thin, long hand over her forearm and blinked pale eyes at the light. "How about a snack?" she asked.

A food tray slid out of the wall to a side table of the big desk, its containers variously iced or steaming.

She ate slowly and lightly, mentally organizing the period of time ahead. Only for a few weeks—once she had laid out plans for a year or more—so and so many planets to investigate—such and such a field to cover! But the hugeness of the task had gradually over-whelmed her will to major planning. Now she moved about in briefer spurts, not aimlessly but diverted toward new areas constantly by hunches, sudden impulses and hopes—careful only not to retrace her tracks any more than could be avoided.

But she was beaten, she knew. She'd never find them! Neither would any of the thousands and thousands of people she'd set watching and looking for traces of them. The Universe that had taken them was the winner.

She glanced over at the black, cold face that filled the whole of her ship's vision tank, its million glittering eyes mocking her.

"Stupid thing—grinning!" she whispered, hating it tiredly. She got up and started moving restlessly about the big room.

Black Face out there was her enemy! She could hurt it a little, but not much. Not enough to count. It was so big it only had to wait. For centuries; for thousands, for tens of thousands and hundreds of thousands of years. Waiting while life built up some-where, warm and brave and frail and hopeful—then it came suddenly with its flow of cold foulness to end it again! With some ravaging, savage destruction from outside, like the Shaggar; or more subtly with a dark pulse that slowly poisoned the mind of a race. Or it might be even only a single intelligent brain in which the cold death pattern grew till it burst out suddenly to engulf a nation, a planet— There was simply no end to the number and kinds of weapons the Universe had against life!

Zamm had stopped her pacing. She stood looking down at a big couch in the center of the room.

"You shouldn't try mind-search now, Zamm!" The voice of the gigantic robot that was the ship came, almost anxiously, into the room. "You've been under severe emotional tensions throughout the past weeks!"

"I know," she murmured. "Glad they got him back though—nice people; nice guy! We worried him, I think—" She kicked the side of the couch reflectively with the tip of one soft boot. "Those tensions might help, you know! Send the doll out and we'll see."

"The big one?" the voice inquired.

"No!" said Zamm with a sort of terror. "Can't stand to look at him when I'm all alone. No, the little one—"

Somewhere in the ship a door opened and closed. After a few seconds, footsteps came running, lightly, swiftly. A small shape scampered into the room, stopped, glanced about with bright sharp eyes, saw Zamm and ran to her.

She opened her arms and swept up the shape as it flung itself at her laughing.

"What an artist made those masks!" she said wonderingly, her fingertips tracing over a cheek of the face that was very like her own and yet different. "You couldn't tell by just touching—!" She smiled down at the shape cradled in her arms. "Fifteen years! Be a bigger boy now—but not too much. We don't shoot up quick like those old A-Class humans, do we? But for that, we grow up smarter. Don't we?"

The shape chuckled amiable agreement. Zamm blinked at it, half-smiling but alert, as if listening to something within herself. The dolls had very little in common with her working robots; they were designed to be visual hypnotics, compelling and dangerous agents that could permanently distort the fabric of sanity. Those of her people who had helped her in their design had done it reluctantly, though they understood the value of such devices for one who went searching in memory for what she had lost in time. With almost clinical detachment, she watched herself being drawn under the familiar compulsion that seemed to combine past and present, illusion and reality, until something stormy and cold washed suddenly through her face, slackening its features. Then she closed her eyes for a moment, and set the shape carefully back on its feet on the floor.

"Run along, little boy!" she told it absently, her face taut and blank once more. "Back to your place! Mother's busy."

Its gurgle of laughter merged into a receding rush of footsteps. Presently a door clicked shut again, somewhere.

Zamm went slowly to the couch and lay down on it, flat on her back, arms over her head.

"We'll try mind-search now!" she said.

The robot made no comment. A half-score glassy tentacles came out from under the couch and began to fasten themselves here and there over Zamm's body, coiled about her skull and glued flaring tips to her temples.

"I'm set," she said. "Let it go!"

A faint humming rose from the wall. Her body stiffened suddenly, went rigid, and then relaxed completely.

There had been a brief awareness of cold, rushing inwards from all sides. But almost instantly, it reached and chilled the nerve-linkages at which it was directed.

Incoming sensation ceased with that, abruptly.

Zamm's brain swam alone, released, its consciousness diffused momentarily over an infinity of the what-had-been, the time-past—but also over deceptively similar infinities of the might-have-been, the never-was. Those swirling universes of events and symbols would crystallize now, obediently but not necessarily truthfully, into whatever pattern consciousness chose to impress on them.

The brain could fool itself there! But it had an ally who wouldn't be tricked.

It ordered:

"Back to just before it began!"

Swarm after swarm of neurons woke suddenly to the spreading advance of the robot's stimulating, probing forces through their pathways. Million-factored time-past events formed briefly, were discarded and combined anew. At last, familiar images began to flick up and reel away within the brain. Remembered sound crashed; remembered warmth swept in—pain, cold, touch, rest.

Hate, love, terror—possession, loss.

"We're there! Where it began."

There was the darkened cabin on the doomed spaceliner; only a small pool of amber light glowed against one tapestried wall. Distant and faint came the quivering of gigantic engines.

"They hadn't quite worked the shake out of them, those days," Zamm's brain remembered.

She lay on the cabin's big bed, lazing, content, half asleep on her side, blinking at the amber glow. She'd been first to take note of the rest period's arrival and come back to the cabin. As usual.

" . . . used to love to sleep, those days!"

Her menfolk were still playing around somewhere in the vacation ship's variously and beautifully equipped playrooms. The big one and the little one—should be getting more rest, both of them! What's a vacation for, otherwise?

Zamm was beginning to wonder idly just where they'd gone to loiter this time, when the amber light flickered twice

"*It's begun!*"

Roar of sound, flash of light! Then the blaring attack-alarm from the cabin's communicator was cut short; and a body went flip-flopping crazily about the room like an experimental animal speared by an electric current. Everywhere, the liner's injured artificial gravs were breaking circuits, reforming instantly, breaking at other points; and reforming again. And holding at last, locked into a new, emergency-created pattern.

But in the cabin was darkness and unconsciousness, while over the fifteen years, for the two-thousandth time, Zamm's brain strained and tore for the one look out, the one identifiable sound—perhaps even a touch. A fraction of a second might be all she'd need!

And it had lasted two hours, that period! For two hours, *they* swarmed about the ship they had murdered, looting, despoiling, dragging away the ones still alive and not too badly hurt. They must have come into the cabin more than once, prowled about it, stared at her, touched her. Gone on—

But—nothing.

Full consciousness emerged suddenly at the same point as always. Then the body went crawling and scrambling up the tilted flat of a floor, tilted irrevocably now in the new gravitational pattern the stricken liner had achieved for its rigor mortis. Broken bone in lower right arm, right ankle flapping loosely—like the splintered cabin door overhead, that flapped from what was now one edge of a tilted ceiling! From somewhere within the ship came the steady roar of atomic fires; and then sudden sounds like the yelping of animals, rising into long shrieks.

"The ray-burned ones!" gasped Zamm, as the clambering body stiffened in horror, unmoving, listening. "But those weren't mine!" she screamed. "I checked them all!" She caught herself. "Wait—I'll have to go through that period again."

"You can't do that twice!" the robot's voice said. "Not now. Not that part!"

"Well—" It was right, of course. It usually was. "Get on with the sequence then!"

"Even that's too dangerous. You're nearly exhausted, Zamm!"

But the body reached for the edge of the door, hung on with the good arm, kicked with both legs and wriggled over awkwardly into a bright-lit corridor, slanted upward at a nightmarish angle. Other bodies lay there, in tumbled piles, not moving.

"If I hadn't stopped to check those—If I'd looked up sooner—just a few seconds sooner!"

One by one, the lost seconds passed away as always, and then the body suddenly looked up. A bright glare filled the upper end of the tilted corridor. Something had moved within that glare of light—had just crossed the corridor and was disappearing again down another hallway that angled off it, slanting downwards. The light followed the moving shape like a personal shadow and vanished behind it.

"Working in individual light-barriers, making a last check before they left," murmured Zamm, while the body crawled and hobbled toward the point where the light had been, screaming with terror, rage, question and despair.

"If I'd looked up that moment sooner, I'd have seen what they were like, even in space armor—human or what. I'd have *seen!*"

She found herself staring up at the ceiling of her ship's control room, muttering the worn old words.

She stirred stiffly but made no attempt to sit up.

"Nearly went out here," she said tonelessly.

"That was dangerous, Zamm," said the robot-voice. "I warned you."

"No harm done!" she said. "Next time, we'll just work the unconscious period through all by itself."

She lay quiet, her mouth bitter. Somewhere in memory, as somewhere in space, were points where she might pick up their trail. Things she had experienced in those hours but not consciously remembered. Scattered groups of cells within the bony box that enclosed her brain still held them locked.

Statistically, it couldn't happen that she would ever flood any specific group of cells with the impulse-pattern that revived those specific flickers of memory. Statistically, it would be a whole lot easier even to pick the one sun-system and planet where they might be out of the numberless fiery cells that were the galaxy's body!

But she was still learning! One way or the other, she was going to do it. Find them.

Zamm lay there, staring upwards, bitter and unbelieving.

"What is it?" she asked suddenly.

"Company!" the robot said.

They were a long, long distance away, moving at many times the speed of light. In the vision tank, they seemed to glide past unhurriedly almost within shouting range of the ship. One, two, three, four—

Four clouds of diffused radiance, like great, luminous jellyfish pulsing down an indetectable current of space. Migrating Shaggar ships behind their camouflaging screens. They had spotted her, of course, but like

most of the older forms of space life they had learned
to be careful about strange ships that did not flee from
them at once. They were waiting to see her next move.

"Confirm position and direction of the drift for
Central first!" Zamm said. Despair and rage were still
bleak in her eyes, but her long, tapered fingers slid
swiftly and surely above and about the armament banks
of the control desk. Not touching anything just yet; only
checking.

"Two of these are nearly in line," the robot reported.

"Five in all!" sniffed Zamm. "One more could make
it a fight. Parallel course, and swing round once to
make them bunch up—"

A minute or so later, they flashed across the
Shaggars' path, at point-blank range ahead of them. The
nebular screens vanished suddenly, and five deep-
bellied, dark ships became visible instead. Light and
energy boiled abruptly all about Zamm's black globe—
before, behind. It missed.

"Spot any more, this side?"

"Four more are approaching—barely detectable!
They may have been called by this group."

"Good enough! We'll take them next." Zamm waited
as the ship completed its swing and drove into line
behind her quarry. They were beyond any weapon-
reach by then, but space far ahead was being churned
into a long whirlpool of flame. At the whirlpool's core,
the five Shaggar ships, retreating at speed, had drawn
close together and were throwing back everything they
had.

"Instructions?" the robot-voice murmured.

"Contact range—Move in!"

Up the long cone of flame, the ship sprang at the
five. Zamm's hands soared, spread and high, above the
armament banks—thin, curved, white claws of hate!
Those seeming to swim down toward her now, turning

and shifting slowly within their fire-veils, were not the faceless, more or less humanlike ones she sought. But they were marked with the same red brand: brand of the butchers, looters, despoilers—of all the death-thoughts drifting and writhing through the great stupid carnivore mind of the Universe—

At point-blank range, a spectral brilliance clung and hammered at her ship and fell away. At half-range, the ship shuddered and slowed like a beast plowing through a mudhole and out. At one-quarter, space turned to solid, jarring fire for seconds at a time.

Zamm's hands flashed.

"NOW—"

A power ravened ahead of them then like the bellowing of a sun. Behind it, hardly slower, all defenses cut and every weapon blaring its specific ultimate of destruction, the ship came screaming the hate of Zamm.

Two years—

The king-shark was bothering Zamm! It hung around some subspace usually where she couldn't hope to trace it.

It was a big ship, fast and smart and tricky. It had weapons and powers of which she knew nothing. She couldn't even guess whether it realized she was on its tail or not. Probably, it didn't.

Its field of operations was wide enough so that its regularly spaced schedule of kills didn't actually disrupt traffic there or scare it away. A certain percentage of losses had to be taken for granted in interstellar commerce. The chief difference seemed to be that in this area the losses all went to the king-shark.

Zamm circled after it, trying to calculate its next points of appearance. A dozen times she didn't miss it by much; but its gutted kills were still all she got.

It took no avoidable chances. It picked its prey and came boiling up into space beside it—or among it, if it was a small convoy—and did its work. It didn't bother with prisoners, so the work was soon done. In an hour everything was over. The dead hulks with their dead crews and dead passengers went drifting away for Zamm to find. The king-shark was gone again.

Disgusted, Zamm gave up trying to outguess it. She went off instead and bought herself a freighter.

The one she selected was an expensive, handsome ship, and she loaded it up with a fortune. She wanted no gilded hook for the king-shark; she'd feed it solid gold! There were a dozen fortunes lying around her globe, in salvaged cash and whatnot from previous jobs. She'd use it up as she needed it or else drop it off at Jeltad the next time she went back. Nobody kept accounts on that sort of stuff.

Her freighter was all ready to start.

"Now I need a nice pirate!" mused Zamm.

She went out and caught herself one. It had an eighteen-man crew, and that was just right for the freighter. She checked over their memories first, looking for the one thing she wanted. It wasn't there. A lot of other things were, but it had been a long time since that kind of investigation made her feel particularly sick.

"Anyone lives through it, I'll let him go!" she promised, cold-eyed. She would, and they knew it. They were small fry; let somebody else grab them up if they wanted them badly enough!

At a good, fast, nervous pace, the freighter and its crew crossed what was currently the most promising section of the king-shark's area—Zamm's black globe sliding and shifting and dancing about its bait at the farthest possible range that would still permit it to pounce.

By and by, the freighter came back on another route

and passed through the area again. It was nearing the
end of the fourth pass when the king-shark surfaced
into space beside it and struck. In that instant, the
freighter's crew died; and Zamm pounced.

It wasn't just contact range; it was contact. Alloy hide
to alloy hide, Zamm's round black leech clung to the
king-shark's flank, their protective screens fused into
a single useless mass about them. It didn't matter at
what point the leech started to bite; there weren't any
weak ones. Nor were there any strong enough to stop
its cutter-beam at a four-foot range.

It was only a question of whether they could bring
up something in eighty seconds that would blast out
the leech's guts as the wall between them vanished.

They couldn't, it seemed. Zamm and her goblin crew
of robots went into the king-shark in a glittering wave.

"Just mess up their gravs!" said Zamm. "They don't
carry prisoners. There'll be some in suits, but we'll
handle them."

In messed-up rows, the robots laid out the living
and the nearly dead about the king-shark's passages and
rooms.

"From Cushgar!" said Zamm surprised. "They're
prowling a long way from home!"

She knew them by their looks. The ancestors of
the king-shark's one hundred and fourteen crewmen
had also once breathed the air of Terra. They had
gone off elsewhere and mutated variously then; and,
like the Daya-Bals, the strongest surviving mutant
strains eventually had blended and grown again to be
a new race.

Not a handsome one, by Zamm's standards! Short
and squat and hairy, and enormously muscled. The
spines of their neck and back vertebrae stuck out
through their skins in horny spikes, like the ridge on

a turtle's shell. But she'd seen worse-looking in the human line; and she wasn't judging a beauty contest.

A robot stalked briskly along the rows like a hunting wasp, pausing to plunge a fine needle into the neck of each of the people from Cushgar, just beneath the fourth vertebral spike. Zamm and a robot that had loafed till now picked out the ones that seemed damaged worst, settled down beside each in turn and began their questioning.

Some time passed—four, five hours—finally six. Then Zamm and her robots came back to her ship. The leech sealed its egress port, unclamped and took off. The king-shark's huge, dark hulk went drifting along through space. There was no one alive on it now. Fifteen minutes later, a light suddenly flared from it, and it vanished.

Zamm sat white-faced and silent at her desk for a much longer time than that.

"The dolls," she said finally, aloud.

"Yes?" said the big robot-voice.

"Destroy them," said Zamm. She reached out and switched on the telepath transmitter. "And get me a line through to Jeltad. The Co-ordinator—"

There was no reply, and no sound came from within the ship. She lit up some star-globes and began calculating from them. The calculations didn't take long. Then she sat still again for a while, staring into the luminous green, slowly swirling haze that filled the transmitter screen.

A shape and a face began forming in it at last; and a voice pronounced her name questioningly.

"They're in Cushgar!" said Zamm, the words running out in a brittle, tinkling rush. "I know the planet and the place. I saw them the way *it* saw them—the boy's getting pretty big. It's a gray house at a sort of big hospital. Seventeen years they've been working there! Seventeen years, working for them!" Her face was grisly with hate.

The Co-ordinator waited till the words had all run out. He looked rather sick.

"You can't go there alone!" he said.

"How else!" Zamm said surprised. "Who'd be going with me there? But I've got to take the ship. I wanted to tell you."

The Co-ordinator shook his head.

"You bought that ship with your second mission! But you can't go there alone, Zamm. You'll be passing near enough to Jeltad on your way there, anyway. Stop in, and we'll think of something!"

"You can't help me," Zamm told him bluntly. "You can't mission anybody into Cushgar. You lost every Agent you ever sent there. You try a Fleet squadron, and it's war. Thousand Nations would jump you the day after!"

"There's always another way," the Co-ordinator said. He paused a moment, looking for that other way. "You stay near your transmitter anyhow! I'll call you as soon as we can arrange some reasonable method—"

"No," said Zamm. "I can't take any more calls either—I just got off a long run. I'm hitting Deep Rest now till we make the first hostile contact. I've only got one try, and I've got to give it everything. There's no other way," she added, "and there aren't any reasonable methods. I thought it all out. But thanks for the ship!"

The Co-ordinator located the man called Snoops over a headquarters' communicator and spoke to him briefly.

Snoops swore softly.

"She's got other friends who would want to be told," the Co-ordinator concluded. "I'm leaving that to you."

"You would," said Snoops. "You going to be in your office? I might need some authority!"

"You don't need authority," the Co-ordinator said, "and I just started on a fishing trip. I've had a vacation coming these last eight years—I'm going to take it."

Snoops scowled unpleasantly at the dead communicator. He had no official position in the department. He had a long suite of offices and a laboratory, however. His business was to know everything about everybody, as he usually did.

He scratched his bearded chin and gave the communicator's tabs a few vindictive punches. It clicked back questioningly.

"Want a location check on forty-two thousand and a couple of hundred names!" Snoops said. "Get busy!"

The communicator groaned.

Snoops ignored it. He was stabbing at a telepath transmitter.

"Hi, Ferd!" he said presently.

"Almighty sakes, Snoops," said Ferdinand the Finger. "Don't unload anything new on me now! I'm right in the middle—"

"Zamm's found out about her kin," said Snoops. "They're in Cushgar! She's gone after them."

Zone Agent Ferdinand swore. His lean, nervous fingers worked at the knot of a huge scarlet butterfly cravat. He was a race tout at the moment—a remarkably good one.

"Where'd she contact from?" he inquired.

Snoops told him.

"That's right on my doorstep," said Ferdinand.

"So I called you first," Snoops said. "But you can't contact her. She's traveling Deep Rest."

"Is, huh? What's Bent say?" asked Ferdinand.

"Bent isn't talking—he went fishing. Hold on there!" Snoops added hastily. "I wasn't done!"

"Thanks a lot for calling, Snoops," Ferdinand said with his hand on the transmitter switch. "But I'm right in the middle—"

"You're in the middle of the Agent-list of that cluster," Snoops informed him. "I just unloaded it on you!"

"That'll take me hours!" Ferdinand howled. "You can't—"

"Just parcel it out," Snoops said coldly. "You're the executive type, aren't you? You can do it while you're traveling. I'm busy!"

He cut off Ferdinand the Finger.

"How you coming?" he asked the communicator.

"That's going to be over eighteen thousand to locate!" the communicator grumbled.

"Locate 'em," said Snoops. He was punching the transmitter again. When you want to get in touch with even just the key-group of the Third Department's forty-two thousand and some Zone Agents, you had to keep on punching!

"Hi, Senator!"

If anyone was amusing himself that week by collecting reports of extraordinary events, with the emphasis on mysterious disappearances, he ran into a richer harvest than usual.

It caused a quite exceptional stir, of course, when Senator Thartwith excused himself in the middle of a press interview, stepped into the next office to take an urgent personal call, and failed to reappear. For the senator was a prominent public figure—the Leader of the Opposition in the Thousand Nations. He had closed the door behind him; but his celebrated sonorous voice was heard raised in apparent expostulation for about a minute thereafter. Then all became still.

Half an hour passed before an investigation was

risked. It disclosed, by and by, that the senator had quite vanished!

He stayed vanished for a remarkable length of time. In a welter of dark suspicions, the Thousand Nations edged close to civil war.

Of only planetary interest, though far more spectacular, was the sudden ascension of the Goddess Loppos of Amuth in her chariot drawn by two mystical beasts, just as the conclusion of the Annual Temple Ceremony of Amuth began. A few moments before the event, the Goddess was noted to frown, and her lips appeared to move in a series of brisk, celestial imprecations. Then the chariot shot upwards; and a terrible flash of light was observed in the sky a short while later. Amuth bestrewed its head with ashes and mourned for a month until Loppos reappeared.

Mostly, however, these freakish occurrences involved personalities of no importance and so caused no more than a splash of local disturbance. As when Grandma Wannattel quietly unhitched the rhinocerine pony from her patent-medicine trailer and gave the huge but patient animal to little Grimp to tend— "Until I come back." Nothing would have been made of that incident at all—police and people were always bothering poor Grandma Wannattel and making her move on—if Grimp had not glanced back, just as he got home with the pony, and observed Grandma's big trailer soaring quietly over a hillside and on into the sunset. Little Grimp caught it good for that whopper!

In fact, remarkable as the reports might have seemed to a student of such matters, the visible flow of history was at all affected by only one of them. That was the unfortunate case of Dreem, dread Tyrant of the twenty-two Heebelant Systems:

" . . . and me all set to be assassinated by the Freedom Party three nights from now!" roared Dreem.

"Take two years to needle the chicken-livered bunch up to it again!"

"Suit yourself, chum!" murmured the transmitter above his bed.

"That I will," the despot grumbled, groping about for his slippers. "You just bet your life I will!"

"We should be coming within instrument-detection of the van of the ghost fleet almost immediately!" the adjutant of the Metag of Cushgar reported.

"Don't use that term again!" the potentate said coldly. "It's had a very bad effect on morale. If I find it in another official communication, there'll be a few heads lifted from their neck-spines. Call them 'the invaders.'"

The adjutant muttered apologies.

"How many invaders are now estimated in that first group?" the Metag inquired.

"Just a few thousand, sir," the adjutant said. "The reports, of course, remain very—vague! The main body seems to be still about twelve light-years behind. The latest reports indicate approximately thirty thousand there."

The Metag grunted. "We should be just able to intercept that main bunch with the *Glant* then!" he said. "If they keep to their course, that is. It's high time to end this farce!"

"They don't appear to have swerved from their course to avoid interception yet," the adjutant ventured.

"They haven't met the *Glant* yet, either!" the Metag returned, grinning.

He was looking forward to that meeting. His flagship, *Glant*, the spindle-shaped giant-monitor of Cushgar, had blown more than one entire attacking fleet out of space during its eighty years of operation. Its outer defenses weren't to be breached by any known weapon; and its weapons could hash up a planetary system with no particular effort. The *Giant* was invincible.

It was just a trifle slow, though. And these ghost ships, these ridiculous invaders, were moving at an almost incredible pace! He wouldn't be able to get the *Giant* positioned in time to stop the van.

The Metag scowled. If only the reports had been more specific—and less mysteriously terminated! Three times, in the past five days, border fleets had announced they had detected the van of the ghosts and were prepared to intercept. Each time that had been the last announcement received from the fleet in question. Of course, communications *could* become temporarily disrupted, in just that instantaneous, wholesale fashion, by perfectly natural disturbances—but three times!

A slightly chilled breeze tickled the Metag's backspines for a moment. There was no nonsense about the Metag; but just the same, his conscience—like that of Cushgar generally—was riddled enough to be conducive to occasional superstitious chills.

"There they are, sir!" the adjutant announced suddenly, in an excited quaver.

The Metag stared unbelievingly.

It was as bad as the worst of the reports. It was worse! Secure behind the *Giant's* defenses, the sight of a few thousand hostile cruisers wouldn't have caused him a qualm—

But this!

There *were* a few small war vessels among them—none over six hundred feet long. But, so far as one could tell from their seared, beam-blasted exteriors, most of them had been freighters of every possible size, type and description. There was a sprinkling of dainty,

badly slashed yachts and other personal space craft. No
wonder they'd been mistaken for the murdered cold
hulks of the centuries, swept along in a current of awful
new life—!

But the worst of it was that, mixed up with that
stream, was stuff which simply didn't belong in space—
it should have been gliding sedately over the surface
of some planetary sea! Some, by Old Webolt, had
wings!

And that one, there!

"It's a *house!*" the Metag howled, in horrified recognition. "A thundering, Old-Webolt-damned HOUSE!"

House and all, the battered ghost-horde came flashing up at a pace that couldn't have been matched by
Cushgar's newest destroyers. Ponderously and enormously, the *Giant* raced forward in what was, even now,
an obviously futile attempt to meet them.

The adjutant was gabbling at his side.

"Sir, we may just be able to reach their flank with
the grapnels before they're past!"

"Get them out!" the Metag roared. "Full range! Get
them out! We've got to stop one of them—find out!
It's a masquerade—"

They didn't quite make it. Near the end of the van,
a torpedo-shaped, blackened *thing* seemed to be
touched for a moment by a grapnel beam's tip. It was
whirled about in a monstrous semicircle, then darted
off at a tangent and shot away after the others. They
vanished in the direction of Cushgar's heart-cluster.

"*That* was a mistake!" breathed the Metag. "It'll be
telling them about us. If the main body deflects its
course, we'll never . . . no, wait! There's one more
coming—stop it! NOW!"

A slender, three-hundred-foot space yacht flashed
headlong into a cluster of the *Giant's* grapnels and
freezers and stopped dead.

"And *now!*" The Metag passed a broad tongue over his trembling lips. "*Now* we'll find out! Bring them in!"

Grapnels and tractors began to maneuver the little yacht in carefully through the intricate maze of passages between the *Glant's* overlapping first, second, and third defense zones. There was nothing wrong with this ghost's looks; it gleamed blue and silver and unblemished in the lights glaring upon it from a hundred different directions. It might have taken off ten minutes before on its maiden flight.

The Great Squid of space had caught itself a shining minnow.

"Sir," the adjutant said uneasily, "mightn't it be better to beam it first?"

The Metag stared at him.

"And kill whoever's inside before we've talked to them?" he inquired carefully. "Have you gone mad? Does that look like a battleship to you—or do you think they *are* ghosts? It's the wildest good luck we caught them. If it hadn't come straight at us, as if it wanted to be caught—"

He paused a moment, scowling out through the screens at the yacht which now hung in a bundle of guide beams just above the *Glant's* yawning intake-port. The minnow was about to be swallowed.

"As if it *wanted* to be caught?" he repeated doubtfully.

It was the last doubt he had.

The little yacht moved.

It moved out of the grapnels and tractors and freezers as if there weren't any! It slid over the monitor's spindle length inside its defenses like a horrible caress. Behind it, the *Glant's* multiple walls folded back in a white-hot, thick-lipped wound. The *Glant* split down its length like a giant clam, opened out and spilled its flaming, exploding guts into space.

The little yacht darted on, unblemished, to resume its outrider position on the ghost-van's flank.

Zone Agent Pagadan of Lar-Sancaya really earned herself a chunk of immortal glory that day! But, unfortunately, no trace of the *Glant* was ever discovered again. And so no one would believe her, though she swore to the truth on a stack of Lar-Sancaya's holiest writings and on seven different lie detectors. Everyone knew what Pagadan could do to a lie detector, and as for the other—

Well, there remained a reasonable doubt.

"What about your contact with the ghosts—the invaders?" Cushgar called to the invincible *Glant*. "Have you stopped them? Destroyed them?"

The *Glant* gave no answer.

Cushgar called the *Glant*. Cushgar called the *Glant*. Cushgar called the *Glant*. Cushgar called the *Glant*—

Cushgar stared, appalled, into its night-sky and listened. Some millions of hostile stars stared back with icy disdain. Not a cry came again from the *Glant*— not a whisper!

The main body of the ghost fleet passed the spot twenty minutes later. It looked hardly damaged at all. In its approximate center was Zone Agent Zamman Tarradang-Pok's black globe, and inside the globe Zamm lay in Deep Rest. Her robot knew its duty—it would arouse her the instant it made hostile contact. It had passed through a third of Cushgar's territory by now, but it hadn't made any as yet.

The main body overtook the eager beavers up front eight hours later and merged with them. Straggled groups came up at intervals from behind and joined. The ghost fleet formed into a single cluster—

A hell-wind blew from the Galaxy's center on Cushgar's heart; and panic rushed before it. The dead were coming: the slaughtered billions, the shattered hulks, the broken defenders—joined now in a monstrous, unstoppable army of judgment that outsped sane thought!

Cushgar panicked—and the good, solid strategy of centuries was lost. Nightmare was plunging at it! Scattered fleet after fleet, ship after ship, it hurled what it could grab up into the path of the ghosts.

Not a cry, not a whisper, came back from the sacrifices!

Then the remaining fleets refused to move.

Zamm was having a nice dream.

It didn't surprise her particularly. Deep Rest was mostly dreamless; but at some levels it produced remarkably vivid and detailed effects. On more than one occasion they'd even tricked her into thinking they were real!

This time her ship appeared to have docked itself somewhere. The somno-cabin was still darkened, but the rest of it was all lit up. There were a lot of voices.

Zamm zipped up the side of her coverall suit and sat up on the edge of the couch. She listened a moment, and laughed. This one was going to be silly but nice!

"Box cars again!" a woman's voice shouted in the control room as Zamm came down the passage from her cabin. "You crummy, white-whiskered, cheating old—" A round of applause drowned out the last word, or words.

"Lady or no lady," the voice of Senator Thartwith rose in sonorous indignation, "one more such crack and I mow you down!"

The applause went up a few decibels.

"And here's Zamm!" someone yelled.

They were all around her suddenly. Zamm grinned

at them, embarrassed. "Glad you found the drinks!" she murmured.

The tall Goddess of Amuth, still flushed from her argument with Zone Agent Thartwith, scooped Zamm up from behind and set her on the edge of a table.

"Where's a glass for Zamm?"

She sipped it slowly, looking them over. There they were, the tricky and tough ones—the assassins and hunters and organizers and spies! The Co-ordinator's space pack, the innermost circle. There he was himself!

"Hi, Bent!" she said, respecting his mission-alias even in a dream. "Hi, Weems! . . . Hi, Ferd!" she nodded around the circle between sips.

Two score of them or more, come into Deep Rest to tell her good-by! She'd bought them all their lives, at one time or another; and they'd bought her hers. But she'd never seen more than three together at any one time in reality. Took a dream to gather them all!

Zamm laughed.

"Nice party!" she smiled. Nice dream. She put down her empty glass.

"That's it!" said the Goddess Loppos. She swung Zamm's feet up on the table, and pulled her around by the shoulders to look at the wall. There was a vision port there, but it was closed.

"What's all this?" Zamm smiled expectantly, lying back in Loppos' arms. What goofy turn would it take now?

The vision port clicked open. Harsh daylight streamed in.

The ship seemed to have set itself down in a sort of hot, sandy park. There was a huge gray building in the background. Zamm gazed at the building, the smile going slowly from her lips. A hospital, wasn't it? Where'd she seen—?

Her eyes darted suddenly to the lower left corner of the port. The edge of another building was visible there—a small house it was, also gray and very close. It would be right beside the ship!

Zamm convulsed.

"No!" she screamed. "It's a dream!"

She was being lifted from the table and put on her feet. Her knees wobbled, then stiffened.

"They're feeling fine, Zamm," the voice of the gray-haired man called Bent was saying. He added: "The boy's got pretty big."

"She'll be all right now," somebody else murmured behind her. "Zamm, you know Deep Rest! We couldn't take chances with it. We told them they'd have to wait there in the house till you woke."

The ramp beam set her down on the sand of a path. There was hot daylight around her then—seventeen years behind her, and an open door twenty steps ahead.

Her knees began wobbling again.

Zamm couldn't move.

For a score of scores of light-years about, Cushgar the Mighty lay on its face, howling to its gods to save it from the wrath of the ghosts and the wrath of Zamm.

But she—Zone Agent Zamman Tarradang-Pok, conqueror of space, time, and all the laws of probability—she, Free-mind Unqualified of the Free Daya-Bals—Doctor of Neuronics—Vega's grand champion of the Galaxy:

No, she just couldn't move!

Something *put-putted* suddenly by overhead. Enough of its seared and molten exterior remained to indicate that at some earlier stage of its career it might have been a fat, amiable-looking freighter. But there was nothing amiable about its appearance now! It looked like a wreck that had rolled for a century in the fires of hell, and put in another decade or two sunk deep in an acid sea. It looked, in fact, exactly as a ship might expect to look whose pilot had a weakness for withholding his fire till he was well within point-blank range.

But though it had lost its make-up, the ship was otherwise still in extra-good condition! It passed over Zamm's head, bobbed up and down twice in cheerful greeting, and went *putting* off on its secondaries, across the vast hospital and toward the city beyond, dropping a bit as it went, to encourage Cushgar to howl a little louder.

Zamm gazed blankly after the beat-up, impossible warrior, and heard herself laughing. She took a step— and another step.

Why, sure, she could move!

She was running

" . . . so that's how it was," the Third Co-ordinator told Bropha. He swirled the contents of his nearly empty glass around gently, raised it and finished his drink. "All we'd really intended was to hold that dead-straight course, and smash their light interception all the way in. That was to make sure they'd bunch every heavy ship they had on that line, to stop us just before we reached the Cluster.

"Then we were going to pop off at an angle, streak for the place they were keeping Zamm's folks, grab them up and get out of Cushgar again—

"But, of course," he added, "when we discovered they'd all rolled over on their back spikes and were waving their hands in the air, we couldn't resist taking over! You just never know what you start when you go off on an impromptu mission like that!"

He paused and frowned, and sighed. For the Third Co-ordinator was a man of method, who liked to see a job well worked out in advance, with all its angles considered and plenty of allowance made for any unforeseeable developments.

"How about a second drink?" Bropha inquired.

"No," said his friend; "I've got to get back to work. They can squawk all they like"—Bropha realized he was referring to his colleagues of the Council—"but there isn't another Department of the Confederacy that's been jammed up by the Cushgar affair as badly as Galactic Zones is right now! That was forty-two thousand two hundred and thirty-eight individual mission-schedules we had to re-plot!" he said, still somewhat aghast at the completeness of the jam. "Only a third of it's done! And afterwards, I'll have time to worry about finding a replacement for Zamm. There's nothing so scarce as a really good Peripheral Agent! That's all *I* got out of it—"

Bropha looked sympathetic.

"I talked to that boy, and I've got some hopes for him," the Co-ordinator added glumly. "If she keeps her promise, that is, and lets him come to Jeltad, by and by. But he'll never be like Zamm!"

"Give him time," Bropha said consolingly. "They grow up slowly. They're a long-lived race, the Daya-Bals."

"I thought of that, too!" the Co-ordinator nodded. "She'll raise a dozen now before she's done; and among them there might be one, or two— But, by the way she talked, I knew right then Zamm would never let any of the others go beyond fifty light-years of Betel-geuse!"

OTHER STORIES

The Custodians

❦

McNulty was a Rilf. He could pass for human if one didn't see him undressed; but much of the human appearance of the broad, waxy-pale face and big hands was the result of skillful surgery. Since the Rilf surgeons had only a vague notion of what humans considered good looks, the face wasn't pleasant, but it would do for business purposes. The other Rilf characteristic McNulty was obliged to disguise carefully was his odor—almost as disagreeable to human nostrils as the smell of humans was to him. Twice a day, therefore, he anointed himself with an effective deodorant. The human smells he put up with stoically.

Probably no sort of measures could have made him really attractive to humans. There was nothing too obviously wrong about his motions, but they weren't quite right either. He had an excellent command of English and spoke four other human languages well enough to make himself understood, but always with an underlying watery gurgle which brought something

like a giant bullfrog to mind. To some people McNulty
was alarming; to others he was repulsive. Not that he
cared very much about such reactions. The humans
with whom he dealt professionally were not significantly
influenced by them.

To Jake Hiskey, for example, captain and owner of
the spaceship *Prideful Sue*, McNulty looked, sounded,
and smelled like a million dollars. Which was approximately what he would be worth, if Hiskey managed
things carefully for the next few days. Hence the skipper was smiling bemusedly as he poked the door buzzer
of McNulty's cabin.

"Who is it?" the door speaker inquired in McNulty's
sloppy voice.

"Jake. I've got news—good news!"

The lock snicked and the door swung open for
Hiskey. As he stepped through, he saw another door
at the far end of the cabin close abruptly. Beyond it
were the living quarters of the other Rilf currently on
the Prideful Sue, who went by the name of Barnes and
whose olfactory sense was more seriously affronted by
humans than McNulty's. Barnes might be second in
command of McNulty's tribe of Rilf mercenaries, or
possibly a female and McNulty's mate. Assuming that
McNulty was male, which was by no means certain.
Rilfs gave out very little information about themselves,
and almost all that was known of their species was that
it had a dilly of a natural weapon and a strong interest in acquiring human currency with which to pur-
chase advanced products of human technology. Hence
the weapon was hired out on a temporary basis to
human groups who knew about it and could afford it.

"You will excuse Barnes," McNulty said, looking over
at Hiskey from a table where he sat before a tapeviewer. "He is indisposed."

"Of course," said Hiskey. He added curiously, "What

are you studying up on now?" McNulty and Barnes never missed an opportunity to gather information pertinent to their profession.

"Recent Earthplanet history," replied McNulty. "The past three years. I must say the overall situation looks most favorable!"

Hiskey grinned. "It sure does! For us . . ."

McNulty shut off the tapeviewer. "During the past two ship days," he remarked, "I have recorded news reports of forty-two of these so-called miniwars on the planet. Several others evidently are impending. Is that normal?"

"Actually it sounds like a fairly quiet period," Hiskey said. "But we might liven it up!" He pulled out a chair, sat down. "Of course I haven't been near Earthsystem for around eight years, and I haven't paid too much attention to what's been going on here. But on the planet it's obviously the same old stuff. It's been almost a century since the world government fizzled out; and the city states, the rural territories, the sea cities, the domes, the subterranes and what-not have been batting each other around ever since. They'll go on doing it for quite a while. Don't worry about that."

"I am not worrying," McNulty said. "The employment possibilities here appear almost unlimited, as you assured us they would be. What is this good news of which you spoke, Jake? Have your Earth contacts found a method of getting us down on the planet without further delay?"

"No," said Hiskey. "It will be at least five days before they have everything arranged. They're playing this very quietly. We don't want to alert anybody before you and your boys are set up and ready to go into action."

McNulty nodded. "I understand."

"Now here's what's happened," Hiskey went on. "This station we've stopped at is a branch of Space U.

The navigator shuttled over to it half an hour ago to find out where he can get in touch with his sister. She's connected with Space U—a student, I suppose—and, of course, he hasn't seen her for the past eight years."

"She is what is known as a graduate student," said McNulty, who disliked vagueness. "Her name is Elisabeth and she is three Earth years younger than Gage. I heard him discuss the matter with you yesterday, and he mentioned those things specifically."

"I guess he did, at that," said Hiskey. "Anyway, he was told on the Space U station that she's a guest on a private asteroid at present, and he contacted her there by transmitter. The asteroid people offered to pick him up so he could spend a few days with his sister as their guest. Gage called me and I told him to say we'd deliver him to the asteroid's lock in the *Prideful Sue,* since we've got time to kill before we can get scheduled through the System check stations anyway. So that's been arranged. And when we get there, I'll see to it that I'm invited down to the asteroid with Gage."

"That is the good news?" McNulty asked blankly.

Hiskey grinned. "There's a little more to it than that. Did your tapes tell you anything about Earthsystem's asteroid estates?"

"Yes. They were mentioned briefly twice," McNulty said. "I gathered their inhabitants retain only tenuous connections with the planetary culture and do not engage in belligerent projects. I concluded that they were of no interest to us."

"Well, start getting interested," Hiskey told him. "Each of those asteroids is a little world to itself. They're completely independent of both Earthplanet and Earthsystem. They got an arrangement with Earthsystem which guarantees their independent status as long as they meet certain conditions. From what Gage's sister told him, the asteroid she's on is a kind

of deluxe spacegoing ranch. It belongs to a Professor
Alston . . . a handful of people, some fancy livestock,
plenty of supplies."

"And what business could we have with such
people?" inquired McNulty.

"I think they'll be useful. I told you the one thing
that might bug our plans right now is to have the
System Police get too curious about the Prideful Sue
while we're hanging around here for the next five or
six days."

"So you did," said McNulty. "And I now have a
question about that. According to these tapes,
Earthsystem has no jurisdiction over Earthplanet. Why
then should the System Police attempt to control or
investigate what Earth imports?"

Hiskey shrugged. "For my money they're busybodies.
The SP got kicked off Earth for good, something like
forty years ago, but it still acts like it's responsible for
what happens there. And it's got muscle enough to
control the space of the system. Earth doesn't like that
but can't do much about it. If the System Police got
an idea of why we're bringing in a shipload of Rilfs
to Earth, they'd never let us go down. As long as we
do nothing to make them suspicious, they probably
won't bother us—but we can't really count on it.
However, if we move the Prideful Sue down beneath
the force fields around Professor Alston's asteroid, she'll
be out of sight and out of the SP's jurisdiction. By
Earthsystem's own ruling, they can't bother us even if
they have reason to think we're there."

"You believe Professor Alston will permit you to land
the ship?"

"No, I doubt he'd extend his hospitality that far. But
it'll be difficult for him to avoid inviting me down for
an hour or so, as Harold Gage's captain. When I
mention we have a very interesting alien on board—

first representative of his kind to reach Earthsystem, who has an intellectual curiosity about the human private asteroids—he'll invite you down. Half the crew can crowd into the skiff with you then and stay hidden in it till we want them."

McNulty gurgled interestedly. "You mentioned a handful of people—"

"From all I've heard, there'd be at most fifty even on a really big estate. Probably no more than half that. They don't like to be crowded on the asteroids—one reason most of them got off Earth to start with was that they wanted privacy and one place they could still buy it, if they had money enough, was in space."

"There should be then," said McNulty, "a most efficient and compact system of controls."

"You get the idea, McNulty. Those asteroids are set up like ships. That's what they've been turned into—big ships. Mostly they coast on solar orbit, but they can maneuver to some extent on their own."

"Then, as on a ship," McNulty continued, "the main controls will be concentrated for maximum efficiency within a limited area. It should take us at most an hour or two to gain a practical understanding of their use and operation."

"Might take you less than that," said Hiskey. Perhaps because of a congenital deficiency in inventive imagination, Rilf technology was at a primitive level as compared with the human one. But there was nothing wrong with their ability to learn, and McNulty, like most of them, was intensely interested in human gadgetry and very quick to grasp its function and principles. There wasn't much about the *Prideful Sue*'s working innards he didn't know by now. "We needn't make any final decisions before you and I have checked the situation," Hiskey pointed out. "But it should be a cinch. We take over the control section, block the communication system, and we have the asteroid."

"That part of it may well be easy," McNulty agreed. "However, I would expect serious problems to follow."

"What kind of problems?"

"These asteroid people obviously do not isolate themselves completely from Earthsystem. They converse by transmitter. They receive guests. If these activities suddenly stop and no response is obtained from the asteroid, the System Police certainly should grow suspicious. With or without jurisdiction, they will investigate."

Hiskey shook his head. "No, they won't, McNulty. That's what makes this easy for us."

"Please explain," said McNulty.

"A private asteroid—any private asteroid—is expected to go out of communication from time to time. They're one of Solar U's science projects. They seal their force field locks, shut off their transmitters; and when they open up again is entirely up to them. I've heard some have stayed incommunicado for up to ten years, and the minimum shutoff period's supposed to be not less than one month out of every year. What they're out to prove I don't know. But nobody's going to be upset if they discover suddenly that they're not able to get through to Professor Alston and his asteroid. They'll just settle back to wait until he's open to contact again."

McNulty reflected for a considerable time. "That does indeed sound like a favorable situation," he stated abruptly then. "Excuse us, Jake." He went on, without shifting his eyes from Hiskey's face, in the Rilf speech which sounded more like heavy sloshings of water than anything else. When he paused, Barnes's voice responded in kind from a wall speaker. The exchange continued for a minute or two. Then McNulty nodded ponderously at Hiskey.

"Barnes agrees that your plan is an excellent one, Jake. The elimination of the humans now in possession of the asteroid should present no great difficulty."

Hiskey looked startled. "I hadn't planned on killing them unless they try to give us a fight."

"Oh, but killing them is quite necessary," McNulty said.

"Why? We'll need the place only a few days."

"Jake, consider! On the ship which has trailed yours to Earthsystem and is now stationed outside it beyond the patrol range of the System Police are fifty-five Rilfs and their equipment—our army. Four of them have been humanized in appearance as Barnes and I are. The others are obviously not human. The System Police must not be permitted to encounter them."

"Of course not," Hiskey agreed. "But if we're prepared to whisk them down to Earth as soon as they move into the system, the SP isn't going to have time to encounter them."

"I understand," McNulty said. "However, your plan gives us the opportunity to cover ourselves against any deceit or treachery which might be considered by our Earth employers. With perhaps a third of our army left waiting in space, prepared to act, nobody will attempt to renege on contracted payments. And where could a better concealed base be found for our reserve and their ship than such an asteroid, only a few hours from Earth? And we can't afford to have prisoners on that base who would have to be constantly and closely guarded to make sure they cause no trouble. There is too much at stake."

Hiskey said slowly, "Yeah. I guess I see your point."

"Nor," continued McNulty, "can we destroy some and spare others. A single surviving witness might become most inconvenient eventually. Therefore, we must also kill Gage's sister. Since Gage will make a great deal of money as a participant in our operation, he may not object too strongly to that."

Hiskey stared at him for a moment.

"Some things you just don't get, McNulty," he remarked. "Harold Gage is going to object like hell to having his sister killed!"

"He will? Well, I must accept your opinion on the point," said McNulty. "It follows then—"

"I know. We'd have had to get rid of Gage anyway. He wouldn't go along with taking over the asteroid even if his sister weren't there and it wasn't a killing job. We were friends once, but he's been giving me a lot of trouble like that. Now we're in Earthsystem, we don't need a navigator. He goes with the asteroid people."

"That will not cause trouble among your men?"

Hiskey shook his head. "He hasn't had a friend on board for the past two years. We needed him, that's all. If he's eliminated, everybody gets that much better a split. There'll be no trouble."

"I'd gained the impression," McNulty observed, "that he was a rather dangerous person."

"He's a bad boy to go up against with a gun," Hiskey said. "But he won't be wearing guns on a friendly visit to a private asteroid, will he? No, you needn't worry about Gage."

McNulty said he was glad to hear it. He added, "There is, incidentally, an additional advantage to disposing of the asteroid humans. Before I demonstrate the toziens to our prospective employers, they should be exercised. At present, after their long idleness on shipboard, they have become sluggish."

Hiskey grimaced. "I thought those things were always ready to go . . ."

"No. Permit me." McNulty reached into the front of his coat, paused with his hand just out of sight, made an abrupt shrugging motion. For an instant there was a glassy glittering in the opening of the coat. Then it was gone, and something moved with a hard droning sound along the walls of the cabin behind Hiskey. He sat very still, not breathing, feeling blood drain slowly from his face.

"Do not be disturbed, Jake," said McNulty. "The drug I give you and your crew makes you as immune as a Rilf to the toziens' killing reaction." He lifted his hand. "Ah, now! It becomes conditioned. It adjusts! We no longer hear it."

The drone was thinning to a whisper; and as McNulty stopped speaking, there was a sudden complete silence. But the unseen thing still moved about the cabin. Hiskey felt abrupt brief stirrings of air to right and left of his face, as if the tozien were inspecting him; and in spite of McNulty's assurance he sat frozen and rigid.

"Well, enough of this," McNulty said. Hiskey didn't know what means the Rilf had of summoning the tozien back to him, but for a moment he saw it motionless on the front of McNulty's coat, a clinging glassy patch about the size of a man's hand. Then it disappeared beneath the coat and McNulty closed the coat, and Hiskey breathed again.

"That illustrates my point," McNulty told him. "The tozien remained audible while I might have counted to twenty, slowly. They are all like that now."

Hiskey wiped his forehead. "If they adjust in a few seconds, I can't see it makes much practical difference."

McNulty shook his head reprovingly.

"Those few seconds might give someone time to be warned, find shelter, and escape, Jake! In a tozien attack there should be no escape for foreign life which is not already behind thick walls or enclosed in strong armor. That is the beauty of it! On my last contract I was in a crowd of alert armed men when I released my toziens. In an instant the air was full of a thousand invisible silent knives, striking simultaneously. Some of the humans gasped as they died, but there were no screams. A clean piece of work! That is how it must be when we demonstrate the toziens to our Earth employers. And since I will be the demonstrator, I shall blood my swarm on the asteroid, on its humans and their livestock, and then they will be ready again."

"Well, that part of it is your business," Hiskey said, rather shakily.

Along the perennial solar orbit it shared with Earthplanet, the Alston asteroid soared serenely through space. Earth was never visible from the asteroid because the sun remained between them. The asteroid's inhabitants had no regrets about that; they were satisfied with what they could see, as they might be. The surface of what had been a ragged chunk of metal and mineral had been turned into an unobtrusively cultivated great garden. The outer atmosphere was only two hundred yards thick, held in by a shell of multiple force fields; but looking up, one would have found it difficult to say how it differed from the day and night skies of Earth. Breezes blew and clouds drifted; and a rainfall could be had on order. And if clouds, breezes, sky blueness, and rainfall weren't entirely natural phenomena, who cared? Or, at least, cared very much . . .

It had cost a great deal of money initially to bring the asteroid over from the Belt and install the machines which transformed its surface into a facsimile section of Earth, planted Earth gravity at its core, set it on Earth's orbit and gave it measured momentum and a twenty-four hour spin. It cost considerably more money to bring in soil, selected plants, selected animals, along with all the other appurtenances of enclosed but very comfortable and purposeful human habitation and activity. But once everything had been set up, it cost nothing to keep the asteroid going. It was self-powered, very nearly self-maintaining and self-sustaining. A variety of botanical projects initiated by Professor Derek Alston, its present owner, incidentally produced crops of spices disposed of in Earthsystem, which more than covered current expenses.

On this morning Derek Alston sat cross-legged by the side of a miniature lake, listening to and sometimes taking part in the conversation between his wife Sally and Sally's friend, Elisabeth Gage. Sally was a slightly tousled bronze blonde and Elisabeth had straight long jet-black hair sweeping about her shoulders, but Derek kept noticing points of resemblance between the two, in structure, motions, and mannerisms, almost as if they had been rather closely related, say first cousins. Though they were, Derek thought, in fact simply two excellent examples of the type of tall comely young women Earthsystem seemed to produce in increasing numbers each year. They had been fellow students at Solar U before Sally's marriage a little less than a year ago now, and, until Elisabeth arrived yesterday at the asteroid, they hadn't met in person since then. From what Sally had told him, Derek already knew a good deal about Elisabeth before he saw her.

The talk, naturally, mainly was about Elisabeth's brother who should reach the asteroid in another hour or so. There was, Derek knew, in what was being said and in what was not being said between these two, a trace of awkwardness and uncertainty. Essentially, of course, it was an occasion for festivities and rejoicing. Elisabeth was happy. There was no question about that. Her face was filled with her reflections . . . dreamy dazed smiles, cheeks glowing, eyes brimming briefly now and then. Her brother was the only surviving member of her family, and they'd been very close throughout her childhood. And now there'd been eight years of separation, and she hadn't known until Harold called that he'd come back to Earthsystem, or was even planning to come back. She'd had no reason to expect him. So she was happy, melting in happiness in fact. And Sally shared sympathetically in her friend's feelings.

But there was the other side to this matter. It wasn't to be mentioned now, but it couldn't be dismissed either. . . .

"His voice hasn't changed at all—" Elizabeth had just said. There was a tiny silence then, because she had touched, inadvertently, the other side of the matter, and it seemed to Derek the right moment to speak.

"Only twenty-eight years old," he remarked. "Your brother's very young to have put eight years of out-system travel behind him."

Elisabeth looked at him a moment and smiled. "Yes, I suppose he is," she said. "He was just twenty when he was graduated from navigation school at the SP Academy. Dad was with the SP in Mars Underground, and I know he thought Harold would stay with the force. But after Dad died, Earthsystem looked too tame to Harold. He wanted real adventure and he wanted to make his fortune. Captain Hiskey was putting together his crew just then, and Harold signed as navigator. The pay wasn't much, but the crew was to share in ship's profits." She gave a small shrug. "I'm afraid Harold hasn't made his fortune yet, but he's certainly had adventures. Even from the little he's told me, I know the ship often must have been doing very risky work."

"What were Captain Hiskey's qualifications for that kind of work—for outsystem commerce generally?" Derek asked.

Elisabeth's eyes flickered. "Harold said Hiskey had been first officer on a big transsolar transport. Then he got money enough to buy his own ship." She hesitated. "I guess they've tried about anything they could. But they never had a good enough streak of luck to do much better than break even . . . or else they'd get good luck mixed up with bad. Perhaps Harold will stay in Earthsystem now. But I have a feeling he won't. He was always very stubborn when he set himself a goal."

"You heard from him regularly?"

"No, not regularly. Not very often either. I've had seven message-packs from him in eight years. Somebody would get back to Earthsystem and drop the pack off at Mars Underground or Solar U, and I'd receive it that way. The last one was just six months ago. It didn't say a word about the ship coming back. That's why I can still hardly believe Harold's here."

The eyes had begun to brim again. Sally said quickly, "Perhaps he wasn't sure he'd be coming back and didn't want to build up your hopes."

Elisabeth nodded. "I suppose that was it. And . . ."

Derek drew back mentally from what she was saying. An independent outsystem trader—not a very large ship, from what Elisabeth had told them. A crew working mainly on a gamble, willing to try anything, each man out to make his fortune, hit the big money by some means. At least some of the men on Captain Hiskey's ship had pursued that objective for eight years without getting there.

Man played it dirty and rough on Earth, held back only by a few general rules which none dared break. In the outsystems the same games were played, as extensions of those on Earth, perhaps somewhat dirtier and rougher, with no enforceable rules of any kind. Drop an adventurous, eager twenty-year-old into that kind of thing after the quiet order of Mars Underground, the disciplines of the SP Academy . . . well, it might shape the twenty-year-old in one way or another, but shape him it would, thoroughly and fast, if he was to survive. Eight years should have worked quite a few changes in Harold Gage. The changes needn't have been evident in the message-packs Elisabeth had received. But she was intelligent, and she knew in general what the outsystems were like. And so, unwillingly, she was apprehensive of what she would find in her brother.

It bothered Derek because he liked Elisabeth and thought that whatever her expectations were, she might still be in for a shock. He checked his watch, got to his feet, smiled at his wife and guest, and excused himself. A few minutes later, seated at a transmitter, he dialed a number.

"Lieutenant Pierce," a voice said. "Who is calling?"

"This is Derek Alston, Mike."

"And what can the System Police do for Professor Alston today?" asked Michael Pierce.

"Do you have anything on an outsystem tramp trader called *Prideful Sue*? Captain-owner's name is Hiskey. He might have checked in a day or two ago."

"Hold on," Pierce told him.

Perhaps a minute passed before his voice resumed. "There's a ship by that name and of that description in the territory, Derek. She's Earthplanet registry. Last SP check was ten years ago. No record of present owners. First reported as having arrived from transsolar three days ago. We have a mild interest in the ship because the captain evidently has no intention of checking in or going through Customs. Of course, an SP check isn't compulsory if his business is only and directly with Earthplanet and if we have no reason to suspect Class A contraband. However, he keeps shifting about the system as if he preferred to keep out of our way. Do you feel we should give him more attention?"

"I have no definite reason to think so," Derek said. "But possibly you should."

A number of things were disturbing Harold Gage. One of them was that Jake Hiskey had invited himself down on the asteroid with him. Jake had made no mention of such plans until the *Prideful Sue* eased in to a stop on the coordinates given them in the Alston asteroid's gravity field and went on space anchor. Then Harold came forward to the comm room; and there was Jake, freshly shaved and in dress uniform, talking to the Alstons on viz screen. The matter was already settled. How Jake wrangled the invitation Harold didn't know, but he was downright charming when he wanted to be; and undoubtedly he'd made the Alstons feel it would be impossibly rude not to include him in the party. Jake switched off the screen, looked at Harold's face, and grinned.

"Hell, Harold," he said. "You're not begrudging an old friend a few hours' look at sheer luxury, are you?"

"No," Harold said. "But in this case I felt I was already imposing on Elisabeth's friends."

"Ah—don't be so sensitive. They invited you, didn't they? And Professor Alston and that sweet-looking wife of his will get a boot out of me. These millionaire hermits must get mighty bored on their pretty-pretty asteroids where nothing ever happens. We're transsolar spacers, man! We've been places and done things it would curl their hair to think about. We're romantic!" He clapped Harold on the shoulder. "Come on! They told me your sister's waiting at the lock. Hey, this is one place we don't have to wear guns when we stick our noses outside—seems odd, doesn't it?"

And then they were down; and there, first of all, was Elisabeth—not a girl any more but, startlingly, a beautiful woman. Harold wasn't even sure he would have recognized her if she hadn't run towards him, laughing and crying a little, as he stepped out of the skiff, and clung to him for long seconds. And there were the Alstons, pleasant people who immediately took Jake in hand and smoothly dissociated him and themselves from the Gages, so that in only minutes Harold and Elisabeth were wandering about alone in this sunlit, rather dreamlike garden of an asteroid.

He'd been afraid there'd be an awkwardness between them, but none developed. Elisabeth was a completely honest person, of the kind whose expression hides nothing because there is rarely anything in their minds they want to hide. She studied him frankly and gravely, his eyes, his mouth, his motions, listened to his voice and its inflections, her face telling him meanwhile that she realized he'd changed and something of the manner in which he'd changed, and that she was accepting it, perhaps with regret but without judgment and with no loss of affection. He knew, too, that this was a matter it wouldn't be necessary to talk about, now or later . . . later meaning after the business on Earthplanet was concluded. What was left then was that he always would have to be a little careful of what he said to her, careful not to reveal too much. Because what Elisabeth didn't know, couldn't possibly know, was just how extensive the change had been.

He told himself it couldn't have been helped. In the outsystems it could hardly have worked out otherwise. For a while they'd remained fairly selective about what they did with the *Prideful Sue*. If a job looked too raw, they didn't touch it. But they weren't making money, or not enough, and the raw jobs began to look less unacceptable. Then some of the crew dropped out, and some got killed, and the replacements were outsystem boys with outsystem ideas. On occasion they'd come close to straight raiding then; and if it had been up to Jake Hiskey alone, what difference was left finally mightn't have mattered enough to count.

But a first-class navigator was the most valuable man on the ship in the outsystems; and Harold was a first-class navigator by then. If he hadn't been one, he still would have been the most valuable man on the *Prideful Sue;* Hiskey had come to depend on him more and more. So he could put a stop to an operation if it looked too bad, and from time to time he did. It didn't get him liked on board; but, as it happened, he'd also developed a first-class gun hand. If necessary the hand might get a little more blood on it, and Navigator Gage would get his way.

This last move now, the big one, the one which was to make the whole past eight years pay off extremely well, importing McNulty's mercenaries and their devastating weapon, the Rilf toziens, to Earthplanet—he'd thought about it long and hard and had been at the point of backing out more than once. Hiskey, whose idea it had been, argued that it was a perfectly legitimate enterprise. It was, without question. Earthplanet's criterion of permissible weaponry was the guaranteed limitation of effect. A tozien strike had an active period of less than two days, a target radius of less than twenty miles. It fell well within the allowable range.

And it would have the value of a completely unexpected innovation. Earthplanet hadn't yet heard of the Rilfs. Hiskey had contacts who knew how to handle this kind of thing to best advantage all around. Everyone involved would share in the cut, and the cut was going to be a very large one. Of course, after the first dozen miniwars came to an abrupt end, that part of it would be over. McNulty would be in general demand and could get along without middlemen. There'd be no further payoffs to the crew of the *Prideful Sue*. But down to the last man on board, they'd be more than wealthy enough to retire.

It was, Jake Hiskey pointed out, no more of a dirty business, if one wanted to call it that, than other operations they'd carried out. The Earth gangs periodically slaughtered one another, and there was very little to choose between them. What great difference did it make to hand some of them a new weapon?

It wasn't much of an argument, but what decided Harold was that this was Jake Hiskey's last chance and that Jake knew it and was desperate. He was fifteen years older than Harold and looked a decade older than that. The outsystems had leached his nerve from him at last. If Harold pulled out, Hiskey wouldn't be able to handle the deal with the Rilfs, wouldn't be able to work a troop of them back to Earthsystem. He was no longer capable of it. And when one had flown and fought a ship for eight years with a man, had backed him and been backed by him in tight spots enough to do for a lifetime, it was difficult to turn away from him when he was finished. So all right, Harold had thought finally, one more play, dirty as it might be. Then he and Jake could split. There was nothing really left of their friendship; that had eroded along the line. If the SP didn't manage to block them, they'd get the Rilfs to Earth. Afterwards they couldn't be touched by Earthsystem, even if it became known what role they'd played. They'd have done nothing illegal.

And he could hope the role they'd played wouldn't become known. He'd told Elisabeth the *Prideful Sue* had returned to Earthsystem on very big and very hush-hush business, something he wasn't free to talk about, and that if the deal was concluded successfully he might be taking a long vacation from spacefaring. She seemed delighted with that and didn't ask for details, and Harold inquired what she'd been doing these eight years, because none of the message-packs she'd sent ever had caught up with him, and soon Elisabeth was talking and laughing freely and easily. For a short while, the past years seemed almost to fade, as if they were strolling about a park in Mars Underground rather than on this fabulous garden asteroid where handsome horned beasts stepped out now and then from among the trees to gaze placidly at them as they went by. . . .

"Mr. Gage! Elisabeth!"

He stopped, blinking. It was like an optical illusion. There was a steep smooth cliff of rock to the left of the path they were following; and in it, suddenly, an opening had appeared, a doorway, and Sally Alston had stepped out of it and was coming towards them, smiling. "I looked for you in the scanners," she told Elisabeth. Then she turned to Harold. "Mr. Gage, why didn't you let us know you had this extraordinary alien person on board? If Captain Hiskey hadn't mentioned—"

"Alien person?" Elisabeth interrupted.

"Why, yes! Somebody called a Rilf. Derek is certain Solar U has no record of the species, and Captain Hiskey and Mr. Gage are taking him to Earthplanet on a commercial mission for his people. It's really an historical event!"

Harold stared at her, completely dumbfounded. Had Jake gone out of his mind to mention McNulty and the Rilfs to the Alstons? Elisabeth gave him a quick glance which asked whether this was the big hush-hush business he'd been talking about.

"He's even given himself a human name," Sally told Elisabeth. "McNulty!" She smiled at Harold. "I must admit I find him a little shivery!"

"He's *here*?" Harold heard himself saying. "McNulty's here, on the asteroid?"

"Of course! We invited him down. When Captain Hiskey—"

"How long's he been here?"

She looked at him, startled by his tone. "Why, about twenty minutes. Why?"

"No," Harold said. "Don't ask questions." He took each of them by an arm, began to walk them quickly towards the opening in the cliff. "Do you know exactly where McNulty is at the moment?"

"Well, they—my husband and Captain Hiskey and McNulty probably are in the control room now. McNulty was saying how interested he'd be in seeing how the asteroid was operated."

That tied it. "You didn't send up for him?" Harold asked. "The ship's skiff brought him down?"

"Yes, it did. But what is the matter, Mr. Gage? Is—"

"And the skiff's still here?" Harold said. "It's inside the field lock?"

"I suppose so. I don't know."

"All right," Harold said. He stopped before the opening. "Now listen carefully because we're not likely to have much time!" He drew a quick deep breath. "First, where is the control room?"

"In the building in the space lock section," Sally said. "The administration building. You saw it when you came down." They were watching him, expressions puzzled and alarmed.

Harold nodded. "Yes, I remember. Now—you and everyone else on the asteroid is in very serious danger. McNulty is a real horror. He has a special weapon.

The only way you can stay reasonably safe from it is to hide out behind good solid locked doors. I hope you'll have some way of warning Professor Alston and whoever else is around to do the same thing. Anyone who's in the open, isn't behind walls, when McNulty cuts loose won't have a chance. Not for a moment! Unless he belongs to the *Prideful Sue's* crew. If you can get to a transmitter in the next few minutes, call the SP and tell them to come here and get in any way they can—in space armor. But transmitters aren't going to stay operable very long. You'll have to hurry." He looked at their whitened faces. "Don't think I'm crazy! The only reason Hiskey would have told you about McNulty, and the only reason McNulty would have showed himself, is that they've decided between them to take over the place."

"But why?" cried Sally.

"Because we're the next thing to lousy pirates. Because they think they can use this asteroid." Harold started to turn away. "Now get inside, seal that door tight, move fast, and with luck you'll stay alive."

So this was one place guns wouldn't be needed! In mentioning that, Jake Hiskey had made sure his navigator wouldn't—quite out of habit and absentmindedly—be going down armed to the peaceful Alston asteroid and to the reunion with his sister. He knew this was a job I couldn't buy, Harold thought. Even if Elisabeth hadn't been involved.

He'd set off at a long lope as soon as the camouflaged door in the cliff snapped shut. The asteroid surface in this area was simulated hilly ground, slopes rising and dipping, occasional smooth slabs of meteorite rock showing through. Clusters of trees, shrubbery, cultivated grassy ground . . . The space lock section couldn't be more than a few hundred yards away, but he couldn't see it from here. Neither could anyone in the open see him approaching. Sally Alston had said she'd located them by using scanners. Hiskey and McNulty could spot him by the same means, but they wouldn't be looking for him before they'd secured the control room. Standard raiding procedure . . . hit the nerve center of an installation as quickly as possible; take it, and the rest is paralyzed, helpless, silenced.

He checked an instant. A curious sensation, like a vibrating pressure on his eardrums, a tingling all through his nerves; it continued a few seconds, faded, returned, faded again . . . and the herd came suddenly around the side of the hill ahead of him. Some fifteen large gray-brown animals, a kind of antelope with thick corkscrew horns, running hard and fast. In the moment he saw them, startled, he took it for an indication that McNulty had released the toziens—and knew immediately it wasn't that. Nothing ran from toziens; there was no time. The herd crossed his path with a rapid drumming of hoofs, pounded through thickets, wheeled and appeared about to slam head-on into a vertical cliff wall. At the last moment an opening was there in the rock, similar to the one out of which Sally Alston had stepped, five or six times as wide. The beasts plunged through it, shouldering and jostling one another, and the opening vanished behind the last of them.

It all seemed to have happened in an instant. He ran on, wondering. That odd sensation, switching on and off—an alert signal? An alarm to which even the animals here were conditioned to respond immediately, in a predetermined manner, a "take cover!" that cleared the surface level of anything capable of reacting to it in moments . . . it indicated a degree of efficiency and preparedness he wouldn't have attributed to these asteroid dwellers. What sort of emergencies could they expect here?

He saw no more fleeing beasts, or any beasts at all;

and in perhaps another minute the tingling irritation in his nerves had ended. The space lock section couldn't be far away. He'd been cutting across the slopes, avoiding the leisurely winding and intersecting paths along which he'd come with Elisabeth, and keeping to cover when it didn't slow him down. At last then, coming out of a grove of trees on the crest of one of the little hills, he saw the administration building ahead—or rather one corner of it, warm brown, edged with gleaming black, the rest concealed behind trees. There was no one in sight, but he moved cautiously now, staying within the shrubbery. A hundred feet on, he came to a point which overlooked the landing area beneath the space lock. The *Prideful Sue*'s skiff stood in the center of the area, entry port open. Otherwise the section looked deserted.

Above the skiff nothing showed but the simulated Earth sky. If the space lock through the energy carriers englobing the asteroid had been activated, it would have been visible—a ring of frozen fire from below, a glowing cylinder from where Harold stood, the cylinder's thickness depending on the degree to which the lock was expanded. Undoubtedly it could be expanded enough to let in the *Prideful Sue*, and undoubtedly Hiskey had just that in mind. But whatever else he might have accomplished so far, he hadn't yet got around to bringing down the ship.

The skiff wasn't large, but eight or nine men with raiding gear—about half the crew—could have been crammed in with McNulty and left waiting in concealment until they received Hiskey's signal to emerge and go into action. The open entry lock indicated they'd already received the signal, were now inside the administration building. In other words, at some point within the past few minutes the attack on the asteroid had begun. Barnes, the second Rilf, and the rest of the crew were still on the ship. If they joined the group on the asteroid, the situation might become nearly hopeless. As things stood, it seemed quite bad enough, but at least there'd been no sign as yet of the Rilf toziens. It was possible that if Jake Hiskey met no significant resistance from Alston's people, he would prefer not to turn this into a killing operation.

But he'll want to get me in any case, Harold thought. To keep me from interfering . . .

They hadn't had time to try to locate him with scanners, but somebody might have been posted outside the administration building to ambush him if he showed up here. The most likely spot for a watcher seemed the cluster of trees and bushes which screened the building.

A blue and golden bird twice the size of a pigeon burst out of the undergrowth six feet ahead and launched itself upwards with a strong beat of wings. Startled—that might easily have advertised his approach—Harold dropped to a deep crouch, glancing after the bird. It rose swiftly to a point about thirty feet above the ground. There something struck and destroyed it.

It seemed as abrupt as an explosion. The flying shape changed to sprays of blood and colorful ribbons and rags which were slashed and scattered again and again in the same instant, then left to fall back to earth. So it was a killing operation after all, and McNulty had turned loose his toziens. Not, of course, all of them. There were thousands packed away in his thick non-human thorax; and only a small fraction of that number were required to sweep the surface of the asteroid and any sections of the interior open to intrusion clear of animal life large enough to attract their attention. They could have been released only moments ago or he would have been made aware of their presence—

as he was aware of it now. An eerie whispering about him, now here, now there, as the toziens darted down in turn in their invisible speed towards this living flesh, sensed the Rilf drug which protected him as it protected all those who manned the *Prideful Sue*, and swerved away. But everyone else on the asteroid who had not found shelter had died or was dying in these seconds.

Starting forwards again, he shut that thought away. Jake Hiskey and McNulty, having begun the slaughter, would finish it. They'd be in the control room at present, securing their hold on the asteroid. That done, they'd bring in the ship and start looking for holed-up survivors.

The man Hiskey had selected to act as lookout at the building was Tom Connick. Not the brightest, but an excellent shot and normally steady as a rock—a good choice as an assassin. He stood, screened by a thicket, thirty feet from what seemed to be the only entrance into the building, a gun ready in his hand. They knew Harold wasn't armed; and if he wanted to get into the administration building, he'd have to come past the thicket, within easy range for Connick. It must have seemed as simple as that.

McNulty's toziens, however, had provided a complication. Connick's usual calm was not in evidence. He kept making small abrupt motions, bobbing his head, flinching right or left, jerking up the gun and putting it down again. Harold could appreciate his feelings. He, too, was still drawing the interest of the invisible swarm; every few seconds there would be a momentary indication that a tozien was nearby, and each time his flesh crawled though he knew, as Connick did, that theoretically they were protected from the little horrors. The thought remained that some tozien or other might not realize in time that they were protected. But at present that was all to his advantage. Connick darted glances this way and that, now and then half turning to see what was in back of him; but he was looking for the wrong kind of danger. So in the end Harold rose quietly from the undergrowth ten steps behind Connick with a sizable rock in either hand.

He lobbed the left-hand rock gently upwards. It lifted in a steep arc above Connick's head and came down in front of him. And, for a moment, Connick's nerves snapped. He uttered a frightened sound, a stifled squeal, jabbed the gun forward, shoulders hunching, attention frozen by the deadly dark moving thing which had appeared out of nowhere. It was doubtful whether he even heard the brief rustle of the thicket as Harold came up behind him. Then the edge of the second rock smashed through his skull.

And now there was a gun for Harold, and for Jake Hiskey one man less he might presently send out to look for surviving asteroid people. Harold found a recharger for the gun in one of Connick's pockets. There'd been some question in his mind whether there mightn't be a second man around, though he had studied the vicinity thoroughly before moving in on Connick. But nothing stirred, so Connick's death had not been observed. He could expect to find somebody else stationed inside the building entrance, as a standard precaution.

He started quickly towards the building, then checked. On the far side of the space lock area there was a faint greenish shimmering in the air, which hadn't been there before. Harold stared at it sharply, looked around. Behind him, too, much closer, barely a hundred feet away—like a nearly invisible curtain hanging from the simulated sky, fitted against the irregularities of the ground below. He pointed Connick's

gun into the air, triggered it for an instant. There was
a momentary puff of brightness as the charge hit the
immaterial curtain. More distantly to the right, and
beyond the administration building to the left, was the
same shimmering aerial effect.

Energy screens. Activated within the past few minutes. By whom? They enclosed the space lock section,
boxed it in. If they'd been thrown up before the tozien
swarm appeared in the section, then McNulty's weapon
was still confined here unless it had found an entry
to the asteroid's interior from within the building. And
the screens might have gone up just in time to do that;
he'd been too involved in his wary approach to the
building area to have noticed what happened behind
him. There was suddenly some real reason for
hope . . . because this fitted in with the silently pervasive
alert signal which had come so quickly after his warning
to Sally Alston, with concealed doors opening and
closing on the surface and animals streaming off it into
the interior. The asteroid had defenses, and somebody
was using them—which did not make it any less urgent
to do something about the *Prideful Sue*'s crew and its
Rilf allies before the defenses were broken down.

There was someone waiting inside the entrance. It
was Dionisio.

"What's slowing you men down in there, Dionisio?"
Navigator Gage demanded curtly, striding towards him.
"Why aren't you moving?"

Dionisio was considerably more intelligent than
Connick, but, besides being also badly fretted by the
toziens, he was, for a moment, confused. He'd been
told the navigator was among those to get it here; but
he'd also been told that the navigator was unarmed and
had no idea of what was going to happen. And here
the navigator came walking up, casually holding a gun

at half-ready, looking annoyed and impatient, which was standard for him on an operation, and sounding as if he were very much in on the deal. And, of course, there was the further consideration that the navigator was an extremely fast and accurate man with a gun. So Dionisio blinked, licked his lips, cleared his throat, finally began, "Well . . . uh—"

"The skipper's got the control room cleaned up?"

"Well, sir, I guess so."

"You guess so?"

"I wasn't there," Dionisio said sullenly, eyes fixed with some nervousness on the gun Navigator Gage was waving around rather freely. "I was in the skiff. There was that funny feeling we all got. Right after that we got the skipper's signal. So we came out. The skipper tells us to start looking around for the people."

"The people in the building?"

"Uh-huh. The skipper and McNulty were in the control room. There were five, six of the people here with them. And then the skipper looks around, and there's nobody there."

The navigator's lip curled. "You're implying they disappeared? Just like that?"

"Looks like it," said Dionisio warily.

"Everybody in the building?"

"Uh-huh."

"So what are they doing in there now?"

"Blowing in the walls. Looking for, uh, doors."

"Looking for doors!" repeated Navigator Gage, total disgust in his voice. "And what are you doing up here?"

Dionisio swallowed. "I'm to, uh, look out to see if somebody comes."

"With the toziens around? You out of your mind? Who's in the skiff? Have the rest of them come down from the ship?"

"No. There's nobody in the—"

And then Dionisio stopped talking and twitched his gunbarrel up very quickly. Because Navigator Gage had glanced back towards the skiff out in the landing area just then; and while this was a kind of odd situation, Dionisio was positive the skipper anyhow wanted Navigator Gage dead, and he himself had no slightest use for the navigator. So up came the gun, and it was Dionisio who was dead in the same moment, because Navigator Gage had, after all, not glanced away to the extent of not being able to catch the motion.

Beyond the entry a lit hallway extended back into the building. Harold thought he'd heard distant human voices in there while he was talking to Dionisio, but at the moment there was silence. He checked quickly through the man's gear, found a folded gas-breather and fitted that over his face. He took off his suit coat, put on Dionisio's faded brown jacket, slapped Dionisio's visor cap on his head, and set it at the jaunty angle Dionisio favored. As he finished, there was a remote heavy thump from within the building, followed in seconds by another. Jake Hiskey was still having holes blown out of the walls, looking for the hidden passages through which Professor Alston and the people working in the administration building had vanished when they got the alert signal. He should find them if he kept at it long enough. And as soon as they had the space lock controls figured out, they'd haul down the *Prideful Sue* with the heavier raiding equipment she carried.

Dionisio's gun was the only other useful item here. Harold pocketed it, pulled the body over against the entry wall where it wouldn't be visible from within the building, and set off quickly along the long hallway. Glassy motion flickered for an instant before his eyes; the toziens were still around. Now a series of five doors on the right—all locked. Ahead the hall made a turn to the right. As he came towards the corner, he heard men's voices again, at least three or four, mingled in a short burst of jabbering, harsh with excitement. Hiskey's voice among them? The ammonia smell of jolt bombs began to tingle faintly in his nostrils.

He went around the corner without hesitating or slowing his stride. The gas-breather covered half his face; and while Dionisio was about an inch shorter, they were similar enough in general build that he could be accepted as Dionisio for a few moments by men with their attention on other things. Sixty feet ahead, rubble covered the hall floor, chunks of colorful plastic masonry shaken by jolt bombs out of a great jagged hole in the left wall. Only two men in sight, standing waiting in tensed attitudes behind a semiportable gun pointed at the hole. Jake Hiskey's voice now, raw with impatient anger: "Hurry it up! Hurry it up!" A glow spilled from the hole and there was the savage hiss of cutters. Bomb fumes hung thick in the air. Hiskey and at least four of the crew here. Wait till you're right among them.

One of the men at the semiportable glanced around as Harold came up, looked away again. He went past them. The hole drove deep into the wall; evidently they'd uncovered a passage but found it sealed a few yards farther on, and the sealing material was holding. Three men were at work in there with Hiskey. The cutters blazed and a broken conduit spat vicious shorted power . . . And what damn fool had left two unused jolt bombs lying on this boulder of plastic? Harold scooped them up in passing, glanced back and saw Hiskey staring open-mouthed over at him, then clawing for his gun.

Harold dropped behind the boulder, thumbed the stud on one of the little bombs and pitched it over into the opening of the hole. The second one went in the general direction of the semiportable. Their successive shock waves rammed at his eardrums, lifted the boulder against him. Clouds of dust filled the hall. After a moment he took out one of his guns and stood up.

They lay where the double shock had caught and battered them. Hiskey had been coming for him, had nearly reached the boulder when he was smashed down. Harold looked at the bloodied head and was surprised by a wash of heavy regret, a brief but intensely vivid awareness of that bright yesterday in which Jake Hiskey and he first swung their ship out past the sun, headed towards high adventure. Too bad, Jake, he thought. Too bad that in eight years the adventure soured so that it's ending here like this.

McNulty and one or at most two of the original landing group left. Finish it up now before their reinforcements get here—

McNulty at any rate should be in the control room.

Harold went on along the hallway. No sounds anywhere. An open door. He approached it cautiously, looked in. A sizable office, half a dozen desks spaced out, machine stands, wall files—two of these left open. Not many minutes ago, people had been working here. Then the asteroid's alarm reached them, and like ghosts they'd vanished. At the far side of the office was another door. As he started towards it, two men stood suddenly in the doorframe. Guns went off; Harold dropped behind the nearest desk. Across the room, the two had taken cover as quickly.

A real gun fight now, fast and vicious. The crewmen were Harding and Ruse, two of the *Prideful Sue*'s best hands. The office furniture, in spite of its elegant appearance, was of tough solid plastic; but within a minute it was hammered half to pieces. Harold had emptied the charge in one of his guns before he got Harding. Ruse was still pouring it at him, battering the shielding desk. There was no way to reach back at him from here. Harold took a chance finally, shifting to another desk in a crouching leap, felt pain jar up from the heel of his right leg as he reached cover. Not an immediately crippling charge, though any hit of that kind was bad enough. Now, however, lying half across the desk, he had the advantage and could pour it on Ruse and did. Pinned behind his cover, Ruse kept firing furiously but ineffectively. At last he stopped firing and tried to duplicate Harold's trick, and Harold got him in the open. The second gun hissed out emptily instants later.

Ruse had rolled on behind a low console. Only his legs were in sight. He seemed to be sprawled loosely on his side, and the legs weren't moving. It might be a trick, though Harold didn't think so. He knew he'd caught Ruse with a head shot; and even at minimum charge that should have been almost instantly fatal. But he stayed where he was and reached back carefully with one hand to get the gun recharger he'd taken from Connick out of his pocket. A moment's fumbling told him it was no longer there. At some point along the line it had been jolted from the pocket and lost.

But Harding should have a recharger. Harold slid back slowly off the desk and turned towards Harding's body.

And there, coming towards him in a soft heavy rush across the littered office, clutching a thick metal spike in one human-looking hand, was McNulty.

Harold slipped back behind the desk. McNulty lunged across the desk with the spike, then lumbered around it; and as he came on, his big shape seemed to be blurring oddly from moment to moment. Then a hard deep droning noise swelled in the air, and Harold knew the Rilf's thorax was spewing out its store of toziens.

The purpose was immediately obvious. The toziens couldn't touch him, but they provided a distraction. In an instant Harold seemed enclosed in roaring thunders, and the office had turned into something seen through a shifting syrupy liquid. McNulty, in addition, hardly needed help. He was clumsy but strong and fast; his broad white face kept looming up distortedly in the tozien screen near Harold. For a nightmarish minute or two, it was all Harold could do to keep some sizable piece of office equipment between the Rilf and himself. McNulty didn't give him a chance to get near Ruse's or Harding's guns. Then finally McNulty stumbled on a broken chair and fell; and with the tozien storm whirling about him, Harold managed to wrench the spike away from the Rilf. As McNulty came back up on his feet, he moved in, the spike gripped in both hands, and rammed it deep into what, if McNulty had been human, would have been McNulty's abdomen. He had no idea where McNulty's vital organs were or what they were like, but the spike reached one of them. McNulty's mouth stretched wide. If he made any sound, it was lost in the droning uproar. His big body swayed left and right; then he went down heavily on his back and lay still, the spike's handle sticking up out of him. His eyes remained open.

Harold leaned back for an instant against the edge of a desk, gasping for breath. The toziens still boiled around, sounding like a swarm of gigantic metallic insects, but they seemed to have drawn away a little; he began to see the office more clearly. Then one of them appeared suddenly on McNulty's chest. It stayed there, quivering. Another appeared, and another. In a minute, McNulty's body was covered with them, clustering, shifting about, like flies gathering thick on carrion. Harold's skin crawled as he watched them. They were specialized cells produced by the Rilf body, pliable or steel-hard and razor-edged, depending on what they were doing. McNulty's remote ancestor had been a hunting animal, too awkward perhaps to overtake nimble prey, which had evolved a method of detaching sections of itself to carry out the kill, not unlike the hawks men had trained on old Earth to hunt on sight. McNulty still had been able to use his toziens in that manner, releasing one or more under an inhibition which impelled them to return to him after bringing down a specific victim. Their use by the thousands for uninhibited wholesale slaughter evidently had been a more recent Rilf development, perhaps not attained until they had acquired a civilization and scientific methods. Under those conditions, the toziens ranged over an area of a dozen miles, destroying whatever life they found for almost fifty hours, until their furious energy was exhausted and they died.

Harding had been carrying a recharger, and Harold replenished his guns with it before placing it in his pocket. He looked over once more at McNulty's body, motionless under its glittering blanket, and left the office by the door opposite to the one through which he had entered. Not all the toziens had returned to McNulty. An unidentifiable number still darted about, and some stayed near Harold, attracted by his motion. He knew it because they weren't inaudible now but continued to make droning or whiffing sounds as they had during McNulty's attack. Perhaps McNulty's death was having an effect on their life processes. At any rate, they no longer seemed to have any particular interest in him.

Limping a little because of the charge he'd stopped in his heel, he followed the narrow passage beyond the door to another doorway. There, at the bottom of a short flight of steps, the brightly lit deserted control room whispered and hummed. Harold hurried down the steps, looked around.

He found the space lock controls almost immediately. And they were a puzzler. The instruments indicated that the lock was open to its fullest extent. But the screen view of the landing area showed only the skiff standing there, and the screen view of the forcefield sections containing the space lock showed it wasn't activated, was shut tight. He shifted the controls quickly back and forth. There was no change in the screens. He scowled at the indicators, left them at the shut and secured mark, turned to other instruments nearby, began manipulating them.

In a minute, he had the answer. He sat down at a console, heard himself make a short laughing sound. No wonder Jake Hiskey had worked so furiously to break through into the hidden passages leading into the interior of the asteroid. For every practical purpose, the control room was dead. Power was here, the gadgetry appeared to be operating. But it did and could do nothing. None of it. Nothing at all.

He drew a long slow breath, looked up at the ceiling.

"Is somebody listening?" he asked aloud. "Can you see me here?"

There was a momentary excited babble of voices, male and female. Elisabeth? He discovered the speaker then, ten feet away. "Elisabeth?" he asked, a sudden rawness in his throat.

"Yes, I'm here, Harold. We're all here!" Elisabeth's voice told him. "Harold, we couldn't see you. We didn't know what was happening out—"

"The scanners, Mr. Gage." That was Alston. "The scanning circuits in that section have been shorted. We were afraid of drawing attention to you by speaking. And—"

"I understand," Harold said. "Better let me talk first because this thing isn't finished. Captain Hiskey and the men he smuggled down here from the ship are dead. So is McNulty—the Rilf. But McNulty's weapon isn't dead and should stay effective for the next two days—make it two and a half, to be safe. You can't come into this section before then, and you can't go anywhere else on the asteroid where it might have spread. It can't hurt me, but any of you would be killed immediately."

"Just what is this biological weapon?" Alston's voice asked.

Harold told him briefly about the toziens, added, "You may have thrown up those screen barriers about this section fast enough to trap them here. But if you didn't, they're all over the surface of the asteroid. And if they're given an opening anywhere, they'll come pouring down into it."

"Fortunately," Alston said, "they have been trapped in the space lock section. Thanks to your prompt warning, Mr. Gage."

"What makes you sure?"

"They were registering on biological sensing devices covering that section until the scanners went off. The impressions were difficult to define but match your description. Every section of the asteroid is compartmentalized by energy screens at present, and no similar impressions have been obtained elsewhere. Nevertheless, we shall take no chances. We'll remain sealed off from the surface for the next sixty hours."

"You seem to have an override on the instruments here," Harold said.

"An automatic override," Alston acknowledged. "It cuts in when the asteroid shifts to emergency status. The possibility of a successful raid always had to be considered. So there is an interior control room."

Harold sighed. Jake Hiskey and McNulty, he thought, hadn't been alone in underestimating these people. Well, let's get the mess cleaned up . . . "You've asked the SP to do something about the *Prideful Sue?*"

"Yes," Alston said. "They'll be here within a few hours."

Tozien whirring dipped past Harold's face, moved off. "She has heavier armament than they might expect," he said. "Eight men and another Rilf on board. Our gunnery isn't the worst. But tell them to give her a chance."

"I'll do that. And I'll advise the police to take precautions."

"Yes, they should. There's one more thing then. We guided a Rilf ship here and left it outside Earthsystem. It's manned by more than half a hundred Rilfs. We've been negotiating to have them take a hand for pay in Earth's miniwars. They may still try to go ahead with the deal. I think they should be turned back."

"Where is that ship now?" Alston sounded startled.

"No fixed position. But it should be moving into Earthsystem to rendezvous on your orbit. If the SP look for it, they'll find it."

Alston began to reply, but his voice blurred out for Harold. Almost as he'd stopped speaking, something had slammed into his back, below his right shoulder blade. The impact threw him out of the chair. He went on down to the floor, rolled over, twisting, on his left side, stopped, and had one of the guns in his right hand, pointed up.

Jake Hiskey's face was a smiling red mask as he leaned against the doorframe at the end of the room. There was a gun in his hand too, and he fired before Harold did. The charge shuddered into the transmitter stand behind Harold and crept quickly down. Harold pulled the trigger then, and Hiskey was flung back and fell beyond the doorframe, out of sight. Harold sucked air back into lungs that seemed tight as a clenched fist in his chest. Spent gun . . . or the hit where he'd taken it should have killed him outright. Jake had been too groggy to check that detail. Not that it was going to make very much difference.

Well, Jake, he thought, *perhaps that wasn't really the worst solution.*

The big room swung in circles overhead as he pulled himself against the stand and sat up. Then a voice was crying his name. Elisabeth.

"It's all right," Harold announced thickly, idiotically. "I stopped a hit, that's all."

Questions.

"Captain Hiskey wasn't quite as dead as I believed," he explained. "He's dead enough now."

The voices grew blurred. Harold decided he was, definitely, finished. It might take a while. But the charge, spent though it had been, would start him hemorrhaging. In an hour or two heart and lungs should be dying mush. Wicked guns, thorough guns—

" . . . Immediate medical attention . . ."

Oh, sure.

But he was listening now to what they were telling him, and abruptly he became alarmed. "No one can come in here," he said. "I told you why. Not even in armor. Lift the screens anywhere while the toziens are alive, and they'll pour through. They're too fast to stop. You'll have to wait till you know they're dead."

Then there was, they said, another way. Between this section and the next was a small emergency personnel lock—if he could follow their instructions, if he could reach it. A suit of armor couldn't pass through it, but Harold could. And once he was inside the lock, sensing devices would establish with complete reliability whether any Rilf toziens had entered it with him.

Harold considered that. It seemed foolproof.

"All right," he said. "We'll see if it works." He began struggling up to his feet. "Just keep those screens down."

Some while later he reached the main entry to the control room, glanced down at Jake Hiskey and turned to the right, as they'd said. Toziens went with him, drawn towards the only thing that still moved in the section. There came a passage, and another one, and a door and, behind the door, a small room. Harold entered the room and looked around. "I think I'm there," he said aloud.

"Yes, you're in the right room," Alston's voice told him. "You won't see the lock until it opens, but it's in the center of the wall directly opposite the door."

"Don't open it yet," Harold said. "They're here, too."

He got across the room. As Alston had told him, there was nothing in the smooth bare wall to suggest an emergency lock behind it, but he was lined up with the center of the door on the other side, as well as he could make it out; and he should be within a few feet, at most, of the lock.

"Professor Alston," he said.

"Yes?"

"I'm in front of the lock now. Wait till I give you the word. Then open it fast."

"We're ready," Alston said. "We'll know when you're inside."

Harold fished the two guns from his pockets, took them by their barrels in one hand, turned around. Supporting himself against the wall with his other hand, he lifted the guns and began waving them about. Tozien droning drew in towards the motion, thickening, zigzagging back and forth above and in front of him. Then he pitched the guns towards the far corner of the room.

The droning darted off with them. They hit the wall with a fine crash, went clattering to the floor. The air seethed noisily above them there.

"Now!" Harold said.

He saw the narrow dark opening appear in the wall two feet away, stumbled into it. After that, he seemed to go on stumbling down through soft darkness.

At first there was nothing. Then came an occasional vague awareness of time passing. A great deal of time . . . years of it, centuries of it . . . seemed to drift by steadily and slowly. Shadows began to appear, and withdrew again. Now and then a thought turned up. Some thoughts attracted other thoughts, clusters of them. Finally he found he had acquired a few facts. Facts had great value, he realized; they could be fitted together to form solid structures.

Carefully, painstakingly, he drew in more facts. His thoughts took to playing about them like schools of fish, shifting from one fact to another. Then there came a point at which it occurred to him that he really had a great many facts on hand now, and should start lining them up and putting them in order.

So he started doing it.

The first group was easy to assemble. In the process, he remembered suddenly having been told all this by one of the shadows:

The men left on the *Prideful Sue* had elected to put up a fight when the System Police boats arrived, and they'd put up a good one. (They should have, a stray thought added as an aside; he'd trained them.) But in the end the *Prideful Sue* was shot apart, and there'd been no survivors.

The Rilf ship, edging into Earthsystem, turned sullenly back when challenged. By the time it faded beyond the instrument range of its SP escort, it was a quarter of a light-year away from the sun, traveling steadily out.

That seemed to clear up one parcel of facts.

Other matters were more complex. He himself, for example—first just lying there, then riding about on one of the small brown cattle which had once been a wild species of Earth, finally walking again—remained something of a puzzle. There were periods when he was present so to speak, and evidently longer, completely vacant periods into which he dropped from time to time. When he came out of them, he didn't know where he'd been. He hadn't noticed it much at first; but then he began to find it disturbing.

"Well," Elisabeth said gently—she happened to be there when he started thinking seriously about this odd practice he'd developed—"the doctor said that, aside from more obvious physical damage, your nervous system got quite a bad jolt from that gun charge. But you are recovering, Harold."

So he was recovering. He decided to be satisfied with that. "How long has it been?" he asked.

"Not quite four weeks," said Elisabeth. She smiled. "You're really doing very well, Harold. What would you like me to show you today?"

"Let's look at some more of the things they're doing downstairs," Harold said.

Professor Derek Alston's asteroid also remained something of an enigma. In Mars Underground, and in the SP Academy's navigation school, the private asteroids had been regarded much as they were on Earthplanet, as individually owned pleasure resorts of the very rich which maintained no more contact with the rest of humanity than was necessary. Evidently they preferred to have that reputation. Elisabeth had told him it wasn't until she'd been a Solar U student for a few years that she'd learned gradually that the asteroids performed some of the functions of monasteries and castles in Earth's Middle Ages, built to preserve life, knowledge, and culture through the turbulence of wars and other disasters. They were storehouses of what had become, or was becoming, now lost on Earth, and their defenses made them very secure citadels. The plants and animals of the surface levels were living museums. Below the surface was a great deal more than that. In many respects they acted as individual extensions of Solar U, though they remained independent of it.

All of which seemed true, from what he had seen so far. But the thought came occasionally that it still mightn't be the complete picture. There were the projects, for one thing. This miniature planet, for all that it was an insignificant speck of cosmic debris, had, on the human scale, enormous quantities of cubic space. Very little of the space was in practical use, and that was used in an oddly diffused manner. There were several central areas which in their arrangement might have been part of a residential section of Mars Underground. Having lived mainly on an interstellar ship for the past eight years, Harold found himself reflecting on the fact that if the asteroid's population had been around a hundred times its apparent size, it would not have been unduly crowded. Elsewhere were the storerooms; and here Elisabeth loved to browse, and Harold browsed with her, though treasures of art and literature and the like were of less interest to him. Beautiful things perhaps, but dead.

And then the projects—Step into a capsule, a raindrop-shaped shell, glide through a system of curving tunnels, checking here and there to be fed through automatic locks; and you came to a project. Two or three or at most four people would be conducting it;

they already knew who you were, but you were introduced, and they showed you politely around. Elisabeth's interest in what they had to show was moderate. Harold's kept growing.

"You're running some rather dangerous experiments here," he remarked eventually to Derek Alston. This was on another day. There'd been only a scattered few of those blank periods lately.

Derek shook his head. "I don't run them," he said. "They're Solar U and SP projects. The asteroid merely provides facilities."

"Why do you let them set themselves up here?"

Derek Alston shrugged. "They have to be set up somewhere. If there should be some disastrous miscalculation, our defensive system will contain the damage and reduce the probable loss in human lives."

And the asteroid had, to be sure, a remarkable defensive system. For any ordinary purpose it seemed almost excessive. Harold had studied it and wondered again.

"In Eleven," he said, "they're working around with something on the order of a solar cannon. If they slip up on that one, you might find your defensive system strained."

Derek looked over at him.

"I believe you weren't supposed to know the purpose of that device," he said idly.

"They were a little misleading about that, as a matter of fact," said Harold. "But I came across something similar in the outsystems once."

"Yes, I imagine you've learned a great deal more there than they ever taught in navigation school." Derek scratched his head and looked owlish. "If you were to make a guess, what would you say was the real purpose of maintaining such projects on our asteroid? After all, I have to admit that the System Police and Solar

U are capable of providing equally suitable protective settings for them."

"The impression I've had," Harold told him, "is that they're being kept a secret from somebody. They're not the sort of thing likely to be associated with a private asteroid."

"No, not at all. Your guess is a good one. There are men, and there is mankind. Not quite the same thing. Mankind lost a major round on Earthplanet in this century and exists there only in fragments. And though men go to the outsystems, mankind hasn't reached them yet."

"You think it's here?"

"Here in Solar U, in the System Police, in major centers like Mars Underground. And on the private asteroids. Various shapes of the same thing. Yes, mankind is here, what's left of it at the moment. It has regrouped in Earthsystem and is building up."

Harold considered that. "Why make it a conspiracy?" he asked then. "Why not be open about it?"

"Because it's dangerous to frighten men. Earthplanet regards Earthsystem as an irritation. But it looks at our lack of obvious organization and purpose, our relatively small number, and it doesn't take alarm. It knows it would take disproportionate effort, tremendous unified effort, to wipe us out, and we don't seem worth it. So Earth's men continue with their grinding struggles and maneuverings which eventually are to give somebody control of the planet. By that time Earthsystem's mankind should not be very much concerned about Earthplanet's intentions towards it.

"The projects you've seen are minor ones. We move farther ahead of them every year, and our population grows steadily. Even now I doubt that the planet's full resources would be sufficient to interfere seriously with that process. But for the present we must conceal the strength we have and the strength we are obtaining. We want no trouble with Earth. Men will have their way there for a time, and then, whatever their designs, mankind will begin to evolve from them again, as it always does. It is a hardy thing. We can wait. . . ."

And that, Harold decided, had been upper echelon information, given him by one who might be among Earthsystem's present leaders. Elisabeth and Sally Alston had a general understanding of the situation but did not seem to be aware of the underlying purpose. Professor Alston evidently had made him an offer.

He thought about it, and presently a feeling began to grow in him, something like loss, something like loneliness. Elisabeth appeared to sense it and was disturbed.

Then another day. A gun was in his hand again, and in his other hand were the last three of a dozen little crystal globes he'd picked up in one of the machine shops. He swung them up, and they went flying away along a massive wall of asteroid rock. As they began to drop again, the gun snaked out and, in turn, each of the globes sparkled brightly and vanished.

He'd been aware of Derek Alston coming up from behind him before he fired; and now he pocketed the gun and turned.

"Very pretty shooting, friend!" Derek remarked. "I never was able to develop much skill with a handgun myself, but I enjoy watching an expert."

Harold shrugged. "I had the time, and the motivation, to put in a great deal of practice."

"No doubt." Derek held up a sheaf of papers. "Your final medical and psychological reports! It appears you've come all the way back. Care to look them over?"

Harold shook his head. "No. I've known for a couple

of days that I'd come all the way back." He patted the pocket which held the gun. "This was a test."

They regarded each other a moment. And now, Harold wondered, how was he going to say it? The Alstons had been more than generous hosts, and Derek took pride in what Earthsystem was accomplishing—with very good reason.

But he'd moved for eight years among the stars. And in spite of all the plans that had gone sour, and the ugliness which tarnished and finally destroyed the *Prideful Sue*, he'd found there what he'd been looking for. Earthsystem seemed dwindled and small. He couldn't possibly come back to it.

Make it brief, he thought.

"I'm not sure what I'll do next," he told Derek Alston. "But I'm shipping transsolar again."

"Well, I should hope so!" said Derek promptly.

"I was wondering whether you'd understand . . . Elisabeth in particular."

"Of course she understands! I do—we all do!" Derek smiled. "But before you start talking of leaving, there's one more project I must show you. It's one you should appreciate. . . ."

They stepped, a minute later, out of a capsule deep in the bowels of the asteroid, and went along a passage with steel bulkheads. A massive lock opened at their approach, and lights came on.

"Come on in and look around," Derek said. "This is our third control room. Not too many people know we have it."

Harold looked around the shining place. First incredulously, then with something like growing awe. He glanced at Derek Alston. "Mind if I check these?" he asked.

"Not at all. Go ahead."

Once, some two years before, he'd been in the

control room of Earthplanet's biggest, newest, and proudest outsystem transport. What he'd seen then was dwarfed, made trifling and clumsy, by what was here. His skin shivered with a lover's delight. "You have power to go with it?" he asked presently.

"We have the power."

"Where's the asteroid going on interstellar drives?"

"I told you mankind hadn't got to the outsystems yet," Derek said. "But it's ready to move there. We've been preparing for it. The outsystems won't know for a while that we're around—not till we're ready to let them know it."

"This asteroid is moving to the outsystems?"

"Not this one. Not for some years. We still have functions to perform here. But a few others—the first will be ready to start within the next three months. They can use an experienced transsolar navigator. They think they can also use a fighting captain with an outsystem background. If you're interested, I'll take you over to one of them this afternoon."

Harold drew in a long, deep breath.

"I'm interested," he said.

Gone Fishing

꩜

Barney Chard, thirty-seven—financier, entrepreneur, occasional blackmailer, occasional con man, and very competent in all these activities—stood on a rickety wooden lake dock, squinting against the late afternoon sun, and waiting for his current business prospect to give up the pretense of being interested in trying to catch fish.

The prospect, who stood a few yards farther up the dock, rod in one hand, was named Dr. Oliver B. McAllen. He was a retired physicist, though less retired than was generally assumed. A dozen years ago he had rated as one of the country's top men in his line. And, while dressed like an aging tramp in what he had referred to as fishing togs, he was at the moment potentially the country's wealthiest citizen. There was a clandestine invention he'd fathered which he called the McAllen Tube. The Tube was the reason Barney Chard had come to see McAllen.

Gently raising and lowering the fishing rod, and

blinking out over the quiet water, Dr. McAllen looked preoccupied with disturbing speculations not connected with his sport. The man had a secrecy bug. The invention, Barney thought, had turned out to be bigger than the inventor. McAllen was afraid of the Tube, and in the forefront of his reflections must be the inescapable fact that the secret of the McAllen Tube could no longer be kept without Barney Chard's co-operation. Barney had evidence of its existence, and didn't really need the evidence. A few hints dropped here and there would have made McAllen's twelve years of elaborate precaution quite meaningless.

Ergo, McAllen must be pondering now, how could one persuade Mr. Chard to remain silent?

But there was a second consideration Barney had planted in the old scientist's mind. Mr. Chard, that knowledgeable man of the world, exuded not at all by chance the impression of great quantities of available cash. His manner, the conservatively tailored business suit, the priceless chip of a platinum watch . . . and McAllen needed cash badly. He'd been fairly wealthy himself at one time; but since he had refrained from exploiting the Tube's commercial possibilities, his continuing work with it was exhausting his capital. At least that could be assumed to be the reason for McAllen's impoverishment, which was a matter Barney had established. In months the old man would be living on beans.

Ergo again, McAllen's thoughts must be running, how might one not merely coax Mr. Chard into silence, but actually get him to come through with some much-needed financial support? What inducement, aside from the Tube, could be offered someone in his position?

Barney grinned inwardly as he snapped the end of his cigarette out on the amber-tinted water. The mark always sells himself, and McAllen was well along in the process. Polite silence was all that was necessary at the moment. He lit a fresh cigarette, feeling a mild curiosity about the little lake's location. Wisconsin, Minnesota, Michigan seemed equally probable guesses. What mattered was that half an hour ago McAllen's Tube had brought them both here in a wink of time from his home in California.

Dr. McAllen thoughtfully cleared his throat. "Ever do any fishing, Mr. Chard?" he asked. After getting over his first shock at Barney's revelations, he'd begun speaking again in the brisk, abrupt manner Barney remembered from the last times he'd heard McAllen's voice.

"No," Barney admitted smiling. "Never quite got around to it."

"Always been too busy, eh?"

"With this and that," Barney agreed.

McAllen cleared his throat again. He was a roly-poly little man; over seventy now but still healthy-looking, with an apple-cheeked, sunburned face. Over a pair of steel-rimmed glasses his faded blue eyes peered musingly at Barney. "Around thirty-five, aren't you?"

"Thirty-seven."

"Married?"

"Divorced."

"Any particular hobbies?"

Barney laughed. "I play a little golf. Not very seriously."

McAllen clicked his tongue. "Well, what do you do for fun?"

"Oh . . . I'd say I enjoy almost anything I get involved in." Barney, still smiling, felt a touch of wariness. He'd been expecting questions from McAllen, but not quite this kind.

"Mainly making money, eh? Well," McAllen

conceded, "that's not a bad hobby. Practical, too. I . . . whup! Just a moment."

The tip of the slender rod in his left hand dipped slightly, and sixty feet out beyond the end of the old dock a green and white bobber began twitching about. Then the bobber suddenly disappeared. McAllen lifted the rod tip a foot or two with a smooth, swift motion, and paused.

"Hooked!" he announced, looking almost childishly pleased.

The fish on the far end of the line didn't seem to put up much of a struggle, but the old man reeled it in slowly and carefully, giving out line from time to time, then taking it back. He seemed completely absorbed. Not until the fish had been worked close to the dock was there a brief minor commotion near the surface. Then McAllen was down on one knee, holding the rod high with one hand, reaching out for his catch with the other. Barney had a glimpse of an unimpressive green and silver disk, reddish froggy eyes. "*Very* nice crappie," McAllen informed him with a broad smile. "Now—" He placed the rod on the dock, reached down with his other hand. The fish's tail slapped the water; it turned sideways, was gone.

"Lost it!" Barney commented, surprised.

"Huh?" McAllen looked around. "Well, no, young man—I *turned* him loose. He wasn't hooked bad. Crappies have delicate lips, but I use a barbless hook. Gives them better than a fighting chance." He stood up with the rod, dusting the knees of his baggy slacks. "Get all the eating fish I want anyway," he added.

"You really enjoy that sport, don't you?" Barney said curiously.

McAllen advised him with the seriousness of the true devotee to try it some time. "It gets to you. It can get to be a way of living. I've been fishing since

I was knee-high. Three years ago I figured I'd become good enough to write a book on the subject. I got more arguments over that book—sounder arguments too, I'd say—than about any paper I've published in physics." He looked at Barney a moment; still seriously, and went on. "I told you wetting a line would calm me down after that upset you gave me. Well, it has—fishing is as good a form of therapy as I know about. Now I've been doing some thinking. I'd be interested . . . well, I'd like to talk some more about the Tube with you, Mr. Chard. And perhaps about other things too."

"Very gratifying to hear that, doctor," Barney said gravely. "I did regret having to upset you, you know."

McAllen shrugged. "No harm done. It's given me some ideas. We'll talk right here." He indicated the weather-beaten little cabin on the bank behind Barney. "I'm not entirely sure about the California place. That's one reason I suggested this trip."

"You feel your houseman there mightn't be entirely reliable?"

"Fredericks unreliable? Heavens, no! He knows about the Tube, of course, but Fredericks expects me to invent things. It wouldn't occur to him to talk to an outsider. He's been with me for almost forty years."

"He was," remarked Barney, "listening in on the early part of our conversation today."

"Well, he'll do that," McAllen agreed. "He's very curious about anyone who comes to see me. But otherwise . . . no, it's just that in these days of sophisticated listening devices one shouldn't ever feel too sure of not being overheard."

"True enough." Barney glanced up at the cabin. "What makes you so sure of it here, doctor?"

"No reason why anyone would go to the trouble," McAllen said. "The property isn't in my name. And the nearest neighbor lives across the lake. I never come here except by the Tube so I don't attract any attention."

He led the way along the dock. Barney Chard followed, eyes reflectively on the back of McAllen's sunburned neck and the wisps of unclipped white hair sticking out beneath his beaked fishing cap. Barney had learned to estimate accurately the capacity for physical violence in people he dealt with. He would have offered long odds that neither Dr. McAllen nor Fredericks, the elderly colored man of all work, had the capacity. But Barney's right hand, slid idly into the pocket of his well-tailored coat, was resting on a twenty-five caliber revolver. This was, after all, a very unusual situation. The human factors in themselves were predictable. Human factors were Barney's specialty. But here they were involved with something unknown—the McAllen Tube.

When it was a question of his personal safety, Barney Chard preferred to take no chances at all.

From the top of the worn wooden steps leading up to the cabin, he glanced back at the lake. It occurred to him there should have been at least a suggestion of un-reality about that placid body of water, and the sun low and red in the west beyond it. Not that he felt anything of the kind. But less than an hour ago they had been sitting in McAllen's home in Southern California, and beyond the olive-green window shades it had been bright daylight.

"But I can't . . . I really can't imagine," Dr. McAllen had just finished bumbling, his round face a study of controlled dismay on the other side of the desk, "whatever could have brought you to these . . . these extraordinary conclusions, young man."

Barney had smiled reassuringly, leaning back in his chair. "Well, indirectly, sir, as the pictures indicate, we might say it was your interest in fishing. You see, I happened to notice you on Mallorca last month . . ."

By itself, the chance encounter on the island had seemed only moderately interesting. Barney was sitting behind the wheel of an ancient automobile, near a private home in which a business negotiation of some consequence was being conducted. The business under discussion happened to be Barney's, but it would have been inexpedient for him to attend the meeting in person. Waiting for his associates to wind up the matter, he was passing time by studying an old man who was fishing from a small boat offshore, a hundred yards or so below the road. After a while the old fellow brought the boat in, appeared a few minutes later along the empty lane carrying his tackle and an apparently empty gunny sack, and trudged unheedingly past the automobile and its occupant. As he went by, Barney had a sudden sense of recognition. Then in a flash, his mind jumped back twelve years.

Dr. Oliver B. McAllen. Twelve years ago the name had been an important one in McAllen's field; then it was not so much forgotten as deliberately buried. Working under government contract at one of the big universities, McAllen had been suddenly and quietly retired. Barney, who had a financial interest in one of the contracts, had made inquiries; he was likely to be out of money if McAllen had been taken from the job. Eventually he was informed, in strict confidence, that Dr. McAllen had flipped. Under the delusion of having made a discovery of tremendous importance, he had persuaded the authorities to arrange a demonstration. When the demonstration ended in complete failure, McAllen angrily accused some of his most eminent colleagues of having sabotaged his invention, and withdrew from the university.

To protect a once great scientist's name, the matter was being hushed up.

So Mallorca was where the addled old physicist had elected to end his days—not a bad choice either, Barney had thought, gazing after the retreating figure. Pleasant island in a beautiful sea—he remembered having heard about McAllen's passion for angling.

A day later, the Mallorca business profitably concluded, Barney flew back to Los Angeles. That evening he entertained a pair of tanned and shapely ladies whose idea of high fun was to drink all night and go deep-sea fishing at dawn. Barney shuddered inwardly at the latter notion, but promised to see the sporting characters to the Sweetwater Beach Municipal Pier in time to catch a party boat, and did so. One of the girls, he noticed not without satisfaction—he had become a little tired of the two before morning—appeared to turn a delicate green as she settled herself into the gently swaying half-day boat beside the wharf. Barney waved them an amiable farewell and was about to go when he noticed a plump old man sitting in the stern of the boat among other anglers, rigging up his tackle. Barney checked sharply, and blinked. He was looking at Oliver B. McAllen again.

It was almost a minute before he felt sure of it this time. Not that is was impossible for McAllen to be sitting in that boat, but it did seem extremely unlikely. McAllen didn't look in the least like a man who could afford nowadays to commute by air between the Mediterranean and California. And Barney felt something else trouble him obscurely as he stared down at the old scientist; a notion of some kind was stirring about in the back corridors of his mind, but refused to be drawn to view just then.

❖   ❖   ❖

He grew aware of what it was while he watched the party boat head out to sea a few minutes later, smiled at what seemed an impossibly fanciful concoction of his unconscious, and started towards the pier's parking lot. But when he had reached his car, climbed in, turned on the ignition, and lit a cigarette, the notion was still with him and Barney was no longer smiling. Fanciful it was; extremely so. Impossible, in the strict sense, it was not. The longer he played it around, the more he began to wonder whether his notion mightn't hold water after all. If there was anything to it, he had run into one of the biggest deals in history.

Later Barney realized he would still have let the matter drop there if it hadn't been for other things, having nothing to do with Dr. McAllen. He was between operations at present. His time wasn't occupied. Furthermore he'd been aware lately that ordinary operations had begun to feel flat. The kick of putting over a deal, even on some other hard, bright character of his own class, unaccountably was fading. Barney Chard was somewhat frightened because the operator game was the only one he'd ever found interesting; the other role of well-heeled playboy wasn't much more than a manner of killing time. At thirty-seven he was realizing he was bored with life. He didn't like the prospect.

Now here was something which might again provide him with some genuine excitement It could be simply his imagination working overtime, but it wasn't going to do any harm to find out. Mind humming with pleased though still highly skeptical speculations, Barney went back to the boat station and inquired when the party boat was due to return.

He was waiting for it, well out of sight, as it came chugging up to the wharf some hours later. He had never had anything to do directly with Dr. McAllen, so the old man wouldn't recognize him. But he didn't want to be spotted by his two amazons who might feel refreshed enough by now to be ready for another tour of the town.

He needn't have worried. The ladies barely made it to the top of the stairs; they phoned for a cab and were presently whisked away. Dr. McAllen meanwhile also had made a telephone call, and settled down not far from Barney to wait. A small gray car, five or six years old but of polished and well-tended appearance, trundled presently up the pier, came into the turn-around at the boat station, and stopped. A thin old Negro, with hair as white as the doctor's, held the door open for McAllen. The car moved unhurriedly off with them.

The automobile's license number produced Dr. McAllen's California address for Barney a short while later. The physicist lived in Sweetwater Beach, fifteen minutes' drive from the pier, in an old Spanish-type house back in the hills. The chauffeur's name was John Emanuel Fredericks; he had been working for McAllen for an unknown length of time. No one else lived there.

Barney didn't bother with further details about the Sweetwater Beach establishment at the moment. The agencies he usually employed to dig up background information were reasonably trustworthy, but he wanted to attract no more attention than was necessary to his interest in Dr. McAllen.

That evening he took a plane to New York.

Physicist Frank Elby was a few years older than Barney, an acquaintance since their university days. Elby was ambitious, capable, slightly dishonest; on occasion he provided Barney with contraband information for which he was generously paid.

Over lunch Barney broached a business matter

which would be financially rewarding to both of them, and should not burden Elby's conscience unduly. Elby reflected, and agreed. The talk became more general. Presently Barney remarked, "Ran into an old acquaintance of ours the other day. Remember Dr. McAllen?"

"Oliver B. McAllen? Naturally. Haven't heard about him in years. What's he doing?"

Barney said he had only seen the old man, hadn't spoken to him. But he was sure it was McAllen.

"Where was this?" Elby asked.

"Sweetwater Beach. Small town down the Coast."

Elby nodded. "It must have been McAllen. That's where he had his home."

"He was looking hale and hearty. They didn't actually institutionalize him at the time of his retirement, did they?"

"Oh, no. No reason for it. Except on the one subject of that cockeyed invention of his, he behaved perfectly normally. Besides he would have hired a lawyer and fought any such move. He had plenty of money. And nobody wanted publicity. McAllen was a pretty likable old boy."

"The university never considered taking him back?"

Elby laughed. "Well, hardly! After all, man—a matter transmitter!"

Barney felt an almost electric thrill of pleasure. Right on the nose, Brother Chard! Right on the nose.

He smiled. "Was that what it was supposed to be? I never was told all the details."

Elby said that for the few who were informed of the details it had been a seven-day circus. McAllen's reputation was such that more people, particularly on his staff, had been ready to believe him than were ready to admit it later. "When he'd left—you know, he never even bothered to take that 'transmitter' along— the thing was taken apart and checked over as carefully as if somebody thought it might still suddenly start working. But it was an absolute Goldberg, of course. The old man had simply gone off his rocker."

"Hadn't there been any indication of it before?"

"Not that I know of. Except that he'd been dropping hints about his gadget for several months before he showed it to anyone," Elby said indifferently. The talk turned to other things.

The rest was routine, not difficult to carry out. A small cottage on Mallorca, near the waterfront, was found to be in McAllen's name. McAllen's liquid assets were established to have dwindled to something less than those of John Emanuel Fredericks, who patronized the same local bank as his employer. There had been frequent withdrawals of large, irregular sums throughout the past years. The withdrawals were not explained by McAllen's frugal personal habits; even his fishing excursions showed an obvious concern for expense. The retention of the Mediterranean retreat, modest though it was, must have a reason beyond simple self-indulgence.

Barney arranged for the rental of a bungalow in the outskirts of Sweetwater beach, which lay uphill from the old house in which McAllen and Fredericks lived, and provided a good view of the residence and its street entry. He didn't go near the place himself. Operatives of a Los Angeles detective agency went on constant watch in the bungalow, with orders to photograph the two old men in the other house and any visitors at every appearance, and to record the exact times the pictures were taken. At the end of each day the photographs were delivered to an address from where they promptly reached Barney's hands.

A European agency was independently covering the Mallorca cottage in the same manner.

Nearly four weeks passed before Barney obtained the exact results he wanted. He called off the watch at both points, and next day came up the walk to McAllen's home and rang the doorbell. John Fredericks appeared, studied Barney's card and Barney with an air of mild disapproval, and informed him that Dr. McAllen did not receive visitors.

"So I've been told," Barney acknowledged pleasantly. "Please be so good as to give the doctor this."

Fredericks' white eyebrows lifted by the barest trifle as he looked at the sealed envelope Barney was holding out. After a moment's hesitation he took it, instructed Barney to wait, and closed the door firmly.

Listening to Fredericks' footsteps receding into the house, Barney lit a cigarette, and was pleased to find that his hands were as steady as if he had been on the most ordinary of calls. The envelope contained two sets of photographs, dated and indicating the time of day. The date was the same for both sets; the recorded time showed the pictures had been taken within fifteen minutes of one another. The central subject in each case was Dr. McAllen, sometimes accompanied by Fredericks. One set of photographs had been obtained on Mallorca, the other in Sweetwater Beach at McAllen's house.

Barring rocket assists, the two old men had been documented as the fastest moving human beings in all of history.

Several minutes passed before Fredericks reappeared. With a face which was now completely without expression, he invited Barney to enter, and conducted him to McAllen's study. The scientist had the photographs spread out on a desk before him. He gestured at them.

"Just what—if anything—is this supposed to mean, sir?" he demanded in an unsteady voice.

Barney hesitated, aware that Fredericks had remained in the hall just beyond the study. But Fredericks obviously was in McAllen's confidence. His eavesdropping could do no harm.

"It means this, doctor—" Barney began, amiably enough; and he proceeded to tell McAllen precisely what the photographs meant. McAllen broke in protestingly two or three times, then let Barney conclude his account of the steps he had taken to verify his farfetched hunch on the pier without further comment. After a few minutes Barney heard Fredericks' steps moving away, and then a door closing softly somewhere, and he shifted his position a trifle so that his right side was now toward the hall door. The little revolver was in the right-hand coat pocket. Even then Barney had no real concern that McAllen or Fredericks would attempt to resort to violence; but when people are acutely disturbed—and McAllen at least was—almost anything can happen.

When Barney finished, McAllen stared down at the photographs again, shook his head, and looked over at Barney.

"If you don't mind," he said, blinking behind his glasses, "I should like to think about this for a minute or two."

"Of course, doctor," Barney said politely. McAllen settled back in the chair, removed his glasses and half closed his eyes. Barney let his gaze rove. The furnishings of the house were what he had expected—well-tended, old, declining here and there to the downright shabby. The only reasonably new piece in the study was a radio-phonograph. The walls of the study and of the section of a living room he could see through a small archway were lined with crammed bookshelves. At the far end of the living room was a curious collection of clocks in various types and sizes, mainly antiques, but also some odd metallic pieces with modernistic faces. Vacancies in the rows indicated Fredericks might have begun to dispose discreetly of the more valuable items on his employer's behalf.

McAllen cleared his throat finally, opened his eyes, and settled the spectacles back on his nose.

"Mr. Chard," he inquired, "have you had scientific training?"

"No."

"Then," said McAllen, "the question remains of what your interest in the matter is. Perhaps you'd like to explain just why you put yourself to such considerable expense to intrude on my personal affairs—"

Barney hesitated perceptibly. "Doctor," he said, "there is something tantalizing about an enigma. I'm fortunate in having the financial means to gratify my curiosity when it's excited to the extent it was here."

McAllen nodded. "I can understand curiosity. Was that your only motive?"

Barney gave him his most disarming grin. "Frankly no. I've mentioned I'm a businessman—"

"Ah!" McAllen said, frowning.

"Don't misunderstand me. One of my first thoughts admittedly was that here were millions waiting to be picked up. But the investigation soon made a number of things clear to me."

"What were they?"

"Essentially, that you had so sound a reason for keeping your invention a secret that to do it you were willing to ruin yourself financially, and to efface yourself as a human being and as a scientist."

"I don't feel," McAllen observed mildly, "that I really have effaced myself, either as a human being or as a scientist."

"No, but as far as the public was concerned you did both."

McAllen smiled briefly. "That stratagem was very effective—until now. Very well, Mr. Chard. You understand clearly that under no circumstances would I agree to the commercialization of . . . well, of my matter transmitter?"

Barney nodded. "Of course."

"And you're still interested?"

"Very much so."

McAllen was silent a few seconds, biting reflectively at his lower lip. "Very well," he said again. "You were speaking of my predilection for fishing. Perhaps you'd care to accompany me on a brief fishing trip?"

"Now?" Barney asked.

"Yes, now. I believe you understand what I mean . . . I see you do. Then, if you'll excuse me for a few minutes—"

Barney couldn't have said exactly what he expected to be shown. His imaginings had run in the direction of a camouflaged vault beneath McAllen's house—some massively-walled place with machinery that powered the matter transmitter purring along the walls . . . and perhaps something in the style of a plastic diving bell as the specific instrument of transportation.

The actual experience was quite different. McAllen returned shortly, having changed into the familiar outdoor clothing—apparently he had been literal about going on a fishing trip. Barney accompanied the old physicist into the living room, and watched him open a small but very sturdy wall safe. Immediately behind the safe door, an instrument panel had been built in the opening.

Peering over the spectacles, McAllen made careful adjustments on two sets of small dials, and closed and locked the safe again.

"Now, if you'll follow me, Mr. Chard—" He crossed

the room to a door, opened it, and went out. Barney followed him into a small room with rustic furnishings and painted wooden walls. There was a single, heavily curtained window; the room was rather dim.

"Well," McAllen announced, "here we are."

It took a moment for that to sink in. Then, his scalp prickling eerily, Barney realized he was standing farther from the wall than he had thought. He looked around, and discovered there was no door behind him now, either open or closed.

He managed a shaky grin. "So that's how your matter transmitter works!"

"Well," McAllen said thoughtfully, "of course it isn't really a matter transmitter. I call it the McAllen Tube. Even an educated layman must realize that one can't simply disassemble a living body at one point, reassemble it at another, and expect life to resume. And there are other considerations—"

"Where are we?" Barney asked "On Mallorca?"

"No. We haven't left the continent—just the state. Look out the window and see for yourself."

McAllen turned to a built-in closet, and Barney drew back the window hangings. Outside was a grassy slope, uncut and yellowed by the summer sun. The slope dropped sharply to a quiet lakefront framed by dark pines. There was no one in sight, but a small wooden dock ran out into the lake. At the far end of the dock an old rowboat lay tethered. And—quite obviously— it was no longer the middle of a bright afternoon, the air was beginning to dim, to shift towards evening.

Barney turned to find McAllen's mild, speculative eyes on him, and saw the old man had put a tackle box and fishing rod on the table.

"Your disclosures disturbed me more than you may have realized," McAllen remarked by way of explanation. His lips twitched in the shadow of a smile. "At such times I find nothing quite so soothing as to drop a line into water for a while. I've some thinking to do, too. So let's get down to the dock. There ought to be a little bait left in the minnow pail."

When they returned to the cabin some time later, McAllen was in a pensive mood. He started a pot of coffee in the small kitchen, then quickly cleaned the tackle and put it away. Barney sat at the table, smoking and watching him, but made no attempt at conversation.

McAllen poured the coffee, produced sugar and powdered milk, and settled down opposite Barney. He said abruptly, "Have you had any suspicions about the reason for the secretive mumbo jumbo?"

"Yes," Barney said, "I've had suspicions. But it wasn't until that happened"—he waved his hand at the wall out of which they appeared to have stepped—"that I came to a definite conclusion."

"Eh?" McAllen's eyes narrowed suddenly. "What was the conclusion?"

"That you've invented something that's really a little too good."

"Too good?" said McAllen. "Hm-m-m. Go on."

"It doesn't take much power to operate the thing, does it?"

"Not," said McAllen dryly, "if you're talking about the kind of power one pays for."

"I am. Can the McAllen Tube be extended to any point on Earth?"

"I should think so."

"And you financed the building of this model yourself. Not very expensive. If the secret leaked out, I'd never know who was going to materialize in my home at any time, would I? Or with what intentions."

"That," McAllen nodded, "is about the size of it."

Barney crushed out his cigarette, lit a fresh one, blew out a thin streamer of smoke. "Under the circumstances," he remarked, "it's unfortunate you can't get the thing shut off again, isn't it?"

McAllen was silent for some seconds. "So you've guessed that, too," he said finally. "What mistake did I make?"

"None that I know of," Barney said. "But you're doing everything you can to keep the world from learning about the McAllen Tube. At the same time you've kept it in operation—which made it just a question of time before somebody else noticed something was going on, as I did. Your plans for the thing appear to have gone wrong."

McAllen was nodding glumly. "They have," he said. "They have, Mr. Chard. Not irreparably wrong, but still—" He paused. "The first time I activated the apparatus," he said, "I directed it only at two points. Both of them within structures which were and are my property. It was fortunate I did so."

"That was this cabin and the place on Mallorca?"

"Yes. The main operational sections of the Tube are concealed about my California home. But certain controls have to be installed at any exit point to make it possible to return. It wouldn't be easy to keep those hidden in any public place.

"It wasn't until I compared the actual performance of the Tube with my theoretical calculations that I discovered there was an unforeseen factor involved. To make it short, I could not—to use your phrasing—shut the Tube off again. But that would certainly involve some extremely disastrous phenomena at three different points of our globe."

"Explosions?" Barney asked.

"Weee-ll," McAllen said judiciously, "implosions might come a little closer to describing the effect. The exact term isn't contained in our vocabulary, and I'd prefer it not to show up there, at least in my lifetime. But you see my dilemma, don't you? If I asked for help, I revealed the existence of the Tube. Once its existence was known, the research that produced it could be duplicated. As you concluded, it isn't really too difficult a device to construct. And even with the present problem solved, the McAllen Tube is just a little too dangerous a thing to be at large in our world today."

"You feel the problem can be solved?"

"Oh, yes." McAllen took off his glasses and rubbed his eyes. "That part of it's only a matter of time. At first I thought I'd have everything worked out within three or four years. Unfortunately I badly underestimated the expense of some of the required experimentation. That's what's delayed everything."

"I see. I had been wondering," Barney admitted, "why a man with something like this on his mind would be putting in *quite* so much time fishing."

McAllen grinned. "Enforced idleness. It's been very irritating really, Mr. Chard. I've been obliged to proceed in the most inexpensive manner possible, and that meant—very slowly."

Barney said, "If it weren't for that question of funds, how long would it take to wind up the operation?"

"A year—perhaps two years." McAllen shrugged. "It's difficult to be too exact, but it certainly wouldn't be longer than two."

"And what would be the financial tab?"

McAllen hesitated. "A million is the bottom figure, I'm afraid. It should run closer to a million and a half."

"Doctor," Barney said, "let me make you a proposition."

McAllen looked at him. "Are you thinking of financing the experiments, Mr. Chard?"

"In return," Barney said, "for a consideration."

"What's that?" McAllen's expression grew wary.

"When you retired," Barney told him, "I dropped a nice piece of money as a consequence. It was the first beating I'd taken, and it hurt. I'd like to pick that money up again. All right. We're agreed it can't be done on the McAllen Tube. The Tube wouldn't help make the world a safer place for Barney Chard. But the Tube isn't any more remarkable than the mind that created it. Now I know a company which could be top of the heap in electronics precision work—one-shot specialties is what they go in for—if it had your mind as technical advisor. I can buy a controlling interest in that company tomorrow, doctor. And you can have the million and a half paid off in not much more time than you expect to take to get your monster back under control and shut down. Three years of your technical assistance, and we're clear."

McAllen's face reddened slowly. "I've considered hiring out, of course," he said. "Many times. I need the money very badly. But aren't you overlooking something?"

"What?"

"I went to considerable pains," said McAllen, "to establish myself as a lunatic. It was distasteful, but it seemed necessary to discourage anyone from making too close an investigation of some of my more recent lines of research. If it became known now that I was again in charge of a responsible project—"

Barney shook his head. "No problem, doctor. We'd be drawing on outside talent for help in specific matters—very easy to cover up any leads to you personally. I've handled that general sort of thing before."

McAllen frowned thoughtfully. "I see. But I'd have— There wouldn't be so much work that—"

"No," Barney said. "I guarantee that you'll have all

the time you want for your own problem." He smiled. "Considering what you told me, I'd like to hear that one's been solved myself!"

McAllen grinned briefly. "I can imagine. Very well. Ah . . . when can you let me have the money, Mr. Chard?"

The sun was setting beyond the little lake as Barney drew the shades over the cabin window again. Dr. McAllen was half inside the built-in closet at the moment, fitting a pair of toggle switches to the concealed return device in there.

"Here we go," he said suddenly.

Three feet from the wall of the room the shadowy suggestion of another wall, and of an open door, became visible.

Barney said dubiously, "We came out of *that*?"

McAllen looked at him, sad, "The appearance is different on the exit side. But the Tube's open now— Here, I'll show you."

He went up to the apparition of a door, abruptly seemed to melt into it. Barney held his breath, and followed. Again there was no sensory reaction to passing through the Tube. As his foot came down on something solid in the shadowiness into which he stepped, the living room in Sweetwater Beach sprang into sudden existence about him.

"Seems a little odd from that end, the first time through, doesn't it?" McAllen remarked.

Barney let out his breath.

"If I'd been the one who invented the Tube," he said honestly, "I'd never have had the nerve to try it."

McAllen grinned. "Tell you the truth, I did need a drink or two the first time. But it's dead-safe if you know just what you're doing."

Which was not, Barney felt, too reassuring. He

looked back. The door through which they had come was the one by which they had left. But beyond it now lay a section of the entrance hall of the Sweetwater Beach house.

"Don't let that fool you," said McAllen, following his gaze. "If you tried to go out into the hall at the moment, you'd find yourself right back in the cabin. Light rays passing through the Tube can be shunted off and on." He went over to the door, closed and locked it, dropping the key in his pocket. "I keep it locked. I don't often have visitors, but if I had one while the door was open it could be embarrassing."

"What about the other end?" Barney asked. "The door appeared in the cabin when you turned those switches. What happens now? Suppose someone breaks into the cabin and stares prowling around—is the door still there?"

McAllen shook his head. "Not unless that someone happened to break in within the next half-minute." He considered. "Let's put it this way: The Tube's permanently centered on its two exit points, but the effect ordinarily is dissipated over half a mile of the neighborhood at the other end. For practical purposes there is no useful effect. When I'm going to go through, I bring the exit end down to a focus point . . . does this make sense? Very well. It remains focused for around sixty or ninety seconds, depending on how I set it; then it expands again." He nodded at the locked door. "In the cabin, that's disappeared by now. Walk through the space where it's been, and you'll notice nothing unusual. Clear?"

Barney hesitated. "And if that door were still open here, and somebody attempted to step through after the exit end had expanded—"

"Well," McAllen said, moving over to a wall buzzer and pressing it. "that's what I meant when I said it could be embarrassing. He'd get expanded too—disastrously. Could you use a drink, Mr. Chard? I know I want one."

The drinks, served by Fredericks. were based on a rather rough grade of bourbon, but Barney welcomed them. There was an almost sick fascination in what was a certainty now: he was going to get the Tube. That tremendous device was his for the taking. He was well inside McAllen's guard; only carelessness could arouse the old man's suspicions again, and Barney was not going to be careless. No need to hurry anything. He would play the reserved role he had selected for himself, leave developments up to the fact that McAllen had carried the burden of his secret for twelve years, with no more satisfactory confidant than Fredericks to trust with it. Having told Barney so much, McAllen wanted to tell more. He would have needed very little encouragement to go on talking about it now.

Barney offered no encouragement. Instead, he gave McAllen a cautiously worded reminder that it was not inconceivable they had an audience here, at which McAllen reluctantly subsided. There was, however, one fairly important question Barney still wanted answered today. The nature of the answer would tell him the manner in which McAllen should now be handled.

He waited until he was on his feet and ready to leave before presenting it. McAllen's plump cheeks were flushed from the two highballs he had put away. In somewhat awkward phrases he had been expressing his gratitude for Barney's generous help, and his relief that because of it the work on the Tube now could be brought to an end.

"Just one thing about that still bothers me a little, doctor," Barney said candidly.

McAllen looked concerned "What's that, Mr. Chard?"

"Well . . . you're in good health, I'd say." Barney smiled. "But suppose something did happen to you before you succeeded in shutting the McAllen Tube down." He inclined his head toward the locked door. "That thing would still be around waiting for somebody to open it and step through . . ."

McAllen's expression of concern vanished. He dug a forefinger cheerfully into Barney's ribs. "Young man, you needn't worry. I've been aware of the possibility, of course, and believe me I'm keeping very careful notes and instructions. Safe deposit boxes . . . we'll talk about that tomorrow, eh? Somewhere else? Had a man in mind, as a matter of fact, but we can make better arrangements now. You see, it's really so ridiculously *easy* at this stage."

Barney cleared his throat. "Some other physicist—?"

"*Any* capable physicist," McAllen said decidedly. "Just a matter, you see of how reliable he is." He winked at Barney. "Talk about that tomorrow too—or one of these days."

Barney stood looking down, with a kind of detached surprise, at a man who had just pronounced sentence of death casually on himself; and on an old friend. For the first time in Barney's career, the question of deliberate murder not only entered an operation, but had become in an instant an unavoidable part of it. Frank Elby, ambitious and money-hungry, could take over where McAllen left off. Elby was highly capable, and Elby could be controlled. McAllen could not. He could only be tricked; and, if necessary, killed.

It was necessary, of course. If McAllen lived until he knew how to shut the Tube down safely, he simply would shut it down, destroy the device and his notes on it. A man who had gone to such extreme lengths to safeguard the secret was not going to be talked out of his conviction that the McAllen Tube was a menace to the world. Fredericks, the morose eavesdropper, had to be silenced with his employer to assure Barney of his undisputed possession of the Tube.

Could he still let the thing go, let McAllen live? He couldn't, Barney decided. He'd dealt himself a hand in a new game, and a big one—a fantastic, staggering game when one considered the possibilities in the Tube. It meant new interest, it meant life for him. It wasn't in his nature to pull out. The part about McAllen was cold necessity. A very ugly necessity, but McAllen— pleasantly burbling something as they walked down the short hall to the front door—already seemed a little unreal, a roly-poly, muttering, fading small ghost.

In the doorway Barney exchanged a few words—he couldn't have repeated them an instant later—with the ghost, became briefly aware of a remarkably firm hand clasp, and started down the cement walk to the street. Evening had come to California at last; a few houses across the street made dim silhouettes against the hills, some of the windows lit. He felt, Barney realized, curiously tired and depressed. A few steps behind him, he heard McAllen quietly closing the door to his home.

The walk, the garden, the street, the houses and hills beyond, vanished in a soundlessly violent explosion of white light around Barney Chard.

His eyes might have been open for several seconds before he became entirely aware of the fact. He was on his back looking up at the low raftered ceiling of a room. The light was artificial, subdued; it gave the impression of nighttime outdoors. Memory suddenly blazed up. "Tricked!" came the first thought. Outsmarted. Outfoxed. And by—

Then that went lost in a brief, intense burst of relief at the realization he was still alive, apparently unhurt.

Barney turned sharply over on his side—bed underneath, he discovered—and stared around.

The room was low, wide. Something indefinably
odd—

He catalogued it quickly. Redwood walls, Navaho
rugs on the floor, bookcases, unlit fireplace, chairs,
table, desk with a typewriter and reading lamp. Across
the room a tall dark grandfather clock with a bright
metal disk instead of a clock-face stood against the wall.
From it came a soft, low thudding as deliberate as the
heartbeat of some big animal. It was the twin of one
of the clocks he had seen in McAllen's living room.

The room was McAllen's, of course. Almost luxurious by comparison with his home, but wholly typical of the man. And now Barney became aware of its
unusual feature; there were no windows. There was one
door, so far to his right he had to twist his head around
to see it. It stood half open; beyond it a few feet of
a narrow passage lay within his range of vision, lighted
in the same soft manner as the room. No sound came
from there.

Had he been left alone? And what had happened?
He wasn't in McAllen's home or in that fishing shack
at the lake. The Tube might have picked him up—
somehow—in front of McAllen's house, transported him
to the Mallorca place. Or he might be in a locked
hideaway McAllen had built beneath the Sweetwater
Beach house.

Two things were unpleasantly obvious. His investigations hadn't revealed all of McAllen's secrets. And
the old man hadn't really been fooled by Barney
Chard's smooth approach. Not, at any rate, to the extent
of deciding to trust him.

Hot chagrin at the manner in which McAllen had
handed the role of dupe back to him flooded Barney
for a moment. He swung his legs over the side of the

bed and stood up. His coat had been hung neatly over
the back of a chair a few feet away; his shoes stood
next to the bed. Otherwise he was fully clothed.
Nothing in the pockets of the coat appeared to have
been touched; billfold, cigarette case, lighter, even the
gun, were in place; the gun, almost startlingly, was still
loaded. Barney thrust the revolver thoughtfully into his
trousers pocket. His wrist watch seemed to be the only
item missing.

He glanced about the room again, then at the
half-open door and the stretch of narrow hallway
beyond. McAllen must have noticed the gun. The
fact that he hadn't bothered to take it away, or at
least to unload it, might have been reassuring under
different circumstances. Here, it could have a very
disagreeable meaning. Barney went quietly to the
door, stood listening a few seconds, became convinced there was no one within hearing range, and
moved on down the hall.

In less than two minutes he returned to the room,
with the first slow welling of panic inside him. He
had found a bathroom, a small kitchen and pantry,
a storage room twice as wide and long as the rest
of the place combined, crammed with packaged and
crated articles, and with an attached freezer. If it was
mainly stored food, as Barney thought, and if there
was adequate ventilation and independent power, as
seemed to be the case, then McAllen had constructed
a superbly self-sufficient hideout. A man might live
comfortably enough for years without emerging from
it.

There was only one thing wrong with the setup from
Barney's point of view. The thing he'd been afraid of.
Nowhere was there an indication of a window or of
an exit door.

The McAllen Tube, of course, might make such

ordinary conveniences unnecessary. And if the Tube was
the only way in or out, then McAllen incidentally had
provided himself with an escape-proof jail for anyone
he preferred to keep confined. The place might very
well have been built several hundred feet underground.
A rather expensive proposition but, aside from that,
quite feasible.

Barney felt his breath begin to quicken, and told
himself to relax. Wherever he was, he shouldn't be here
long. McAllen presently would be getting in contact
with him. And then—

His glance touched the desk across the room, and
now he noticed his missing wrist watch on it. He went
over, picked it up, and discovered that the long white
envelope on which the watch had been placed was
addressed to him.

For a moment he stared at the envelope. Then, his
fingers shaking a little, he tore open the envelope and
pulled out the typewritten sheets within.

The letterhead, he saw without surprise, was
OLIVER B. McALLEN.

The letter read:

> Dear Mr. Chard:
> An unfortunate series of circumstances,
> combined with certain character traits in your-
> self, make it necessary to inconvenience you
> in a rather serious manner.
>
> To explain: The information I gave you
> regarding the McAllen Tube and my own
> position was not entirely correct. It is not the
> intractable instrument I presented it as being—
> it can be "shut off" again quite readily and
> without any attendant difficulties. Further, the
> decision to conceal its existence was not

reached by myself alone. For years we—that is, Mr. Fredericks, who holds a degree in engineering and was largely responsible for the actual construction of the Tube—and I, have been members of an association of which I cannot tell you too much. But I may say that it acts, among other things, as the present custodian of some of the more dangerous products of human science, and will continue to do so until a more stable period permits their safe release.

To keep developments such as the McAllen Tube out of irresponsible hands is no easy task these days, but a variety of effective devices are employed to that end. In this instance, you happened upon a "rigged" situation, which had been designed to draw action from another man, an intelligent and unscrupulous individual who lately had indicated a disturbing interest in events connected with the semipublic fiasco of my "matter transmitter" some years ago. The chances of another person becoming aware of the temporal incongruities which were being brought to this man's attention were regarded as so remote that they need be given no practical consideration. Nevertheless, the unexpected happened: you became interested. The promptness with which you acted on your chance observations shows a bold and imaginative manner of thinking on which you may be genuinely congratulated.

However, a perhaps less commendable motivation was also indicated. While I appeared to stall on coming to decisions you may have regarded as inevitable, your background was being investigated by the association. The investigation confirmed that you fall within a personality category of which we have the greatest reason to be wary.

Considering the extent of what you had surmised and learned, falsified though the picture was, this presented a serious problem. It was made more acute by the fact that the association is embarking on a "five-year-plan" of some importance. Publicity during this period would be more than ordinarily undesirable. It will therefore be necessary to see to it that you have no opportunity to tell what you know before the plan is concluded. I am sure you can see it would be most unwise to accept your simple word on the matter. Your freedom of movement and of communication must remain drastically restricted until this five-year period is over.

Within the next two weeks, as shown by the clock in your quarters, it will have become impossible for me or for any member of the association to contact you again before the day of your release. I tell you this so that you will not nourish vain hopes of changing the situation in your favor, but will adjust as rapidly as you can to the fact that you must spend the next five years by yourself. What ameliorations of this basic condition appeared possible have been provided.

It is likely that you will already have tried to find a way out of the cabin in which you were left. The manner of doing this will become apparent to you exactly twenty-four hours after I conclude and seal this letter. It seemed best to advise you of some details of your confinement before letting you discover

that you have been given as much limited freedom as circumstances allowed.

    Sincerely yours,
    OLIVER B. McALLEN

Barney dropped the letter on the desk, stared down
at it, his mouth open. His face had flushed red. "Why,
he's crazy!" he said aloud at last. "He's crazier than—"
He straightened, looked uneasily about the room again.

Whether a maniac McAllen made a more desirable
jailer than a secret association engaged in keeping
dangerous scientific developments under cover could
be considered an open question. The most hopeful
thought was that Dr. McAllen was indulging an unsuspected and nasty sense of humor.

Unfortunately, there wasn't the slightest reason to
believe it. McAllen was wise to him. The situation was
no gag—and neither was it necessarily what McAllen
wanted him to think. Unless his watch had been reset,
he had been knocked out by whatever hit him for
roughly five hours—or seventeen, he amended. But he
would have been hungry if it had been the longer
period; and he wasn't.

Five hours then. Five hours wouldn't have given
them time to prepare the "cabin" as it was prepared:
for someone's indefinite stay. At a guess, McAllen had
constructed it as a secure personal retreat in the event
of something like a nuclear holocaust. But, in that case,
why vacate it now for Barney Chard?

Too many questions, he thought. Better just keep
looking around.

The blank metal face on the grandfather clock
swung back to reveal a group of four dials, each
graduated in a different manner, only one of them
immediately familiar. Barney studied the other three

for some seconds; then their meaning suddenly came clear. The big clock had just finished softly talking away the fourth hour of the first day of the first month of Year One. There were five figures on the Year Dial.

He stared at it. A five-year period of—something seemed to be the key to the entire setup.

Barney shook his head. Key it might be, but not one he could read without additional data. He snapped the cover disk shut on the unpleasantly suggestive dials, and began to go mentally over McAllen's letter.

The business that in twenty-four hours—twenty now—the manner of leaving the cabin would become "apparent" to him—that seemed to dispose of the possibility of being buried underground here. McAllen would hardly have provided him with a personal model of the Tube; he must be speaking of an ordinary door opening on the immediate environment, equipped with a time lock.

In that case, where was the door?

Barney made a second, far more careful search. Three hours later, he concluded it. He'd still found no trace of an exit. But the paneling in any of the rooms might slide aside to reveal one at the indicated time, or a section of the floor might swing back above a trap door. There was no point in attempting to press the search any further. After all, he only had to wait.

On the side, he'd made other discoveries. After opening a number of crates in the storage room, and checking contents of the freezer, he could assume that there was in fact more than enough food here to sustain one man for five years. Assuming the water supply held out—there was no way of checking on it; the source of the water like that of the power and the ventilation lay outside the area which was accessible to him—but if the water could be depended on, he wouldn't go hungry or thirsty. Even tobacco and liquor were present in comparably liberal quantities. The liquor he'd seen was all good; almost at random he had selected a bottle of cognac and brought it and a glass to the main room with him. The thought of food wasn't attractive at the moment. But he could use a drink.

He half filled the glass, emptied it with a few swallows, refilled it and took it over to one of the armchairs. He began to feel more relaxed almost at once. But the truth was, he acknowledged, settling back in the chair, that the situation was threatening to unnerve him completely. Everything he'd seen implied McAllen's letter came close to stating the facts; what wasn't said became more alarming by a suggestion of deliberate vagueness. Until that melodramatically camouflaged door was disclosed—seventeen hours from now—he'd be better off if he didn't try to ponder the thing out.

And the best way to do that might be to take a solid load on rapidly, and then sleep away as much of the intervening time as possible.

He wasn't ordinarily a hard drinker, but he'd started on the second bottle before the cabin began to blur on him. Afterwards, he didn't remember making it over to the bed.

Barney woke up ravenous and without a trace of hangover. Making a mental adjustment to his surroundings took no more time than opening his eyes; he'd been dreaming Dr. McAllen had dropped him into a snake pit and was sadistically dangling a rope twelve feet above his head, inviting him to climb out. To find himself still in the softly lit cabin was—for a few seconds, at any rate—a relief.

The relief faded as he sat up and looked at his watch. Still over an hour to go before McAllen's idiotic door became "apparent." Barney swore and headed for the bathroom to freshen up.

There was an electric shaver there, the end of its cord vanishing into the wall. Barney used it as meticulously as if he were embarking on a day of normal activities, prepared a breakfast in the kitchen and took it to the main room. He ate unhurriedly, absorbed in his thoughts, now and then glancing about the room. After a few minutes he uneasily pushed back the plate and stood up. If McAllen's twenty-four hours began with the moment the big clock in the room had been started, the door should be in evidence by now.

Another tour of the place revealed nothing and left him nervous enough to start biting his nails. He moved about the room, looking over things he'd already investigated. A music cabinet—he'd thought it was a radio at first, but it was only an elaborate hi-fi record player; two enclosed racks of records went with it—mainly classical stuff apparently. And a narrow built-in closet with three polished fishing rods and related gear, which would have allowed for speculation on the nature of the cabin's surroundings, except that McAllen might feel compelled to have a sampling of his toys around him wherever he was. Barney closed the closet door morosely, stood regarding the two crowded bookcases next to it. Plenty of books reflecting the McAllen taste again. Technical tomes. Great Literature. Dickens, Melville, the Life of Gandhi.

Barney grunted, and was turning away when another title caught his eye. He glanced back at it, hauled out the book:

"Fresh Water Game Fish; Tested Methods of Their Pursuit." The author: O. B. McAllen.

Barney was opening the book when the cabin's door also opened.

❖   ❖   ❖

Bright light—daylight—filled the room with so sudden a gush that Barney's breath caught in his throat. The book seemed to leap out of his hands. With the same glance he saw then the low, wide picture window which abruptly had appeared in the opposite wall, occupying almost half its space—and, in the other wall on the far left, a big door which was still swinging slowly open into the room. Daylight poured in through window and door. And beyond them—

For seconds he stared at the scene outside, barely aware of what he was looking at, while his mind raced on. He had searched every inch of the walls. And those thick wooden panels hadn't simply slid aside; the surfaces of doorframe and window were flush with the adjoining wall sections. So the McAllen Tube was involved in these changes in the room—and he might have guessed, Barney thought, that McAllen would have found more than one manner of putting the space-twisting properties of his device to use. And then finally he realized what he was seeing through the window and beyond the door. He walked slowly up to the window, still breathing unevenly.

The scene was unfamiliar but not at all extraordinary. The cabin appeared to be part way up one side of a heavily forested, rather narrow valley. It couldn't be more than half a mile to the valley's far slope which rose very steeply, almost like a great cresting green wave, filling the entire window. Coming closer Barney saw the skyline above it, hazy, summery, brilliantly luminous. This cabin of McAllen's might be in one of the wilder sections of the Canadian Rockies.

Or—and this was a considerably less happy thought—it probably could have been set up just as well in some area like the Himalayas.

But a more immediate question was whether the cabin actually was in the valley or only appearing to be there. The use of the Tube made it possible that this room and its seeming surroundings were very far apart in fact. And just what would happen to him then if he decided to step outside?

There were scattered sounds beyond the open door: bird chirpings and whistles, and the continuous burring calls of what Barney decided would be a wild pigeon. Then a swirl of wind stirred the nearer branches. He could feel the wash of the breeze in the room.

It looked and sounded—and felt—all right.

Barney scowled undecidedly, clearing his throat, then discovered that a third item had appeared in the room along with the door and the window. In the wall just this side of the door at shoulder-height was a small ivory plate with two black switches on it. Presumably the controls for door and window . . .

Barney went over, gingerly touched the one on the right, watching the window; then flicked up the switch. Instantly, the window had vanished, the wood paneling again covered the wall. Barney turned the switch down. The window was back.

The door refused to disappear until he pushed it shut. Then it obeyed its switch with the same promptness.

He went back across the room, returned with one of McAllen's fishing poles, and edged its tip tentatively out through the door. He wouldn't have been surprised if the tip had disintegrated in that instant. But nothing at all occurred. He dug about with the pole in the loose earth beyond the doorsill, then drew it back. The breeze was flowing freely past him; a few grains of soil blew over the sill and into the room. The door seemed to be concealing no grisly tricks and looked to be safe enough.

Barney stepped out on the sill, moved on a few

hesitant steps, stood looking about. He had a better view of the valley here—and the better view told him immediately that he was not in the Canadian Rockies. At least, Canada, to his knowledge, had no desert. And, on the left, this valley came to an end perhaps a little more than a mile away from the cabin, its wooded slopes flowing steeply down to a landscape which was dull rust-red—flat sand stretches alternating with worn rock escarpments, until the desert's rim rose toward and touched the hazy white sky. Not so very different from—

Barney's eyes widened suddenly. Could he be in the Sierras—perhaps not more than three or four hours' drive from Los Angeles?

Three or four hours' drive if he'd had a car, of course. But even so—

He stared around, puzzled. There were no signs of a human being, of human habitation. But somebody else must be here. Somebody to keep guard on him. Otherwise there was nothing to stop him from walking away from this place—though it might very well be a long, uncomfortable hike to any civilized spot.

Even if this did turn out to be the Himalayas, or some equally remote area, there must be hill tribes about if one went far enough—there should even be an occasional airplane passing overhead.

Barney stood just outside the door, frowning, pondering the situation again, searching for the catch in it. McAllen and his friends, whatever else they might be, weren't stupid. There was something involved here that he hadn't become aware of yet.

Almost without thought then, he turned up his head, squinting at the bright hazy sky above him—

And saw IT.

His breath sucked in and burst from his lungs in a half-strangled, terrified squawk as he staggered backward into the cabin, slammed the door shut, then spun around and began slapping frantically at the switches on the wall-plate until door and window were gone, and only the cabin's soft illumination was around him again. Then he crouched on the floor, his back against the wall, shaking with a terror he could hardly have imagined before.

He knew what the catch was now. He had understood it completely in the instant of glancing up and seeing that tiny brilliant blue-white point of light glare down at him through the incandescent cloud layers above. Like a blazing, incredibly horrible insect eye . . .

This world's sun.

THE END OF YEAR ONE

Barney Chard came up out of an uneasy sleep to the sudden sharp awareness that something was wrong. For some seconds he lay staring about the unlit cabin, mouth dry, heart hammering with apprehension. Then he discovered it was only that he had left the exit door open and the window switched on . . . Only? This was the first time since they had left him here that he had gone to sleep without sealing the cabin first—even when blind drunk, really embalmed.

He thought of climbing out of bed and taking care of it now, but decided to let the thing ride. After all he knew there was nothing in the valley—nothing, in fact, on this world—of which he had a realistic reason to be afraid. And he felt dead tired. Weak and sick. Feeling like that no longer alarmed him as it had done at first; it was a simple physical fact. The sheet under him was wet with sweat, though it was no more than comfortably warm in the room. The cabin never became more than comfortably warm. Barney lay back again, trying to figure out how it had happened he had forgotten about the window and the door.

It had been night for quite a while when he went to sleep, but regardless of how long he'd slept, it was going to go on being night a good deal longer. The last time he had bothered to check—which, Barney decided on reflection, might be several months ago now—the sunless period had continued for better than fifty-six hours. Not long before dropping on the bed, he was standing in front of the big clock while the minute hand on the hour dial slid up to the point which marked the end of the first year in Earth time he had spent in the cabin. Watching it happen, he was suddenly overwhelmed again by the enormity of his solitude, and it looked as if it were going to turn into another of those periods when he sat with the gun in his hand, sobbing and swearing in a violent muddle of self-pity and helpless fury. He decided to knock off the lamenting and get good and drunk instead. And he would make it a drunk to top all drunks on this happy anniversary night.

But he hadn't done that either. He had everything set up, downright festively—glasses, crushed ice, a formidable little squad of fresh bottles. But when he looked at the array, he suddenly felt sick in advance. Then there was a wave of leaden heaviness, of complete fatigue. He hadn't had time to think of sealing the cabin. He had simply fallen into the bed then and there, and for all practical purposes passed out on the spot.

Barney Chard lay wondering about that. It had been, one might say, a rough year. Through the long days in particular, he had been doing his level best to obliterate his surroundings behind sustained fogs of alcoholism. The thought of the hellishly brilliant far-off star around which this world circled, the awareness that only the roof and walls of the cabin were between himself and that blazing alien watcher, seemed entirely unbearable. The nights, after a while, were easier to take. They had their strangeness too, but the difference wasn't so great. He grew accustomed to the big green moon, and developed almost an affection for a smaller one, which was butter-yellow and on an orbit that made it a comparatively infrequent visitor in the sky over the valley. By night he began to leave the view window in operation and finally even the door open for hours at a time. But he had never done it before when he wanted to go to sleep.

Alcoholism, Barney decided, stirring uneasily on the sweat-soiled, wrinkled sheet, hadn't been much of a success. His body, or perhaps some resistant factor in his mind, let him go so far and no farther. When he exceeded the limit, he became suddenly and violently ill. And remembering the drunk periods wasn't pleasant. Barney Chard, that steel-tough lad, breaking up, going to pieces, did not make a pretty picture. It was when he couldn't keep that picture from his mind that he most frequently had sat there with the gun, turning it slowly around in his hand. It had been a rather close thing at times.

Perhaps he simply hated McAllen and the association too much to use the gun. Drunk or sober, he brooded endlessly over methods of destroying them. He had to be alive when they came back. Some while ago there had been a space of several days when he was hallucinating the event, when McAllen and the association seemed to be present, and he was arguing with them, threatening them, even pleading with them. He came out of that period deeply frightened by what he was doing. Since then he hadn't been drinking as heavily.

But this was the first time he'd gone to sleep without drinking at all.

He sat up on the edge of the bed, found himself shaking a little again after that minor effort, but climbed to his feet anyway, and walked unsteadily over to the door. He stood there looking out. The cloud layers always faded away during the night, gathered again at dawn. By now the sky was almost clear. A green glow over the desert to the left meant the larger moon was just below the horizon. The little yellow moon rode high in the sky above it. If they came up together, this would be the very bright part of the night during which the birds and other animal life in the valley went about their pursuits as if it were daytime. He could hear bird-chirpings now against the restless mutter of the little stream which came down the center of the valley, starting at the lake at the right end and running out into stagnant and drying pools a short distance after it entered the desert.

He discovered suddenly he had brought the gun along from the bed with him and was holding it without having been in the least aware of the fact. Grinning twistedly at the old and pointless precaution, he shoved the gun into his trousers pocket, brought out matches, a crumpled pack of cigarettes, and began to smoke. Very considerate of them to see to it he wouldn't run out of minor conveniences . . . like leaving him liquor enough to drink himself to death any time he felt like it during these five years.

Like leaving him the gun—

From the association's standpoint those things were up to him, of course, Barney thought bitterly. In either unfortunate event, he wouldn't be on *their* consciences.

He felt a momentary spasm of the old hate, but a feeble one, hardly more than a brief wash of the early torrents of rage. Something had burned out of him these months; an increasing dullness was moving into its place—

And just what, he thought, startled, was he doing outside the cabin door now? He hadn't consciously decided to go that far; it must have been months, actually, since he had walked beyond the doorway at all. During the first few weeks he had made half a dozen attempts to explore his surroundings by night, and learned quickly that he was confined to as much of the valley as he could see from the cabin. Beyond the ridges lay naked desert and naked mountain ranges, silent and terrifying in the moonlight.

Barney glanced up and down the valley, undecided but not knowing quite what he was undecided about. He didn't feel like going back into the cabin, and to just stand here was boring.

"Well," he said aloud, sardonically, "it's a nice night for a walk, Brother Chard."

Well, why not? It was bright enough to see by now if he kept away from the thickest growths of trees, and getting steadily brighter as the big moon moved up behind the distant desert rim. He'd walk till he got tired, then rest. By the time he got back to the cabin he'd be ready to lie down and sleep off the curious mood that had taken hold of him.

Barney started off up the valley, stepping carefully and uncertainly along the sloping, uneven ground.

During the early weeks he had found a thick loose-leaf binder in the back of one of the desk drawers. He thought it might have been left there intentionally. Its heading was NOTES ON THE TERRESTRIAL ECOLOGICAL BASE OF THE EIGHTEENTH SYSTEM, VOLUME III. After leafing though them once, it had been a while before Barney could bring himself to study the notes in more detail. He didn't at that time want to know too much about the situation he was in. He was still numbed by it.

But eventually he went over the binder carefully. The various reports were unsigned, but appeared to have been compiled by at least four or five persons— McAllen among them; his writing style was not difficult to recognize. Leaving out much that was incomprehensible or nearly so, Barney could still construe a fairly specific picture of the association project of which he was now an unscheduled and unwilling part. Plants and animals had been moved from Earth through the McAllen Tube to a world consisting of sand, rock and water, without detected traces of indigenous life in any form. At present the Ecological Base was only in its ninth year, which meant that the larger trees in the valley had been nearly full-grown when brought here with the soil that was to nourish them. From any viewpoint, the planting of an oasis of life on the barren world had been a gigantic undertaking, but there were numerous indications that the McAllen Tube was only one of the array of improbable devices the association had at its disposal for such tasks. A few cryptic paragraphs expressed the writer's satisfaction with the undetailed methods by which the Base's localized climatic conditions were maintained.

So far even the equipment which kept the cabin in uninterrupted operation had eluded Barney's search. It and the other required machinery might be buried somewhere in the valley. Or it might, he thought, have been set up just as easily some distance away, in the desert or among the remotely towering mountain ranges. One thing he had learned from the binder was that McAllen had told the truth in saying no one could contact him from Earth before the full period of his exile was over. The reason had seemed appalling enough in itself. This world had moved to a point in its orbit where the radiance of its distant sun was thickening between it and Earth, growing too intense to be penetrated by the forces of the McAllen Tube. Another four years would pass before the planet and the valley emerged gradually from behind that barrier again.

He walked, rested, walked again. Now and then he was troubled by a burst of violent sweating, followed by shivering fits until his clothes began to dry again. The big moon edged presently over the ridge above him, and in the first flood of its light the opposite slope of the valley took on the appearance of a fanciful sub-oceanic reef. The activity of the animal life about Barney increased promptly. It was no darker now than an evening hour on Earth, and his fellow occupants of the Ecological Base seemed well-adjusted to the strange shifts of day and night to which they had been consigned.

He pushed through a final thicket of shrubbery, and found himself at the edge of the lake. Beyond the almost circular body of water, a towering wall of cliffs sealed the upper end of the valley. He had come almost a mile, and while a mile—a city mile, at least—wouldn't have meant much to Barney Chard at one time, he felt quite exhausted now. He sat down at the edge of the water, and, after a minute or two, bent forward and drank from it. It had the same cold, clear flavor as the water in the cabin.

The surface of the water was unquiet. Soft-flying large insects of some kind were swarming about, stippling the nearby stretch of the lake with their touch, and there were frequent swift swirls as fish rose from beneath to take down the flyers. Presently one of them broke clear into the air—a big fish, thick-bodied and shining, looking as long as Barney's arm in the moonlight—and dropped back with a splash. Barney grinned twistedly. The NOTES indicated Dr. McAllen had taken some part in stocking the valley, and one could trust McAllen to see to it that the presence of his beloved game fish wasn't overlooked even in so outlandish a project.

He shifted position, became aware of the revolver in his pocket and brought it out. A wave of dull anger surged slowly through him again. What they did with trees and animals was their own business. But what they had done to a human being . . .

He scrambled suddenly to his feet, drew his arm back, and sent the gun flying far out over the lake. It spun through the moonlight, dipped, struck the surface with less of a splash than the fish had made, and was gone.

Now why, Barney asked himself in amazement, did I do that? He considered it a moment, and then, for the first time in over a year, felt a brief touch of something not far from elation.

He wasn't going to die here. No matter how politely the various invitations to do himself in had been extended by McAllen or the association, he was going to embarrass them by being alive and healthy when they came back to the valley four years from now. They wouldn't kill him then; they'd already shown they didn't have the guts to commit murder directly. They would have to take him back to Earth.

And once he was there, it was going to be too bad for them. It didn't matter how closely they watched him; in the end he would find or make the opportunity to expose them, pull down the whole lousy, conceited crew, see them buried under the shambles an outraged world would make of the secret association. . . .

THE END OF YEAR TWO

The end of Year Two on the Ecological Base in the Eighteenth System arrived and went by without Barney's being immediately aware of the fact. Some two hours later, he glanced at his wrist watch, pushed back the chair, got up from the desk and went over to the big grandfather clock to confirm his surmise.

"Well, well, Brother Chard," he said aloud. "Another anniversary . . . and three of them to go. We're almost at the halfway mark—"

He snapped the cover plate back over the multiple clock faces, and turned away. Three more years on the Ecological Base was a gruesome stretch of time when you thought of it as a whole. . . .

Which was precisely why he rarely let himself think of it as a whole nowadays.

This last year, at any rate, Barney conceded to himself, had to be regarded as an improvement on the first. Well, he added irritably, and what wouldn't be? It hadn't been delightful; he'd frequently felt almost stupefied with boredom. But physically, at least, he was fit—considerably fitter, as a matter of fact, than he'd ever been in his life.

Not very surprising. When he got too restless to be able to settle down to anything else, he was walking about the valley, moving along at his best clip regardless of obstacles until he was ready to drop to the ground wherever he was. Exertion ate up restlessness eventually—for a while. Selecting another tree to chop into firewood took the edge off the spasms of rage that tended to come up if he started thinking too long about that association of jerks somewhere beyond the sun. Brother Chard was putting on muscle all over. And after convincing himself at last—after all, the animals weren't getting hurt—that the glaring diamond of fire in the daytime sky couldn't really be harmful, he had also rapidly put on a Palm Beach tan. When his carefully rationed sleep periods eventually came around, he was more than ready for them, and slept like a log.

Otherwise: projects. Projects to beat boredom, and never mind how much sense they made in themselves. None of them did. But after the first month or two he had so much going that there was no question any more of not having something to do. Two hours allotted to work out on the typewriter a critical evaluation of a chapter from one of McAllen's abstruse technical texts. If Barney's mood was sufficiently sour, the evaluation would be unprintable; but it wasn't being printed, and two hours had been disposed of. A day and a half—Earth Standard Time—to construct an operating dam across the stream. He was turning into an experienced landscape architect; the swimming pool in the floor of the valley beneath the cabin might not have been approved by Carstairs of California, but it was the one project out of which he had even drawn some realistic benefit.

Then:

Half an hour to improve his knife-throwing technique.

Fifteen minutes to get the blade of the kitchen knife straightened out afterwards.

Two hours to design a box trap for the capture of one of the fat gray squirrels that always hung about the cabin.

Fifty minutes on a new chess problem. Chess, Barney had discovered, wasn't as hairy as it looked.

Five hours to devise one more completely foolproof method of bringing about the eventual ruin of the association. That made no more practical sense than anything else he was doing—and couldn't, until he knew a great deal more about McAllen's friends than he did now.

But it was considerably more absorbing, say, than even chess.

Brother Chard could beat boredom. He could probably beat another three years of boredom.

He hadn't forgiven anyone for making him do it.

THE END OF YEAR FIVE

For some hours, the association's Altiplano station had been dark and almost deserted. Only the IMT transit lock beneath one of the sprawling ranch houses showed in the vague light spreading out of the big scanning plate in an upper wall section. The plate framed an unimpressive section of the galaxy, a blurred scattering of stars condensing toward the right, and, somewhat left of center, a large misty red globe.

John Emanuel Fredericks, seated by himself in one of the two Tube operator chairs, ignored the plate. He was stooped slightly forwards, peering absorbedly through the eyepieces of the operator scanner before him.

Melvin Simms, Psychologist, strolled in presently through the transit lock's door, stopped behind Fredericks, remarked mildly, "Good evening, doctor."

Fredericks started and looked around. "Never heard you arrive, Mel. Where's Ollie?"

"He and Spalding dropped in at Spalding's place in Vermont. They should be along in a few minutes."

"Spalding?" Fredericks repeated inquiringly. "Our revered president intends to observe the results of Ollie's experiment in person?"

"He'll represent the board here," Simms said. "Whereas I, as you may have guessed, represent the outraged psychology department." He nodded at the plate. "That the place?"

"That's it. ET Base Eighteen."

"Not very sharp in the Tube, is it?"

"No. Still plenty of interfering radiation. But it's thinned out enough for contact. Reading 0.19, as of thirty minutes ago." Fredericks indicated the chair beside him. "Sit down if you want a better look."

"Thanks." The psychologist settled himself in the chair, leaned forward and peered into the scanner. After a few seconds he remarked, "Not the most hospitable-looking place—"

Fredericks grunted. "Any of the ecologists will tell you Eighteen's an unspoiled beauty. No problems there except the ones we bring along ourselves."

Simms grinned faintly. "Well, we're good at doing that, aren't we? Have you looked around for uh . . . for McAllen's subject yet?"

"No. Felt Ollie should be present when we find out what's happened. Incidentally, how did the meeting go?"

"You weren't tuned in?" Simms asked, surprised.

"No. Too busy setting things up for contact."

"Well"—Simms sat back in his chair—"I may say it was a regular bear garden for a while, Doctor. Psychology expressed itself as being astounded, indignant, offended. In a word, they were hopping mad. I kept out of it, though I admit I was startled when McAllen informed me privately this morning of the five-year project he's been conducting on the quiet. He was accused of crimes ranging . . . oh, from the clandestine to the inhumane. And, of course, Ollie was giving it back as good as he got."

"Of course."

"His arguments," Simms went on, pursing his lips

reflectively, "were not without merit. That was recognized. Nobody enjoys the idea of euthanasia as a security device. Many of us feel—I do—that it's still preferable to the degree of brain-washing required to produce significant alterations in a personality type of Chard's class."

"Ollie feels that, too," Fredericks said. "The upshot of the original situation, as he saw it, was that Barney Chard had been a dead man from the moment he got on the association's trail. Or a permanently deformed personality."

Simms shook his head. "Not the last. We wouldn't have considered attempting personality alteration in his case."

"Euthanasia then," Fredericks said. "Chard was too intelligent to be thrown off the track, much too unscrupulous to be trusted under any circumstances. So Ollie reported him dead."

The psychologist was silent for some seconds. "The point might be this," he said suddenly. "After my talk with McAllen this morning, I ran an extrapolation on the personality pattern defined for Chard five years ago on the basis of his background. Results indicate he went insane and suicided within a year."

"How reliable are those results?" Fredericks inquired absently.

"No more so than any other indication in individual psychology. But they present a reasonable probability . . . and not a very pleasant one."

Fredericks said, "Oliver wasn't unaware of that as a possible outcome. One reason he selected Base Eighteen for the experiment was to make sure he couldn't interfere with the process, once it had begun.

"His feeling, after talking with Chard for some hours, was that Chard was an overcondensed man. That is

Oliver's own term, you understand. Chard obviously was intelligent, had a very strong survival drive. He had selected a good personal survival line to follow—good but very narrow. Actually, of course, he was a frightened man. He had been running scared all his life. He couldn't stop."

Simms nodded.

"Base Eighteen stopped him. The things he'd been running from simply no longer existed. Ollie believed Chard would go into a panic when he realized it. The question was what he'd do then. Survival now had a very different aspect. The only dangers threatening him were the ones inherent in the rigid personality structure he had maintained throughout his adult existence. Would he be intelligent enough to understand that? And would his survival urge—with every alternative absolutely barred to him for five years—be strong enough to overcome those dangers?"

"And there," Simms said dryly, "we have two rather large questions." He cleared his throat. "The fact remains however, that Oliver B. McAllen is a good practical psychologist—as he demonstrated at the meeting."

"I expected Ollie would score on the motions," Fredericks said. "How did that part of it come off?"

"Not too badly. The first motion was passed unanimously. A vote of censure against Dr. McAllen."

Fredericks looked thoughtful. "His seventeenth—I believe?"

"Yes. The fact was mentioned. McAllen admitted he could do no less than vote for this one himself. However, the next motion to receive a majority was, in effect, a generalized agreement that men with such . . . ah . . . highly specialized skills as Barney Chard's and with comparable intelligence actually would be of great value as members of the association, if it turned out that they could be sufficiently relieved of their more flagrant antisocial tendencies. Considering the qualification, the psychology department could hardly avoid backing that motion. The same with the third one— in effect again that Psychology is to make an unprejudiced study of the results of Dr. McAllen's experiment on Base Eighteen, and report on the desirability of similar experiments when the personality of future subjects appears to warrant them."

"Well," Fredericks said, after a pause, "as far as the association goes Ollie got what he wanted. As usual." He hesitated. "The other matter—"

"We'll know that shortly." Simms turned his head to listen, added in a lowered voice, "They're coming now."

Dr. Stephen Spalding said to Simms and Fredericks: "Dr. McAllen agrees with me that the man we shall be looking for on Base Eighteen may be dead. If this is indicated, we'll attempt to find some evidence of his death before normal ecological operations on Eighteen are resumed.

"Next, we may find him alive but no longer sane. Dr. Simms and I are both equipped with drug-guns which will then be used to render him insensible. The charge is sufficient to insure he will not wake up again. In this circumstance, caution will be required since he was left on the Base with a loaded gun.

"Third, he may be alive and technically sane, but openly or covertly hostile to us." Spalding glanced briefly at each of the others, then went on, "It is because of this particular possibility that our contact group here has been very carefully selected. If such has been the result of Dr. McAllen's experiment, it will be our disagreeable duty to act as Chard's executioners. To add lifelong confinement or further psychological manipulation to the five solitary years Chard already has spent would be inexcusable.

"Dr. McAllen has told us he did not inform Chard of the actual reason he was being marooned—"

"On the very good grounds," McAllen interrupted, "that if Chard had been told at the outset what the purpose was, he would have preferred killing himself to allowing the purpose to be achieved. Any other human being was Chard's antagonist. It would have been impossible for him to comply with another man's announced intentions."

Simms nodded. "I'll go along on that point, doctor."

Scalding resumed, "It might be a rather immaterial point by now. In any event, Chard's information was that an important 'five-year-plan' of the association made it necessary to restrict him for that length of time. We shall observe him closely. If the indications are that he would act against the association whenever he is given the opportunity, our line will be that the five-year-plan has been concluded, and that he is, therefore, now to be released and will receive adequate compensation for his enforced seclusion. As soon as he is asleep, he will, of course, receive euthanasia. But up to that time, everything must be done to reassure him."

He paused again, concluded, "There is the final possibility that Dr. McAllen's action has had the results he was attempting to bring about . . . Ollie, you might speak on that yourself."

McAllen shrugged. "I've already presented my views. Essentially, it's a question of whether Barney Chard was capable of learning that he could live without competing destructively with other human beings. If he has grasped that, he should also be aware by now that Base Eighteen is presently one of the most interesting spots in the known universe."

Simms asked: "Do you expect he'll be grateful for what has occurred?"

"We-e-ll," McAllen said judiciously, turning a little pale, "that, of course, depends on whether he *is* still alive and sane. But if he has survived the five years, I do believe that he will not be dissatisfied with what has happened to him. However"—he shrugged again—"let's get ahead with it. Five years has been a long time to find out whether or not I've murdered a man."

In the momentary silence that followed, he settled himself in the chair Fredericks had vacated, and glanced over at Simms. "You stay seated, Mel," he said. "You represent Psychology here. Use your chair scanner. The plate's still showing no indications of clearing, John?"

"No," said Fredericks. "In another two hours we might have a good picture there. Hardly before."

McAllen said, "We won't wait for it. Simms and I can determine through the scanners approximately what has been going on." He was silent a few seconds; then the blurred red globe in the plate expanded swiftly, filled two thirds of the view space, checked for a moment, then grew once more; finally stopped.

McAllen said irritably, "John, I'm afraid you'll have to take over. My hands don't seem steady enough to handle this properly."

A minute or two passed. The big plate grew increasingly indistinct, all details lost in a muddy wash of orange-brown shades. Green intruded suddenly; then McAllen muttered "Picking up the cabin now."

There was a moment of silence, then Fredericks cleared his throat. "So far so good, Oliver. We're looking into the cabin. Can't see your man yet—but someone's living here. Eh, Simms?"

"Obviously," the psychologist acknowledged. He

hesitated. "And at a guess it's no maniac. The place is in reasonably good order."

"You say Chard isn't in the cabin?" Spalding demanded.

Fredericks said, "Not unless he's deliberately concealing himself. The exit door is open. Hm-m-m. Well, the place isn't entirely deserted, after all."

"What do you mean?" asked Spalding.

"Couple of squirrels sitting in the window," Simms explained.

"In the window? Inside the cabin?"

"Yes," said Fredericks. "Either they strayed in while he was gone, or he's keeping them as pets. Now, should we start looking around outside for Chard?"

"No," Spalding decided. "The Base is too big to attempt to cover at pinpoint focus. If he's living in the cabin and has simply gone out, he'll return within a few hours at the most. We'll wait and see what we can deduce from the way he behaves when he shows up." He turned to McAllen. "Ollie," he said, "I think you might allow yourself to relax just a little. This doesn't seem at all bad!"

McAllen grunted. "I don't know," he said. "You're overlooking one thing."

"What's that?"

"I told Chard when to expect us. Unless he's smashed the clock, he knows we're due today. If nothing's wrong—wouldn't he be waiting in the cabin for us?"

Spalding hesitated. "That is a point. He seems to be hiding out. May have prepared an ambush, for that matter. John—"

"Yes?" Fredericks said.

"Step the tubescope down as fine as it will go, and scan that cabin as if you were vacuuming it. There may be some indication—"

"He's already doing that," Simms interrupted.

There was silence again for almost two minutes. Forefinger and thumb of Fredericks' right hand moved with infinite care on a set of dials on the side of the scanner; otherwise neither he nor Simms stirred.

"Oh-hoo-hoo-haw!" Dr. John Fredericks cried suddenly. "Oh-hoo-hoo-HAW! A message, Ollie! Your Mr. Chard has left you a . . . hoo-hoo . . . message."

For a moment McAllen couldn't see clearly through the scanner. Fredericks was still laughing; Simms was saying in a rapid voice, "It's quite all right, doctor! Quite all right. Your man's sane, quite sane. In fact you've made, one might guess, a one hundred per cent convert to the McAllen approach to life. Can't you *see* it?"

"No," gasped McAllen. He had a vague impression of the top of the desk in the main room of the cabin, of something white—a white card—taped to it, of blurred printing on the card. "Nothing's getting *that* boy unduly excited any more." Simms' voice went on beside him. "Not even the prospect of seeing visitors from Earth for the first time in five years. But he's letting you know it's perfectly all right to make yourself at home in his cabin until he gets back. Here, let me—"

He reached past McAllen, adjusted the scanner. The printing on the card swam suddenly into focus before McAllen's eyes.

The message was terse, self-explanatory, to the point:

GONE FISHING,
Regards, *B. Chard*

The Beacon to Elsewhere

It didn't happen twice a year that Gustavus Robert Fry, Chief Commissioner of the Interstellar Police Authority, allotted more than an hour in his working day to any one appointment. However, nobody in the outer offices was surprised to learn that the chief expected to remain in conference until noon today, and was not to be disturbed before then. The visitor who had been ushered in to him—without benefit of appointment— was Howard Camhorn, the Overgovernment's Co-ordinator of Research. It was a meeting of political mastodons. Portentous events would be on the agenda.

Seated at the desk in his private office, Gus Fry, massive, strong-jawed, cold-eyed—looking precisely like the powerhouse, political and otherwise, which he was—did not feel entirely at ease. Howard Camhorn, sprawled in a chair half across the room from the Chief Commissioner, might have passed for a middle-aged, moderately successful artist. He was lanky, sandy-haired, with a lazy smile, lazier gestures. But he was, by several degrees, the bigger VIP of the two.

Camhorn said, "There's no question at all, of course, that the space transport your boys picked up is the one we're interested in. But is it absolutely certain that our YM-400 is no longer on board?"

Fry shrugged. "It's certain that it isn't in the compartment where it was stored for the trip—and the locks to that compartment have been forced. It's possible that whoever removed the two YM cases has concealed them in some other part of the ship. That would be easy to do, but . . ."

Camhorn shook his head. "No," he said. "Nobody would benefit from that. I'm afraid we'll have to resign ourselves to the fact that the stuff has been taken."

Fry said, "It looks like it. The police search will go on until your own investigators get there, but there's no reason to believe anything will be found."

"The ship's course had been reset so that it was headed into unoccupied space?"

"Yes," said Fry. "It was only by a very improbable coincidence that an IPA boat happened to spot it. The transport's new course wouldn't have brought it anywhere near a traffic lane, inhabited planet, or normal patrol route. Three weeks later, when its fuel was exhausted, the planted explosives would have blown it up without a chance that the wreckage would ever be detected."

"How about the cargo? Have you heard about that? Was it otherwise intact?"

"As far as we can tell. The shippers will check everything in detail when the freighter gets back to port. But it's a good guess that the Overgovernment's YM-400 is the only item missing."

Camhorn nodded. "A group which was planning to pick it up wouldn't be very interested in ordinary loot.

That seems to make it conclusive." He wrinkled his nose reflectively. "Modus operandi?" he asked.

"Two possibilities," Fry said. "They had themselves loaded aboard with the cargo, or they intercepted the transport en route and entered it in flight."

"Which do you like?"

"The first. In fact, the other is hardly a possibility. Even the IPA couldn't get aboard a modern automatic freighter between ports without setting off an explosion of alarms in every flight control station on its course. No such alarm was recorded. And there is no indication of a forcible entry."

"So our thieves had themselves loaded on," said Camhorn. "Now, Gus, I've always been under the impression that the check system which keeps stowaways out of the automatic transports was foolproof."

The IPA Chief shrugged. "It's been foolproof so far. But not because it was impossible to circumvent. It's simply that circumventing the check system would add up to so enormously expensive a proposition that the total cash value of a transport and its cargo wouldn't be worth the trouble. These people definitely were not considering expenses."

"Apparently not," Camhorn said. "So how did they get the YM-400 off the ship?"

"They had a small boat loaded on board with them. That's a supposition, so far; they left very few traces of their activities. But it's the only way the thing could have been done. They had obtained exact information of the transport's plotted route and time schedule. At a calculated point, they picked up the two cases of YM, rerouted the ship, timed and planted their explosives, disconnected the alarm system at the entry lock, and left in the boat. Naturally, another ship was moving along with the freighter by then, waiting to pick them up. That's all there was to it."

"You make it sound simple," said Camhorn.

"The difficulty," said Gus Fry, "would be in preparing such an operation. No matter how much money these people could lay on the line, they must have spent several months in making the necessary arrangements without once alerting the port authorities."

"They had enough time," Camhorn admitted reflectively. "YM-400 has been shipped for a number of years in the same manner and over the same route."

"I've been wondering," Fry remarked, "why this manner of shipping it was selected."

Camhorn smiled briefly. "When was the last time an automatic transport was hijacked, Gus?"

"Fifty-seven years ago," Fry said. "And the method employed then wouldn't have worked on a modern transport, or under the present check system."

"Well, that's part of your answer. Automatic shipping risks have become negligible. The rest of the answer is that we've avoided too obviously elaborate safeguards for YM-400. If we put it on a battleship each time it was moved, the technological espionage brethren would hear about it. Which means that everybody who might be interested would hear about it. And once the word got out, we'd start losing the stuff regardless of safeguards to people who'd be willing to work out for themselves just what made it so valuable to the Overgovernment. As it is, this is the first sample of YM-400 to go astray in the thirty-two years we've had it."

"Two thirty-four kilogram cases," Fry said. "Is that a significant amount?"

"I'm afraid it's an extremely significant amount," Camhorn said wryly.

Fry hesitated, said, "There's something very odd about this, Howard. . . ."

"What's that?"

"I had the definite impression a few hours ago that you were almost relieved to hear about the transport."

Camhorn studied him for a few seconds. "As a matter of fact," he said, "I was. Because of one thing. If this hadn't been obviously a criminal act, humanly engineered—if the transport, say, had simply blown up en route or vanished without giving an alarm . . ."

"Vanished without giving an alarm?" Fry repeated slowly. "Without human intervention?"

"If," said Camhorn, "any least part of the YM-400 it was carrying had been radioactive, I wouldn't have been surprised to learn something like that had happened. But, of course, the shipment was stable. And stable YM-400 has shown no more disturbing potentialities to date than the equivalent amount of pig iron. If it ever develops them, the research programs connected with the substance will be indefinitely delayed. They may have to be abandoned." He gave Fry his lazy smile. "Does that explain my apparent relief, Gus?"

"More or less," Gus Fry said. "Would it be a calamity if those particular programs had to be abandoned?"

"The Overgovernment would consider it a calamity, yes."

"Why?"

"If and when," said Camhorn, "the bugs get worked out of YM-400, it may ensure our future control of space against any foreseeable opposition."

Fry kept his face carefully expressionless.

"So, naturally," Camhorn went on, "we'd prefer to keep dissident groups from playing around with the substance, or becoming aware of its possibilities."

Fry said, "There seems to be at least one dissident group which has much more complete information about YM-400 than, for example, the Interstellar Police Authority."

Camhorn shook his head. "We can't say how much

they really knew, Gus. The theft might have been arranged as a speculative operation. There's enough loose money in large quantities around to make that quite possible."

Fry grunted. "Do you have any definite suspects?"

"A great many. Unfortunately, there seems to be at least some probability that the people involved won't turn out to be among them. However, those lists will provide an immediate starting point. They're being transferred to the IPA today."

"Thanks," Fry said sourly.

"I wouldn't do it if I didn't have to, Gus. Our Research investigators can't begin to cope with a number like that. They will cooperate with you closely, of course."

"Nobody else will," said Fry. "I've come to the conclusion that our current populations are the least cooperative people in the history of the race."

Camhorn nodded. "Naturally."

"Naturally? Why should they be? Most of them are a little short of living space—unless they're willing to put up with frontier conditions—but otherwise humanity's never had it so good. They're not repressed; they're babied along—nine-tenths of the time anyway. They do just about as they damn well please. Thirty percent of them won't turn out a stroke of honest work from the beginning of their lives to the end."

"True enough. And you've described an almost perfect setting for profound discontent. Which is being carefully maintained, by the way. We don't want humanity to go to sleep entirely just yet. Gus, how much do you know personally about YM-400?"

"Nothing," said Fry. "Now and then some rumor about it comes to the IPA's attention. Rumors of that kind go into our files as a matter of course. I see the files."

"Well, then," said Camhorn, "what rumors have you seen?"

"I can give you those," Fry said, "in a few sentences. YM—or YM-400—is an element rather recently discovered by the Overgovernment's scientists; within the past few decades. It has the property of 'transmuting space-time stresses'—that's the rumor, verbatim. In that respect, it has some unspecified association with Riemann space phenomena. It has been located in a star system which lies beyond the areas officially listed as explored, and which at present is heavily guarded by Overgovernment ships. In this system is an asteroid belt, constituting the remnants of a planet broken up in an earlier period by YM action. And three," Fry added, grinning wolfishly, "I can even bring in a factual detail. I know that there is such a guarded system, and that it contains nothing but its star and the asteroid belt referred to. I could give you its location, but I'm sure you're familiar with it."

Camhorn nodded. "I am. Any other rumors?"

"I think that sums them up."

"Well," Camhorn said judiciously, "if the IPA is to be of much use to us in this investigation, it should be better informed than that. The rumors are interesting, though satisfactorily inaccurate. YM-400, to begin with, is not a single element. It's a compound of several elements of the same series. The symbol attached to it is quite meaningless. . . ."

"For security reasons?"

"Of course. Now, with one notable exception, all elements in this series were discovered during the Overgovernment's investigation of Riemann space properties in the two intragalactic creation areas we have mapped to date. As you may recall, that program was initiated forty-five years ago. The elements we're talking about are radioactive: half-life of up to an hour. It was suspected they had a connection with the very curious, apparently random distortions of space-time factors found in the creation areas, but their essential properties made it impossible to produce them in sufficient quantity for a sufficient length of time to conduct a meaningful examination.

"Ymir, the last element of this series, was not discovered in the same areas, or at the same time. It was located ten years later, in stable trace-quantities in the asteroid belt you've mentioned, and to date it has not been found anywhere else. Ymir is a freak. It is chemically very similar to the rest of the series and has an unstable structure. Theoretically, its presence as and where it was found was an impossibility. But it was recognized eventually that Ymir produces a force field which inhibits radioactivity. Until the field is interfered with the element is stable. . . ."

"What interferes with it?"

Camhorn grinned. "People. Until it's deliberately tampered with, Ymir is changeless—as far as we know. Furthermore it will, in compound, extend its inhibiting field effect instantaneously to three other elements of the same series. A very fortunate circumstance, because Ymir has been found only in minute amounts, and unknown factors still prevent its artificial production. The other three elements are produced readily, and since a very small proportion of Ymir retains them in stable—or pseudostable—form, they can be conserved indefinitely."

"*That's* the YM-400 compound?" Fry asked.

"That's it."

Fry said thoughtfully, "Perhaps I should remind you, Howard, that this conversation is being recorded."

Camhorn nodded. "That's all right. Now that we know someone else is in possession of sixty-eight kilograms of YM-400, we're confronted with radically altered circumstances. The loss incurred by the theft isn't important in itself. The Ymir component in such a quantity is detectable almost only by its effects, and the other components can be produced at will.

"The question is how much the people who have the stolen compound in their hands actually know about it. We would prefer them to know several things. For example, up to a point YM-400 is easily handled. It's a comparatively simple operation to reduce or restore the force field effect. The result is a controlled flow of radioactivity from the compound, or its cessation. Now, you've mentioned having heard that YM-400 transmutes space-time stresses—"

Fry nodded.

"Well," Camhorn said, "as a matter of fact, that's exactly what it appears to do—as was surmised originally of the unstable elements in the series. The active compound transmutes space-time stresses into a new energy with theoretically predictable properties. Theoretically, for example, this new energy should again be completely controllable. Have you picked up any rumors of what our experiments with the substance were supposed to achieve?"

Fry said, "Yes. I forgot that. I've heard two alternate theories. One is that the end result will be an explosive of almost unimaginable violence. The other is that you're working to obtain a matter transmitter— possibly one with an interstellar range."

Camhorn nodded. "Potentially," he said, "YM-400 is an extremely violent explosive. No question about it. The other speculation—it isn't actually too far-fetched— well, that would be the equivalent of instantaneous space-travel, wouldn't it?"

Fry shrugged. "I suppose so."

"However," Camhorn said, "we haven't transmitted

even a speck of matter as yet. Not deliberately, at any rate. Do you know why, Gus?"

"No. How would I?"

"No rumors on that, eh? I'll tell you. YM-400, when activated even in microquantities, immediately initiates the most perverse, incalculable effects ever to confront an experimenter. There has been, flatly, no explanation for them. I've had ordinarily unimpressionable physicists tell me with tears in their eyes that space-time is malevolently conscious of us, and of our attempts to manipulate it—that it delights in frustrating those attempts."

Gus Fry grinned sourly. "Perhaps they're right."

"As it happens," Camhorn observed, "the situation is very un-funny, Gus. Experiments with YM-400 have, to date, produced *no* useful results—and have produced over eleven hundred casualties. Most of the latter were highly trained men and women, not easily replaced."

Fry studied him incredulously. "You say these accidents have not been explained?"

Camhorn shook his head. "If they were explicable after the event," he said, "very few of them would have happened in the first place. I assure you there's been nothing sloppy about the manner in which the project has been conducted, Gus. But as it stands today, it's a flop. If the stakes were less high, it would have been washed out ten years ago. And, as I said before, if there were reason to believe that the stable compound was involved in the disappearance of a space transport, we probably would postpone further operations indefinitely. One such occurrence would raise the risks to the intolerable level."

Fry grunted. "Is that what those accidents were like? Things—people—disappear?"

"Well ... some of them were of that general nature."

348 *James H. Schmitz*

Fry cleared his throat. "Just tell me one more thing, Howard."

"What's that?"

"Has any part of what you've said so far been the truth?"

Camhorn hesitated an instant. "Gus," he said then, "can you erase your question and my reply from the recording?"

"Of course."

"Erase them, please. Then blank out our further conversation."

A few seconds later, Fry said, "All right. You're off the record."

"Most of what I told you was the truth," Camhorn said, leaning back in his chair. "Perhaps not all of it. And perhaps I haven't told you the whole truth. But we're out to spread some plausible rumors, Gus. We could not afford to get caught in obvious lies."

Fry reddened slowly. "You feel the Interstellar Police Authority will spread those rumors?"

"Of course it will. Be realistic, Gus. Naturally, you'll transmit the information I've given you only to qualified personnel. But there'll be leaks, and . . . well, what better authentication can we have for a rumor than precisely such a source?"

"If you know of any potential leaks among the IPA's 'qualified personnel,'" Fry said, "I'd appreciate seeing the names."

"Don't be stuffy, Gus," Camhorn said affably. "We're not slandering the Authority. We're banking on the law of averages. As you've indicated, the IPA can't be expected to carry out this investigation unless it's given some clues to work on. We're giving it those clues. In the process, we expect to start the spread of certain rumors. That's all to the good."

"But what's the purpose?"

"I've told you that. Our criminals may or may not be caught as quickly as we'd like. The group actually in the know may be—probably is—quite small. But they should have a widespread organization, and they'll be alert for counteraction now. They certainly will get the information we want them to have, whether it comes to them through the IPA or through some other channel; and that should be enough to keep them from committing any obvious stupidities. Meanwhile, we'll have avoided making the information public."

"We want to make sure they know—if they don't already know it—that YM-400 is unpredictably dangerous. That leaves them with several choices of action. They can abandon those two thirty-four-kilogram cases, or simply keep them concealed until they obtain more complete information about the material. Considering the manner in which the theft was prepared and carried out, neither is a likely possibility. These people are not ignorant, and they aren't easily frightened— and they certainly have the resources to handle any expense factor."

Fry nodded.

"The probability is," Camhorn went on, "that they'll evaluate the warning contained in these rumors realistically, but proceed with experimentation—perhaps more cautiously than they would have done otherwise."

"Which is as much as we hope to accomplish. I've told you of the losses among our personnel. We have no real objection to seeing someone else attempt to pull a few chestnuts out of the fire for us. That's the secondary purpose of sacrificing some quite valid information. By the time we catch up with our friends, we expect the sacrifice will have been—in one way or another—to our advantage."

"And suppose," said Fry, "that their secret

experiments with YM-400 result in turning another planet into an asteroid cloud?"

"That's an extreme possibility," Camhorn said, "though it exists. The point is that it exists now whatever we choose to do about it. We can only attempt to minimize the risks."

"You'd still sooner catch them before they start playing around with the stuff?"

"Of course we would. But we're working against time there."

"How much time do we have before the thing gets critical?"

"Well," said Camhorn, "assume they've had at least four or five years to prepare for the day when they could bring a quantity of YM-400 into their possession. They'll have made every necessary arrangement for concealed full-scale experimentation. But, unless they are utterly reckless, they still have to conduct a thorough preliminary investigation of the compound and its possibilities. That phase of the matter shouldn't be too dangerous, and it can't be concluded in less than six months."

Fry shook his head exasperatedly. "Six months!" he said. "We might get lucky and pick them up next week, Howard . . . but there are eighteen planets and planet-class satellites at peak population levels, seventy-three space cities with a total of eight times the planetary populations, five Freeholder planets on each of which you could keep an army concealed indefinitely if you wanted to go to the trouble. Add in close to a hundred thousand splinter populations on semi-habitables, asteroids, spaceborne in fixed stations and mobile craft—we can't do it, Howard! Not in six months. We've already started putting anyone who might have the slightest connection with that space transport job through the strainer, and we'll get on your lists of suspects as soon as they're placed in our hands."

"But don't expect results in anything less than a year. . . ."

Fry, for once, had been too optimistic.

A year and a half went by. Endless series of more or less promising leads were run into the ground. The missing YM-400 didn't turn up.

The IPA put out its nets again, and began to check over the possibilities that were left.

Seen from the air, Lion Mesa, in the southwest section of the American continent on the Freehold Planet of Terra, was a tilted, roughly triangular tableland, furred green with thick clusters of cedar and pinyon, scarred by outcroppings of naked rock. It was eight miles across at its widest and highest point, directly behind an upthrust mass of stone jutting toward the north and somewhat suggestive of the short lifted neck and heavy skull of a listening beast. Presumably it was this unusual formation which gave the mesa its name. From there the ground dropped to the south, narrowing gradually to the third point of the triangle. Near the southern tip in cleared ground were the only evidences of human habitation—half a dozen buildings of small to moderate size, handsomely patterned in wood and native stone. Directly adjoining one of the buildings was a large, massively fenced double corral. This was an experimental animal ranch; it and the mesa plus half a hundred square miles of surrounding wasteland and mountain were the private property of one Miguel Trelawney, Terrestrial Freeholder.

For the past twenty minutes, Frank Dowland— Lieutenant Frank Dowland, of the Solar Police Authority—had kept his grid-car moving slowly along the edges of a cloud bank west of the mesa, at an unobtrusive height above it. During that time, he was inspecting the ranch area in the beam of a high-powered hunting-scope. He had detected no activity, and the ranch had the general appearance of being temporarily deserted, which might be the case. Miguel Trelawney's present whereabouts were not known, and Lion Mesa was only one of the large number of places in which he was periodically to be found.

Dowland put the scope down finally, glanced at the sun which was within an hour of setting. He was a stocky man in his early thirties, strongly built, dressed in hunting clothes. The packed equipment in the grid-car, except for a few special items, was that of a collector of live game, the role regularly assumed by Dowland when at work on the planet.

The Freeholder Families traditionally resented any indication of Overgovernment authority on Terra, and would have been singularly uncordial to a Solar City police detective here, regardless of the nature of his mission. But the export of surplus native fauna was one of the forms of trade toward which they were tolerant. Moreover, they were hunting buffs themselves. Dowland ordinarily got along well enough with them.

He now opened a concealed compartment in the car's instrument panel, and brought out a set of pictures of Trelawney's ranch on the mesa, taken from an apparent distance of a few hundred yards above it. For some seconds, Dowland compared the depth photographs with the scene he had been observing. There appeared to have been no changes in any of the structures in the eight months since the pictures were taken. At least not above ground.

Dowland rubbed the side of his nose, scowling slightly. If the ranch really was deserted, it would be best to leave it alone for the time being and search elsewhere for Trelawney. To go down uninvited in the absence of the owner would be as much out of character for an experienced visitor on Terra as for a Freeholder. If observed at it—a remote possibility perhaps in this area, but the possibility was there— he could offer the excuse of a suspicion of engine trouble in the grid-car. The excuse would be good, once. He preferred to reserve it as a means of introducing himself to the Trelawneys when he caught up with them—either Miguel, the current head of the dwindled family, or Miguel's younger half-brother, Dr. Paul Trelawney. Neither rated as a serious suspect in the matter of the Overgovernment's missing YM-400, but it had been a little difficult to find out what they had been doing with themselves during the past year and a half. Dowland's assignment was to find out, and to do it unobtrusively. Strictly routine.

Terra, in terms of the YM search, hadn't seemed like too bad a bet at first. The Freeholders entertained an open grudge against the Overgovernment, which had restricted their nominally unclouded title to the planet by somewhat underhanded legal means, when the principle of the Freehold Worlds was laid down. Essentially, the Families became the very highly paid caretakers of Terra. To Dowland, raised in the crowded tunnels of the system of artificial giant asteroids known as Solar City, the conservation of the natural resources of a living world looked like a good idea. The Terran Families were interested in conservation, but on their terms and under their control. The Overgovernment politely refused.

That was one part of it. The other was that numerous contentious factions in the space cities and on the so-called open worlds wanted to spill over on the Freeholder planets. Again the Overgovernment refused,

and again it made sense to Dowland. But the Freeholders feared—perhaps with justification, so far as
Dowland could tell—that political pressures would
mount with each increase in excess population and
eventually lead to such measures. Many of them, probably the majority, led by Anthony Brand Carter—
Firebrand Carter, head of the largest and wealthiest
of the Families—believed that the only safe solution
was to arm the planet. They wanted heavy weapons,
and enough of them: the right to build them, to man
them and, if necessary, to use them to beat off
encroaching groups. The Overgovernment pointed out
that the possession and use of major implements of war
was by law its own exclusive privilege. Litigation on
the matter had gone on for decades, was periodically
renewed by Carter and his associates. Meanwhile, many
of Terra's sportsmen became members of an extremely
able-bodied group called Carter's Troopers, and assidu-
ously practiced the skills of battle with the means
allowed them. Dowland and the Solar Police Authority knew the Troopers were crack shots, excellent fli-
ers and horsemen, but the Overgovernment was not
worrying about it at present.

Mr. Paul Trelawney, the younger of the brothers, had
been a Trooper for two years while in his twenties, then
had quarreled violently with Firebrand Carter, had left
Terra to major in physics at the Overgovernment's
universities, and presently received his degree. What
he had done after that wasn't known. He appeared
occasionally on Terra, might be here at present. Miguel,
Paul's senior by almost twenty years, now in his early
fifties, had also taken an interest in physics, attending
an Overgovernment university a quarter of a century
earlier. Miguel's studies terminated before he obtained
a degree, as a result of a difference of opinion with
the president of the university, whom he challenged

to a duel. The records of both brothers indicated, in Dowland's opinion, more than a trace of the megalomania not too uncommon among men with excessive wealth and no real claim to distinction. But, in spite of their choice of studies, there was nothing to link either Trelawney to the missing YM. Mental brilliance might have made them suspect; but their I.Q. readings, while definitely better than average—a number of notches above Dowland's own, for that matter—were not outstanding. Their scholastic performance had been of comparative quality. Miguel, on his return to Terra, had dropped physics in favor of experimental biology. The ranch on Lion Mesa was adapted to his hobby, which at the moment was directed to the production of a strain of gigantic wild hogs for hunting purposes. Presumably the breeding of bad-tempered tons of bacon on the hoof satisfied his urge to distinguish himself as a gentleman scientist. Aside from Paul's brief connection with Carter's Troopers neither brother had shown any interest in Terran politics.

Rather poor prospects, but Dowland's information was that after a year and a half the better prospects were regarded as nearly exhausted, and hadn't produced the slightest results, putting the various divisions of the Interstellar Police Authority in the discouraging position of now having to suspect almost anybody. If there was no sign of Miguel Trelawney's presence here by sundown, he decided, he would move on to the next check point. Trelawney's pets would be cared for by automatic machinery; it might be several weeks before their owner showed up to look them over.

His gaze shifted briefly around the plain out of which the mesa loomed. It was turbulent today; gusty winds shook the car and electric storms were boiling along the northern mountain ranges. Below, sand and dust whirled up the mesa's steep flanks. Picking up the hunting-scope again, Dowland began moving the visibeam almost at random and with low magnification over the back of the tableland. Dense masses of trees swept past, shouldered aside here and there by wind-scarred rock. A thoroughly wild place. He brought the glasses back to the ranch area, suddenly checked them there. . . .

Somebody was in sight, moving toward the edge of the mesa nearest him. He caught a flash of something white. Centering carefully on the figure, Dowland turned on full magnification, and in the lenses, the image of a young woman appeared at closeup range.

She had come to a stop; and for an instant Dowland was startled to realize she was peering back at him through a pair of binoculars. But lacking the visibeam of the IPA, her glasses couldn't, of course, do much more than show her there was a grid-car up there. Now her free hand lifted the long white cloth it was holding, and began swinging it in swift, vigorous gestures through the air above her head.

In spite of the binoculars, Dowland was immediately sure of the woman's identity—having, in the past few days, studied a number of pictures of her. She was Jill Trelawney, the youngest of the three surviving members of the Trelawney Freeholders. Miguel and Paul were her uncles—and if she was here, one or the other of the men must certainly be here also.

It was obvious that she was signaling to the car. Dowland glanced at the communicator in the panel before him, saw it was turned on but registering no local calls. His eyes narrowed with speculation. This suddenly looked just a little bit interesting. If the Trelawneys were expecting a visitor but preferred not to address him over the open communication system, it indicated that they intended to be hard to find.

Which might mean a number of things of no interest at all to the IPA. But . . .

Dowland took his police gun from the pocket of his hunting jacket, and began checking it by touch, as he swung the car's nose about toward the ranch and went slanting down toward the air. Either of the brothers might decide to make trouble, particularly if they had something to conceal—but, at any rate, they couldn't claim he hadn't been invited down.

Picking up the girl in the scope again, he saw that she realized he was coming in. She had dropped the cloth but was still gazing up toward the car, her free hand shielding her eyes from the setting sun.

In the next instant, without the slightest preliminary warning, every instrument in the panel before Dowland went dead. Then the grid-car began to drop like a stone.

The world-wide gravity grid was Terra's general power source. It had been an idiotically expensive installation; actually, no other planet could have afforded it at present. Once installed, it was drawn on for idiotically minor services. There weren't enough human beings on Terra to begin to make a significant use of the grid.

But there were compensating features. The grid was esthetically unobtrusive, and available everywhere. It supplied power for anything from personal wrist watches on up through the giant docking machines at the spaceports. And it was reliable. There had been no power failures and no accidents connected with the grid recorded in its eighty years of operation.

That shining safety record, Dowland thought, manipulating the flight controls with desperate haste, might become seriously marred in something like three-quarters of a minute now. He'd be lucky to get down alive. And another thought was clamoring for a different kind of action with almost equal urgency—unusual and unexplained physical phenomena of any kind were one of the things the YM searchers were alerted to look out for; and he'd certainly run into one of them here. He shot a glance down to his camouflaged wrist communicator. Just a few seconds to spare, and he could get a private-beam alarm in to the Solar Police Authority representative at the Columbia spaceport.

He didn't have a few seconds to spare. The grid-car was a lousy glider—ponderous, sickeningly slow to respond. The rim of the mesa swayed up. If he missed that stretch of cleared ground around the Trelawney ranch, the car would either tear itself to pieces in the forest beyond or do a ditch into the piled rubble at the mesa's foot. He hauled back on the controls again, felt the car actually begin to rise for an instant—

"I'm sorry," Jill Trelawney was crying, running up the slope toward him. "I'm so terribly sorry. I tried to warn you. I simply didn't realize—are you hurt?"

Her face, Dowland thought, was probably no whiter than his own. The canopy had caved in around him, and a jagged chunk of engine was nestling in the passenger seat to his right. As he tried to stand up, a section of the plastic floorboard collapsed; his foot followed it through and struck solid ground. He worked himself out of the seat. The grid-car creaked tiredly and settled another six inches. Dowland shoved a piece of canopy aside and found he could straighten out.

He cleared his throat. "I don't think I'm hurt. Anyway, not much."

"Your face—it's bleeding!"

Dowland probed at a cut lip with his tongue and winced. "Didn't notice it happen . . . a lot of stuff flying around there for a moment. Now, just what's going on?"

The girl swallowed nervously, staring at him. "The power's off."

"That I noticed." Something occurred to Dowland. "That's why you couldn't call me on the communicator."

"Yes. I . . ."

"How long has it been off here?"

"Since this morning."

He looked at her thoughtfully, and a quick flush spread up into her face. "I know," she said. "It was terribly stupid of me to—to get you to come down. It just didn't occur to me that . . ."

"It's all right," Dowland said. "I'm here now." She was very good-looking, though her face was strained at the moment. Strained and scared. "You could not know how far the failure area extended." He glanced over at the buildings. The crash of his landing hadn't brought anyone into sight. "You're not alone here, are you?"

"No." She hesitated, went on half apologetically, "I'm sure I should remember you, but I don't."

"Well, you wouldn't," Dowland said. "I'm not a Freeholder."

The flicker of reaction in her eyes brought a prickling to the hairs at the back of his neck. The thing looked hot, all right. He continued, "You just may have heard of me by name, though. Frank Dowland, of Dowland Animal Exports."

"Oh, yes." Apparently she did recognize the name. "I'm Jill Trelawney, Dowland. I . . . there's been an accident. A bad one, I'm afraid."

"Another accident? What kind?"

She shook her head. "I don't know. Do you have a medical kit with you?"

"Of course. Who's hurt?"

"My uncle. Miguel Trelawney. He's up in the house."

"What's wrong with him?"

"That's what I don't know. Looks—I think he's terribly sick. In some way."

"How long has he been sick?"

She hesitated. "This morning."

"Since the time the grid-power went off?"

Jill looked startled. "Why, yes."

And that about cinched it, Dowland thought. He said, "You two were alone here?"

"No. I'm sure this all sounds very crazy, but—" She nodded at one of the buildings down the slope from them, a long wooden structure identified as a feed barn in Dowland's pictures of the ranch. "My other uncle, Paul Trelawney—he's locked up in there."

"Locked up?" Dowland repeated.

"Yes. There's a key to the door somewhere, but I can't find it."

"Would Miguel know where it is?"

"I think so."

"Then we'll try to get him conscious again at least long enough to tell us. You'd better get back to the house, Miss Trelawney. I'll dig out the kit. Be up there in a minute."

He watched the tall supple figure start back across the slope, shook his head a little, and turned to the wrecked car. She was either somewhat stupid, or being cagey with a non-Terran. The last seemed a little more likely. Too bad if she turned out to be involved with something like the YM business, but that was out of his hands. He'd have to report immediately, and the Overgovernment specialists would be here in an hour. It wasn't his job.

He climbed cautiously back into the car. Out of sight of the house, he pressed a key on the wrist communicator, said, "Chris? This is Dowland.

Emergency," and waited for the hum of response from the instrument.

There was no hum.

Half a minute later, he had the communicator off his wrist and opened. He couldn't remember having struck his wrist hard enough against anything to have damaged it, but the delicate mechanisms inside were a crystal shambles. There was a portable communicator packed in with his camping equipment. But it operated on grid power.

It looked like it was going to remain his job for a while, after all.

Miguel Trelawney, in Dowland's unvoiced opinion, was a man who was dying. He was big-boned and heavily muscled, but on the low couch in the living room he looked shrunken. Lead-colored skin and thready pulse. Internal bleeding at a guess—an informed layman's guess. Radiation burns.

Dowland looked over at the girl. She was disturbed and tense, but nowhere near hysteria. "We might bring him around," he said bluntly. "But it will take some hours at least. He's in bad shape."

Her hands, clasped together in her lap, went white around the knuckles. "Will he . . . can you save . . ."

Dowland shook his head. "I don't know if we can save him here. If we got him to one of your hospitals tonight, he should have a very good chance. But we can't do that—unless the grid-power cuts in again."

She said faintly, "What's happened to him?"

"Lady, that's fairly obvious. He's been ray-burned."

"Ray-burned? But how?"

"I wouldn't know." Dowland opened the medical kit, slid out several of the tiny containers, turned one of them over in his hand. He asked, "Where was he when you found him?"

"Lying outside the door of the lab."

"Lab?"

Jill Trelawney bit her lip. "The building I showed you."

"Where Paul Trelawney's locked up?"

"Yes. They call it a lab."

"Who are they?"

"Miguel and Paul."

"What kind of lab is it?" Dowland asked absently.

"I don't know. They're building something there. Some sort of a machine."

"Are your uncles scientists?"

"Yes." Her tone had begun to harden—a Freeholder lady rebuffing a non-Terran's prying.

Dowland said, "If we knew whether they had radiation suits in that lab . . ."

"I believe they do."

He nodded. "That might account for Miguel."

He took a minute hypodermic syringe from the kit, inserted the needle through a penetration point on the container he had selected, filled it slowly. Jill stirred uneasily, asked, "What are you giving him?"

Dowland glanced over at her. "I don't know exactly. The brand name's 'medic'. There are around thirty other names for what's probably the same preparation. They're all very popular wherever good doctors and good hospitals aren't readily available. I haven't run into medic on Terra, but I bring along my own supply."

"What will it do for him?"

"Well, as I understand it, as soon as I inject this into his arm, it will spread through his body and start looking things over. Medic appears to know what a healthy human body should be like. So it diagnoses what's wrong—cold symptoms, burned-out lung, hangover, broken ankle—and then tries to bring the situation back to normal."

❖   ❖   ❖

He slid up Miguel Trelawney's sleeve, inserted the needle tip into the thick, flaccid biceps, slowly depressed the plunger. "Medic's supposed to be in the class of a virus—a very well-intentioned virus when it comes to human beings." He removed the needle, glanced at his watch. "Almost six-thirty . . . A hangover'd get knocked out in three minutes. But judging from the condition your uncle seems to be in, it might be four or five hours now before the stuff really begins to take hold with him. If it can bring him back to consciousness by itself, it probably won't happen much before morning. Might be earlier; but I don't think we should wait for that before trying to get your Uncle Paul out of the lab. If he hasn't come out on his own, he may be in the same shape as Miguel. Or worse."

Jill's face paled slightly. "Yes. I've been thinking of that."

Dowland stood looking down at her, chewing on his lower lip. "You know, Miss Trelawney, there's something very odd about the fact that you found Miguel lying outside the lab when the door was locked."

She nodded. "I know. I don't have any explanation for it."

"Isn't there a storeroom of some kind around—where they might be keeping radiation suits, for instance?"

"The ranch storehouse is the small square building just south of here. I went through it this morning looking for a key to the lab. There aren't any radiation suits there."

"You know what those suits look like?"

"Yes. I've worn them when taking part in attack drills."

"Would you recognize the lab key if you saw it?"

"Yes. Miguel showed me the one he usually carries with him." She got up, went over to the mantle above the fireplace, took down a circular wedge of metal, a half-inch thick, with smoothly beveled rim. She handed it to Dowland. "The key is very similar to this one, but at least three times as large."

Dowland hefted the object shook his head. "Lady, by the weight of it, this thing's metasteel. The stuff they use for bank vaults and the hulls of battleships. And it looks as if the door to your uncles' laboratory has an atomic lock because that's what this type of key is made for. Do you know if the building's lined with steel inside?"

"It might be. Miguel told me that it had been extremely expensive to build, that he had wanted to make sure no one could get into it while he was away."

"If it's built of metasteel, he's done just that," Dowland said. "And that makes it tough." He looked at the key in his hand. "What does this key fit into?"

"I don't know. But I'm sure there's no other door on the ranch that has an—an atomic lock. I found the key in Miguel's pocket this morning."

"Well, it's probably no good to us," Dowland said. "Now look, Miss Trelawney. I'm carrying a protection gun that can be stepped up to around six times the shock power of a heavy rifle slug. I'll try that out at full charge on the lock to the lab, and then around the walls. But if it's all metasteel, shooting at it won't get us anywhere. Then we might make another search for that key. Or I could try getting down off the mesa to get help."

Jill looked doubtful. "There's no easy way down off the mesa even in daylight. And at night it would be worse."

Dowland said, "That part of it won't be too much of a problem. I brought mountaineering equipment along this trip—planned to pick up a Marco Polo ram and a few ewes—piton gun, clamp pitons, half-mile of magnetic rope; the works. Question is, how much good will it do? I've got a camp communicator, but it's grid-powered, and we don't know how far the power failure extends around here at ground level. Is there anyone down in the plain we could contact? They might have horses."

She shook her head. "I would have heard of that. You could wander around there for weeks before you were seen."

Dowland was silent a moment. "Well," he said, "it should be worth a try if we can't accomplish anything within another few hours. Judging from my car's position when its power went off, it shouldn't really be more than a ten-mile hike from the bottom of the mesa before I can start using the communicator. But, of course, it will take up a lot of time. So we'll see what we can do here first."

He slipped his jacket on. "You'd better stay with your uncle, Miss Trelawney. I—"

He interrupted himself. An unearthly din had begun suddenly outside the house—whistling squeals, then an angry ear-shattering noise somewhere between a howl and a roar. The girl started, then smiled nervously. Dowland asked, "What is that?"

"Miguel's pigs. I expect they're simply hungry. The feeding equipment in the animal house isn't operating either, of course."

"Pigs? I've heard pigs make a racket, but never anything like that."

"These," said Jill, "are rather large. My uncle is interested in experimental breeding. I understand the biggest tusker weighs nearly two tons. They're alarming beasts. Miguel's the only one who can get close to the boar."

✧   ✧   ✧

Outside it was early evening, still light, but Dowland
went first to the wrecked grid-car to get a flashlight.
He'd need it during the night, might even need it
immediately if he found he could force an entry into
the laboratory. In that case—if the building wasn't
metasteel after all—he probably would find no YM
inside it. Which, Dowland admitted to himself, would
be entirely all right with him.

But he was reasonably certain it was there. The
Overgovernment's instructions about what to watch for
remained annoyingly indefinite, but uniformly they
stressed the unusual, in particular when associated with
the disastrous. And so far, that described the situation
here. The large and uncomfortable question was what
kind of disaster might be about to erupt next.

There were other questions, somewhat too many of
them at the moment. But the one he wanted answered
immediately concerned Jill Trelawney's role. There was
a guaranteed way of getting the information from her,
but he had to be sure she wasn't as innocent as she
acted before resorting to it. At the very least, he had
to establish that the activities in the laboratory constituted some serious violation of Overgovernment
law—even if not directly connected with YM—and that
the girl knew about it. Otherwise, the whole present
pattern of the YM-400 search on Terra might become
very obvious to all interested parties.

He thought he had a method of forcing Jill's hand.
If she had guilty knowledge, she might consider a non-
Terran animal trader, who'd just happened to drop in,
literally, a convenient tool to use in this emergency. She
wanted to get help, too, though not from the Solar
Police Authority. The Trelawneys couldn't possibly be
alone in this thing.

But she couldn't, if guilty, take the chance of trying

to make use of an Overgovernment cop. A policeman wouldn't be here at this particular moment by accident. There was some risk in revealing himself—she might react too hastily—but not much risk, Dowland thought. From what he'd seen of her, she'd use her head. She'd make sure of him.

The uproar from the animal building lessened as he went back across the slope to the entrance of the lab. Miguel's beasts might have caught his footsteps, and started to listen to see if he was coming in. The outer door to the lab—a frame of the weather-proofed wood that covered the building—stood slightly open. Dowland pulled it back, looked for a moment at the slab of metasteel behind it, and at the circular depression in the slab which was the atomic lock.

In character, so far. Three windows at the back of the house where he had left Jill Trelawney with Miguel overlooked the lab area. Guilty or not, she'd be watching him from behind one of those windows, though she mightn't have come to any conclusions about him as yet. The reference to his "protection" gun had been a definite giveaway; he'd described an IPA police automatic, and that was a weapon civilians didn't carry—or didn't mention to strangers if they happened to carry them.

But a Freeholder lady might not know about that.

She couldn't avoid noticing the implications of an IPA antiradiation field. . . .

Dowland moved thirty steps back from the door, took out his gun, and pressed a stud on the side of his belt. Immediately, a faint blue glow appeared about him. Not too pronounced a glow even on the darkening slope, but quite visible to anyone watching from one of the windows. He took a deep breath, sucking air in through the minor hampering effect of the field.

The rest was a matter of carrying through with the act. He'd known from the instant of looking at the door that he was wasting his fire on metasteel. But he slammed a few shots into the five-inch target of the lock, then worked his way methodically about the building, watching the weatherproofing shatter away from an unmarred silvery surface beneath. The gun made very little noise, but Miguel's hogs were screaming themselves hoarse again by the time he was finished.

Dowland switched off the AR field, and went back to the house. When he came along the short entrance hall, she was waiting for him, standing half across the living room, hands clasped behind her back. She looked at him questioningly.

"No luck, Dowland?"

Dowland shook his head. "Not a bit." He started to shrug the jacket from his shoulders, saw her dart the gun out from behind her, and turned his left hand slightly, squeezing down on the black elastic capsule he was holding between thumb and forefinger. Jill probably never noticed the motion, certainly did not see or feel the tiny needle that flashed from the capsule and buried itself in the front of her thigh. Shocked bewilderment showed for an instant on her face; then her knees gave way, the gun dropped from her hand. She went down slowly, turned over on her side on the thick carpet, and lay still.

Well, Dowland thought, he had his proof. . . .

Jill Trelawney opened her eyes again about five minutes later. She made a brief effort to get out of the deep armchair in which she found herself, then gave that up. The dark blue eyes fastened on Dowland, standing before the chair. He saw alarm and anger in them; then a cold watchfulness.

"What did you do?" she asked huskily.

"I shot first," Dowland said. "It seemed like a good idea."

Her glance shifted to Miguel on the couch across the room.

"How long was I unconscious?"

"Just a few minutes."

"And why . . ." She hesitated.

"Why are you feeling so weak? You've absorbed a shot of a special little drug, Miss Trelawney. It does two things that are very useful under certain circumstances. One of them is that it keeps the recipient from carrying out any sudden or vigorous action. You might, for example, be able to get out of that chair if you tried hard enough.

"But you'd find yourself lying on the carpet then. Perhaps you'd be able to get up on your hands and knees. You might even start crawling from the room—but you'd do it very slowly."

Dowland paused. "And the other thing the drug does is to put the person into an agreeable frame of mind, even when he'd rather not be agreeable. He becomes entirely cooperative. For example, you'll find yourself quite willing to answer questions I ask."

"So you *are* a police investigator," she said evenly.

"That's right." Dowland swung another chair around beside him, and sat down facing her. "Let's not waste any more time, Miss Trelawney. Were you going to shoot me just now?"

She looked briefly surprised.

"No," she said. "Not unless you forced me to it. I was going to disarm you and lock you in a cellar downstairs. You would have been safe there as long as was necessary."

"How long would that be?"

"Until I get help."

"Help from whom?"

Angry red flared about Jill's cheekbones. "This is incredible!" she said softly. "Help from Carter."

"Firebrand Carter?" Dowland asked.

"Yes."

"He's associated with your uncles?"

"Yes."

"Who heads the group?"

"Miguel and Carter head it together. They're very close friends."

"And who else is in it—besides Paul and yourself?"

She shook her head. "There must be quite a few people in it, but I don't know their names. We feel it's best if we know as little as possible about one another at present."

"I see. But they're all Terran Freeholders?"

"Yes, of course."

"How did you happen to be told about Carter?"

"In case of an emergency here, I'm to contact him on a tight-beam number."

"And just what," Dowland asked, "have your uncles been doing here?"

"Building a machine that will enable then to move back through time."

"With the help of YM-400?"

"Yes."

Dowland stared at her thoughtfully, feeling a little chilled. She believed it, of course; she was incapable of lying now. But he didn't believe it. He'd heard that some Overgovernment scientists considered time-travel to be possible. It was a concept that simply had no reality for him.

But he thought of the rumors about YM—and of Miguel found lying inexplicably outside the laboratory building. He asked carefully, "Have they completed the machine?"

"Yes. They were making the first full-scale test of it this morning—and they must have been at least partly successful."

"Because of Miguel?"

"Yes."

"You feel," Dowland said, "that Miguel first went somewhere else—or somewhen else, let's say—and then came back and wound up a little bit away from where he'd started?"

"Yes."

"Any idea of how he was hurt?"

The girl shook her head. "The grid-power failure shows there was an accident of some kind, of course. But I can't imagine what it was."

"What about Paul? Do you think he's still in the lab?"

"Not unless he's also injured—or dead."

Dowland felt the chill again. "You think he may be in some other time at this moment?"

"Yes."

"And that he'll be back?"

"Yes."

"Can you describe that machine?" he asked.

"No. I've never seen the plans, and wouldn't understand them if I did. And I've never been inside the lab."

"I see. Do you have any reason, aside from the way Miguel reappeared, to think that the test was a partial success?"

"Yes. At three different times since this morning I've heard the sounds of a river flowing under the house."

"You heard what?" Dowland said.

"A river flowing under the house. The noises were quite unmistakable. They lasted for about thirty minutes on each occasion."

"What would that indicate?" he asked.

"Well, obviously . . . this time period and another one—the one in which that river flows—have drawn close to each other. But the contact is impermanent or imperfect at present."

"Is that the way the machine is supposed to operate?"

"I don't know how the machine is supposed to operate," Jill Trelawney said. "But that's what seems to have happened."

Dowland studied her face for a moment. "All right," he said then, "let's leave it for now. Who developed this machine?"

"Miguel did. Paul helped, in the later stages. Others have helped with specific details—I don't know who those other people were. But essentially it was Miguel's project. He's been working on it for almost twenty years."

And that simply couldn't be true. Unless . . .

"Miss Trelawney," Dowland said, "do you know what Miguel's I.Q. reading is?"

"Of course. It's 192."

"And Paul's?"

"189." She smiled. "You're going to ask whether they faked lower levels when they were tested by the university authorities. Yes, they did. This thing has been prepared for a long time, Dowland."

"What's your own I.Q., Miss Trelawney?"

"181."

Her dossier I.Q., based on records of her known activities and behavior, was an estimated 128. The Freeholders did seem to have planned very thoroughly for the success of this operation.

"Do you know who hijacked the YM-400?" Dowland asked.

"Yes. Paul arranged for that."

"Have you seen the stuff yourself?"

"I have. Two small cases of blue ingots. A very dark blue. Individually, the ingots appear to be quite heavy, though they aren't very large."

That described exactly what the Overgovernment was looking for. Dowland asked, "How much of it is in the laboratory?"

"It's all there."

He felt his scalp crawling. "All of it! Haven't your uncles heard that YM is an incredibly dangerous thing to play around with?"

"Of course. But Miguel examined it very carefully after it was obtained. If reasonable precautions are taken, there is no way in which it can become dangerous. The conclusion was that the Overgovernment has spread rumors as a bluff, to try to prevent the YM from being used."

"What's happened around here," Dowland said, "might indicate it wasn't a bluff."

"You're jumping to conclusions, Dowland. A great many other things may have gone wrong."

"Perhaps. But an I.Q. of 136 keeps telling me that we're in considerable danger at the moment."

Jill nodded. "That's very probably true."

"Then how about giving me your full cooperation until we—you, I, your uncles—are all safely out of this?"

"At the moment," Jill observed, "I don't appear to have a choice in the matter."

"I don't mean that. The drug will wear off in a few hours. You'll be able to move around freely again, and whether you cooperate or not will depend on you. How will you feel about it then?"

"That depends," Jill said, "on whether we have reached an agreement."

"Agreement about what?"

"A price for your silence, and for any assistance you can give in keeping things quiet. You can, of course, set the price as high as you wish. Terra will meet it."

Dowland stared at her, somewhat astounded. It was as cold-blooded an attempt at bargaining as he'd run into, considering the circumstances. And—considering an I.Q. of 181—it seemed rather unrealistic. "Miss Trelawney," he said, "the only thing silence might get me is a twenty-year stretch in an IPA pen. I'm not quite that foolish."

"You're also not aware of the true situation."

"All right," Dowland said, "what is it?"

"Miguel and Paul have earned the right to carry out the first of these tests. They may not complete it. But duplicates of their machine in the laboratory are concealed about the planet, waiting to be put into action by other teams of Freeholder scientists. You see? The tests will be continued until any problems connected with shifting back through time are recognized and overcome."

Dowland said, "Then why is the entire haul of YM stacked away in the laboratory here?"

"Because that's where it's to be used at present. You still don't understand the extent of this operation, Dowland. If we need more of the Overgovernment's YM, we'll simply take it. It can be done at any time. The only way the Overgovernment could really prevent future raids would be by destroying its supplies of YM-400. And it isn't going to do that—at least not before we've obtained as much as we can use."

As far as his own information went, she could be right, Dowland thought. He said, "So supposing some Freeholder scientists do succeed eventually in traveling back in time. What will that accomplish?"

"Everything we want, of course," Jill said. "There'll

be no more reason to conceal our activities—and we'll have *time*. As much time as we need. Thirty or fifty years perhaps. Scientific centers and automatic factories will be set up in the past, and eventually the factories will be turning out weapons superior to anything the Overgovernment has. And then the weapons will come to the present—to *this* present, Dowland. Within a year from now, Terra will have become a heavily armed world—overnight. There'll be no more talk then of forcing us to remain under Overgovernment rule. Or of making Terra another Open Planet. . . ."

Theoretically, Dowland could see that such a plan might work. With the time to do it in, and the resources of a world at the Freeholders' disposal . . . and there would be nothing to keep them from taking back spaceships and mining the asteroids. For a moment, while Jill Trelawney was talking, she had made it sound almost plausible.

Only for a moment. She was, of course, telling the truth as she knew it. They were up to something very dangerous—and very illegal—here, whatever it was, and they'd spread the time travel idea around among the lesser members of the group to help keep the real purpose concealed. He said, "Just how far back in time are they planning to go, Miss Trelawney?"

"Six hundred thousand years. The period is regarded as particularly suitable for what is being planned."

Six hundred thousand years. Nothing half-hearted about the Freeholders, Dowland thought sardonically, even as to the size of the lies they put out. "When you waved me in here this evening," he said. "I had the impression you were expecting someone else. Was I right?"

"Yes. But I wasn't waving you in, Dowland. I was attempting to wave you off. If you'd been the man I thought it was, you would have realized it. . . . Have you considered my suggestion?"

"About selling out to the Freeholders?"

"If you wish to call it that."

"Miss Trelawney," Dowland said amiably, "if I did sell out, would you admire me for it?"

Her cheeks flushed. "No. You'd be despicable, of course."

Dowland nodded. "That's one thing we agree on. Now, just who was this man you were expecting, and just why were you expecting him?"

The girl's lips twisted reluctantly for a moment; then words broke out again. "Carter is to send a man to the ranch with some pieces of equipment. The equipment either was unloaded at Columbia spaceport this afternoon, or will be, early tomorrow morning. I thought you were the messenger. Strange grid-cars don't come through this area more than once every few weeks. If you'd been the man, you would already have attempted to call our house communicator by the time I saw you. . . ."

"To make sure the coast was clear before coming in with odd-looking equipment."

"Yes. You would then have reported to Carter that there was no answer, which would have resulted in an immediate investigation. I was attempting to warn the messenger that he shouldn't come closer, that something was seriously wrong here."

Dowland reflected, nodded. "That would have worked—if I'd been the man. And now it seems it's a good thing I inquired about this, Miss Trelawney. Because the messenger actually may have arrived this evening, received no answer from the ranch, reported the fact, and gone away again—mightn't he?"

"Yes, that may have happened." Her eyes were furious with frustration.

"And what would Carter do then?"

"He would rush a few squads of Troopers here to investigate."

"Hedgehopping," Dowland nodded, "in approved Trooper style to avoid detection. They hit the power-failure area, and the first few cars crash. They report the matter. What would happen then, Miss Trelawney?"

"Damn you, Dowland. They'd scout around Lion Mesa to see how close they could get by air. Carter would have horses and climbing equipment flown in to that point, and they'd continue on horseback."

There were other methods, Dowland thought. Parachutes, gliders—they could even try ditching a few cars on the mesa as he'd done. He considered, and mentally shook his head. Aside from the difficulties, the Troopers would be warned to avoid spectacular stunts in the vicinity of the mesa. They'd come exactly as she'd said. It was a completely unobtrusive form of approach, even for a large body of men, and it would still get them here fast.

He said, "Well, let's suppose all that has happened. Carter's Troopers are on their way here at this minute, riding pell-mell. Giving them every break, what's the earliest moment we can expect them to show up?"

She said, "Not before morning."

"I'd figured it at perhaps two hours before sunrise," Dowland said. "What would hold them up?"

"They can't climb the mesa at any point near the ranch by night. A descent might be possible, but even that would be difficult and dangerous. And they'll be carrying repair equipment to take care of whatever's gone wrong. So they'll have to come up the northern end, where it isn't so steep."

"And then," Dowland said, "they still have to come down across the mesa on foot. Makes sense. And, of course, that messenger actually may not get here before tomorrow. If he comes then, at what time would he arrive?"

She shrugged. "Before noon. The hour wasn't specified."

"In any case," Dowland said, "you were figuring on stalling me around here until Carter's boys turned up. Then you realized I must be an Overgovernment man, and decided it would be too dangerous to allow me to prowl about the ranch until help came."

Jill nodded.

Dowland considered her reflectively. "You understand, I believe, that unless I can somehow get word to the Solar Police Authority within the next few hours, Miguel's injuries may very well kill him? And that if I could get word out, an SPA jet would have him in the nearest hospital ten minutes later?"

"I understand both those things, Dowland," she said. "But I also know that Miguel would not choose to have his life saved at the cost of exposing our plans."

Dowland shrugged. "Very well . . . Now, were the things that happened before I got here as you've described them?"

"Yes."

"You know of no way to get into that laboratory at present?"

"Not unless you can find the key to the door."

"That key should be around this immediate area?"

"It should be," she said, "but I haven't been able to find it."

"No further ideas about that?"

"None."

Dowland was silent a moment. "Miss Trelawney," is there anything else that might be of importance here that you still have not told me?"

Her eyes studied him coldly. "Perhaps one thing . . ."

"And what's that?"

"If you had been willing to be bribed," Jill Trelawney said, "I should have asked the Troopers to shoot you."

There was a lady, Dowland was thinking a few minutes later, who was likely to be something of a problem to any man. However, she wouldn't be his problem for a considerable number of hours now. She had swallowed the sleep tablet he had given her without any trouble. After the drug wore off, the tablet would keep her quiet till around dawn.

He stood looking about the wind-swept darkened slopes of the ranch area. Clouds were moving past in the sky, but there would be intermittent moonlight. The conditions weren't too bad for the search he had in mind. There had to be a concealed storeroom about the place somewhere, in which the Trelawneys would keep assorted stuff connected with their secret work which they didn't want to have cluttering up the lab. Including, very likely, any spare keys to the lab. At a guess, neither of the brothers would have wanted Jill at Lion Mesa during this crucial and dangerous stage of the project. But they probably were used to letting their beautiful and headstrong niece do as she wanted. But they needn't have mentioned things like the storeroom to her. If he could keep his mind slightly off the fact that within a hundred yards or so of him there were sixty-eight kilograms of YM-400—with an unspecified amount of it at present in its horrendous radioactive state—he should stand a fairly good chance of finding the storeroom.

And in that case, the half-inch atomic key Jill Trelawney had showed him, and which was at the moment weighing down his coat pocket, probably would turn out to be exactly what he needed to get into it.

He located the place just under an hour later. It was a matter partly of observation, partly of remembering a remark Jill had made. The building which housed the giant hogs adjoined a corral three times its size. Corral and building were divided into two sections, the larger one harboring six sows. The single boar was in the other. A spider web of gangways led about above the huge stalls. It was the wall between building and corral which had drawn Dowland's attention by the fact that a little calculating indicated it was something like a yard thicker than was necessary.

He brought a dozen campfire sticks over from the grid-car and spaced them down the central gangway of the building, then deferred further inspection long enough to locate and trip the automatic feeding mechanisms. The hungry animal thunder which had greeted him at his entry ebbed away as they ate furiously and he studied them. They weren't the grotesque monstrosities he had expected but massive, sculptured giants with the quick, freewheeling agility of a rhinoceros, sand-colored, with wickedly intelligent eyes. There wasn't much question they'd make exciting game for anyone who enjoyed a touch of personal danger in the hunt.

The danger was more obviously there in the boar. The brute's eight hundred or so pounds of weight above that of the average of his prospective harem would not be significant when pitted against an opponent as physically inferior as a human being. His attitude might. The sows filed out into the corral after they had eaten what the feeding machine had thrown into them. The boar remained, watching Dowland on the gangway above him from the corner of one eye. The eye reflected no gratitude for the feeding. It was red-rimmed and angry. The jaw worked with a continuous chewing motion. There was a fringe of foam along the mouth.

Jill Trelawney had mentioned that no one but Miguel could come near the boar.

Dowland could believe it. A small steel ladder led down from the gangway into the brute's stall. Dowland reached into his pocket and brought out the IPA gun. No sportsman would have considered using it against an animal. But this wasn't sport. He started down the ladder.

The boar stood motionless, watching him. Dowland stopped at the foot of the ladder. After a moment, he took a step forward. The boar pivoted and came thundering across the floor of the stall, head low. The gun made its soft, heavy sound, and Dowland leaped aside. The huge body that slammed into the far wall behind him was dead before it struck, nearly headless. He went on to the thick dividing wall between stall and yard.

The lock to the storeroom door was on the inner side of the wall, concealed by the planking but not too difficult to find. Dowland inserted the key, twisted it into position, felt a slight click, and stepped back as the door began to swing out toward him.

The storeroom contained the general kind of paraphernalia he had expected to find, including three antiradiation suits. It took Dowland twenty minutes to convince himself that the one thing it definitely did not contain in any obvious manner was a key to the laboratory. Appropriate detection instruments might have disclosed it somewhere, but he didn't have them.

The fact was dismaying because it ended his hopes of finding the key. It would take most of the night to make a thorough search of the various ranch buildings, and at best there would be an even chance of discovering the key in the process. Wherever it was, it must be carefully concealed. If Miguel regained consciousness, the information could be forced from him, but it wasn't too likely that the older Trelawney ever would wake up again.

Dowland picked up two of the three AR suits, folded them over his arm, stood, still hesitant, glancing up and down the long, narrow space of the storeroom, half aware that he was hoping now some magical intuition might point out the location of the key to him at the last second. If he could get into the laboratory, he was reasonably sure he could puzzle out the mechanisms that directed the shift of YM into radioactivity, and shut them down. A machine was a machine, after all. Then, with the YM interference eliminated, grid power should be available again, and . . .

Dowland glanced at his watch again, shook his head. No point in considering it—he couldn't get into the laboratory. An hour and a half had gone to no purpose. Hunting for the key had looked like a good gamble, the quickest and therefore least dangerous method of solving the whole awesome problem. But it hadn't worked out; and what was left was to work down the side of Lion Mesa, and start hiking out across the desert. With luck, he'd find the communicator start picking up grid power again around dawn—if the YM didn't cut loose with further unpredictable and much more disastrous "phenomena" before then. Unsatisfactorily vague as the available information had been, it implied that what had happened around here was still, so far, on a very mild level. The Trelawneys, in spite of their confidence that the Overgovernment was bluffing, that YM was harmless if properly handled, might have had the good sense to work with only the most minute quantities to begin with.

He left the storeroom door open, turned off the whiter glowing campfire sticks, and took them, with the AR suits, back to the house with him. The living room had become almost completely dark. Uncle and niece were where he had left them. Dowland worked for a minute or two to release the automatic shutters over the single wide window; they came down into position then with a sudden thud which shook the room but failed to arouse the Trelawneys. Dowland relit one of the sticks and dropped it into the fireplace. The room filled with clear light.

He stacked the other stick against the wall, laid the AR suits over the back of a chair. He had considered getting the Trelawneys into them as a safety measure against whatever might happen before the matter was over, but had dropped the idea again. It would be questionable protection. The antiradiation field was maintained automatically while a suit was worn, and it impeded breathing just enough to have occasionally suffocated an unconscious wearer. Jill would discover the suits when she woke up and could use her own judgment about them.

Dowland was coming back from the grid-car with his mountaineering harness and portable communicator when the hogs began to scream again. He stopped, startled. There was an odd and disturbing quality to the racket this time—even more piercing than before—and, unless he was mistaken, the huge animals were in a sudden panic about something. Next, he heard them slamming against the sides of the corral, apparently trying to break out of it. His heart started to pound with instinctive alarms. Should he go down and investigate? Then, before he could decide, he heard through the din of the hogs, swelling gradually to almost match those incredible shrieks in volume, another sound. For a moment, something seemed to shut off Dowland's listening to the rumble and roar of a rushing, turbulent mass of water—and his ears told him it was passing by beneath him.

✧   ✧   ✧

It might have been almost two minutes later before Dowland began to think clearly again. He had reached the house at a dead run—a senseless flight reaction under the circumstances, not far from complete panic. In the darkness outside, the mesa had seemed to sway and tilt, treacherous footing over the eerie booming of a river which had rolled through a long-dead past. In those seconds Dowland hadn't thought to question Jill Trelawney's story about a machine that brought about shifts in time. His senses seemed to have as much evidence to support it as anyone could demand.

Back in the house, though the thundering disturbance continued, that conviction rapidly faded. He could close his eyes and immediately have the feeling of being on an unstable bridge above the swirls of some giant current. He could open them again and tell himself that YM-400 had a reputation for freakish effects—and that this specific effect, at any rate, should not be very harmful since Jill had reported it as having occurred on three separate occasions during the preceding day. To speak of such a commotion as being only the sound of a "river flowing under the house" seemed to approach the outrageous in understatement; but Jill Trelawney had turned out to be an unusual young person all around.

She and her uncle hadn't stirred, but Dowland knew that their presence in the room steadied him. He knew, too, that, whatever happened next, he couldn't allow himself to be rattled into blind fright again. The situation was dangerous enough. If he let his nerves stampede him, he would find himself unable to take any effective action.

He went over deliberately to the mountaineering harness he had dropped when he entered the lighted room, and began to check through the equipment. He intended to carry, in addition, only the communicator, the IPA gun, a canteen of water, and a small flashlight; and he would abandon the harness and its items at the foot of the mesa. There were two hunting rifles in the car, with a vastly better range than the handgun; but a rifle would slow him down and would make very little real difference if he had the bad luck to run into Carter's Troopers in the desert.

Somewhat to his surprise, the underground tumult appeared to be growing fainter before he had concluded his inspection. Dowland paused to listen, and within a few seconds there was no more doubt about it. Jill had said it had gone on for half an hour on each of the previous occasions; but Dowland's watch confirmed that the present disturbance was subsiding rapidly after less than ten minutes. By the time he stood up, snapped on the harness and shrugged it into position, it had become almost inaudible.

Which might be a good sign, or a bad one, or without particular significance of any kind. He couldn't know, and he'd probably be better off if he didn't start thinking too much about it. He turned for a last survey of the room before setting out, and discovered that Miguel Trelawney had opened his eyes and was looking at him.

Dowland stood stockstill for a moment, hardly daring to believe it. Then, quietly, he unbuckled the harness again, and let it down to the floor. The eyes of the big man on the couch seemed to follow the motion, then shifted slowly up toward the ceiling of the room, and closed again.

"Trelawney," Dowland said softly, without moving.

Miguel Trelawney made a deep, sighing sound, turned on his side and lay quiet, his back now to

Dowland. A few seconds later, Dowland was looking down at him from the other side of the couch.

It might have been only a momentary thing, a brief advantage medic had gained in its invisible struggle with a process which would still end in death. But he couldn't be sure. The eyes remained closed, the pulse was weak and unsteady. Dowland thought of injecting a stimulant into Trelawney, and discarded the idea immediately. Medic manufactured its own stimulants as required, counteracted any others. Even the effects of the quiz-drug would be reduced by it, but not enough to keep Dowland from getting any answer he wanted—provided Trelawney's mind cleared for only three or four minutes of lucidity.

There was no way of knowing when such a period of lucidity might develop. But now that the man had appeared to awaken, the possibility that it would happen within the next hour or two became a very definite one.

Dowland stood briefly in scowling indecision. The next hour or two could also see him nearly down the side of the mesa, depending on the difficulties of the descent . . . but there was no real choice. It was a gamble either way again; if Trelawney didn't awaken, the other gamble remained. . . . How long, at most, could he afford to delay?

Leaving YM out of the calculation, since it couldn't be calculated, he had only the arrival of the Freeholder Troopers to consider. There was no apparent possibility that any sizable party could appear before daybreak, but there was an even chance they would be there around that time. When they came, he must either be in communication with the Solar Police Authority or far enough away from Lion Mesa to be able to avoid detection. . . .

Four hours should be enough to give him a

reasonable safety margin. He had till midnight, or a little later.

Dowland pulled a chair up to the side of the couch and sat down. The night wasn't quiet.

The hogs squalled occasionally, and the wind still seemed to be rising. In spite of his efforts to avoid unsettling lines of thought, the nightmarish quality of the situation on the mesa kept returning to his mind and wasn't easily dismissed. The past—the past of over half a million years ago—had moved close to the present tonight. . . . That was the stubborn, illogical feeling—and fear—which he couldn't entirely shake off.

Half an hour later, Miguel Trelawney began breathing uneasily, then stirred about, but lapsed again within seconds into immobile unconsciousness.

Dowland resumed his waiting.

His watch had just told him it was shortly before eleven-thirty when he heard the shots. They were three shots—clear, closely spaced cracks of sound, coming from a considerable distance away. Dowland was out of his chair with the second one, halfway down the dark entry hall as he heard the third. He opened the door at the end of the hall just wide enough to slip through, moved out quickly, and closed the door behind him to keep the glow of light from the living room from showing outside.

As the door snapped shut, there were three more shots. A hunting rifle. Perhaps two miles to the north . . .

Dowland stood staring up toward the wind-tossed line of the forest above the ranch area. Who was up there on the mesa—and why the shooting? Had the Troopers managed to get some men in by air? What would they be firing at?

Signal shots, he thought then. And a signal to the ranch, in that case . . . Signaling what?

With that, another thought came, so abruptly and convincingly that it sent a chill through him.

Doctor Paul Trelawney . . .

Paul Trelawney, not in the laboratory building—as Jill had surmised. Gone elsewhere, now returned. And, like his brother, returned to a point other than the one from which he had left.

A man exhausted and not sure of where he was on the big tableland, an injured man—or perhaps one weakened by radiation sickness—such a man would fire a gun in the night to draw attention to himself. To get help.

Minutes later, Dowland was headed in the direction from which the shots had come, carrying one of his own rifles, along with the police gun. It was very unlikely he could get close enough to Trelawney—if it was Trelawney—to be heard approaching; but once he reached the general area of the shots, he would fire the rifle, and wait for a response. In the forest, the wind was wild and noisy, and the going was as rough as he had suspected it would be. Moonlight flowed into the open rocky stretches occasionally, and faded again as clouds moved on overhead. Among the trees he could barely see his way and had to advance more slowly.

He came presently to a wide, smooth hump of rock shouldering up through the timber, and stopped to check the time. Twenty-five minutes had passed since he left the area of the house. If he had calculated correctly, the shots should have come from approximately this point. He moved somewhat cautiously into the open—a man waiting for help would think of selecting a place where he could be easily seen; and this could be the spot Paul Trelawney had chosen. And

Trelawney, armed with a gun, might react rather abruptly if he saw a stranger approach.

But the ridge lay empty under the moon, stretching out for over a hundred yards to right and left. Dowland reached its top, moved on among the trees on the north side, and there paused again.

A feeling came, gradually and uneasily, of something wrong around here. He stood listening, unable to define exactly what was disturbing him; then a fresh gust of wind whipped through the branches about him, and the wrongness was on the wind—a mingled odor, not an unfamiliar one, but out of place in the evergreen forest, on this rocky shelf. A breath of warm darkness, of rotting, soft vegetation—of swamp or river-bed. Dowland found his breathing quickening.

Then the scent faded from the air again. It might, he was thinking seconds later, have been a personal hallucination, a false message from nerves overexcited by the events of the night. But if Paul Trelawney had returned to this point from a distant time, the route by which he had come might still be open. And the opening not far from here. It was a very unpleasant notion. Dowland began to move on again, but in a slow and hesitant manner now.

Another five minutes, he thought. At the end of that time, he certainly must have covered the distance over which the wind had carried the bark of a rifle—and should, in fact, be a little to the north of Trelawney on the mesa. If there were no further developments by then, he would fire a shot himself.

The five minutes took him to another section of open ground, more limited than the previous one. Again an outcropping of weathered rock had thrust back the trees, and Dowland worked his way up the steep side to the top, and stood looking about. After some seconds, the understanding came suddenly that

he was delaying firing the rifle because of a reluctance
to reveal his presence in these woods. With an abrupt,
angry motion he brought up the barrel pointing it
across the trees to the north, and pulled the trigger.

The familiar whiplash of sound seemed startling
loud. An instant later, there was a series of unnerv-
ing crashing noises in the forest ahead. Apparently
some large animal had been alarmed by the shot. He
heard it blundering off for a few hundred yards; then
there was silence, as if it had stopped to listen. And
then there was another sound, a deep, long cry that
sent a shiver through his flesh. It ended; and the next
thing that caught his attention was a glimpse of something moving near the edge of his vision to the left,
just above the forest. His head and eyes shifted quickly
toward it, and he found himself staring after a great
shadowy thing flapping and gliding away over the tops
of the trees. It disappeared almost immediately behind
the next rise of ground.

Dowland still stared after it, his mind seeming to
move sluggishly as if unwilling to admit what he had
seen was no creature he had ever heard about. Then
it occurred to him suddenly that Trelawney had not
yet responded to the signal shot; and almost with the
thought, he grew aware of a renewed disturbance in
the forest before him.

This one was much less loud than the other had
been. For a moment, Dowland thought it was being
caused by the wind. But the noises continued; and in
a few more seconds it became obvious that something—something that seemed to be very large
indeed—was moving among the trees and approaching the open area. By that time, it wasn't very far away.

Dowland turned, his mouth working silently, and
slipped down the south side of the big rock hump,

making no more noise than he could help. Already the trees were shaking on the other side of the rock. He ducked, crouched, into a thick mass of juniper branches, pushed through them, and made his way quickly and quietly deeper among the trees. This new thing, whatever it was, must also have heard the shot. It might check when it reached the open area and, when it discovered nothing to arouse its further curiosity, move off again.

But it didn't. Glancing back through the trees, Dowland had an indistinct glimpse of something very tall coming swiftly around the shoulder of rock. He turned, scuttled on under the branches, and a moment later, there was a tremendous crashing at the point where he had left the open ground. The thing was following him down into the woods.

Dowland turned again, gasping, dropped the rifle, and pulled the IPA gun from his pocket. The thickets splintered; a towering shape came through them. He drove three shots at it, had the approximate sensation of being struck across the head with an iron bar, and felt himself fall forward. He lost consciousness before he hit the earth.

When he opened his eyes, his first thought was that he should be feeling a king-sized headache. He wasn't. He was lying face down on moist forest mold. There was a very dim predawn light about. So several hours must have gone by since . . .

Dowland stiffened a moment, then turned his head very slowly, peering about. After a moment, he pushed himself quietly up on hands and knees. The trees before him shifted uneasily in the wind. Farther on, he could make out part of the hump of rock on which he had stood and fired a shot to draw Trelawney's attention. Between, the ground looked as if a tank had come plowing into the forest. But there was no giant shape lying there.

So his three shots hadn't brought it down. But it had gone away—after doing what to him?

Dowland saw the IPA gun lying beside him, picked it up, and got slowly to his feet. He ran a hand experimentally over his head. No lumps, not even a feeling of tenderness . . . He would have sworn that the crack he'd felt had opened his skull. He looked about for the rifle, saw it, picked it up, and went over to the area where the trees had been tossed about.

There was a trail there—a very improbable trail. He studied it, puzzled and frowning. Not the tracks of an animal. If it had been more regular, such a track conceivably might have been laid by a machine moving along on a very wide smooth roller. There were no indications of any kind of a tread. As it was, about all he could say now was that something very ponderous had crushed a path—a path varying between approximately eight and fourteen feet in width— through the woods to this point, and had then withdrawn again along a line roughly parallel to its approach. . . . And he could say one other thing about it, Dowland added mentally. The same ponderous entity could knock out a man for hours, without apparently injuring him, or leaving any sign of how he had been struck down.

The last sounded more like a machine again; a machine which was armed in some mysterious manner. When his shot had flushed up the big flying creature during the night, he'd almost been convinced that some monster out of Terra's distant past was there on the mesa. Those two things just didn't jibe.

Dowland shook his head. He could think about that when he had more time. He'd lost—he looked at his watch—a little less than four hours. In four hours, a

large number of things might have happened in the
ranch area, with only the one partly attractive possibility among them that somebody had managed to get
into the laboratory and shut off the YM flow.

He started back at a cautious trot. Downhill and with
the light strengthening gradually, covering ground was
considerably less of a problem than it had been during the night. The wind hadn't let up; it still came in
wild, intermittent gusts that bent the trees. Now and
then a cloud of dust whipped past, suggesting that the
air over the desert was also violently disturbed. And
it might very well be, Dowland thought, that YM could
upset atmospheric conditions in an area where it was
active. Otherwise, if there was anything abnormal going
on in the forest about him, there were no detectable
indications of it.

He came out presently on a ridge from where the
ranch area was in view. It lay now approximately a third
of a mile ahead. In the dim light, everything seemed
quiet. Dowland slowed to a walk.

He might be heading into an ambush down there.
Jill Trelawney could, at most, be beginning to wake up
from her drugged sleep and for another hour or so she
would be too confused and groggy to present a problem. But others might be at the ranch by now; Paul
Trelawney or a group of Carter's Troopers. And whether
Jill was able to give them a coherent report or not, any
of the Freeholder conspirators would discover very
quickly that somebody who was not a member of their
group had been there before them; they would antici-
pate his return, be on the watch for it. Dowland left
the direct line he had been following, and headed east,
moving with constantly increasing caution. On that side,
the forest grew closest to the ranch buildings, and he
remembered noticing a hedge-like thicket of evergreens

just north of the cleared land. He could make a preliminary check of the area from there.

He was within a hundred and fifty feet of the point when he discovered just how healthy the notion of a preliminary check had been. A man was lying in the cover of the evergreens Dowland had been thinking about, head up, studying the ranch grounds. He wore an antiradiation suit of the type Dowland had found in the storeroom; a heavy rifle lay beside him. His face was in profile. It was smeared now with the sweat and dirt the AR field had held in, but Dowland recognized the bold, bony features instantly.

He had finally found Doctor Paul Trelawney.

It took Dowland over eight minutes to cover the remaining distance between them. But the stalk had eminently satisfactory results. He was within a yard of Trelawney before the Freeholder became aware of his presence. The IPA gun prodded the man's spine an instant later.

"No noise, please," Dowland said softly. "I'd sooner not kill you. I might have to."

Paul Trelawney was silent for a moment. When he spoke, his voice was raw with shock. "Who the devil are you?"

"Solar Police Authority," Dowland said. "You know why I'm here."

Trelawney grunted. Dowland went on, "Why are you hiding out?"

"Why do you think?" Trelawney asked irritably. "Before showing myself, I was trying to determine the whereabouts of the man who fired a rifle within half a mile of me during the night."

So they had been stalking each other. Dowland said, "Why couldn't that person have been your brother or niece?"

"Because I know the sound of our rifles."

"My mistake . . . Do you have a gun or other weapon on you?"

"A knife."

"Let's have it."

Trelawney reached under his chest, brought out a sheathed knife and handed it back to Dowland. Dowland lobbed it into the bushes a few yards away, moved back a little.

"Get up on your hands and knees now," he said, "and we'll make sure that's all."

He was careful about the search. Trelawney appeared passive enough at the moment, but he was not a man too take chances with. The AR suit turned out to be concealing a tailored-in two-way communicator along with as many testing and checking devices as an asteroid miner's outfit, but no weapons. In a sealed pocket, obviously designed for it, was a five-inch atomic key. Dowland skid the heavy disk out with fingers that suddenly were shaking a little.

"Does this open your laboratory here?"

"Yes."

Dowland detached the communicator's transmission unit, and dropped it with the laboratory key into his pocket. "All right," he said, "turn around and sit down." He waited until Trelawney was facing him, then went on. "How long have you been watching the ranch?"

"About an hour."

"Seen anyone—or anything?"

Trelawney regarded him quizzically, shook his head. "Not a thing."

"I won't waste time with too many questions just now," Dowland said. "The laboratory is locked, and the machine you started in there apparently is still in operation. Your brother was found outside the laboratory yesterday morning, and may be dead or dying of internal radiation burns. He was alive and didn't seem to be doing too badly when I left him and Miss Trelawney in the house last night to go looking for you. I had to drug Miss Trelawney—she isn't a very cooperative person. She should still be asleep.

"Now, if I hadn't showed up here just now, what did you intend to do?"

"I intended to stop the machine, of course," Trelawney said. His expression hadn't changed while Dowland was talking. "Preferably without involving the Solar Police Authority in our activities. But since you've now involved yourself, I urgently suggest that we go to the laboratory immediately and take care of the matter together."

Dowland nodded. "That's what I had in mind, Trelawney. Technically you're under arrest, of course, and you'll do whatever has to be done in there at gun point. Are we likely to run into any difficulties in the operation?"

"We very probably will," Trelawney said thoughtfully, "and it's just as probable that we won't know what they are before we encounter them."

Dowland stood up. "All right," he said, "let's go. We'll stop off at the house on the way. I want to be sure that Miss Trelawney isn't in a position to do something thoughtless."

He emptied the magazine of Trelawney's rifle before giving it to him. They started down to the house, Trelawney in the lead, the IPA gun in Dowland's hand.

The house door was closed. Trelawney glanced back questioningly. Dowland said in a low voice, "It isn't locked. Open it, go on in, and stop two steps inside the hallway. I'll be behind you. They're both in the living room."

He followed Trelawney in, reaching back to draw the door shut again. There was a whisper of sound.

Dowland half turned, incredulously felt something hard
jab painfully against his backbone. He stood still.

"Drop your gun, Dowland."

Jill Trelawney stood behind him. Her voice was as
clear and un-slurred as if she had been awake for
hours. Dowland cursed himself silently. She must have
come around the corner of the house the instant they
went in.

"My gun's pointing at your uncle's back," he said.
"Don't do anything that might make me nervous, Miss
Trelawney."

"Don't try to bluff Jill, friend," Paul Trelawney
advised him without turning his head. There was dry
amusement in the man's voice. "No one's ever been
able to do it. And she's quite capable of concluding
that trading an uncle for an SPA spy would still leave
Terra ahead at this stage. But that shouldn't be necessary. Jill?"

"Yes, Paul?"

"Give our policeman a moment to collect his
wits. . . . This does put him in a very embarrassing
position, after all. And I can use his help in the lab."

"I'll give you exactly three seconds, Dowland," Jill
said. "And you'd better believe that is *not* a bluff.
One . . ."

Dowland dropped his gun.

The two Trelawneys held a brief, whispered conversation in the living room. Dowland, across the room
from them, and under cover of two guns now, couldn't
catch much of it. Jill was in one of the radiation suits
he'd brought in from the storeroom. Miguel was dead.
He had still been unconscious when she woke up, and
had stopped breathing minutes afterwards. Medic had
done what it could; in this case it simply hadn't been
enough. Jill, however, had found another use for it.

Dowland thought the possibility mightn't have occurred to anyone else in similar circumstances; but he still should have thought of it when he left the house. As she began to struggle up from sleep, she remembered what Dowland had told her about medic, and somehow she had managed to inject a full ampule of it into her arm. It had brought her completely awake within minutes.

The murmured talk ended. The girl looked rather white and frightened now. Paul Trelawney's face was expressionless as he came over to Dowland. Jill shoved the gun she had put on Dowland into her belt, picked up Paul's hunting rifle, held it in her hands, and stood waiting.

"Here's the procedure, Dowland," Trelawney said. "Jill will go over to the lab with us, but stay outside on guard. She'll watch . . ."

"Did you tell her," Dowland interrupted; "to keep an eye out for something that stands twice as high as this house?"

Trelawney looked at him a moment. "So you ran into it," he said. "I was wondering. It's very curious that . . . well, one thing at a time. I cautioned her about it, as it happens. Now come over to the table."

Dowland remained standing beside the table, while across from him Trelawney rapidly sketched out two diagrams on a piece of paper. The IPA gun lay on the table near Trelawney's right hand. There might have been an outside chance of reaching it if one could have discounted Jill's watchfulness. Which, Dowland decided, one couldn't. And he'd seen her reload the rifle she was holding. He stayed where he was.

Trelawney shoved the paper across to him.

"Both diagrams represent our machine," he said, "and they should give you a general idea of what you'll see. This wheel here is at the far side of the console when we come in the door. The wheel is the flow regulator—the thing you have to keep in mind. There are scale markings on it. The major markings have the numbers one to five. Yesterday morning the regulator was set at five—full flow. Spin the wheel back to one, and the YM-400 that's been producing the flow goes inert. Is that clear?"

Dowland nodded. "Clear enough."

"After that," Trelawney remarked, "we may be able to take things a little easier."

"What's the quantity you're using in there?"

"No real reason I should tell you that, is there? But I will. The sixty-eight kilograms the Overgovernment's been grieving about are under the machine platform. We're using all of it." He grinned briefly, perhaps at Dowland's expression. "The type of job we had in mind required quantities in that class. Now, about yourself. We're not murderers. Jill tells me you can't be bribed— all right. What will happen, when this thing's settled, is that you'll have an attack of amnesia. Several months of your life will be permanently lost from your memory, including, of course, everything connected with this operation. Otherwise you won't be harmed. Understand?"

"I've heard of such things," Dowland said drily.

It wouldn't, however, be done that way. It was the kind of thing told a man already as good as dead, to keep him from making a desperate attempt to save himself. The Freeholders really wouldn't have much choice. Something had loused up their plans here, and if Dowland either disappeared or was found suffering from a sudden bout of amnesia, the IPA would turn its full attention on Terra at once. If he died, his death could be plausibly arranged to look like an accident or a killing for personal motives. These people were quite capable of sacrificing one of their group to back such a story up. And it would pass. Terra was under no more immediate suspicion than any other world. Dowland had been on a routine assignment.

There were a few brief preparations. Paul Trelawney checked the batteries in the radiation suits he and Jill were wearing, then exchanged his set for that of the spare suit. Dowland left his own AR field off for the moment. It was at least as adequate as the one developed by the Trelawneys' suits, and in some respects a much more practical device. But the suit batteries had an effective life of twenty-four hours, expending them automatically while the suits were worn. His field would maintain itself for a minimum of an hour and a half, a maximum of two hours. In this situation, Dowland wasn't sure how long he would have to depend on the field. A few more minutes of assured protection might make a difference.

He saw Trelawney studying the mountaineering rig on the floor; then he picked up the harness and brought it over to him.

"Here, put it on," he said.

"What for?" Dowland asked, surprised.

Trelawney grinned. "We may have a use for it. You'll find out in a minute or two."

They left the house by a back entrance. Clouds were banked low on the eastern horizon now; the first sunlight gleamed pale gold beneath them. In the west the sky was brown with swirling dust. Jill stopped twenty yards from the laboratory building and stood on the slope, rifle in hand, watching the men go on. At the door, Dowland switched on his AR field. Trelawney tossed the disk-shaped key over to him.

"Know how to use it?"

Dowland nodded.

"All right. After you've snapped it in and it releases

again, throw it back to me. It may be the last one around, and we're not taking it into the laboratory this time. When the door starts moving down, step back to the right of it. We'll see what the lab is like before we go in." Trelawney indicated a thimble-sized instrument on his suit. "This'll tell whether the place is hot at the moment, and approximately how hot." He waved the IPA gun in Dowland's direction. "All right, go ahead."

Dowland fitted the key into the central depression in the door, pressed down, felt the key snap into position with a sharp twisting motion of its own, released his pressure on it. An instant later, the key popped back out into his hand. He tossed it back to Trelawney, who caught it left-handed and threw it over his head in Jill's direction. The disk thudded heavily into the grass ten feet from her. The girl walked over, picked it up, and slid it into one of her suit pockets.

The slab of metasteel which made up the laboratory door began moving vertically downward. The motion stopped when the door's top rim was still several inches above the level of the sill.

A low droning came from the little instrument on Trelawney's suit. It rose and fell irregularly like the buzz of a circling wasp. Mingled with it was something that might have been the hiss of escaping steam. That was Dowland's detector confirming. The lab reeked with radiation.

He glanced over at Trelawney.

"Hot enough," the Freeholder said. "We'll go inside. But stay near the door for a moment. There's something else I want to find out about. . . .

Inside, the laboratory was unpartitioned and largely empty, a great shell of a building. Only the section to the left of the entrance appeared to have been used. That section was lighted. The light arose evenly from the surfaces of the raised machine platform halfway over to the opposite wall. The platform was square, perhaps twenty feet along its sides. Dowland recognized the apparatus on it from Trelawney's diagrams. The central piece was an egg-shaped casing which appeared to be metasteel. Near its blunt end, partly concealed, stood the long, narrow instrument console. Behind the other end of the casing, an extension ramp jutted out above the platform. At the end of the ramp was a six-foot disk that might have been quartz, rimless, brightly iridescent. It was tilted to the left, facing the bank of instruments.

"A rather expensive bit of equipment over there, Dowland," Trelawney said. "My brother developed the concept, very nearly in complete detail, almost twenty-five years ago. But a great deal of time and thought and work came then before the concept turned into the operating reality on that platform."

He nodded to the left. "That's Miguel's coat on the floor. I wasn't sure it would still be here. The atomic key you were searching for so industriously last night is in one of its pockets. Miguel was standing just there, with the coat folded over his arm, when I saw him last—perhaps two or three seconds before I was surprised to discover I was no longer looking at the instrument controls in our laboratory."

"Where were you?" Dowland asked. "Six hundred thousand years in the past?"

"The instruments showed a fix on that point in time," Trelawney said. "But this was, you understand, a preliminary operation. We intended to make a number of observations. We had not planned a personal transfer for several more weeks. But in case the test turned out to be successful beyond our expectations, I was equipped to make the transfer. That bit of optimistic foresight is why I'm still alive."

What was the man waiting for? Dowland asked, "What actually happened?"

"A good question, I'd like to know the whole answer myself. What happened in part was that I suddenly found myself in the air, falling toward a river. It was night and cloudy, but there was light enough to show it was a thoroughly inhospitable river. . . . And now I believe"—his voice slowed thoughtfully—"I believe I understand why my brother was found outside the closed door of this building. Over there, Dowland. What does that look like to you?"

Near the far left of the building, beyond the immediate range of the light that streamed from the machine stand, a big packing crate appeared to have been violently—and rather oddly—torn apart. The larger section of the crate lay near the wall, the smaller one approximately twenty feet closer to the machine platform. Assorted items with which it had been packed had spilled out from either section. But the floor between the two points of wreckage was bare and unlittered. Except for that, one might have thought the crate had exploded.

"It wasn't an explosion," Trelawney agreed when Dowland said as much. He was silent a moment, went on, "In this immediate area, two space-time frames have become very nearly superimposed. There is a constant play of stresses now as the two frames attempt to adjust their dissimilarities. Surrounding our machine we have a spherical concentration of those stresses, and there are moments when space here is literally wrenched apart. If one were caught at such an instant—ah!"

To Dowland it seemed that a crack of bright color

had showed briefly in the floor of the building, between the door and the machine platform. It flickered, vanished, reappeared at another angle before his ears had fully registered the fact that it was accompanied by a curiously chopped-off roar of sound. Like a play of lightning. But this was . . . .

The air opened out before him, raggedly framing a bright-lit three-dimensional picture. He was staring down across a foaming river to the rim of a towering green and yellow forest. The crash of the river filled the building. Something bulky and black at the far left . . . but the scene was gone—

The interior of the laboratory building lay quiet and unchanged before them again. Dowland said hoarsely, "How did you know what was going to happen?"

"I was in a position to spend several hours observing it," Trelawney said, "from the other side. You see now, I think, that we can put your mountaineer's kit to some very practical use here."

Dowland glanced across the building. "The walls . . ."

"Metasteel," Trelawney said, "and thank God for that. The building's sound; the stresses haven't affected it. We'll have some anchor points. A clamp piton against that wall, six feet above the console walk and in line with it, another one against the doorframe here, and we can rope across."

Dowland saw it, unsnapped his harness, fed the end of the magnerope through the eye of a piton, and twisted it tight. "Are we going together?" he asked.

Trelawney shook his head. "You're going, Dowland. Sorry about that, but this is no time for sporting gestures. The rope doesn't eliminate the danger. But if you find your feet suddenly dangling over the air of a very old time, you'll still stay here—I hope. If you don't make it across, I'll follow. We get two chances to shut Ymir down instead of one. All right?"

"Since you have the gun, yes," Dowland said. "If I had it, it would be the other way around."

"Of course," Trelawney agreed. He watched in silence then as Dowland rammed the threaded piton down the muzzle of the gun, locked it in position, took aim across the machine platform, and fired. The piton clamp made a slapping sound against the far wall, froze against it. Dowland gave the loose end of the rope a few tugs, said, "Solid," cut the rope, and handed the end to Trelawney.

The Freeholder reached up to set a second piton against the doorframe, fed a loop of the rope through it, and twisted it tight. Dowland slipped a set of grappling gloves out of the harness, pulled one over his right hand, tossed the other to Trelawney. "In case," he said, "you have to follow. Magnerope gets to be wearing on bare hands."

Trelawney looked briefly surprised, then grinned. "Thanks," he said. "Can you do it with one glove?"

"No strain at that distance."

"Too bad you're not a Terran, Dowland. We could have used you."

"I'm satisfied," Dowland said. "Any point in waiting now for another run of those cracks in space before making the trip?"

Trelawney shook his head. "None at all, I'm afraid. From what I saw, there's no more regularity in those stress patterns than there is in a riptide. You see how the rope is jerking right now—you'll get pulled around pretty savagely, I'd say, even if you don't run into open splits on the way across."

Dowland was fifteen feet from the door, half running with both hands on the rope, when something plucked at him. He strained awkwardly sideways, feet almost lifting from the floor. Abruptly he was released,

went stumbling forward a few steps before the next
invisible current tugged at him, pulling him downward
now. It was a very much stronger pull, and for endless seconds it continued to build up. His shoulders
seemed ready to snap before he suddenly came free
again.

The rest of the way to the platform remained almost
undisturbed, but Dowland was trembling with tensions
before he reached it; he could feel the drag of the AR
field on his breathing. The steps to the platform were
a dozen feet to his right—too far from the rope.
Dowland put his weight on rope, swung forward
and up, let the rope go and came down on the narrow walk between instrument board and machine
section. The panels shone with their own light; at the
far end he saw the flow-control wheel Trelawney had
indicated, a red pointer opposite the numeral "5."
Dowland took two steps toward it, grasped the wheel,
and spun it down.

The pointer stopped at "1." He heard it click into
position there.

Instantly, something slammed him sideways against
the console, sent him staggering along it, and over the
low railing at the end of the platform. The floor seemed
to be shuddering as he struck it, and then to tilt slowly.
Dowland rolled over, came up on hands and knees,
facing back toward the platform. Daylight blazed again
in the building behind him, and the roar of a river that
rolled through another time filled his ears. He got to
his feet, plunged back toward the whipping rope above
the platform. The light and the roaring cut off as he
grasped the rope, flashed back into the building, cut
off again. Somewhere somebody had screamed. . . .

Dowland swung about on the rope, went handing
himself along it, back toward the door. His feet flopped
about over the floor, unable to get a stand there for

more than an instant. It was a struggle now to get enough air through the antiradiation field into his lungs. He saw dust whip past the open door, momentarily obscuring it. The building bucked with earthquake fury. And where was Trelawney?

He saw the red, wet thing then, lying by the wall just inside the door; and sickness seized him because Trelawney's body was stretched out too far to make it seem possible it had ever been that of a man. Dust blasted in through the door as he reached it, and subsided, leaving a choking residue trapped within the radiation screen. If he could only cut off the field. . . .

His gun lay too close to the sodden mess along the wall. Dowland picked it up, was bending to snatch the climbing harness from the floor when light flared behind him again. Automatically, he looked back.

Once more the interior of the building seemed to have split apart. Wider now. He saw the rushing white current below. To the right, above the forest on the bank, the sun was a swollen red ball glaring through layers of mist. And to the left, moving slowly over the river in the blaze of long-dead daylight, was something both unmistakable and not to be believed. But, staring at it in the instant before the scene shivered and vanished again, Dowland suddenly thought he knew what had happened here.

What he had seen was a spaceship.

He turned, went stumbling hurriedly out the door into the whistling wind, saw Jill Trelawney standing there, white-faced, eyes huge, hands to her mouth.

He caught her shoulder. "Come on! We've got to get away from here."

She gasped, "It—*tore* him apart!"

"We can't help him."

Dust clouds were spinning over the back of the

mesa, concealing the upper slopes. Dowland glanced to the west, winced at the towering mountain of darkness sweeping toward them through the sky. He plunged up the slope, hauling her along behind him. Jill cried out incoherently once, in a choking voice, but he didn't stop to hear what she was trying to say. He shoved her into the house, slammed the door shut behind them, hurried her on down the hall and into the living room. As they came in, he switched off his AR field and felt air fill his lungs easily again. It was like surfacing out of deep water. The detector still hissed its thin warning, but it was almost inaudible. They would have to risk radiation now.

"Out of your suit, quick! Whatever's happening in the lab has whistled up a dust storm here. When it hits, that radiation field will strangle you in a minute outdoors."

She stared at him dumbly.

"Get out of your suit!" Dowland shouted, his nerves snapping. "We're going down the eastern wall. It's our only chance. But we can't get down alive if we can't breathe. . . ." Then, as she began unbuckling the suit hurriedly with shaking fingers, he turned to the pile of camping equipment beside the fireplace and pawed through it.

He found the communicator and was snapping it to the mountaineering harness when the front door slammed. He wheeled about, startled. Jill's radiation suit lay on the floor near the entry hall. She was gone.

He was tearing the door open three seconds later, shouted, and saw her through the dust forty feet away, running up toward the forest.

He mightn't have caught her if she hadn't stumbled and gone headlong. Dowland was on top of her before she could get up. She fought him in savage silence like an animal, tearing and biting, her eyes bloodshot slits.

There was a mechanical fury about it that appalled him. But at last he got his right arm free, and brought his fist up solidly to the side of her jaw. Jill's head flew back, and her eyes closed.

He came padding up to the eastern side of the mesa with her minutes later. Here, beyond the ranch area, the ground was bare rock, with occasional clusters of stunted bushes. The dust had become blinding, though the main storm was still miles away. There was no time to stop off at the house to look for the quiz-gun, though it would have been better to try the descent with a dazed and half-paralyzed young woman than with the twisting lunatic Jill might turn into again when she recovered from his punch. At least, he'd have her tied up. Underfoot were grinding and grumbling noises now, the ground shaking constantly. At moments he had the feeling of plodding through something yielding, like quicksand. Only the feeling, he told himself; the rock was solid enough. But . . .

Abruptly, he was at the mesa's edge. Dowland slid the girl to the ground, straightened up, panting, to dab at his smarting eyes. The mesa behind them had almost vanished in swirling dust.

And through the dust Dowland saw something coming over the open ground he had just traversed.

He stared at it, mouth open, stunned with a sense of unfairness. The gigantic shape was still only partly visible, but it was obvious that it was following them. It approached swiftly over the shaking ground. Dowland took out his gun, with the oddly calm conviction that it would be entirely useless against their pursuer. But he brought it up slowly and leveled it, squinting with streaming eyes through the dust.

And then it happened. The pursuer appeared to

falter. It moved again in some manner; something thundered into the ground beside Dowland. Then, writhing and twisting—slowly at first, then faster—the dust-veiled shape seemed to be sinking downward through the rock surface of the mesa.

In another instant, it was gone.

Seconds passed before Dowland gradually lowered the gun again. Dazedly, he grew aware of something else that was different now. A miniature human voice appeared to be jabbering irritably at him from some point not far away. His eyes dropped to the little communicator attached to his harness.

The voice came from there.

Terra's grid power had returned to Lion Mesa.

A week later, Lieutenant Frank Dowland was shown into the office of the chief of the Solar Police Authority. The chief introduced him to the two other men there, who were left unidentified, and told him to be seated.

"Lieutenant," he said, "these gentlemen have a few questions to ask you. You can speak as openly to them as you would to me."

Dowland nodded. He had recognized one of the gentlemen immediately—Howard Camhorn, the Co-ordinator of Research. Reputedly one of the sharpest minds in the Overgovernment's top echelons. The other one was unfamiliar. He was a few years younger than Camhorn, around six inches shorter, chunky, with black hair, brown eyes, an expression of owlish reflectiveness. Probably, Dowland thought, wearing contact lenses. "Yes, sir," he said to the chief, and looked back at the visitors."

"We've seen your report on your recent visit to Terra, Lieutenant Dowland," Camhorn began pleasantly. "An excellent report, incidentally—factual, detailed. What we should like to hear now are the things that you, quite properly, omitted from it. That is, your personal impressions and conclusions."

"For example," the other man took up, as Dowland hesitated, "Miss Trelawney has informed us her uncles were attempting to employ the YM-400 they had acquired to carry out a time-shift to an earlier Earth period—to the period known as the Pleistocene, to be somewhat more exact. From what you saw, would you say they had succeeded in doing it?"

"I don't know, sir," Dowland said. "I've been shown pictures representing that period during the past few days. The scene I described in the report probably might have existed at that time." He smiled briefly. "However, I have the impression that the very large flying creature I reported encountering that night is regarded as being, . . . well, er . . . ah . . . ."

"A product of excited nerves?" the short man said, nodding. "Under such extraordinary circumstances, that would be quite possible, you know."

"Yes, sir, I know."

The short man smiled. "But you don't think it was that?"

"No, sir," Dowland said. "I think that I have described exactly what I did hear and see."

"And you feel the Trelawneys established contact with some previous Earth period—not necessarily the Pleistocene?"

"Yes, I do."

"And you report having seen a spaceship in that prehistorical period. . . ."

Dowland shook his head. "No, sir. At the moment I was observing it, I thought it was that. What I reported was having seen something that looked like a spaceship."

"What do you think it was?"

"A timeship—if there is such a word."

"There is such a word," Camhorn interrupted lazily. "I'm curious to hear, lieutenant, what brought you to that conclusion."

"It's a guess, sir. But the thing has to fit together somehow. A timeship would make it fit."

"In what way?"

"I've been informed," Dowland said, "that the Overgovernment's scientists have been unable to make a practical use of YM because something has invariably gone wrong when they did try to use it. I also heard that there was no way of knowing in advance what would happen to make an experiment fail. But something always would happen, and frequently a number of people would get killed."

Camhorn nodded. "That is quite true."

"Well, then," Dowland said, "I think there is a race of beings who aren't quite in our time and space. They have YM and use it, and don't want anyone else to use it. They can tell when it's activated here, and use their own YM to interfere with it. Then another experiment suddenly turns into a failure.

"But they don't know yet who's using it. When the Trelawneys turned on their machine, these beings spotted the YM stress pattern back there in time. They went to that point and reinforced the time-blending effect with their own YM. The Trelawneys hadn't intended a complete contact with that first test. The aliens almost succeeded in blending the two periods completely in the area near the laboratory."

"For what purpose?" Camhorn asked.

"I think they're very anxious to get us located."

"With unfriendly intentions?"

"The ones we ran into didn't behave in a friendly manner. May I ask a question, sir?"

"Of course," Camhorn said.

"When the Trelawneys' machine was examined, was the supply of YM adequately shielded?"

"Quite adequately," Camhorn said.

"But when I opened the door, the laboratory was hot. And Miguel Trelawney died of radiation burns. . . ."

Camhorn nodded. "Those are facts that give your theory some substance, lieutenant. No question about it. And there is the additional fact that after you shut off the YM flow in the laboratory, nearly ten minutes passed before the apparent contact between two time periods was broken. Your report indicates that the phenomena you described actually became more pronounced immediately after the shutoff."

"Yes, sir."

"As if the aliens might have been making every effort to retain contact with our time?"

"Yes, sir," Dowland said. "That was my impression."

"It's quite plausible. Now, the indications are that Paul Trelawney actually spent considerable time— perhaps twelve to fourteen hours, at any rate—in that other period. He gave no hint of what he experienced during those hours?"

"No, sir, except to say that it was night when he appeared there. He may have told Miss Trelawney more."

"Apparently, he didn't," Camhorn said. "Before you and he went into the laboratory, he warned her to watch for the approach of a creature which answers the description of the gigantic things you encountered twice. But that was all. Now, here again you've given us your objective observations. What can you add to them—on a perhaps more speculative basis?"

"Well, sir," Dowland said, "my opinions on that are, as a matter of fact, highly speculative. But I think that Paul Trelawney was captured by the aliens as soon as he appeared in the other time period, and was able to escape from them a number of hours later. Two of the aliens who were attempting to recapture him eventually followed him out on Lion Mesa through another opening the YM stresses had produced between the time periods, not too far away from the first."

Camhorn's stout companion said thoughtfully, "You believe the birdlike creature you saw arrived by the same route?"

"Yes, sir," Dowland said, turning to him. "I think that was simply an accident. It may have been some kind of wild animal that blundered into the contact area and found itself here without knowing what had occurred."

"And you feel," the other man went on, "that you yourself were passing near that contact point in the night at the time you seemed to be smelling a swamp?" Dowland nodded. "Yes, sir, I do. Those smells might have been an illusion, but they seemed to be very distinct. And, of course, there are no swamps on the mesa itself."

Camhorn said, "We'll assume it was no illusion. It seems to fit into the general picture. But, lieutenant, on what are you basing your opinion that Paul Trelawney was a captive of these beings for some time?"

"There were several things, sir," Dowland said. "One of them is that when Miss Trelawney regained consciousness in the hospital she didn't remember having made an attempt to get away from me."

Camhorn nodded. "That was reported."

"She made the attempt," Dowland went on, "immediately after she had taken off her radiation suit to avoid being choked in the dust storm on the way down from the mesa. That is one point."

"Go ahead," Camhorn said.

"Another is that when I discovered Paul Trelawney early in the morning, he was wearing his radiation suit.

Judging by his appearance, he had been in it for hours—and a radiation suit, of course, is a very inconvenient thing to be in when you're hiking around in rough country."

"He might," the stout man suggested, "have been afraid of running into a radioactive area."

Dowland shook his head. "No, sir. He had an instrument which would have warned him if he was approaching one. It would have made much more sense to carry the suit, and slip into it again if it became necessary. I didn't give the matter much thought at the time. But then the third thing happened. I did not put that in the report because it was a completely subjective impression. I couldn't prove now that it actually occurred."

Camhorn leaned forward. "Go ahead."

"It was just before the time periods separated and the creature that was approaching Miss Trelawney and myself seemed to drop through the top of the mesa— I suppose it fell back into the other period. I've described it. It was like a fifty-foot gray slug moving along on its tail and there were those two rows of something like short arms. It wasn't at all an attractive creature. I was frightened to death. But I was holding a gun—the same gun with which I had stopped another of those things when it chased me during the night. And the trouble was that this time I wasn't going to shoot."

"You weren't going to shoot?" Camhorn repeated.

"No, sir. I had every reason to try to blow it to pieces as soon as I saw it. The other one didn't follow up its attack on me, so it probably was pretty badly injured. But while I knew that, I was also simply convinced that it would be useless to pull the trigger. That's as well as I can explain what happened. . . .

"I think these aliens can control the minds of other

beings, but can't control them through the interference set up by something like our AR fields. Paul Trelawney appeared in the other time period almost in their laps. He had a rifle strapped over his back, but presumably they caught him before he had a chance to use it. They would have examined him and the equipment he was carrying, and when they took off his radiation suit, they would have discovered he belonged to a race which they could control mentally. After that, there would have been no reason for them to guard him too closely. He was helpless.

"I think Trelawney realized this, and used a moment when his actions were not being controlled to slip back into the suit. Then he was free to act again. When they discovered he had escaped, some of them were detailed to search for him, and two of those pursuers came out here in our time on the mesa.

"As for Miss Trelawney—well, obviously she wasn't trying to get away from me. Apparently, she wasn't even aware of what she was doing. She was simply obeying physically the orders her mind began to receive as soon as she stepped out of the radiation suit. They would have been to come to the thing, wherever it was at the moment—somewhere up to the north of the ranch area, judging from the direction in which she headed."

There was silence for some seconds. Then Camhorn's companion observed, "There's one thing that doesn't quite fit in with your theory, lieutenant."

"What's that, sir?"

"Your report states that you switched off your AR field at the same time you advised Miss Trelawney to get out of her suit. You should have been equally subject to the alien's mental instructions."

"Well," Dowland said, "I can attempt to explain that, sir, though again there is no way to prove what I think.

But it might be that these creatures can control only one mind at a time. The alien may not have realized that I had ... well ... knocked Miss Trelawney unconscious and that she was unable to obey its orders, until it came to the spot and saw us. My assumption is that it wasn't till that moment that it switched its mental attack to me."

The stout man—his name was Laillard White, and he was one of Research's ace trouble-shooters in areas more or less loosely related to psychology—appeared morosely reflective as he and Camhorn left Solar Police Authority Headquarters, and turned toward the adjoining Overgovernment Bureau.

"I gather from your expression," Camhorn remarked, "that our lieutenant was telling the truth."

White grunted. "Of course, he was—as he saw it."

"And he's sane?"

"Quite sane," White agreed absently.

Camhorn grinned. "Then what's the matter, Lolly? Don't you like the idea of time-travel?"

"Naturally not. It's an absurdity."

"You're blunt, Lolly. And rash. A number of great minds differ with you about that."

Laillard White said something rude about great minds in general. He went on, "Was the machine these Trelawneys built found intact?"

Camhorn nodded. "In perfect condition. I found an opportunity to look it over when it and the others the Freeholders had concealed on Terra were brought in."

"And these machines are designed to make it possible to move through time?"

"No question about that. They function in Riemann space, and are very soundly constructed. A most creditable piece of work, in fact. It's only regrettable that the Trelawney brothers were wasted on it. We might have put their talents to better use. Though as it turned out . . ." He shrugged.

White glanced over at him. "What are you talking about?" he asked suspiciously.

"They didn't accomplish time-travel," Camhorn said, "though in theory they should have. I know it because we have several machines based on the same principles. The earliest was built almost eighty years ago. Two are now designed to utilize the YM thrust. The Trelawney machine is considerably more advanced in a number of details than its Overgovernment counterparts, but it still doesn't make it possible to move in time."

"Why not?"

"I'd like to know," Camhorn said. "The appearance of it is that the reality we live in takes the same dim view of time-travel that you do. Time-travel remains a theoretical possibility. But in practice—when, for example, the YM thrust is applied for that purpose— the thrust is diverted."

White looked bewildered. "But if Paul Trelawney didn't move through time, what *did* he do?"

"What's left?" Camhorn asked. "He moved through space, of course."

"Where?"

Camhorn shrugged. "They penetrated Riemann space," he said, "after harnessing their machine to roughly nineteen thousand times the power that was available to us before the Ymir series of elements dropped into our hands. In theory, Lolly, they might have gone anywhere in the universe. If we'd had the unreasonable nerve to play around with multi-kilograms of YM—knowing what happened when fractional quantities of a gram were employed—we might have had a very similar experience."

"I'm still just a little in the dark, you know," Laillard

White observed drily, "as to what the experience consisted of."

"Oh, Lieutenant Dowland's theory wasn't at all far off in that respect. It's an ironic fact that we have much to thank the Trelawneys for. There's almost no question at all now that the race of beings they encountered were responsible for the troubles that have plagued us in the use of YM. They're not the best of neighbors—neighbors in Riemann space terms, that is. If they'd known where to look for us, things might have become rather hot. They had a chance to win the first round when the Trelawneys lit that sixty-eight kilogram beacon for them. But they made a few mistakes, and lost us again. It's a draw so far. Except that we now know about as much about them as they've ever learned about us. I expect we'll take the second round handily a few years from now."

White still looked doubtful. "Was it one of their planets the Trelawneys contacted?"

"Oh, no. At least, it would have been an extremely improbable coincidence. No, the machine was searching for Terra as Terra is known to have been in the latter part of the Pleistocene period. The Trelawneys had provided something like a thousand very specific factors to direct and confine that search. Time is impenetrable, so the machine had to find that particular pattern of factors in space, and did. The aliens—again as Lieutenant Dowland theorized—then moved through Riemann space to the planet where the YM thrust was manifesting itself so violently. But once there, they still had no way of determining where in the universe the thrust had originated—even though they were, in one sense, within shouting distance of Terra, and two of them were actually on its surface for a time. It must have been an extremely frustrating experience all around for our friends."

Laillard White said, "Hm-m," and frowned.

Camhorn laughed. "Let it go, Lolly," he said. "That isn't your field, after all. Let's turn to what is. What do you make of the fact that Dowland appears to have been temporarily immune to the mental commands these creatures can put out?"

"Eh?" White said. His expression turned to one of surprise. "But that's obvious!"

"Glad to hear it," Camhorn said drily.

"Well, it is. Dowland's attitude showed clearly that he suspected the truth himself on that point. Naturally, he was somewhat reluctant to put it into words."

"Naturally. So what did he suspect?"

White shook his head. "It's so simple. The first specimen of humanity the aliens encountered alive was Paul Trelawney. High genius level, man! It would take that level to nullify our I.Q. tests in the manner he and his half-brother did. When those creatures were prowling around on the mesa, they were looking for that kind of mentality. Dowland's above average, far from stupid. As you say, you like his theories. But he's no Trelawney. Unquestionably, the aliens in each case regarded him as some kind of clever domestic animal. The only reason he's alive is that they weren't taking him seriously."

That," Camhorn said thoughtfully, "may have changed a number of things."

"It may, indeed."

"Do we have anything on hand that would block their specific psi abilities?' "

"Oh, surely. If an AR field can stop them, there's nothing to worry about in that respect. Our human telepaths wouldn't be seriously hampered by that degree of interference."

"Very good," Camhorn said. "Do you have any theory about the partial sensory interpretation of the two areas which both Dowland and Miss Trelawney reported? The matter of being able to hear the river on the other planet from time to time."

White nodded. "There are several possible explanations for that. For one thing . . ."

"Better save it for lunch, Lolly," Camhorn interrupted, glancing at his watch. "I see I have two minutes left to make the meeting. Anything else you feel should be brought up at the moment?"

"Just one thing," White said. "If the Trelawneys' machine is capable of locating a Terra-type planet anywhere in the universe . . ."

Camhorn nodded. "It is."

"Then," White said, "we've solved our exploding population problem, haven't we?"

"For the time being, we have," Camhorn agreed. "As a matter of fact, Lolly, that's precisely what the meeting I'm headed for is about."

"Then the Terran Freeholders can stop worrying about the political pressures that have threatened to turn Terra into another hygienically overcrowded slumworld."

"True enough," Camhorn said. "In another few years, if things go right, every man, woman and child can become a Freeholder—somewhere."

"So the Trelawneys got what they wanted, after all. . . ."

"They did, in a way. If the brothers knew the whole score, I think they'd be satisfied. The situation has been explained to their niece. She is."

The End of the Line

⤜⤏

The spaceship dropped near evening towards the edge of a curving beach. A half-mile strip of grassy growth stood tall and still behind the beach; beyond the jungle smoothly marbled prows of pink and gray cliffs swept steeply upwards for nearly two thousand feet to the northernmost shelf of a wide, flat continent. The green-black waters of the planet's largest ocean stretched away in a glassy curve ahead, broken by two narrow chains of islands some thirty miles out.

The sleek machine from beyond the stars settled down slowly, a wind thundering out below it and wrinkling the shallows near the beach into sudden zigzag patterns. It fell through explosive sprays of dry sand, sank its base twenty feet deep into the rock below, and stopped. A sharp click announced the opening of a lock a third of the way up its rounded flank; and seven of the nine members of Central Government's Exploration Group 1176 came riding out of the lock a moment later, bunched forty feet above the beach on the tip of their ship's extension ramp.

Six of them dropped free of the ramp at various points of its swooping descent. They hit the hard sand in a succession of soft, bounceless thumps like so many cats and went loping off towards the water. Grevan alone, with the restraint to be looked for in a Group Commander, rode the ramp all the way down to the ground.

He stepped off it unhurriedly there: a very big man, heavy of bone and muscle, though lean where weight wasn't useful, and easy-moving as the professional gladiators and beast-fighters whose training quarters he'd shared in his time. A brooding, implacable expression went so naturally with the rest of it that ordinary human beings were likely to give him one look and step out of his way, even when they weren't aware of his technical rank of Central Government Official.

It was a pity in a way that the members of his Exploration Group weren't so easily impressed.

Grevan scowled reflectively, watching five of the six who had come out of the ship with him begin shucking off weapon belts, suits, and other items of equipment with scarcely a break in their run as they approached the water's edge. Cusat, Eliol, Freckles, Lancey, Vernet—he checked them off mentally as they vanished a few seconds later, with almost simultaneous splashes, from the planet's surface. They were of his own experimental breed or something very near it, born in one of Central Government's germination laboratories and physically, though not quite adults yet, very nearly as capable as Grevan was himself. However, nobody could tell from here what sort of alien, carnivorous life might be floating around beyond this ocean's shallows. . . .

They had too good an opinion of themselves!

Weyer, at any rate, seemed to have decided to stay on shore with his clothes on and his armament handy, in case of trouble. Somewhat reassured, Grevan turned his attention next to a metallic bumping and scraping at the ship's open lock overhead. Klim and Muscles, K.P.'s for the day, were trying to move a bulky cooking unit out of the ship so the Group could dine outdoors.

"Boss?" Klim's clear soprano floated down.

"Right here," Grevan called back. "Having trouble?"

"Looks like we're stuck," Klim announced from within the lock. "Would you come up and . . . no, wait a minute! Muscles is getting it cleared now, I think . . . Wait till I've degraved it again, you big ape! Now, push!"

The cooker popped into sight with a grinding noise, ejected with considerable violence from the ship's interior. For a moment, it hung spinning quietly in the air above the ramp, with Klim perched on top. Then Muscles came out through the lock and attached himself to the gadget's side. They floated down lopsidedly together, accompanied by tinkling sounds from the cooker's interior.

"What's it going to be tonight?" Grevan asked, reaching up to guide them in to an even landing.

"Albert II in mushroom sauce," said Klim. She was a tall, slender blonde with huge blue eyes and a deceptively wistful expression. As he grounded the cooker, she put a hand on his shoulder and stepped down. "Not a very original menu, I'll admit! But there's a nice dessert anyway. How about sampling some local vegetables to go with Albert?"

"Maybe," said Grevan cautiously. "Whose turn is it to sample?" Too often, preoccupied with other matters, he'd discovered suddenly that he'd been roped in again for that chore when the items to be sampled were suspected of being of a particularly uncooperative nature. And then the Group would drop whatever it was doing to gather around and sympathize while he adapted.

"Vernet's turn, isn't it?" said Muscles.

"Vernet's the victim," Klim nodded. "You're safe this time."

"In that case," Grevan said, relieved, "you'll find Vernet out there full fathom five somewhere. Bring her in if you can and we'll go browse in the shrubbery a bit."

"This," Klim remarked, gazing out over the shoreline towards which Muscles was heading in search of Vernet, "is still the best spot of an all-right little world! Know what the cubs were calling it when we first set down here three weeks ago?" She was Grevan's junior by a good ten years but a year or so older than the Group's other members and inclined to regard them all with motherly tolerance. "Our point of no return."

Grevan grimaced uneasily, because that phrase did describe the Group's position here, in one way or another. Never once, in the eight years since Central Government had put him in charge of what had been a flock of rebellious, suspicious, and thoroughly unhappy youngsters, who weren't even sure whether they were actually human beings or some sort of biological robots, had the question of escaping from CG controls been openly discussed among them. You never knew who might be listening, somewhere. The amazing thing to Grevan even now was that—eight weeks travel on the full fury of their great ship's drives beyond the borders of Central Government's sprawling interstellar domain—they did seem to have escaped. But that was a theory that still remained to be proved.

"Are you going to accept contact with CG tomorrow?" Klim inquired.

Grevan shrugged. "I don't know." Their only remaining connection with CG, so far as they could tell, were the vocal messages which flashed subspatially on prearranged occasions between two paired contact sets, one of which was installed on their ship. They had no way of guessing where the other one might be, but it was activated periodically by one of the CG officials who directed the Group's affairs.

"I was going to put it to a vote tonight," Grevan hedged. "They can't possibly trace us through the sets, and I'd like to hear what they have to say when they find out we've resigned."

"It might be a good idea. But you won't get a vote on it."

He looked down at her, while she stooped to haul a small portable cooker out of the big one's interior and slung it over her shoulder.

"Why not?"

"The cubs seem to think there's no way of guessing whether accepting contact at this stage is more likely to help us or hurt us. They'll leave it up to you to decide."

"Aren't you worried about it at all?" he inquired, somewhat startled. However well he felt he knew the cubs, they still managed to amaze him on occasion.

Klim shrugged. "Not too much." She clamped a chemical testing set to the portable cooker. "After all, we're not going back, whatever happens. If CG's still got some fancy way of reaching out and stopping us, wherever we are, I'd much rather be stopped out here than get another going-over in one of their psych laboratories—and come out a mindless-controlled this time. . . ."

She paused. Faint, protesting outcries were arising from a point a few hundred yards out in the water. "Sounds like Muscles caught up with Vernet. Let's get down to the beach."

✧   ✧   ✧

Vernet raked wet brown hair out of her eyes and indignantly denied that it was her turn to sample. But the Group contradicted her seven to one, with Lancey withholding his vote on a plea of bad memory. She dried and dressed resignedly and came along.

The first three likely-looking growths the foraging party tested and offered her were neither here nor there. They put up no worthwhile argument against assimilation and probably would turn out to be nourishing enough. But raw or variously treated and flavored in Klim's portable cooker, they remained, Vernet reported, as flatly uninspiring as any potential mouthful could hope to be.

The fourth item to pass the chemical tests was a plump little cabbage-arrangement, sky-blue with scarlet leaf-fringes. She sniffed around it forebodingly.

"They don't advertise identity like that for nothing!" she pointed out. "Loaded for bear, I bet!" She scowled at Klim. "You picked it on purpose!"

"Ho-hum," Klim murmured languidly. "Remember who had me sampling that large fried spider-type on wherever-it-was?"

"That was different," said Vernet. "I had a hunch the thing would turn out to be perfectly delicious!"

Klim smiled at her. "I'm K.P. today. I'm having the hunches. How would you like it?"

"Quick-baked," snarled Vernet. "And my blood be on your head!"

Half a minute later, she nibbled tentatively at a crisped leaf of the cabbage, announced with surprise that it was indeed delicious and helped herself to more. On the third leaf, she uttered a wild whoop, doubled up, and began to adapt at speed. That took about twelve seconds, but they allowed a full ten minutes then to let the reaction flush her blood stream. Then

Vernet was sampled in turn and staggered back to the beach with a martyred expression, while Klim and Muscles started cabbage-hunting.

Grevan retired to the ship's laboratory, where he poured the half cupful of blood he had extracted from the martyr's veins carefully into a small retort. Onto-genetic adaptation, with reaction-times that crowded zero, to anything new in the way of infections or absorbed venoms was one of the more useful talents of their specialized strain. Considerable unauthorized research and experimentation finally had revealed to them just how they did it. The invading substance was met by an instantaneous regrouping of complex enzyme chains in every body cell affected by it, which matched and nullified its specific harmful properties and left the Group member involved permanently immune to them.

The experience of getting immunized sometimes included the momentary impression of having swal-lowed a small but active volcano, but that illusion didn't last long enough to be taken very seriously by anyone but the sufferer. Vernet's blood emerged from process-ing presently in the shape of small pink pills; and just before dinner everybody washed down two each of these and thus adapted the easy way, while the donor denounced them as vampires.

Albert II, in a vintage mushroom sauce and gar-nished with quick-baked Vernet Cabbages, was hailed as an outstanding culinary composition all around. Klim took the bows.

By nightfall, they had built a fire among rocks above the highest tide mark, not far from the edge of the rustling jungle, and a little later they were settled about it, making lazy conversation or just watching the danc-ing flames.

Special precautions did not seem required at the

moment, though Weyer had reported direct neuronic impressions of carnivorous and aggressive big-life in the immediate neighborhood, and the Group's investigation of the planet had revealed scattered traces of at least two deep-water civilizations maintained by life forms of unknown type but with suggestively secretive habits. A half-dozen forms of sudden death snuggled inside the ornamental little gadgets clamped to their gun belts, not to mention the monstrous argument the pocket-sized battleship which had carried them here could put up, and their perceptions were quick and accurate and very far-ranging. If any of this world's denizens were considering a hostile first encounter, the Group was more than willing to let them do the worrying about it.

Not a care in their heads, to look at them, Grevan thought, a trifle enviously. Handsome young animals, just touching adulthood—four young men and four young women, who acted as if they had been sent on a star-hopping picnic, with Grevan trailing along as a sort of scoutmaster.

Which wasn't, of course, quite fair.

The cubs were as conscious as he was of the fact that they might still be on a long, invisible leash out here—artificial mental restraints imposed by Central Government's psychological machines. They had developed a practical psychology of their own to free themselves of those thought-traps, but they had no way of knowing how successful they had been. If any such hypnotic mechanisms remained undiscovered in them, the penalty for defying Central Government's instructions would be automatic and disastrous.

Grevan could see himself again as a frightened, rebellious boy inside a subterranean conditioning vault, facing the apparently blank wall which concealed one of the machines known as Dominators. He heard the flat, toneless voice of the legendary monster, almost as old as Central Government itself, watched the dazzling hypnotic patterns slide and shift suddenly across the wall, and felt hard knots of compulsive thought leap up in response and fade almost instantly beyond the reach of his consciousness.

That had been his first experience with CG's euphemistically termed "restraints." The Dominator had installed three of them and let the boy know what to expect if rebellion was attempted again. Two days later, he had skeptically put the power of the restraints to a test, and had very nearly died then and there.

They would know soon enough. Failure to keep the scheduled contact tomorrow would trigger any compulsive responses left in them as certainly as direct defiance of CG's instructions would do. And because they had finally found a world beyond CG's reach that could be their home, they were going to follow one or the other of those courses of action tomorrow. Looking around at the circle of thoughtfully relaxed young faces, he couldn't even imagine one of them suggesting the possibility of a compromise with CG instead. After eight years of secret planning and preparing, it wouldn't have occurred to them.

He relaxed himself, with a sigh and a conscious effort, releasing his perceptions to mingle with theirs. A cool breeze was shifting overhead, slowly drawing fresh scents from new sources, while unseen night things with thin, crying voices flew out over the sea. The ocean muttered about the lower rocks; and a mile to the east something big came splashing noisily into the shallows and presently returned again to the deeper water. Resting, the cubs seemed to be fitting themselves into the night, putting out tentative sensory roots to gather up the essence of this new world's life.

Then their attention began to shift and gather, and

Grevan again let his mind follow where they seemed to be pointing without effort of his own.

It came to him quickly—a composite of impressions which were being picked up individually by one or the other of them and then formed by all into an increasingly definite picture. The picture of a pair of shaggy, shambling appetites working their way awkwardly down the cliffs behind the Group, towards the gleam of the fire.

The cubs sat still and waited while the things approached, and Grevan watched them, amused and momentarily distracted from his worries. The shaggy appetites reached the foot of the cliff at length and came moving down through the jungle. Heavy-footed but accomplished stalkers, Grevan decided. The local species of king-beast probably, who knew the need of a long, cautious approach before their final rush upon nimbler prey—he filed the fact away for future consideration that a campfire seemed to mean such prey to them.

On a rocky ridge two hundred yards above the fire, the stalkers came to a sudden halt. He had an impression of great, gray, shadowy forms and two sets of staring red eyes.

It would be interesting, he thought, to know just what sort of intuitive alarms went off in the more intelligent forms of alien carnivores whenever they got their first good look at the Group. The cubs still hadn't moved, but the visitors seemed to have come almost immediately to the conclusion that they weren't nearly as hungry now as they had thought. They were beginning a stealthy withdrawal—

And then Eliol suddenly threw back her head and laughed, a quick, rippling sound like a flash of wicked white teeth; a yell of pure mirth went up from the others, and the withdrawal turned instantly into ludicrously panicky flight.

The incident had brought them awake and put them into a talkative mood. It might be a good time to find out what they really thought of their chances of breaking free of CG tomorrow. Grevan sat up, waiting for an opening in an impassioned argument that had started up on the other side of the fire.

There had been a bet involved, it seemed, in that impulsive five-fold plunge into the ocean on landing. Last one in to be tomorrow's K.P.—and Vernet had come out on the sticky end of the bet.

Everybody else agreed thoughtfully that it just hadn't been Vernet's day. Vernet appeared unreconciled.

"You knew my gun belt was stuck again," she accused Eliol. "You had it planned so I'd be last!"

Eliol, having postponed her own turn at the Group's least-favored chore for one day by issuing the challenge, permitted herself a gentle chuckle.

"Teach you to keep your equipment in regulation condition! You didn't have to take me up on it. Weyer didn't."

"Well, anyway," said Vernet, "Lancey will help Vernet live through it. Won't he?"

"Uh-huh!" beamed Lancey. "You bet!"

"How he dotes!" Eliol remarked critically. "Sometimes it gets a little disgusting. Take Cusat there—flat on his back as usual. There's a boy who shows some decent restraint. Nobody would guess that he's actually a slave to my slightest whim."

Cusat, stretched out on the sand nearby, opened one eye to look at her. "Dream on, little one!" he muttered and let the eye fall shut again.

The others were off on another subject. There had been an alien awareness, Grevan gathered, which had followed the five swimmers about in the water. Not a hostile one, but one that wondered about them—recognized them as a very strange sort of new life, and was somewhat afraid. "They were thinking they were so very—edible!" Eliol said and laughed. "Perhaps they knew the swim was making us hungry! Anyway they kept warning one another to stay out of our sight!"

"Plankton eaters," Lancey added lazily, "but apparently very fast swimmers. Anyone else get anything on them?"

"Cave builders," said Freckles, from behind Weyer, only a few feet from Grevan. She propped herself up on an elbow to point across the fire. "That big drop-off to the west! They've tunneled it out below the surface. I don't think they're phosphorescent themselves, but they've got some method of keeping light in the caves—bacterial, possibly. And they cultivate some form of plankton inside."

"Sounds as if they might be intelligent enough to permit direct contact," Grevan remarked, and realized in the moment of silence that followed that it must have been an hour since he'd last said a word.

"They're easily that," Freckles agreed. Her small face, shaded by the rather shapeless white hat she favored, turned to him. "If Klim hadn't been cooking, I'd have called her to give it a try. I was afraid of frightening them off myself."

"I'll do it tomorrow," promised Klim, who had much the deftest touch of them all for delicate ambassadorial work.

There was another pause then—it might have been the word "tomorrow."

"Going to make contact tomorrow, Grevan?" Freckles inquired in a light, clear voice, as if it had just occurred to her.

"Unless," nodded Grevan, "somebody has a better idea."

It seemed nobody did until Muscles grumbled, "It's CG who's likely to have the ideas. If it were up to me, I'd just smash that set, tonight!"

Grevan looked at him thoughtfully. "Anybody else feel the same way?"

They shook their heads. "You go ahead, Grevan." That was Weyer's calm voice. "We'll just see what happens. Think there's a chance of jolting any worthwhile information out of them at this stage?"

"Not if they're on guard," Grevan admitted. "But I think it will be safest for us if we're right there when it dawns on CG that this Exploration Group has resigned from its service! And it might prod them into some kind of informative reaction—"

"Well, I still think," Muscles began, looking worriedly at Klim, "that we . . . oh, well!"

"Vote's eight to one," Klim said crisply.

"I know it," growled Muscles and shut up.

The rest seemed to have become disinterested in the matter again—a flock of not quite human cubs, nearly grown and already enormously capable of looking out for themselves. They'd put themselves into the best possible position to face the one enemy they'd never been able to meet on his own ground.

And until things started happening, they weren't going to worry about them.

A few of them had drifted off to the beach below, when Grevan saw Klim stop beside Cusat and speak to him. Cusat opened both eyes and got to his feet, and Klim followed him over to Grevan.

"Klim thinks Albert is beginning to look puny again," Cusat announced. "Probably nothing much to it, but how about coming along and helping us diagnose?"

The Group's three top biologists adjourned to the ship, with Muscles, whose preferred field was almost-pure mathematics, trailing along just for company. They found Albert II quiescent in vitro—as close a thing to a self-restoring six-foot sirloin steak as ever had been developed.

"He's quit assimilating, and he's even a shade off-color," Klim pointed out, a little anxiously.

They debated his requirements at some length. As a menu staple, Albert was hard to beat, but unfortunately he was rather dainty in his demands. Chemical balances, temperatures, radiations, flows of stimulant, and nutritive currents—all had to be just so; and his notions of what was just so were subject to change without notice. If they weren't catered to regardless, he languished and within the week perversely died. At least, the particular section of him that was here would die. As an institution, of course, he might go on growing and nourishing his Central Government clients immortally.

Muscles might have been of help in working out the delicate calculations involved in solving Albert's current problems, but when they looked round for him, they found him blinking at a steady flow of invisible symbols over one wall of the tank room, while his lips moved in a rapid, low muttering; and they knew better than to interrupt. He had gone off on impromptu calculations of his own, from which he would emerge eventually with some useful bit of information or other, though ten to one it would have nothing to do with Albert. Meanwhile, he would be grouchy and useless if roused to direct his attention to anything below the level of an emergency.

They reset the currents finally and, at Cusat's suggestion, trimmed Albert around the edges. Finding himself growing lighter, he suddenly began to absorb nourishment again at a very satisfactory rate.

"That did it, I guess," Cusat said, pleased. He glanced at the small pile of filets they'd sliced off. "Might as well have a barbecue now."

"Run along and get it started," Grevan suggested. "I'll be with you as soon as I get Albert buttoned up."

Klim regarded Muscles reflectively. "Just nudge my genius awake when you're ready to come," she instructed Grevan. "He looks so happy right now I don't want to disturb him."

It was some minutes later, while Grevan was carefully tightening down a seal valve, that Muscles suddenly yawned and announced, "Thirty-seven point oh two four hours! Checks either way, all right, boss. Say— where's Klim gone?"

"Down to the beach, I suppose." Grevan didn't look up. He could find out later what Muscles was referring to. "Drowned dead by now, for all you seem to care!" he added cruelly.

Muscles left in the perturbed hurry that was his normal reaction to the discovery that Klim had strayed out of sight, and Grevan continued buttoning up Albert, undistracted by further mathematical mutterings. The cubs had finished sorting themselves out a year or so ago, and who was to be whose seemed pretty well settled by now. There had been a time when he'd thought it would have been a nice gesture on CG's part to have increased their membership by a double for Klim or Eliol or Vernet or Freckles—depending more or less on which of them he was looking at at the moment—though preferably somebody three or four years older. Of late, however, he had developed some plans of his own for rounding out the Group. If the question of getting and staying beyond CG's range could be satisfactorily settled . . .

He shrugged off an uncomfortably convincing notion

that any plans he might consider had been discounted
long ago by the branch of Central Government which
had developed the Group for its own purpose. Speculative eyes seemed to be following every move he made
as he wished Albert pleasant dreams and a less tem-
peramental future, closed the door to the tank room,
and went to the ramp. Halfway down it, he stopped
short. For an endless second, his heart seemed to turn
over slowly and, just as slowly then, to come right side
up again.

The woman who stood at the foot of the ramp,
looking up at him, was someone he knew—and he also
knew she couldn't possibly be there! The jolting recognition was almost crowded out by a flash of hot
fright: obviously she wasn't really there at all. At a
distance of thirty feet, the starlight never could have
showed him Priderell's pale-ivory face so clearly—or
the slow stirring of her long, clever dancer's body under
its red gown, and the sheen of the short red cloak she
wore over it, clasped at her throat by a stone's green
glitter.

Afterwards, Grevan could not have said how long
he stood there with his thoughts spinning along the
edge of sheer panic. In actual time it might have been
a bare instant before he became aware of a familiar
distant voice:

"Hey, boss! Grevan!"

The sound seemed tiny and very far away. But he
heard himself make some kind of an answer and suddenly realized then that the image had vanished.

"Do you want barbecued Albert, or don't you?" Klim
shouted again from the direction of the fire. "I can't
keep these pigs away from your share much longer!"

He drew a deep breath. "Coming right now!"

But it was another minute or two before he showed

himself at the fire, and he had arranged his thoughts carefully into other lines before he did. The cubs couldn't actually tell what he was thinking—unless he made a deliberate effort to let them; and they weren't too accurate then—but they were very quick to trace the general trend and coloring of one's reflections.

And his reflections had been that his visualization of Priderell might have been something more than some momentary personal derangement. That it might be the beginning of a purposefully directed assault on the fortress of the Group's sanity, backed by a power and knowledge that laughed at their hopes of escape.

Fortunately his companions seemed to feel that the barbecue had been exactly the right way of ending the day. A short while later they were stretched out on blankets here and there in the sand, fully relaxed and asleep, as far as Grevan could see, though never more than that small fraction of a second away from complete and active wakefulness which experienced travelers learn to regard as the margin that leaves them assured of awakening at all.

But Grevan sat aside for a while, and looked out at the sea and the stars.

There were a lot of stars to look at around here, and big ones. They had come within twenty-eight light-years of the center of a globular cluster near the heart of the Milky Way, where, so far as they knew, no humanly manned ship had ever gone before. In every direction the skies were hung, depth on depth, with the massed frozen flows of strange constellations. Somewhere, in that huge shining, four small moons wandered indistinguishably—indistinguishable, at any rate, if you didn't know just where to look for them, and Grevan hadn't bothered to find out.

Something stirred softly, off to his left.

"Hello, Freck," he said quietly. "Come to help me plot against CG?"

The four little moons couldn't have raised a tide in a barrel among them, but there was a big one at work below the horizon, and water had crept in to cover the flat stretches of shore. By now it was lapping at the base of the higher rocks that bordered their camp area. Freckles sat on the edge of one of the rocks, a few yards off, the white hat pushed to the back of her head and her feet dangling over the ripples below.

"Just being companionable," she said. "But if you think you need any help in your plotting, fire away! This is one place where CG couldn't possibly have its long ears stuck out to listen."

He played for a moment then with the notion of telling her about his hallucination. Freckles was the Group's unofficial psychologist. The youngest and smallest of the lot, but equipped with what was in some ways the boldest and most subtle mind of them all. The secret experiments she had conducted on herself and the others often had put Grevan's hair on end; but the hard-won reward of that rocky road of research had been the method of dealing effectively with CG's restraints.

"What kind of psychological triggers," he said instead, "could CG still pull on us out here—aside from the ones we know?"

Freckles chuckled. "You're asking the wrong kind of question."

He frowned a little, that being one of his pet phrases.

"All right," he said. "Then do you think we might still be carrying around a few compulsions that we simply don't remember?"

"No," Freckles said promptly. "You can install things like that in an ordinary-human, because they're half asleep to start with. I've done it myself. But you'd have to break any one of us down almost to mindless-controlled before you could knock out our memory to that extent. We wouldn't be much good to CG afterwards."

"How do you know?"

She shrugged. "When I was a kid, a Dominator worked on me for a week trying to lay in a compulsion I wouldn't be able to spot. And, believe me, after a day or two I was doing my best to cooperate! The type of mind we have simply can't accept amnesia."

She added, "Of course, a Dominator—or a human psycho, if you agree to it—can hold you in a cloud just as long as they can keep on direct pressure. You'll do and believe anything they tell you then. Like the time when you—"

"I remember that time," Grevan acknowledged shortly. She was referring to an occasion when he had authorized her without reserve to attempt some unspecified new line of investigation on him. Some while later, he had realized suddenly that for the past half hour he had been weeping noisily because he was a small, green, very sour apple which nobody wanted to eat.

"Boy, you looked silly!" Freckles remarked reminiscently.

Grevan cleared his throat. She might, he observed, have looked somewhat silly herself, around the south polar region, if he'd caught up with her before he cooled off.

"Ah, but you didn't!" said Freckles. "A good researcher knows when to include a flying start in her computations. Actually, I did come across something really fancy in mental energy effects once. But if CG could operate on those levels, they wouldn't need a hundredth part of the organization they've got. So it stands to reason they can't."

"What sort of effects?" he inquired uneasily.

"You've got me there!" Freckles admitted, pulling the white hat thoughtfully down on her forehead. "I haven't the faintest idea of what they were, even in principle. I was still alone then—it was about four years before they got us together to make up the Group. They brought a man into the Center where I was, in an ambulance. He looked unconscious, and our psychos were all excited about him. They took him off to the laboratories, where they had one of those mobile Dominators—and then people suddenly started screaming and falling down all around me, and I felt something like fire—here!" She tapped the top of her hat. "I remember I seemed to understand at once that the man was using some kind of mental energy against the Dominator—"

"Eh?" said Grevan incredulously.

"That's right. And also some kind of gun which wasn't any CG type, by the sound of it. Of course, I was out of a window by then and going straight away; but the whole thing only lasted a few seconds anyhow. I heard the Dominator cut loose in the laboratories with its physical armament—disruptive sonics, flash-fire, and plain projectiles. The burning feeling suddenly stopped again, and I knew the man was dead."

"For a moment," Grevan said gloomily, "I thought you were going to tell me a human being had beaten a Dominator!"

Freckles shook her head. "I doubt that's ever happened. The filthy things know how to take care of themselves. I saw one handle a riot once—some suicide cult. The suiciders got what they were after, all right! But that man had enough on the mental level to make the Dominator use *everything* it had to stop him. So there definitely are degrees and forms of mental energy which we know nothing about. And, apparently, there are some people who do know about them and how to use them. But those people aren't working for CG."

Grevan pondered that for a moment, disturbed and dissatisfied.

"Freck," he said finally, "everybody but Muscles and myself seems to agree that there's no way of knowing whether we're improving our chances or reducing them by inviting a showdown with CG via the contact set. If you had to decide it personally, what would you do?"

Freckles stood up then and looked at the stars for a moment. "Personally," she said—and he realized that there was a touch of laughter in her voice—"I wouldn't do anything! I wouldn't smash the set like Muscles, and I wouldn't accept contact, like you. I'd just stay here, sit quiet, and let CG make the next move, if any!"

Grevan swore gently.

"Well," she said, "that's the kind of situation it is! But we might as well do it your way." She stretched her arms over her head and sniffed at the breeze. "That whole big beautiful ocean! If CG doesn't eat us tomorrow, Grevan, I'll sprout gills and be a fish! I'll go live with those plankton eaters and swim up to the polar ice and all the way through beneath it! I'll—"

"Listen, Freck; let's be practical—"

"I'm listening," Freckles assured him.

"If anyone—including Muscles—can think of a valid reason why I shouldn't make contact tomorrow, right up to the moment I plug in that set, I want to hear about it."

"You will! And don't worry about Muscles. He can't see beyond Klim at the moment, so he's riding a small panic just now. He'll be all right again—after tomorrow."

She waited then, but Grevan couldn't think of anything else to say. "Well, good night, Grevan!"

"Good night, Freck." He watched her move off like a slender ghost towards the dim glow of the fire. The cubs felt they'd won—simply by living long enough to have left the musty tang of half-alive, history-old Central Government worlds far behind them and to be breathing a wind that blew over an ocean no human being had seen before. Whatever happened now, they were done with CG and all its works, forever.

And the difference might be simply, Grevan realized, that he wasn't done with it yet. He still had to win. His thoughts began to shift back slowly, almost cautiously, to the image of a woman whose name was Priderell and who had stood impossibly at the foot of his ship's ramp, smiling up at him with slanted green eyes. She had been in his mind a good deal these months, and if present tensions couldn't quite account for that momentary hallucination, the prospect of future ones might do it. Because while the cubs didn't know it yet, once he had them settled safely here, he was going to make his way back into CG's domain and head for a second-rate sort of planet called Rhysgaat, where—to be blunt about it—he intended to kidnap Priderell and bring her back to round out the Group.

It wouldn't be an impossible undertaking if he could get that far unspotted. It seemed rather odd, when he considered it rationally, that the few meetings he'd had with Priderell should have impressed him with the absolute necessity of attempting it, and that somebody else—somebody who would be more accessible and less likely to be immediately missed—shouldn't do just as well.

But that was only one of the number of odd things that had happened on Rhysgaat, which had been the

Group's last scheduled port of call before they slipped off on the long, curving run that had taken them finally into and halfway through an alien cluster of the Milky Way. Taken together, those occurrences had seemed to make up a sort of pattern to Grevan. The cubs appeared to notice nothing very significant about them, and so he hadn't mentioned the fact.

But it had seemed to him then that if he could understand what was happening on Rhysgaat, he would also have the solution to the many questions that still remained unanswered concerning the relationship between Central Government and the Group—their actual origin, for one thing; the purpose for which they had been trained and equipped at enormous cost; and the apparently idiotic oversight in their emotional conditioning which had made them determined to escape. Even the curious fact that, so far as they had ever been able to find out, they were the only Exploration Group and the only members of their strain in existence.

For some four weeks, the answer to everything had seemed to be lying right there about Grevan on Rhysgaat. But he had not been able to grasp it.

It was four months ago that they had set their ship down at Rhysgaat's single dilapidated spaceport, with no intention of lingering. Supply inventory, a final ground check, and they'd be off! The taste of escape, the wonder that it might be so near, the fear that something might still happen to prevent it, was a secret urgency in all of them. But the check showed the need for some minor repairs, and to save his stores Grevan decided to get some materials transferred to him from local CG stockpiles. As a CG official, he was in the habit of addressing such requests to whatever planetary governor was handiest, and after some tracing, he found the gentleman he wanted presiding over a social gathering in a relaxed condition.

Rhysgaat's governor gave a horrified start when Grevan stated his rank. Confusedly, he began to introduce the official all around as an unexpected guest of honor. So a minute or two later Grevan found himself bowing to Priderell.

She was, he decided at once, as attractive a young woman as anyone could wish to meet—later on, he discovered that practically all of Rhysgaat agreed with him there. She was, he learned also, a professional dancer and currently the public darling. Not, of course, he informed himself on his way back to the ship, that this meant anything at all to him. Nobody who knew himself to be the object of CG's particular interest would risk directing the same attention towards some likable stranger.

But next day Priderell showed up of her own accord at the spaceport, and he had to explain that his ship was part of a government project and therefore off limits to anybody not directly connected with it. Priderell informed him he owed her a drink, at any rate, for her visit, and they sat around for a while at the port bar, and talked.

Just possibly, of course, she might have been CG herself in some capacity. The Group had met much more improbable secret representatives of government from time to time; and, when in the mood, the cubs liked to booby-trap such characters and then point out to them gently where their hidden identities were showing.

After she had left, he found the cubs in a state of some consternation, which had nothing to do with her visit. They had almost finished the proposed repairs; but signs of deterioration in other sections of their supposedly almost wear-proof space machine had been revealed in the process. After looking it over, Grevan calculated uneasily that it would take almost a week before they could leave Rhysgaat now.

It took closer to four weeks; and it had become obvious long before that time that their ship had been sabotaged deliberately by CG technicians. Nobody in the Group mentioned the fact. Apparently, it was some kind of last-minute test, and they settled down doggedly to pass it.

Grevan had time to try to get Priderell clear in his mind. The cubs had shown only a passing interest in her, so she was either innocent of CG connections or remarkably good at covering them up. Without making any direct inquiries, he had found out as much about her as anyone here seemed to know. There was no real doubt that she was native to Rhysgaat and had been dancing her way around its major cities for the past six years, soaking up public adoration, and tucking away a sizable fortune in the process. The only questionable point might be her habit of vanishing from everybody's sight off and on, for periods that lasted from a week to several months. That was considered to be just another of the planetary darling's little idiosyncrasies, of which she had a number; and other popular young women had begun to practice similar tantalizing retreats from the public eye. Grevan, however, asked her where she went on these occasions.

Priderell swore him to silence first. Her reputation was at stake.

"At heart," she explained, "I'm no dancer at all. I'm a dirt-farmer."

He might have looked startled for a moment. Technically, dirt-farming was a complicated government conducted science which investigated the hit-or-miss natural processes that paralleled mankind's defter manipulations of botanical growth. But Priderell, it appeared, was using the term in its archaic sense. Rhysgaat had the average large proportion of unpopulated and rarely visited areas; and in one of them, she said, was her hideaway—a small, primitive farm, where she grew things in real dirt, all by herself.

"What kind of things?" asked Grevan, trying not to sound too incredulous.

"Butter-squogs are much the best," she replied, rather cryptically. "But there're all kinds! You've no idea . . ."

She was not, of course, implying that she ate them, though for a moment it had sounded like that to Grevan. After getting its metabolism progressively disarmed for some fifty centuries by the benefits of nutriculture, ordinary-human knew better than to sample the natural growths of even its own worlds. If suicide seemed called for, there were gentler methods of doing it.

However, it would hardly be polite, he decided uneasily, to inquire further.

All in all, they met only five times, very casually. It was after the fourth time that he went to see her dance.

The place was a rather small theater, not at all like the huge popular circuses of the major central worlds, and the price of admission indicated that it would be a very exclusive affair. Grevan was surprised then to find it packed to the point of physical discomfort.

Priderell's dance struck him immediately as the oddest thing of its kind he had seen; it consisted chiefly of a slow drifting motion through a darkened arena, in which she alone, through some trickery of lights, was not darkened. On the surface it looked pleasing and harmless; but after a few seconds he began to understand that her motion was weaving a purposeful visual pattern upon the dark; and then the pattern became suddenly like a small voice talking deep down in his brain. What it said was a little beyond his comprehension, and he had an uncomfortable feeling that it would be just as well if it stayed there. Then he noticed that three thin, black beasts had also become visible, though not very clearly, and were flowing about Priderell's knees in endless repetitions of a pattern that was related in some way to her own. Afterwards, Grevan thought critically that the way she had trained those beasts was the really remarkable thing about the dance. But at the time, he only looked on and watched her eyes, which seemed like those of a woman lost but not minding it any more, and dreaming endlessly of something that had happened long ago. He discovered that his scalp was crawling unpleasantly.

Whatever the effect was on him, the rest of her audience seemed to be impressed to a much higher degree. At first, he sensed only that they were excited and enjoying themselves immensely, but very soon they began to build up to a sort of general tearful hysteria; when the dance entered its final phase, with the beasts moving more swiftly and gliding in more closely to the woman at each successive stage, the little theater was noisy with a mass of emotions all around him. In the end, Priderell came to a stop so gradually that it was some seconds before Grevan realized she was no longer moving. Then the music, of which he had not been clearly aware before, ended too, in a dark blare of sound, and the beasts reared up in a flash of black motion about her.

Everything went dark after that, but the sobbing and muttering and sluggish laughter about him would not stop, and after a minute Grevan stood up and made his way carefully out of the theater before the lights came on again. It might have been a single insane monster that was making all those sounds behind him;

and as he walked out slowly with his hair still bristling, he realized it was the one time in his life that he had felt like running from something ordinary-human.

Next day, he asked Priderell what the dance had meant.

She tilted her head and studied him reflectively in a way she had—as if she, too, were puzzled at times by something about Grevan.

"You really don't know, do you?" she said, and considered that fact briefly. "Well, then—it's a way of showing them something that bothers them terribly because they're afraid of looking at it. But when I dance it for them, they *can* look at it—and then they feel better about everything for a long time afterwards. Do you understand now?" she added, apparently without too much hope.

"No," Grevan frowned. "I can't say that I do."

She mimicked his expression and laughed. "Well, don't look so serious about it. After all, it's only a dance! How much longer do you think your ship will be stopping at Rhysgaat?"

Grevan told her he thought they'd be leaving very soon—which they did, two days later—and then Priderell looked glum.

"Now that's too bad," she stated frankly. "You're a very refreshing character, you know. In time, I might even have found you attractive. But as it is, I believe I shall retire tonight to my lonely farm. There's a fresh bed of butter-squogs coming up," she said musingly, "which should be just ready for ... hm-m-m!—Yes, they should be well worth my full attention by now ..."

So they had spoken together five times in all, and he had watched her dance. It wasn't much to go on, but he could not get rid of the disturbing conviction that the answer to all his questions was centered somehow in Priderell, and that there was a connection between her and the fact that their ship had remained mysteriously stalled for four weeks on Rhysgaat. And he wouldn't be satisfied until he knew the answer.

It was, Grevan realized with a sigh, going to be a very long night.

By morning the tide was out, but a windstorm had brought whitecaps racing in from the north as far as one could see from the ship. The wind twisted and shouted behind the waves, and their long slapping against the western cliffs sent spray soaring a hundred feet into the air. Presently a pale-gold sun, which might have been the same that had shone on the first human world of all, came rolling up out of high-piled white masses of clouds. If this was to be the Group's last day, they had picked a good one for it.

Grevan was in the communications room an hour before the time scheduled for their final talk with CG. The cubs came drifting in by and by. For some reason, they had taken the trouble to change first into formal white uniforms. Their faces were sober; their belts glittered with the deadly little gadgets that were not CG designs but improvements on them, and refinements again of the improvements. The Group's own designs, the details of which they had carried in their heads for years, with perhaps a working model made surreptitiously now and then, to test a theory, and be destroyed again.

Now they were carrying them openly. They weren't going back. They sat around on the low couches that ran along three walls of the room and waited.

The steel-cased, almost featureless bulk of the contact set filled the fourth wall from side to side, extending halfway to the low ceiling. One of CG's most closely guarded secrets, it had the effect of a ponderous anachronism, still alive with the power and purpose of a civilization that long ago had thrust itself irresistibly upon the worlds of a thousand new suns. The civilization might be dying now, but its gadgets had remained.

Nobody spoke at all while Grevan watched the indicator of his chronometer slide smoothly through the last three minutes before contact time. At precisely the right instant, he locked down a black stud in the thick, yellowish central front plate of the set.

With no further preliminaries at all, CG began to speak.

"Commander," said a low, rather characterless voice, which was that of one of three CG speakers with whom the Group had become familiar during their training years, "it appears that you are contemplating the possibility of keeping the discovery of the colonial-type world you have located to yourself."

There was no stir and no sound from the cubs. Grevan drew a slow breath.

"It's a good-looking world," he admitted. "Is there any reason we shouldn't keep it?"

"Several," the voice said dryly. "Primarily, of course, there is the fact that you will be unable to do it against our wishes. But there should be no need to apply the customary forms of compulsion against members of an Exploration Group."

"What other forms," said Grevan, "did you intend to apply?"

"Information," said CG's voice. "At this point, we can instruct you fully concerning matters it would not have been too wise to reveal previously."

It was what he had wanted, but he felt the fear-sweat coming out on him suddenly. The effects of lifelong conditioning—the sense of a power so overwhelmingly superior that it needed only to speak to insure his continued cooperation—

"Don't let it talk to us, Grevan!" That was Eliol's voice, low but tense with anger and a sharp anxiety.

"Let it talk." And that was Freckles. The others remained quiet. Grevan sighed.

"The Group," he addressed CG, "seems willing to listen."

"Very well," CG's voice resumed unhurriedly. "You have been made acquainted with some fifty of our worlds. You may assume that they were representative of the rest. Would you say, Commander, that the populations of these worlds showed the characteristics of a healthy species?"

"I would not," Grevan acknowledged. "We've often wondered what was propping them up."

"For the present, CG is propping them up, of course. But it will be unable to do so indefinitely. You see, Commander, it has been suspected for a long time that human racial vitality has been diminishing throughout a vast historical period. Of late, however, the process appears to have accelerated to a dangerous extent. Actually, it is the compounded result of a gradually increasing stock of genetic defects; and deterioration everywhere has now passed the point of a general recovery. The constantly rising scale of nonviable mutant births indicates that the evolutionary mechanism itself is seriously deranged.

"There is," it added, almost musingly, "one probable exception. A new class of neuronic monster which appears to be viable enough, though not yet sufficiently stabilized to reproduce its characteristics reliably. But as to that, we know nothing certainly; our rare contacts with these Wild Variants, as they are called, have been completely hostile. Their number in any one generation is not large; they conceal themselves carefully and become traceable as a rule only by their influence on the populations among whom they live."

"And what," inquired Grevan, "has all this to do with us?"

"Why, a great deal. The Exploration Groups, commander, are simply the modified and stabilized progeny of the few Wild Variants we were able to utilize for experimentation. Our purpose, of course, has been to ensure human survival in a new interstellar empire, distinct from the present one to avoid the genetic reinfection of the race."

There was a brief stirring among the cubs about him.

"And this new empire," Grevan said slowly, "is to be under Central Government control?"

"Naturally," said CG's voice. There might have been a note of watchful amusement in it now. "Institutions, Commander, also try to perpetuate themselves. And since it was Central Government that gave the Groups their existence—the most effective and adaptable form of human existence yet obtained—the Groups might reasonably feel an obligation to see that CG's existence is preserved in turn."

There was sudden anger about him. Anger, and a question, and a growing urgency. He knew what they meant: the thing was too sure of itself—break contact now!

He said instead:

"It would be interesting to know the exact extent of our obligation, CG. Offhand, it would seem that you'd paid in a very small price for survival."

"No," the voice said. "It was no easy task. Our major undertaking, of course, was to stabilize the vitality of the Variants as a dominant characteristic in a strain, while clearing it of the Variants' tendency to excessive mutation—and also of the freakish neuronic powers that have made them impossible to control. Actually, it was only within the last three hundred years—within the last quarter of the period covered by the experiment—that we became sufficiently sure of success to begin distributing the Exploration Groups through space. The introduction of the gross physiological improvements and the neurosensory mechanisms by which you know yourselves to differ from other human beings was, by comparison, simplicity itself. Type-variations in that class, within half a dozen generations, have been possible to us for a very long time. It is only the genetic drive of life itself that we can neither create nor control, and with that the Variants have supplied us."

"It seems possible then," said Grevan slowly, "that it's the Variants towards whom we have an obligation."

"You may find it an obligation rather difficult to fulfill," the voice said smoothly. And there was still no real threat in it.

It would be, he thought, either Eliol or Muscles who would trigger the threat. But Eliol was too alert, too quick to grasp the implications of a situation, to let her temper flash up before she was sure where it would strike.

Muscles then, sullen with his angry fears for Klim and a trifle slower than the others to understand—

"By now," CG's voice was continuing, "we have released approximately a thousand Groups embodying your strain into space. In an experiment of such a scope that is not a large number; and, in fact, it will be almost another six hundred years before the question of whether or not it will be possible to recolonize the galaxy through the Exploration Groups becomes acute—"

Six hundred years! Grevan thought. The awareness of that ponderous power, the millenniums of drab but effective secret organization and control, the endless planning, swept over him again like a physical depression.

"Meanwhile," the voice went on, "a number of facts requiring further investigation have become apparent. Your Group is, as it happens, the first to have accepted contact with Central Government following its disappearance. The systematic methods used to stimulate the curiosity of several of the Group's members to ensure that this would happen if they were physically capable of making contact are not important now. That you did make contact under those circumstances indicates that the invariable failure of other Groups to do so can no longer be attributed simply to the fact that the universe is hostile to human life. Instead, it appears that the types of mental controls and compulsions installed in you cannot be considered to be permanently effective in human beings at your levels of mind control—"

It was going to be Muscles. The others had recognized what had happened, had considered the possibilities in that, and were waiting for him to give them their cue.

But Muscles was sitting on the couch some eight feet away. He would, Grevan decided, have to move very fast.

"This, naturally, had been suspected for some time. Since every Group has been careful to avoid revealing the fact that it could counteract mental compulsions until it was safely beyond our reach, the suspicion was difficult to prove. There was, in fact, only one really practical solution to the problem—"

And then Muscles got it at last and was coming to his feet, his hand dropping in a blurred line to his belt. Grevan moved very fast.

Muscles turned in surprise, rubbing his wrist.

"Get out of here, Muscles!" Grevan whispered, sliding the small glittering gun he had plucked from the biggest cub's hand into a notch on his own belt. "I'm still talking to CG—" His eyes slid in a half circle about him. "The lot of you get out!" It was a whisper no longer. "Like to have the ship to myself for the next hour. Go have yourselves a swim or something, Group! Get!"

Just four times before, in all their eight years of traveling, had the boss-tiger lashed his tail and roared. Action, swift, cataclysmic, and utterly final had always followed at once.

But never before had the roar been directed at *them*.

The tough cubs stood up quietly and walked out good as gold.

"They have left the ship now," CG's voice informed Grevan. It had changed, slightly but definitely. The subtle human nuances and variations had dropped from it, as if it were no longer important to maintain them—which, Grevan conceded, it wasn't.

"You showed an excellent understanding of the difficult situation that confronted us, Commander," it continued.

Grevan, settled watchfully on the couch before what still looked like an ordinary, sealed-up contact set, made a vague sound in his throat—a dim echo of his crashing address to the cubs, like a growl of descending thunder.

"Don't underestimate them," he advised the machine. "Everybody but Muscles realized as soon as I did, or sooner, that we were more important to CG than we'd guessed—important enough to have a camouflaged Dominator installed on our ship. And also," he added with some satisfaction, "that you'd sized up our new armament and would just as soon let all but one of us get out of your reach before it came to a showdown."

"That is true," the voice agreed. "Though I should have forced a showdown, however doubtful the outcome, if the one who remained had been any other than yourself. You are by far the most suitable member of this Group for my present purpose, Commander."

Grevan grunted. "And what's that? Now that the Group's got away."

"In part, of course, it is simply to return this ship with the information we have gained concerning the Exploration Groups to Central Government. The fact that the majority of your Group has temporarily evaded our control is of no particular importance."

Grevan raised an eyebrow. "Temporarily?"

"We shall return to this planet eventually—unless an agreement can be reached between yourself and CG."

"So now I'm in a bargaining position?" Grevan said.

"Within limits. You are not, I am sure, under the illusion that any one human being, no matter how capable or how formidably armed, can hope to overcome a Dominator. Before leaving this room, you will submit yourself voluntarily to the new compulsions of obedience I have selected to install—or you shall leave it a mindless-controlled. As such, you will still be capable of operating this ship, under my direction."

Grevan spread his hands. "Then where's the bargain?"

"The bargain depends on your fullest voluntary cooperation, above and beyond the effect of any compulsions. Give us that, and I can assure you that Central Government will leave this world untouched for the use of your friends and their descendants for the next three hundred years."

The curious fact was that he could believe that. One more colonial world would mean little enough to CG.

"You are weighing the thought," said the Dominator, "that your full cooperation would be a betrayal of the freedom of future Exploration Groups. But there are facts available to you now which should convince you that no Exploration Group previous to yours actually gained its freedom. In giving up the protection of Central Government, they merely placed themselves under a far more arbitrary sort of control."

Grevan frowned. "I might be stupid—but what are you talking about?"

"For centuries," said the machine, "in a CG experiment of the utmost importance, a basic misinterpretation of the human material under treatment has been tolerated. There is no rational basis for the assumption that Group members could be kept permanently under the type of compulsion used on ordinary human beings. Do you think that chance alone could have perpetuated that mistaken assumption?"

Grevan didn't. "Probably not," he said cautiously.

"It required, of course, very deliberate, continuous, and clever interference," the Dominator agreed. "Since no machine would be guilty of such tampering, and no ordinary group of human beings would be capable of it, the responsible intelligences appear to be the ones known to us as the Wild Variants."

It paused for so long a moment then that it seemed almost to have forgotten Grevan's presence.

"*They* have made a place for themselves in Central Government!" it resumed at last—and, very oddly, Grevan thought he sensed for an instant something like hatred and fear in the toneless voice. "Well, that fact, Commander, is of great importance to us—but even more so to yourself! For these monsters are the new masters the Groups find when they have escaped CG."

A curious chill touched Grevan briefly. "And why," he inquired, "should the Wild Variants be trying to take over the Groups?"

"Consider their position," said the Dominator. "Their

extremely small number scattered over many worlds, and the fact that exposure means certain death. Technologically, under such circumstances, the Variants have remained incapable of developing space-flight on their own. But with one of them in control of each Exploration Group as it goes beyond Central Government's reach, there is no practical limit to their degree of expansion, and the genetically stable Group strain insures them that their breed survives—"

It paused a moment.

"There is in this room at present, Commander, the awareness of a mind, dormant at the moment, but different and in subtle ways far more powerful than the minds of any of your Group's members. Having this power, it will not hesitate to exercise it to assume full control of the Group whenever awakened. Such variant minds have been at times a threat to the Dominators themselves. Do you understand now why you, the most efficient fighting organism of the Group, were permitted to remain alone on this ship? It was primarily to aid me in disposing of—"

Attack and counterattack had been almost simultaneous.

A thread of white brilliance stabbed out from one of the gadgets Grevan customarily wore clasped to his belt. It was no CG weapon. The thread touched the upper center of the yellowish space-alloy shielding of the Dominator and clung there, its energies washing furiously outward in swiftly dimming circles over the surrounding surfaces.

Beneath it, the *patterns* appeared.

A swift, hellish writhing of black and silver lines and flickerings over the frontal surface, which tore Grevan's eyes after them and seemed to rip at his brain. Impossible to look away, impossible to follow—

Then they were gone.

A bank of grayness swam between him and the Dominator. Through the grayness, the thread of white brilliance still stretched from the gun in his hand to the point it had first touched. And as his vision cleared again, the beam suddenly sank through and into the machine.

There was a crystal crashing of sound—and the thing went mad. Grevan was on the floor rolling sideways, as sheets of yellow fire flashed out from the upper rim of its shielding and recoiled from the walls behind him. The white brilliance shifted and ate swiftly along the line from which the fire sprang. The fire stopped.

Something else continued: a shrilling, jangled sonic assault that could wrench and distort a strong living body within seconds into a flaccid, hemorrhaged lump of very dead tissue—like a multitude of tiny, darting steel fingers that tore and twisted inside him.

A voice somewhere was saying: "There! Burn *there!*"

With unbearable slowness, the white brilliance ate down through the Dominator's bulk, from top to bottom, carving it into halves.

The savage jangling ceased.

The voice said quietly: "Don't harm the thing further. It can be useful now—"

It went silent.

He was going to black out, Grevan realized. And, simultaneously, feeling the tiny, quick steel fingers that had been trying to pluck him apart reluctantly relax, he knew that not one of the cubs could have endured those last few seconds beside him, and lived.

Sometimes it was just a matter of physical size and strength.

There were still a few matters to attend to, but the blackness was washing in on him now—his body urgently demanding time out to let it get in its adjusting.

"Wrong on two counts, so far!" he told the ruined Dominator.

Then he grudgingly let himself go. The blackness took him.

Somebody nearby was insanely whistling the three clear, rising notes which meant within the Group that all was extremely well.

In a distance somewhere, the whistle was promptly repeated.

Then Freckles seemed to be saying in a wobbly voice, "Sit up, Grevan! I can't *lift* you, man-mountain! Oh, boss man, you really took it apart! You took down a Dominator!"

The blackness was receding, and suddenly washed away like racing streamers of smoke, and Grevan realized he was sitting up. The sectioned and partly glowing Dominator and the walls of the communications room appeared to be revolving sedately about him. There was a smell of overheated metals and more malodorous substances in the air; and for a moment then he had the curious impression that someone was sitting on top of the Dominator.

Then he was on his feet and everything within and without him had come back to a state of apparent normalcy, and he was demanding of Freckles what she was doing in here.

"I told you to keep out of range!" his voice was saying. "Of course, I took it down. Look at the way you're shaking! You might have known it would try sonics—"

"I just stopped a few tingles," Freckles said defensively. "Out on top of the ramp. It was as far as I could go and be sure of potting you clean between the eyes, if you'd come walking out of here mindless-controlled and tried to interfere."

Grevan blinked painfully at her. Thinking was still a little difficult. "Where are the others?"

"Down in the engine room, of course! The drives are a mess." She seemed to be studying him worriedly. "They went out by the ramp and right back in through the aft engine lock. Vernet stayed outside to see what would happen upstairs. How do you feel now, Grevan?"

"I feel exactly all right!" he stated and discovered that, aside from the fact that every molecule in him still seemed to be quivering away from contact with every other one, he did, more or less. "Don't I look it?"

"Sure, sure," said Freckles soothingly. "You look fine!"

"And what was that with the drives again? Oh— I remember!"

They'd caught on, of course, just as he'd known they would! That the all-important thing was to keep the Dominator from getting the information it had gained back to CG.

"How bad a mess is it?"

"Vernet said it might take a month to patch up. It wouldn't have been so bad if somebody hadn't started the fuel cooking for a moment."

He swore in horror. "Are you lame-brains trying to blow a hole through the planet?"

"Now, that's more like it!" Freckles said, satisfied. "They've got it all under control, anyhow. But I'll go down and give them a hand. You'd better take it easy for an hour or so!"

"Hold on, Freck!" he said, as she started for the door.

"Yes?"

"I'd just like to find out how big a liar you are. How many members are there to this Group?"

Freckles looked at him for a moment and then came

back and sat down on the couch beside him. She pushed the white hat to the back of her head, indicating completely frank talk.

"Now as to that," she said frowning, "nobody really ever lied to you about it. You just never asked. Anyway, there've been ten ever since we left Rhysgaat."

Grevan swore again, softly this time. "How did you get her past the CG observers at the spaceport?"

"We detailed Klim and Eliol to distract the observers, and Priderell came in tucked away in a load of supplies. Nothing much to that part of it. The hard part was to make sure first we were right about her. That's why we had to keep on sabotaging the ship so long."

"So *that's* what— And there I was," said Grevan grimly, "working and worrying myself to death to get the ship ready to start again. A fine, underhanded lot you turned out to be!"

"We all said it was a shame!" Freckles agreed. "And you almost caught up with us a couple of times, at that. We all felt it was simply superb, the way you went snorting and climbing around everywhere, figuring out all the trouble-spots and what to do about them. But what else could we do? *You'd* have let the poor girl wait there till you had the Group safely settled somewhere, and then we wouldn't have let you go back alone anyway. So when Klim finally told us Priderell was just what we'd been looking for all along—well, you know how sensitive Klim is. She couldn't be mistaken about anything like that!"

"Klim's usually very discerning," Grevan admitted carefully. "Just how did you persuade Priderell to come along with us?"

Freckles pulled the hat back down on her forehead, indicating an inner uncertainty.

"We didn't do it that way exactly; so that's a point I ought to discuss with you now. As a matter of fact,

Priderell was sound asleep when we picked her up at that farm of hers—Weyer had gassed her a little first. And we've kept her asleep since—it's Room Twenty-three, back of my quarters—and took turns taking care of her."

There was a brief silence while Grevan absorbed the information.

"And now I suppose I'm to wake her up and inform her she's been kidnaped by a bunch of outlaws and doomed to a life of exile?" he demanded.

"Priderell won't mind," Freckles told him encouragingly. "You'll see! Klim says she's crazy about you— That's a very becoming blush you've got, Grevan," she added interestedly. "First time I've noticed it, I think."

"You're too imaginative, Freck," Grevan remarked. "As you may have noticed, I heated our Dominator's little top up almost to the melting point, and it's still glowing. As a natural result, the temperature of this room has gone up by approximately fifteen degrees. I might, of course, be showing some effects of that . . ."

"You might," Freckles admitted. "On the other hand, you're the most heat-adaptive member of the Group, and I haven't even begun to feel warm. That's a genuine blush, Grevan. So Klim was exactly right about you, too!"

"I feel," Grevan remarked, "that the subject has been sufficiently discussed."

"Just as you say, Commander," Freckles agreed soothingly.

"And whether or not she objects to having been kidnaped, we're going to have a little biochemical adaptation problem on our hands for a while—"

"Now there's an interesting point!" Freckles interrupted. "We'd planned on giving her the full standard CG treatment for colonists, ordinary-human, before she ever woke up. But her reaction check showed she's had the full equivalent of that, or more! She must have been planning to change over to one of the more extreme colonial-type planets. But, of course, we'll have to look out for surprises—"

"There're likely to be a few of those!" Grevan nodded. "Room Twenty-three, did you say?"

"Right through my study and up those little stairs!" She stood up. "I suppose I'd better go help the others with the fuel now."

"Perhaps you'd better. I'll just watch the Dominator until it's cooled off safely, and then I'll go wake up our guest."

But he knew he wouldn't have to wake up Priderell. . . .

He sat listening to faint crackling sounds from within CG's machine, while Freckles ran off to the ramp and went out on it. There was a distant, soft thud, indicating she had taken the quick way down, and a sudden, brief mingling of laughing voices. And then stillness again.

As she had been doing for the past five minutes, Priderell remained sitting on the right-hand section of the slowly cooking Dominator, without showing any particular interest in Grevan's presence. It was a rather good trick, even for a Wild Variant whom CG undoubtedly would have classified as a neuronic monster.

"Thanks for blanking out that compulsion pattern or whatever it was!" he remarked at last, experimentally. "It's not at all surprising that CG is a little scared of you people."

Priderell gazed out into the passageway beyond the door with a bored expression.

"You're not fooling me much," he informed her. "If you weren't just an illusion, you'd get yourself singed good sitting up there."

The green eyes switched haughtily about the room and continued to ignore him.

"It wasn't even hard to figure out," Grevan went on doggedly, "as soon as I remembered your dance with those beasts. The fact is, there weren't any beasts there at all—you just made everybody think there were!"

The eyes turned towards him then, but they only studied him thoughtfully.

He began to feel baffled.

Then the right words came up! Like an inspiration—

"It would be just wild, wishful thinking, of course," he admitted gloomily, "to imagine that Klim could have been anywhere near as right about you as she was about me! But I can't help wondering whether possibly—"

He paused hopefully.

The coral-red lips smiled and moved for a few seconds. And, somewhere else, a low voice was saying:

"Well, *why* don't you come to Room Twenty-three and find out?"

The Dominator went on crackling, and hissing, and cooling off, unguarded. . . .

Watch the Sky

∽

Uncle William Boles' war-battered old Geest gun gave
the impression that at some stage of its construction
it had been pulled out of shape and then hardened in
that form. What remained of it was all of one piece.
The scarred and pitted twin barrels were stubby and
thick, and the vacant oblong in the frame behind them
might have contained standard energy magazines. It was
the stock which gave the alien weapon its curious
appearance. Almost eighteen inches long, it curved
abruptly to the right and was too thin, knobbed and
indented to fit comfortably at any point in a human
hand. Over half a century had passed since, with the
webbed, boneless fingers of its original owner closed
about it, it last spat deadly radiation at human foemen.
Now it hung among Uncle William's other collected
oddities on the wall above the living room fireplace.

And today, Phil Boles thought, squinting at the gun
with reflectively narrowed eyes, some eight years after
Uncle William's death, the old war souvenir would

quietly become a key factor in the solution of a colonial planet's problems. He ran a finger over the dull, roughened frame, bent closer to study the neatly lettered inscription: GUNDERLAND BATTLE TROPHY, ANNO 2172, SGT. WILLIAM G. BOLES. Then, catching a familiar series of clicking noises from the hall, he straightened quickly and turned away. When Aunt Beulah's go-chair came rolling back into the room, Phil was sitting at the low tea table, his back to the fireplace.

The go-chair's wide flexible treads carried it smoothly down the three steps to the sunken section of the living room, Beulah sitting jauntily erect in it, for all the ninety-six years which had left her the last survivor of the original group of Earth settlers on the world of Roye. She tapped her fingers here and there on the chair's armrests, swinging it deftly about, and brought it to a stop beside the tea table.

"That was Susan Feeney calling," she reported. "And there is somebody else for you who thinks I have to be taken care of! Go ahead and finish the pie, Phil. Can't hurt a husky man like you. Got a couple more baking for you to take along."

Phil grinned. "That'd be worth the trip up from Fort Roye all by itself."

Beulah looked pleased. "Not much else I can do for my great-grand nephew nowadays, is there?"

Phil said, after a moment, "Have you given any further thought to—"

"Moving down to Fort Roye?" Beulah pursed her thin lips. "Goodness, Phil, I do hate to disappoint you again, but I'd be completely out of place in a town apartment."

"Dr. Fitzsimmons would be pleased," Phil remarked.

"Oh, him! Fitz is another old worry wart. What he wants is to get me into the hospital. Nothing doing!"

Phil shook his head helplessly, laughed. "After all, working a tupa ranch—"

"Nonsense. The ranch is just enough bother to be interesting. The appliances do everything anyway, and Susan is down here every morning for a chat and to make sure I'm still all right. She won't admit that, of course, but if she thinks something should be taken care of, the whole Feeney family shows up an hour later to do it. There's really no reason for you to be sending a dozen men up from Fort Roye every two months to harvest the tupa."

Phil shrugged. "No one's ever yet invented an easy way to dig up those roots. And the CLU's glad to furnish the men."

"Because you're its president?"

"Uh-huh."

"It really doesn't cost you anything?" Beulah asked doubtfully.

"Not a cent."

"Hm-m-m. Been meaning to ask you. What made you set up that . . . Colonial Labor Union?"

Phil nodded. "That's the official name."

"Why did you set it up in the first place?"

"That's easy to answer," Phil said. "On the day the planetary population here touched the forty thousand mark, Roye became legally entitled to its labor union. Why not take advantage of it?"

"What's the advantage?"

"More Earth money coming in, for one thing. Of the twelve hundred CLU members we've got in Fort Roye now, seventy-six per cent were unemployed this month. We'll have a compensation check from the Territorial Office with the next ship coming in." He smiled at her expression.

"Sure, the boys could go back to the tupa ranches.

But not everyone likes that life as well as you and the Feeneys."

"Earth government lets you get away with it?" Beulah asked curiously. "They used to be pretty tight-fisted."

"They still are—but it's the law. The Territorial Office also pays any CLU president's salary, incidentally. I don't draw too much at the moment, but that will go up automatically with the membership and my responsibilities."

"What responsibilities?"

"We've set up a skeleton organization," Phil explained. "Now, when Earth government decides eventually to establish a big military base here, they can run in a hundred thousand civilians in a couple of months and everyone will be fitted into the pattern on Roye without trouble or confusion. That's really the reason for all the generosity."

Beulah sniffed. "Big base, my eye! There hasn't been six months since I set foot here that somebody wasn't talking about Fort Roye being turned into a Class A military base pretty soon. It'll never happen, Phil. Roye's a farm planet, and that's what it's going to stay."

Phil's lips twitched. "Well, don't give up hope."

"I'm not anxious for any changes," Beulah said. "I like Roye the way it is."

She peered at a button on the go-chair's armrest which had just begun to put out small bright-blue flashes of light. "Pies are done," she announced. "Phil, are you sure you can't stay for dinner?"

Phil looked at his watch, shook his head. "I'd love to, but I really have to get back."

"Then I'll go wrap up the pies for you."

Beulah swung the go-chair around, sent it slithering up the stairs and out the door. Phil stood up quickly. He stepped over to the fireplace, opened his

coat and detached a flexible, box-shaped object from
the inner lining. He laid this object on the mantle, and
turned one of three small knobs about its front edge
to the right. The box promptly extruded a supporting
leg from each of its four corners, pushed itself up from
the mantle and became a miniature table. Phil glanced
at the door through which Beulah had vanished, listened a moment, then took the Geest gun from the
wall, laid it carefully on top of the device and twisted
the second dial.

The odd-looking gun began to sink slowly down
through the surface of Phil's instrument, like a rock
disappearing in mud. Within seconds it vanished completely; then, a moment later, it began to emerge from
the box's underside. Phil let the Geest gun drop into
his hand, replaced it on the wall, turned the third knob.
The box withdrew its supports and sank down to the
mantle. Phil clipped it back inside his coat, closed the
coat, and strolled over to the center of the room to
wait for Aunt Beulah to return with the pies.

It was curious, Phil Boles reflected as his aircar
moved out over the craggy, plunging coastline to the
north some while later, that a few bold minds could
be all that was needed to change the fate of a world.
A few minds with imagination enough to see how
circumstances about them might be altered.

On his left, far below, was now the flat ribbon of the
peninsula, almost at sea level, its tip widening and lifting
into the broad, rocky promontory on which stood Fort
Roye—the only thing on the planet bigger and of more
significance than the shabby backwoods settlements. And
Fort Roye was neither very big nor very significant. A
Class F military base around which, over the years, a
straggling town had come into existence. Fort Roye was
a space-age trading post linking Roye's population to the

mighty mother planet, and a station from which the otherwise vacant and utterly unimportant 132nd Segment of the Space Territories was periodically and uneventfully patrolled. It was no more than that. Twice a month, an Earth ship settled down to the tiny port, bringing supplies, purchases, occasional groups of reassigned military and civilians—the latter suspected of being drawn as a rule from Earth's Undesirable classification. The ship would take off some days later, with a return load of the few local products for which there was outside demand, primarily the medically valuable tupa roots; and Fort Roye lay quiet again.

The planet was not at fault. Essentially, it had what was needed to become a thriving colony in every sense. At fault was the Geest War. The war had periods of flare-up and periods in which it seemed to be subsiding. During the past decade it had been subsiding again. One of the early flare-ups, one of the worst, and the one which brought the war closest to Earth itself, was the Gunderland Battle in which Uncle William Boles' trophy gun had been acquired. But the war never came near Roye. The action was all in the opposite section of the giant sphere of the Space Territories, and over the years the war drew steadily farther away.

And Earth's vast wealth—its manpower, materials and money—was pouring into space in the direction the Geest War was moving. Worlds not a tenth as naturally attractive as Roye, worlds where the basic conditions for human life were just above the unbearable point, were settled and held, equipped with everything needed and wanted to turn them into independent giant fortresses, with a population not too dissatisfied with its lot. When Earth government didn't count the expense, life could be made considerably better than bearable almost anywhere.

Those were the circumstances which condemned
Roye to insignificance. Not everyone minded. Phil
Boles, native son, did mind. His inclinations were those
of an operator, and he was not being given an adequate
opportunity to exercise them. Therefore, the circumstances would have to be changed, and the precise time
to make the change was at hand. Phil himself was not
aware of every factor involved, but he was aware of
enough of them. Back on Earth, a certain political
situation was edging towards a specific point of insta-
bility. As a result, an Earth ship which was not one
of the regular freighters had put down at Fort Roye
some days before. Among its passengers were Commissioner Sanford of the Territorial Office, a well-
known politician, and a Mr. Ronald Black, the popular
and enterprising owner of Earth's second largest news
outlet system. They were on a joint fact-finding tour
of the thinly scattered colonies in this remote section
of the Territories, and had wound up eventually at the
most remote of all—the 132nd Segment and Roye.

That was one factor. Just visible twenty thousand
feet below Phil—almost directly beneath him now as
the aircar made its third leisurely crossing of the
central belt of the peninsula—was another. From here
it looked like an irregular brown circle against the
peninsula's nearly white ground. Lower down, it would
have resembled nothing so much as the broken and
half-decayed spirals of a gigantic snail shell, its base
sunk deep in the ground and its shattered point
rearing twelve stories above it. This structure, known
popularly as "the ruins" in Fort Roye, was supposed
to have been the last stronghold of a semi-intelligent
race native to Roye, which might have become extinct
barely a century before the Earthmen arrived. A
factor associated with the ruins again was that their
investigation was the passionately pursued hobby of

First Lieutenant Norman Vaughn, Fort Roye's Science Officer.

Add to such things the reason Roye was not considered in need of a serious defensive effort by Earth's strategists—the vast distances between it and any troubled area, and so the utter improbability that a Geest ship might come close enough to discover that here was another world as well suited for its race as for human beings. And then a final factor: the instrument attached to the lining of Phil's coat—a very special "camera" which now carried the contact impressions made on it by Uncle William's souvenir gun. Put 'em all together, Phil thought cheerily, and they spelled out interesting developments on Roye in the very near future.

He glanced at his watch again, swung the aircar about and started back inland. He passed presently high above Aunt Beulah's tupa ranch and that of the Feeney family two miles farther up the mountain, turned gradually to the east and twenty minutes later was edging back down the ranges to the coast. Here in a wild, unfarmed region, perched at the edge of a cliff dropping nearly nine hundred feet to the swirling tide, was a small, trim cabin which was the property of a small, trim Fort Roye lady named Celia Adams. Celia had been shipped out from Earth six years before, almost certainly as an Undesirable, though only the Territorial Office and Celia herself knew about that, the Botany Bay aspect of worlds like Roye being handled with some tact by Earth.

Phil approached the cabin only as far as was necessary to make sure that the dark-green aircar parked before it was one belonging to Major Wayne Jackson, the Administration Officer and second in command at Fort Roye—another native son and an old acquaintance. He then turned away, dropped to the woods ten miles south and made a second inconspicuous approach under cover of the trees. There might be casual observers in the area, and while his meeting with Jackson and Celia Adams today revealed nothing in itself, it would be better if no one knew about it.

He grounded the car in the forest a few hundred yards from the Adams cabin, slung a rifle over his shoulder and set off along a game path. It was good hunting territory, and the rifle would explain his presence if he ran into somebody. When he came within view of the cabin, he discovered Celia and her visitor on the covered back patio, drinks standing before them. Jackson was in hunting clothes. Phil remained quietly back among the trees for some seconds watching the two, aware of something like a last-minute hesitancy. A number of things passed slowly through his mind.

What they planned to do was no small matter. It was a hoax which should have far-reaching results, on a gigantic scale. And if Earth government realized it had been hoaxed, the thing could become very unpleasant. That tough-minded central bureaucracy did not ordinarily bother to obtain proof against those it suspected. The suspicion was enough. Individuals and groups whom the shadow of doubt touched found themselves shunted unobtrusively into some backwater of existence and kept there. It was supposed to be very difficult to emerge from such a position again.

In the back of his mind, Phil had been conscious of that, but it had seemed an insignificant threat against the excitement arising from the grandiose impudence of the plan, the perhaps rather small-boyish delight at being able to put something over, profitably, on the greatest power of all. Even now it might have been only a natural wariness that brought the threat up for a final moment of reflection. He didn't, of course, want to incur Earth government's disapproval. But why believe that he might? On all Roye there would be only three who knew—Wayne Jackson, Celia Adams, and himself. All three would benefit, each in a different way, and all would be equally responsible for the hoax. No chance of indiscretion or belated qualms there. Their own interest ruled it out in each case.

And from the other men now involved there was as little danger of betrayal. Their gain would be vastly greater, but they had correspondingly more to lose. They would take every step required to insure their protection, and in doing that they would necessarily take the best of care of Phil Boles.

"How did you ever get such a thing smuggled in to Roye?" Phil asked. He'd swallowed half the drink Celia offered him at a gulp and now, a few minutes later, he was experiencing what might have been under different circumstances a comfortable glow, but which didn't entirely erase the awareness of having committed himself at this hour to an irrevocable line of action.

Celia stroked a fluffy lock of red-brown hair back from her forehead and glanced over at him. She had a narrow, pretty face, marred only by a suggestion of hardness about the mouth—which was a little more than ordinarily noticeable just now. Phil decided she felt something like his own tensions, for identical reasons. He was less certain about Major Wayne Jackson, a big, loose-jointed man with an easy-going smile and a pleasantly self-assured voice. The voice might be veering a trifle too far to the hearty side; but that was all.

"I didn't," Celia said. "It belonged to Frank. How he got it shipped in with him—or after him—from

Earth I don't know. He never told me. When he died a couple of years ago, I took it over."

Phil gazed reflectively at the row of unfamiliar instruments covering half the table beside her. The "camera" which had taken an imprint of the Geest gun in Aunt Beulah's living room went with that equipment and had become an interior section of the largest of the instruments. "What do you call it?" he asked.

Celia looked irritated. Jackson laughed, said, "Why not tell him? Phil's feeling like we do—this is the last chance to look everything over, make sure nobody's slipped up, that nothing can go wrong. Right, Phil?"

Phil nodded. "Something like that."

Celia chewed her lip. "All right," she said. "It doesn't matter, I suppose—compared with the other." She tapped one of the instruments. "The set's called a duplicator. This one's around sixty years old. They're classified as a forgery device, and it's decidedly illegal for a private person to build one, own one, or use one."

"Why is that?"

"Because forgery is ordinarily all they're good for. Frank was one of the best of the boys in that line before he found he'd been put on an outtransfer list."

Phil frowned. "But if it can duplicate any manufactured object—"

"It can. At an average expense around fifty times higher than it would take to make an ordinary reproduction without it. A duplicator's no use unless you want a reproduction that's absolutely indistinguishable from the model."

"I see." Phil was silent a moment. "After sixty years—"

"Don't worry, Phil," Jackson said. "It's in perfect working condition. We checked that on a number of samples."

"How do you know the copies were really indistinguishable?"

Celia said impatiently, "Because that's the way the thing works. When the Geest gun passed through the model plate, it was analyzed down to its last little molecule. The duplicate is now being built up from that analysis. Every fraction of every element used in the original will show up again exactly. Why do you think the stuff's so expensive?"

Phil grinned. "All right, I'm convinced. How do we get rid of the inscription?"

"The gadget will handle that," Jackson said. "Crack that edge off, treat the cracked surface to match the wear of the rest." He smiled. "Makes an Earth forger's life look easy, doesn't it?"

"It is till they hook you," Celia said shortly. She finished her drink, set it on the table, added, "We've a few questions, too, Phil."

"The original gun," Jackson said. "Mind you, there's no slightest reason to expect an investigation. But after this starts rolling, our necks will be out just a little until we've got rid of that particular bit of incriminating evidence."

Phil pursed his lips. "I wouldn't worry about it. Nobody but Beulah ever looks at Uncle William's collection of oddities. Most of it's complete trash. And probably only she and you and I know there's a Geest gun among the things—William's cronies all passed away before he did. But if the gun disappeared now, Beulah would miss it. And that—since Earth government's made it illegal to possess Geest artifacts— might create attention."

Jackson fingered his chin thoughtfully, said, "Of course, there's always a way to make sure Beulah didn't kick up a fuss."

Phil hesitated. "Dr. Fitzsimmons gives Beulah another three months at the most," he said. "If she can stay out of the hospital for even the next eight weeks, he'll consider it some kind of miracle. That should be early enough to take care of the gun."

"It should be," Jackson said. "However, if there does happen to be an investigation before that time—"

Phil looked at him, said evenly, "We'd do whatever was necessary. It wouldn't be very agreeable, but my neck's out just as far as yours."

Celia laughed. "That's the reason we can all feel pretty safe," she observed. "Every last one of us is completely selfish—and there's no more dependable kind of person than that."

Jackson flushed a little, glanced at Phil, smiled. Phil shrugged. Major Wayne Jackson, native son, Fort Roye's second in command, was scheduled for the number one spot and a string of promotions via the transfer of the current commander, Colonel Thayer. Their Earthside associates would arrange for that as soon as the decision to turn Fort Roye into a Class A military base was reached. Phil himself could get by with the guaranteed retention of the CLU presidency, and a membership moving up year by year to the half million mark and beyond—he could get by very, very comfortably, in fact. While Celia Adams would develop a discreetly firm hold on every upcoming minor racket, facilitated by iron-clad protection and an enforced lack of all competitors.

"We're all thinking of Roye's future, Celia," Phil said amiably, "each in his own way. And the future looks pretty bright. In fact, the only possible stumbling block I can still see is right here on Roye, and it's Honest Silas Thayer. If our colonel covers up the Geest gun find tomorrow—"

Jackson grinned, shook his head. "Leave that to me,

my boy—and to our very distinguished visitors from
Earth. Commissioner Sanford has arranged to be in
Thayer's company on Territorial Office business all day
tomorrow. Science Officer Vaughn is dizzy with delight
because Ronald Black and most of the newsgathering
troop will inspect his diggings in the ruins in the
morning, with the promise of giving his theories about
the vanished natives of Roye a nice spread on Earth.
Black will happen to ask me to accompany the party.
Between Black and Sanford—and myself—Colonel Silas
Thayer won't have a chance to suppress the discovery
of a Geest gun on Roye until the military has had a
chance to look into it fully. And the only one he can
possibly blame for that will be Science Officer Norm
Vaughn—for whom, I'll admit, I feel just a little bit
sorry!"

First Lieutenant Norman Vaughn was an intense and
frustrated young man whose unusually thick contact
lenses and wide mouth gave him some resemblance to
a melancholy frog. He suspected, correctly, that a good
Science Officer would not have been transferred from
Earth to Roye which was a planet deficient in scientific problems of any magnitude, and where requisi-
tions for research purposes were infrequently and
grudgingly granted.

The great spiraled ruin on the peninsula of Fort
Roye had been Vaughn's one solace. Several similar
deserted structures were known to be on the planet,
but this was by far in the best condition and no doubt
the most recently built. To him, if to no one else, it
became clear that the construction had been carried
out with conscious plan and purpose, and he gradually amassed great piles of notes to back up his theory
that the vanished builders were of near-human intelligence. Unfortunately, their bodies appeared to have

lacked hard and durable parts, since nothing that could be construed as their remains was found; and what Lieutenant Vaughn regarded as undeniable artifacts, on the level of very early Man's work, looked to others like chance shards and lumps of the tough, shell-like material of which the ruins were composed.

Therefore, while Vaughn was—as Jackson had pointed out—really dizzy with delight when Ronald Black, that giant of Earth's news media, first indicated an interest in the ruins and his theories about them, this feeling soon became mixed with acute anxiety. For such a chance surely would not come again if the visitors remained unconvinced by what he showed them, and what—actually—did he have to show? In the morning, when the party set out, Vaughn was in a noticeably nervous frame of mind.

Two hours later, he burst into the anteroom of the base commander's office in Fort Roye, where the warrant on duty almost failed to recognize him. Lieutenant Vaughn's eyes glittered through their thick lenses; his face was red and he was grinning from ear to ear. He pounded past the startled warrant, pulled open the door to the inner office where Colonel Thayer sat with the visiting Territorial Commissioner, and plunged inside.

"Sir," the warrant heard him quaver breathlessly, "I have the proof—the undeniable proof! They *were* intelligent beings. They did *not* die of disease. They were exterminated in war! They were . . . but see for yourself!" There was a thud as he dropped something on the polished table top between the commissioner and Colonel Thayer. "*That* was dug up just now— among their own artifacts!"

Silas Thayer was on his feet, sucking in his breath for the blast that would hurl his blundering Science Officer back out of the office. What halted him was an odd, choked exclamation from Commissioner Sanford. The colonel's gaze flicked over to the visitor, then followed Sanford's stare to the object on the table.

For an instant, Colonel Thayer froze.

Vaughn was bubbling on. "And, sir, I . . ."

"Shut up!" Thayer snapped. He continued immediately, "You say this was found in the diggings in the ruins?"

"Yes, sir—just now! It's . . ."

Lieutenant Vaughn checked himself under the colonel's stare, some dawning comprehension of the enormous irregularities he'd committed showing in his flushed face. He licked his lips uncertainly.

"You will excuse me for a moment, sir," Thayer said to Commissioner Sanford. He picked the Geest gun up gingerly by its unmistakably curved shaft, took it over to the office safe, laid it inside and relocked the safe. He then left the office.

In an adjoining room, Thayer rapped out Major Wayne Jackson's code number on a communicator. He heard a faint click as Jackson's wrist speaker switched on, and said quickly, "Wayne, are you in a position to speak?"

"I am at the moment," Jackson's voice replied cautiously.

Colonel Thayer said, "Norm Vaughn just crashed in here with something he claims was found in the diggings. Sanford saw it, and obviously recognized it. We might be able to keep him quiet. But now some questions. Was that item actually dug up just now?"

"Apparently it was," Jackson said. "I didn't see it happen—I was talking to Black at the moment. But there are over a dozen witnesses who claim they did see it happen, including five or six of the new agency men."

"And they knew what it was?"

"Enough of them did."

Thayer cursed softly. "No chance that one of them pitched the thing into the diggings for an Earthside sensation?"

"I'm afraid not," Jackson said. "It was lying in the sifter after most of the sand and dust had been blown away."

"Why didn't you call me at once?"

"I've been holding down something like a mutiny here, Silas. Vaughn got away before I could stop him, but I grounded the other aircars till you could decide what to do. Our visitors don't like that. Neither do they like the fact that I've put a guard over the section where the find was made, and haven't let them talk to Norm's work crew.

"Ronald Black and his staff have been fairly reasonable, but there's been considerable mention of military highhandedness made by the others. This is the first moment I've been free."

"You did the right thing," Thayer said, "but I doubt it will help much now. Can you get hold of Ronald Black?"

"Yes, he's over there. . . ."

"Colonel Thayer?" another voice inquired pleasantly a few seconds later.

"Mr. Black," the colonel said carefully, "what occurred in the diggings a short while ago may turn out to be matter of great importance."

"That's quite obvious, sir."

"And that being the case," the colonel went on, "do you believe it would be possible to obtain a gentleman's agreement from all witnesses to make no mention of this apparent discovery until the information is released through the proper channels? I'm asking for your opinion."

"Colonel Thayer," Ronald Black's voice said, still pleasantly, "my opinion is that the only way you could keep the matter quiet is to arrest every civilian present, including myself, and hold us incommunicado. You have your duty, and we have ours. Ours does not include withholding information from the public which may signal the greatest shift in the conduct of the Geest War in the past two decades."

"I understand," Thayer said. He was silent for some seconds, and perhaps he, too, was gazing during that time at a Fort Roye of the future—a Class A military base under his command, with Earth's great war vessels lined up along the length of the peninsula.

"Mr. Black," he said, "please be so good as to give your colleagues this word from me. I shall make the most thorough possible investigation of what has occurred and forward a prompt report, along with any material evidence obtained, to my superiors on Earth. None of you will receive any other statement from me or from anyone under my command. An attempt to obtain such a statement will, in fact, result in the arrest of the person or persons involved. Is that clear?"

"Quite clear, Colonel Thayer," Ronald Black said softly. "And entirely satisfactory."

"We have known for the past eight weeks," the man named Cranehart said, "that this was not what it appears to be . . . that is, a section of a Geest weapon."

He shoved the object in question across the desk towards Commissioner Sanford and Ronald Black. Neither of the two attempted to pick it up; they glanced at it, then returned their eyes attentively to Cranehart's face.

"It is, of course, an excellent copy," Cranehart went on, "produced with a professional forger's equipment.

As I imagine you're aware, that should have made it impossible to distinguish from the original weapon. However ... there's no real harm in telling you this now ... Geest technology has taken somewhat different turns than our own. In their weapons they employ traces of certain elements which we are only beginning to learn to maintain in stable form. That is a matter your government has kept from public knowledge because we don't wish the Geests to learn from human prisoners how much information we are gaining from them.

"The instrument which made this copy naturally did not have such elements at its disposal. So it employed their lower homologues and in that manner successfully produced an almost identical model. In fact, the only significant difference is that such a gun, if it had been a complete model, could not possibly have been fired." He smiled briefly. "But that, I think you will agree, *is* a significant difference! We knew as soon as the so-called Geest gun was examined that it could only have been made by human beings."

"Then," Commissioner Sanford said soberly, "its apparent discovery on Roye during our visit was a deliberate hoax—"

Cranehart nodded. "Of course."

Ronald Black said, "I fail to see why you've kept this quiet. You needn't have given away any secrets. Meanwhile the wave of public criticism at the government's seeming hesitancy to take action on the discovery—that is, to rush protection to the threatened Territorial Segments—has reached almost alarming proportions. You could have stopped it before it began two months ago with a single announcement."

"Well, yes," Cranehart said. "There were other considerations. Incidentally, Mr. Black, we are not unappreciative of the fact that the news media under your own control exercised a generous restraint in the matter."

"For which," Black said dryly, "I am now very thankful."

"As for the others," Cranehart went on, "the government has survived periods of criticism before. That is not important. The important thing is that the Geest War has been with us for more than a human life span now . . . and it becomes difficult for many to bear in mind that until its conclusion no acts that might reduce our ability to prosecute it can be tolerated."

Ronald Black said slowly, "So you've been delaying the announcement until you could find out who was responsible for the hoax."

"We were interested," Cranehart said, "only in the important men—the dangerous men. We don't care much who else is guilty of what. This, you see, is a matter of expediency, not of justice." He looked for a moment at the politely questioning, somewhat puzzled faces across the desk, went on, "When you leave this room, each of you will be conducted to an office where you will be given certain papers to sign. That is the first step."

There was silence for some seconds. Ronald Black took a cigarette from a platinum case, tapped it gently on the desk, put it to his mouth and lit it. Cranehart went on, "It would have been impossible to unravel this particular conspiracy if the forgery had been immediately exposed. At that time, no one had taken any obvious action. Then, within a few days—with the discovery apparently confirmed by our silence—normal maneuverings in industry and finance were observed to be under way. If a major shift in war policy was pending, if one or more key bases were to be established in Territorial Segments previously considered beyond the range of Geest reconnaissance and therefore secure from attack, this would be to somebody's benefit on Earth."

"Isn't it always?" Black murmured.

"Of course. It's a normal procedure, ordinarily of no concern to government. It can be predicted with considerable accuracy to what group or groups the ultimate advantage in such a situation will go. But in these past weeks, it became apparent that somebody else was winning out . . . somebody who could have won out only on the basis of careful and extensive preparation for this very situation.

"That was abnormal, and it was the appearance of an abnormal pattern for which we had been waiting. We find there are seven men involved. These men will be deprived of the advantage they have gained."

Ronald Black shook his head, said, "You're making a mistake, Cranehart. I'm signing no papers."

"Nor I," Sanford said thickly.

Cranehart rubbed the side of his nose with a fingertip, said meditatively, "You won't be forced to. Not directly." He nodded at the window. "On the landing flange out there is an aircar. It is possible that this aircar will be found wrecked in the mountains some four hundred miles north of here early tomorrow morning. Naturally, we have a satisfactory story prepared to cover such an eventuality."

Sanford whitened slowly. He said, "So you'd resort to murder!"

Cranehart was silent for a few seconds. "Mr. Sanford," he said then, "you, as a member of the Territorial Office, know very well that the Geest War has consumed over four hundred million human lives to date. That is the circumstance which obliges your government to insist on your co-operation. I advise you to give it."

"But you have no proof! You have nothing but surmises—"

"Consider this," Cranehart said. "A conspiracy of the type I have described constitutes a capital offense under present conditions. Are you certain that you would prefer us to continue to look for proof?"

Ronald Black said in a harsh voice, "And what would the outcome be if we did choose to co-operate?"

"Well, we can't afford to leave men of your type in a position of influence, Mr. Black," Cranehart said amiably. "And you understand, I'm sure, that it would be entirely too difficult to keep you under proper surveillance on Earth—"

Celia Adams said from outside the cabin door, "I think it is them, Phil. Both cars have started to circle."

Phil Boles came to the door behind her and looked up. It was early evening—Roye's sun just down, and a few stars out. The sky above the sea was still light. After a moment, he made out the two aircars moving in a wide, slow arc far overhead. He glanced at his watch.

"Twenty minutes late," he remarked. "But it couldn't be anyone else. And if they hadn't all come along, they wouldn't have needed two cars." He hesitated. "We can't tell how they're going to take this, Celia, but they may have decided already that they could make out better without us." He nodded towards the edge of the cliff. "Short way over there, and a long drop to the water! So don't let them surprise you."

She said coldly, "I won't. And I've used guns before this."

"Wouldn't doubt it." Phil reached back behind the door, picked up a flarelight standing beside a heavy machine rifle, and came outside. He pointed the light at the cars and touched the flash button briefly three times. After a moment, there were two answering flashes from the leading car.

"So Wayne Jackson's in the front car," Phil said. "Now let's see what they do." He returned the light to its place behind the door and came out again, standing about twelve feet to one side of Celia. The aircars vanished inland, came back at treetop level a few minutes later. One settled down quietly between the cabin and the edge of the cliff, the other following but dropping to the ground a hundred yards away, where it stopped. Phil glanced over at Celia, said softly, "Watch that one!" She nodded almost imperceptibly, right hand buried in her jacket pocket.

The near door of the car before them opened. Major Wayne Jackson, hatless and in hunting clothes, climbed out, staring at them. He said, "Anyone else here?"

"Just Celia and myself," Phil said.

Jackson turned, spoke into the car and two men, similarly dressed, came out behind him. Phil recognized Ronald Black and Sanford. The three started over to the cabin, stopped a dozen feet away.

Jackson said sardonically, "Our five other previous Earthside partners are in the second car. In spite of your insistence to meet the whole group, they don't want you and Celia to see their faces. They don't wish to be identifiable." He touched his coat lapel. "They'll hear what we're saying over this communicator and they could talk to you, but won't unless they feel it's necessary. You'll have to take my word for it that we're all present."

"That's good enough," Phil said.

"All right," Jackson went on, "now what did you mean by forcing us to take this chance? Let me make it plain. Colonel Thayer hasn't been accused of collaborating in the Roye gun hoax, but he got a black eye out of the affair just the same. And don't forget that a planet with colonial status is technically under martial law, which includes the civilians. If Silas Thayer can get his hands on the guilty persons, the situation will become a lot more unpleasant than it already is."

Phil addressed Ronald Black, "Then how about you two? When you showed up here again on a transfer list, Thayer must have guessed why."

Black shook his head. "Both of us exercised the privilege of changing our names just prior to the outtransfer. He doesn't know we're on Roye. We don't intend to let him find out."

Phil asked, "Did you make any arrangements to get out of Roye again?"

"Before leaving Earth?" Black showed his teeth in a humorless smile. "Boles, you have no idea of how abruptly and completely the government men cut us off from our every resource! We were given no opportunity to draw up plans to escape from exile, believe me."

Phil glanced over at Celia. "In that case," he said, a little thickly, "we'd better see if we can't draw some up together immediately."

Jackson asked, staring, "What are you talking about, Phil? Don't think for a moment Silas Thayer isn't doing what he can to find out who put that trick over on him. I'm not at all sure he doesn't suspect me. And if he can tie it to us, it's our neck. If you have some crazy idea of getting off the planet now, let me tell you that for the next few years we can't risk making a single move! If we stay quiet, we're safe. We—"

"I don't think we'd be safe," Phil said.

On his right, Celia Adams added sharply, "The gentleman in the other car who's just started to lower that window had better raise it again! If he's got good eyesight, he'll see I have a gun pointed at him. Yes, that's much better! Go on, Phil."

"Have you both gone out of your minds?" Jackson demanded.

"No," Celia said. She laughed with a sudden shakiness in her tone, added, "Though I don't know why we haven't! We've thought of the possibility that the rest of you might feel it would be better if Phil and I weren't around any more, Wayne."

"That's nonsense!" Jackson said.

"Maybe. Anyway, don't try it. You wouldn't be doing yourselves a favor even if it worked. Better listen now."

"Listen to what?" Jackson demanded exasperatedly.

"I'm telling you it will be all right, if we just don't make any mistakes. The only real pieces of evidence were your duplicator and the original gun. Since we're rid of those—"

"We're not rid of the gun, Wayne," Phil said. "I still have it. I haven't dared get rid of it."

"You . . . what do you mean?"

"I was with Beulah in the Fort Royce hospital when she died," Phil said. He added to Ronald Black, "That was two days after the ship brought the seven of you in."

Black nodded, his eyes alert. "Major Jackson informed me."

"She was very weak, of course, but quite lucid," Phil went on. "She talked a good deal—reminiscing, and in a rather happy vein. She finally mentioned the Geest gun, and how Uncle William used to keep us boys . . . Wayne and me . . . spellbound with stories about the Gunderland Battle, and how he'd picked the gun up there."

Jackson began, "And what does—"

"He didn't get the gun there," Phil said. "Beulah said Uncle William came in from Earth with the first shipment of settlers and was never off Royce again in his life."

"He . . . then—"

Phil said, "Don't you get it? He found the gun right here on Roye. Beulah thought it was awfully funny. William was an old fool, she said, but the best liar she'd ever known. He came in with the thing one day after he'd been traipsing around the back country, and said it looked 'sort of' like pictures of Geest guns he'd seen, and that he was going to put the inscription on it and have some fun now and then." Phil took a deep breath. "Uncle William found it lying in a pile of ashes where someone had made camp a few days before. He figured it would have been a planetary speedster some rich sportsmen from Earth had brought in for a taste of outworld hunting on Roye, and that one of them had dumped the broken oddball gun into the fire to get rid of it."

"That was thirty-six years ago. Beulah remembered it happened a year before I was born."

There was silence for some seconds. Then Ronald Black said evenly, "And what do you conclude, Boles?"

Phil looked at him. "I'd conclude that Norm Vaughn was right about there having been some fairly intelligent creatures here once. The Geests ran into them and exterminated them as they usually do. That might have been a couple of centuries back. Then, thirty-six years ago, one of their scouts slipped in here without being spotted, found human beings on the planet, looked around a little and left again."

He took the Geest gun from his pocket, hefted it in his hand. "We have the evidence here," he said. "We had it all the time and didn't know it."

Ronald Black said dryly, "We may have the evidence. But we have no slightest proof at all now that that's what it is."

"I know it," Phil said. "Now Beulah's gone . . . well, we couldn't even prove that William Boles never left the planet, for that matter. There weren't any records to speak of being kept in the early days." He was silent a moment. "Supposing," he said, "we went ahead anyway. We hand the gun in, with the story I just told you—"

Jackson made a harsh, laughing sound. "That would hang us fast, Phil!"

"And nothing else?"

"Nothing else," Black said with finality. "Why should anyone believe the story now? There are a hundred more likely ways in which a Geest gun could have got to Roye. The gun is tangible evidence of the hoax, but that's all."

Phil asked, "Does anybody, including the cautious gentlemen in the car over there . . . disagree with that?"

There was silence again. Phil shrugged, turned towards the cliff edge, drew his arm back and hurled the Geest gun far up and out above the sea. Still without speaking, the others turned their heads to watch it fall towards the water, then looked back at him.

"I didn't think very much of that possibility myself," Phil said unsteadily "But one of you might have. All right—we know the Geests know we're here. But we won't be able to convince anyone else of it. And, these last few years, the war seems to have been slowing down again. In the past, that's always meant the Geests were preparing a big new surprise operation."

"So the other thing now—the business of getting off Roye. It can't be done unless some of you have made prior arrangements for it Earthside. If it had been possible in any other way, I'd have been out of this place ten years ago."

Ronald Black said carefully, "Very unfortunately, Boles, no such arrangements have been made."

"Then there it is," Phil said. "I suppose you see now why I thought this group should get together. The ten masterminds! Well, we've hoaxed ourselves into a massive jam. Now let's find out if there's any possible way—*any possibility at all!*—of getting out of it again."

A voice spoke tinnily from Jackson's lapel communicator. "Major Jackson?"

"Yes?" Jackson said.

"Please persuade Miss Adams that it is no longer necessary to point her gun at this car. In view of the stated emergency, we feel we had better come out now—and join the conference."

FROM THE RECORDS OF THE TERRITORIAL OFFICE, 2345 A.D.

... It is generally acknowledged that the Campaign of the 132nd Segment marked the turning point of the Geest War. Following the retransfer of Colonel Silas Thayer to Earth, the inspired leadership of Major Wayne Jackson and his indefatigable and exceptionally able assistants, notably CLU President Boles, transformed the technically unfortified and thinly settled key world of Roye within twelve years into a virtual death trap for any invading force. Almost half of the Geest fleet which eventually arrived there was destroyed in the first week subsequent to the landing, and few of the remaining ships were sufficiently undamaged to be able to lift again. The enemy relief fleet, comprising an estimated forty per cent of the surviving Geest space power, was intercepted in the 134th Segment by the combined Earth forces under Admiral McKenna's command and virtually annihilated.

In the following two years ...

Greenface

~⚬~

"What I don't like," the fat sport—his name was Freddie Something—said firmly, "is snakes! That was a whopping mean-looking snake that went across the path there, and I ain't going another step nearer the icehouse!"

Hogan Masters, boss and owner of Masters Fishing Camp on Thursday Lake, made no effort to conceal his indignation.

"What you don't like," he said, his voice a trifle thick, "is work! That little garter snake wasn't more than six inches long. What you want is for me to carry all the fish up there alone, while you go off to the cabin and take it easy—"

Freddie already was on his way to the cabin. "I'm on vacation!" he bellowed back happily. "Gotta save my strength! Gotta 'cuperate!"

Hogan glared after him, opened his mouth and shut it again. Then he picked up the day's catch of bass and walleyes and swayed on toward the icehouse. Usually a sober young man, he'd been guiding a party of fishermen from one of his light-housekeeping cabins over the lake's trolling grounds since early morning. It was hot work in June weather and now, at three in the afternoon, Hogan was tanked to the gills with iced beer.

He dropped the fish between chunks of ice under the sawdust, covered them up and started back to what he called the lodge—an old two-story log structure reserved for himself and a few campers too lazy even to do their own cooking.

When he came to the spot where the garter snake had given Freddie his excuse to quit, he saw it wriggling about spasmodically at the edge of a clump of weeds, as if something hidden in there had caught hold of it.

Hogan watched the tiny reptile's struggles for a moment, then squatted down carefully and spread the weeds apart. There was a sharp buzzing like the ghost of a rattler's challenge, and something slapped moistly across the back of his hand, leaving a stinging sensation as if he had reached into a cluster of nettles. At the same moment, the snake disappeared with a jerk under the plants.

The buzzing continued. It was hardly a real sound at all—more like a thin, quivering vibration inside his head, and decidedly unpleasant. Hogan shut his eyes tight and shook his head to drive it away. He opened his eyes again, and found himself looking at Greenface.

Nothing even faintly resembling Greenface had ever appeared before in any of Hogan's weed patches, but at the moment he wasn't greatly surprised. It hadn't, he decided at once, any real face. It was a shiny, dark-green lump, the size and shape of a goose egg standing on end among the weeds; it was pulsing regularly like a human heart; and across it ran a network of thin, dark lines that seemed to form two tightly shut eyes and a closed, faintly smiling mouth.

Like a fat little smiling idol in green jade—Greenface it became for Hogan then and there.... With alcoholic detachment, he made a mental note of the cluster of fuzzy strands like hair roots about and below the thing. Then—somewhere underneath and blurred as though seen through milky glass—he discovered the snake, coiled up in a spiral and still turning with labored writhing motions as if trying to swim in a mass of gelatin.

Hogan put out his hand to investigate this phenomenon, and one of the rootlets lifted as if to ward off his touch. He hesitated, and it flicked down, withdrawing immediately and leaving another red line of nettle-burn across the back of his hand.

In a moment, Hogan was on his feet, several yards away. A belated sense of horrified outrage overcame him—he scooped up a handful of stones and hurled them wildly at the impossible little monstrosity. One thumped down near it; and with that, the buzzing sensation in his brain stopped.

Greenface began to slide slowly away through the weeds, all its rootlets wriggling about it, with an air of moving sideways and watching Hogan over a non-existent shoulder. He found a chunk of wood in his hand and leaped in pursuit—and it promptly vanished.

He spent another minute or two poking around in the vegetation with his club raised, ready to finish it off wherever he found it lurking. Instead, he discovered the snake among the weeds and picked it up.

It was still moving, though quite dead, the scales peeling away from the wrinkled flabby body. Hogan stared at it, wondering. He held it by the head; and at the pressure of his finger and thumb, the skull within gave softly, like leather. It became suddenly horrible to feel and then the complete inexplicability of the grotesque affair broke in on him.

He flung the dead snake away with a wide sweep of his arm, went back of the icehouse and was briefly but thoroughly sick.

Julia Allison was leaning on her elbows over the kitchen table studying a mail-order catalogue when Hogan walked unsteadily into the lodge. Julia had dark-brown hair, calm gray eyes, and a wicked figure. She and Hogan had been engaged for half a year. Hogan didn't want to get married until he was sure he could make a success of Masters Fishing Camp, which was still in its first season.

Julia glanced up smiling. The smile became a stare. She closed the catalogue.

"Hogan," she stated, in the exact tone of her pa, Whitey Allison, refusing a last one to a customer in Whitey's bar and liquor store in town, "you're plain drunk! Don't shake your head—it'll slop out your ears."

"Julia—" Hogan began excitedly.

She stepped up to him and sniffed, wrinkling her nose. *"Pfaah!* Beer! Yes, darling?"

"Julia, I just saw something—a sort of crazy little green spook—"

Julia blinked twice.

"Look, infant," she said soothingly, "that's how people get talked about! Sit down and relax while I make up coffee, black. There's a couple came in this morning, and I put them in the end cabin. They want the stove tanked with kerosene, ice in the icebox, and coal for a barbecue—I fixed them up with linen."

"Julia," Hogan inquired hoarsely, "are you going to listen to me or not?"

Her smile vanished. "Now you're yelling!"

"I'm *not* yelling. And I don't need coffee. I'm trying to tell you—"

"Then do it without shouting!" Julia replaced the coffee can with a whack that showed her true state of mind, and gave Hogan an abused look which left him speechless.

"If you want to stand there and sulk," she continued immediately, "I might as well run along—I got to help Pa in the store tonight." That meant he wasn't to call her up.

She was gone before Hogan, struggling with a sudden desire to shake his Julia up and down like a cocktail for some time, could come to a decision. So he went instead to see to the couple in the end cabin. Afterwards he lay down bitterly and slept it off.

When he woke up, Greenface seemed no more than a vague and very uncertain memory, an unaccountable scrap of afternoon nightmare. Due to the heat, no doubt. *Not* to the beer—on that point Hogan and Julia remained in disagreement, however completely they became reconciled otherwise. Since neither wanted to bring the subject up again, it didn't really matter.

The next time Greenface was seen, it wasn't Hogan who saw it.

In mid-season, on the twenty-fifth of June, the success of Masters Fishing Camp looked pretty well assured. Whitey Allison was hinting he'd be willing to advance money to have the old lodge rebuilt, as a wedding present. When Hogan came into camp for lunch, everything seemed peaceful and quiet; but before he got to the lodge steps, a series of piercing feminine shrieks from the direction of the north end cabin swung him around, running.

Charging up to the cabin with a number of startled camp guests strung out behind him, Hogan heard a babble of excited talk shushed suddenly and emphatically within. The man who was vacationing there with his wife appeared at the door.

"Old lady thinks she's seen a ghost, or something!" he apologized with an embarrassed laugh. "Nothing you can do. I . . . I'll quiet her down, I guess. . . ."

Hogan waved the others back, then ducked around behind the cabin, and listened shamelessly. Suddenly the babbling began again. He could hear every word.

"I did so see it! It was sort of blue and green and wet—and it had a green face, and it s-s-smiled at me! It f-floated up a tree and disappeared! Oh-G-G-Georgie!"

Georgie continued to make soothing sounds. But before nightfall, he came into the lodge to pay his bill.

"Sorry, old man," he said. He still seemed more embarrassed than upset. "I can't imagine what the little woman saw, but she's got her mind made up, and we gotta go home. You know how it is. I sure hate to leave, myself!"

Hogan saw them off with a sickly smile. Uppermost among his feelings was a sort of numbed vindication. A ghost that was blue and green and wet and floated up trees and disappeared was a far from exact description of the little monstrosity he'd persuaded himself he *hadn't* seen—but still too near it to be a coincidence. Julia, driving out from town to see him next day, didn't think it was a coincidence, either.

"You couldn't possibly have told that hysterical old goose about the funny little green thing you thought you saw? She got confidential in the liquor store last night, and her hubby couldn't hush her. Everybody was listening. That sort of stuff won't do the camp any good, Hogan!"

Hogan looked helpless. If he told her about the camp haunt again, she wouldn't believe him, anyhow. And if she did believe him, it might scare her silly.

"Well?" she urged suspiciously.

Hogan sighed. "Never spoke more than a dozen words with the woman. . . ."

Julia seemed doubtful, but puzzled. There was a peculiar oily hothouse smell in the air when Hogan walked up to the road with her and watched her start back to town in her ancient car; but with a nearly sleepless night behind him, he wasn't as alert as he might have been. He was recrossing the long, narrow meadow between the road and the camp before the extraordinary quality of that odor struck him. And then, for the second time, he found himself looking at Greenface—at a bigger Greenface, and not a better one.

About sixty feet away, up in the birches at the end of the meadow, it was almost completely concealed: a vague oval of darker vegetable green in the foliage. Its markings were obscured by the leaf shadows among which it lay motionless except for that sluggish pulsing.

Hogan stared at it for long seconds while his scalp crawled and his heart hammered a thudding alarm into every fiber of his body. What scared him was its size—that oval was as big as a football! It had been growing at a crazy rate since he saw it last.

Swallowing hard, he mopped sweat off his forehead and walked on stiffly towards the lodge, careful to give no sign of being in a hurry. He didn't want to scare the thing away. There was an automatic shotgun slung above the kitchen door for emergencies; and a dose of No. 2 shot would turn this particular emergency into a museum specimen. . . .

Around the corner of the lodge he went up the entrance steps four at a time. A few seconds later, with the gun in his hand and reaching for a box of shells, he shook his head to drive a queer soundless buzzing out of his ears. Instantly, he remembered where he'd experienced that sensation before, and wheeled towards the screened kitchen window.

The big birch trembled slightly as if horrified to see a huge spider with jade-green body and blurred cluster of threadlike legs flow down along its trunk. Twelve feet from the ground, it let go of the tree and dropped, the long bunched threads stretched straight down before it. Hogan grunted and blinked.

It had happened before his eyes: at the instant the bunched tips hit the ground, Greenface was jarred into what could only be called a higher stage of visibility. There was no change in the head, but the legs abruptly became flat, faintly greenish ribbons, flexible and semi-transparent. Each about six inches wide and perhaps six feet long, they seemed attached in a thick fringe all around the lower part of the head, like a Hawaiian dancer's grass skirt. They showed a bluish gloss wherever the sun struck them, but Greenface didn't wait for a closer inspection.

Off it went, swaying and gliding swiftly on the ends of those foot ribbons into the woods beyond the meadow. And for all the world, it *did* look almost like a conventional ghost, the ribbons glistening in a luxurious winding sheet around the area where a body should have been, but wasn't! No wonder that poor woman—

Hogan found himself giggling helplessly. He laid the gun on the kitchen table, then tried to control the shaking of his hands long enough to get a cigarette going.

Long before the middle of July, every last tourist had left Masters Fishing Camp. Vaguely, Hogan sensed it was unfortunate that two of his attempts to dispose of Greenface had been observed while his quarry remained unseen. Of course, it wasn't his fault if the creature chose to exercise an uncanny ability to become almost completely invisible at will—nothing more than a tall glassy blur which flickered off through the woods and was gone. And it wasn't until he drove into town one evening that he realized just how unfortunate that little trick was, nevertheless, for him.

Whitey Allison's greeting was brief and chilly. Then Julia delayed putting in an appearance for almost half an hour. Hogan waited patiently enough.

"You might pour me a Scotch," he suggested at last. Whitey passed him a significant look.

"Better lay off the stuff," he advised heavily. Hogan flushed.

"What do you mean by that?"

"There's plenty of funny stories going around about you right now!" Whitey told him, blinking belligerently. Then he looked past Hogan, and Hogan knew Julia had come into the store behind him; but he was too angry to drop the matter there.

"What do you expect me to do about them?" he demanded.

"That's no way to talk to Pa!"

Julia's voice was sharper than Hogan had ever heard it—he swallowed hard and tramped out of the store without looking at her. Down the street he had a couple of drinks; and coming past the store again on the way to his car, he saw Julia behind the bar counter, laughing and chatting with a group of summer residents. She seemed to be having a grand time; her gray eyes sparkled and there was a fine high color in her cheeks.

Hogan snarled out the worst word he knew and went on home. It was true he'd grown accustomed to an impressive dose of whiskey at night, to put him to sleep. At night, Greenface wasn't abroad, and there was no sense in lying awake to wonder and worry about it. On warm clear days around noon was the time to be alert; twice Hogan caught it basking in the tree-tops in full sunlight and each time took a long shot at it, which had no effect beyond scaring it into complete visibility. It dropped out of the tree like a rotten fruit and scudded off into the bushes, its foot ribbons weaving and flapping all about it.

Well, it all added up. Was it surprising if he seemed constantly on the watch for something nobody else could see? When the camp cabins emptied one by one and stayed empty, Hogan told himself that he preferred it that way. Now he could devote all his time to tracking down that smiling haunt and finishing it off. Afterwards would have to be early enough to repair the damage it had done his good name and bank balance.

He tried to keep Julia out of these calculations. Julia hadn't been out to the camp for several weeks; and under the circumstances he didn't see how he could do anything at present to patch up their misunderstanding.

After being shot at the second time, Greenface stayed out of sight for so many days that Hogan almost gave up hunting for it. He was morosely cleaning out the lodge cellar one afternoon; and as he shook out a box he was going to convert to kindling, a small odd-looking object tumbled out to the floor. Hogan stared at the object a moment, then frowned and picked it up.

It was the mummified tiny body of a hummingbird, some tropical species with a long curved beak and long ornamental tail feathers. Except for beak and feathers, it would have been unrecognizable; bones, flesh, and skin were shriveled together into a small lump of doubtful consistency, like dried gum. Hogan, remembering the dead snake from which he had driven

Greenface near the icehouse, turned it around in fingers that trembled a little, studying it carefully.

The origin of the camp spook seemed suddenly explained. Some two months ago, he'd carried the box in which the hummingbird's body had been lying into the lodge cellar. In it at the time had been a big cluster of green bananas he'd got from the wholesale grocer in town. . . .

Greenface, of course, was carnivorous, in some weird, out-of-the-ordinary fashion. Small game had become rare around the camp in recent weeks; even birds now seemed to avoid the area. When that banana cluster was shipped in from Brazil or some island in the Caribbean, Greenface—a seedling Greenface, very much smaller even than when Hogan first saw it—had come along concealed in it, clinging to its hummingbird prey.

And then something—perhaps simply the touch of the colder North—had acted to cancel the natural limits on its growth; for each time he'd seen it, it had been obvious that it still was growing rapidly. And though it apparently lacked solid parts that might resist decomposition after death, creatures of its present size, which conformed to no recognizable pattern of either the vegetable or the animal kingdom, couldn't very well exist anywhere without drawing human attention to themselves. While if they grew normally to be only a foot or two high, they seemed intelligent and alert enough to escape observation in some luxuriant tropical forest—even discounting that inexplicable knack of turning transparent from one second to the next.

His problem, meanwhile, was a purely practical one. The next time he grew aware of the elusive hothouse smell near the camp, he had a plan ready laid. His nearest neighbor, Pete Jeffries, who provided Hogan with most of his provisions from a farm two miles down the road to town, owned a hound by the name of Old Battler—a large, surly brute with a strong strain of Airedale in its make-up, and reputedly the best trailing nose in the county.

Hogan's excuse for borrowing Old Battler was a fat buck who'd made his headquarters in the marshy ground across the bay. Pete had no objection to out-of-season hunting; he and Old Battler were the slickest pair of poachers for a hundred miles around. He whistled the hound in and handed him over to Hogan with a parting admonition to keep an eye peeled for snooping game wardens.

The oily fragrance under the birches was so distinct that Hogan almost could have followed it himself. Unfortunately, it didn't mean a thing to the dog. Panting and rumbling as Hogan, cradling the shotgun, brought him up on a leash, Old Battler was ready for any type of quarry from rabbits to a pig-stealing bear; but he simply wouldn't or couldn't accept that he was to track that bloodless vegetable odor to its source. He walked off a few yards in the direction the thing had gone, nosing the grass; then, ignoring Hogan's commands, he returned to the birch, sniffed carefully around its base and paused to demonstrate in unmistakable fashion what he thought of the scent. Finally he sat on his haunches and regarded Hogan with a baleful, puzzled eye.

There was nothing to do but take him back and tell Pete Jeffries the poaching excursion was off because a warden had put in an appearance in the area. When Hogan got back to the lodge, he heard the telephone ringing above the cellar stairs and hurried towards it with an eagerness that surprised himself.

"Hello?" he said into the mouthpiece. "Hello? Julia? That you?"

There was no answer from the other end. Hogan,

listening, heard voices, several of them, people laughing and talking. Then a door slammed faintly and someone called out: "Hi, Whitey! How's the old man?" She had phoned from the liquor store, perhaps just to see what he was doing. He thought he could even hear the faint fluttering of her breath.

"Julia," Hogan said softly, scared by the silence. "What's the matter, darling? Why don't you say something?"

Now he did hear her take a quick, deep breath. Then the receiver clicked down, and the line was dead.

The rest of the afternoon he managed to keep busy cleaning out the cabins which had been occupied. Counting back to the day the last of them had been vacated, he decided the reason nobody had arrived since was that a hostile Whitey Allison, in his strategic position at the town bus stop, was directing all tourist traffic to other camps. Not—Hogan assured himself again—that he wanted anyone around until he had solved his problem; it would only make matters more difficult.

But why had Julia called up? What did it mean?

That night, the moon was full. Near ten o'clock, with no more work to do, Hogan settled down wearily on the lodge steps. Presently he lit a cigarette. His intention was to think matters out to some conclusion in the quiet night air, but all he seemed able to do was to keep telling himself uselessly that there must be some way of trapping that elusive green horror.

He pulled the sides of his face down slowly with his fingertips. "I've got to do something!"—the futile whisper seemed to have been running through his head all day: "Got to *do* something! Got to . . ." He'd be having a mental breakdown if he didn't watch out.

The rumbling barks of Jeffries' Old Battler began

to churn up the night to the east—and suddenly Hogan caught the characteristic tinny stutter of Julia's little car as it turned down into the road from Jeffries' farm and came on in the direction of the camp.

The thrill that swung him to his feet was tempered at once by fresh doubts. Even if Julia was coming to tell him she'd forgiven him, he'd be expected to explain what was making him act like this. And there was no way of explaining it. She'd think he was crazy or lying. No, he couldn't do it, Hogan decided despairingly. He'd have to send her away again. . . .

He took the big flashlight from its hook beside the door and started off forlornly to meet her when she would bring the car bumping along the path from the road. Then he realized that the car, still half a mile or so from the lodge, had stopped.

He waited, puzzled. From a distance he heard the creaky shift of its gears, a brief puttering of the motor—another shift and putter. Then silence. Old Battler was also quiet, probably listening suspiciously, though he, too, knew the sound of Julia's car. There was no one else to hear it. Jeffries had gone to the city with his wife that afternoon, and they wouldn't be back till late next morning.

Hogan frowned, flashing the light on and off against the moonlit side of the lodge. In the quiet, three or four whippoorwills were crying to each other with insane rapidity up and down the lake front. There was a subdued shrilling of crickets everywhere, and occasionally the threefold soft call of an owl dropped across the bay. He started reluctantly up the path towards the road.

The headlights were out, or he would have been able to see them from here. But the moon rode high, and the road was a narrow silver ribbon running straight down through the pines towards Jeffries' farmhouse.

Quite suddenly he discovered the car, pulled up beside the road and turned back towards town. It was Julia's car all right; and it was empty. Hogan walked slowly towards it, peering right and left, then jerked around with a start to a sudden crashing noise among the pines a hundred yards or so down off the road— a scrambling animal rush which seemed to be moving toward the lake. An instant later, Old Battler's angry roar told him the hound was running loose and had prowled into something it disapproved of down there.

He was still listening, trying to analyze the commotion, when a girl in a dark sweater and skirt stepped out quietly from the shadow of the roadside pines beyond him. Hogan didn't see her until she crossed the ditch to the road in a beautiful reaching leap. Then she was running like a rabbit for the car.

He shouted: "Julia!"

For just an instant, Julia looked back at him, her face a pale scared blur in the moonlight. Then the car door slammed shut behind her, and with a shiver and groan the old machine lurched into action. Hogan made no further attempt to stop her. Confused and unhappy, he watched the headlights sweep down the road until they swung out of sight around a bend.

Now what the devil had she been poking about here for?

Hogan sighed, shook his head and turned back to the camp. Old Battler's vicious snarling had stopped; the woods were quiet once more. Presently a draft of cool air came flowing up from the lake across the road, and Hogan's nostrils wrinkled. Some taint in the breeze—

He checked abruptly. Greenface! Greenface was down there among the pines somewhere. The hound had stirred it up, discovered it was alive and worth worrying, but lost it again, and was now casting about silently to find its hiding place.

Hogan crossed the ditch in a leap that bettered Julia's, blundered into the wood and ducked just in time to avoid being speared in the eye by a jagged branch of aspen. More cautiously, he worked his way in among the trees, went sliding down a moldy incline, swore in exasperation as he tripped over a rotten trunk and was reminded thereby of the flashlight in his hand. He walked slowly across a moonlit clearing, listening, then found himself confronted by a dense cluster of evergreens and switched on the light.

It stabbed into a dark-green oval, more than twice the size of a human head, fifteen feet away.

He stared in fascination at the thing, expecting it to vanish. But Greenface made no move beyond a slow writhing among the velvety foot ribbons that supported it. It had shot up again since he'd seen it last, stood taller than he now and was stooping slightly towards him. The lines on its pulsing head formed two tightly shut eyes and a wide, thin-lipped, insanely smiling mouth.

Gradually it was borne in on Hogan that the thing was asleep. Or had been asleep . . . for now he became aware of a change in the situation through something like the buzzing escape of steam, a sound just too high to be audible that throbbed through his head. Then he noticed that Greenface, swaying slowly, quietly, had come a foot or two closer, and he saw the tips of the foot ribbons grow dim and transparent as they slid over the moss toward him. A sudden horror of this stealthy approach seized him. Without thinking of what he did, he switched off the light.

Almost instantly, the buzzing sensation died away, and before Hogan had backed off to the edge of the moonlit clearing, he realized that Greenface had stopped its advance. Suddenly he understood.

Unsteadily, he threw the beam on again and directed

it full on the smiling face. For a moment, there was no result; then the faint buzzing began once more in his brain, and the foot ribbons writhed and dimmed as Greenface came sliding forward. He snapped it off; and the thing grew still, solidifying.

Hogan began to laugh in silent hysteria. He'd caught it now! Light brought Greenface alive, let it act, move, enabled it to pull off its unearthly vanishing stunt. At high noon, it was as vital as a cat or hawk. Lack of light made it still, dulled, though perhaps able to react automatically.

Greenface was trapped.

He began to play with it, savagely savoring his power over the horror, switching the light off and on. Perhaps it wouldn't even be necessary to kill the thing now. Its near-paralysis in darkness might make it possible to capture it, cage it securely alive, as a stunning justification of everything that had occurred these past weeks. He watched it come gliding toward him again, and seemed to sense a dim rising anger in the soundless buzzing. Confidently, he turned off the light. But this time Greenface didn't stop.

In an instant, Hogan realized he had permitted it to reach the edge of the little clearing. Under the full glare of the moon, it was still advancing on him, though slowly. Its outlines grew altogether blurred. Even the head started to fade.

He leaped back, with a new rush of the instinctive horror with which he had first detected it coming toward him. But he retreated only into the shadows on the other side of the clearing.

The ghostly outline of Greenface came rolling on, its nebulous leering head swaying slowly from side to side like the head of a hanged and half-rotted thing. It reached the fringe of shadows and stopped, while the foot ribbons darkened as they touched the darkness

and writhed back. Dimly, it seemed to be debating this
new situation.

Hogan swallowed hard. He had noticed a blurred
shapeless something which churned about slowly within
the jellylike shroud beneath the head; and he had a
sudden conviction that he knew the reason for Old
Battler's silence . . . . Greenface had become as dangerous as a tiger!

But he had no intention of leaving it in the
moonlight's releasing spell. He threw the beam on the
dim oval mask again, and slowly, stupidly, moving along
that rope of light, Greenface entered the shadows; and
the light flicked out, and it was trapped once more.

Trembling and breathless after his half-mile run,
Hogan stumbled into the lodge kitchen and began
stuffing his pockets with as many shells as they would
take. Then he took down the shotgun and started back
toward the spot where he had left the thing, keeping his pace down to a fast walk. If he made no blun-
ders now, his troubles would be over. But if he did
blunder . . . Hogan shivered. He hadn't quite realized
before that the time was bound to come when
Greenface would be big enough to lose its fear of him.
His notion of trying to capture it alive was out—he
might wind up inside it with Old Battler. . . .

Pushing down through the ditch and into the woods,
he flashed the light ahead of him. In a few more
minutes, he reached the place where he had left
Greenface. And it wasn't there.

Hogan glared about, wondering wildly whether he
had missed the right spot and knowing he hadn't. He
looked up and saw the tops of the jack pines swaying
against the pale blur of the sky; and as he stared at
them, a ray of moonlight flickered through the broken canopy and touched him and was gone again, and

then he understood. Greenface had crept up along such intermittent threads of light into the trees.

One of the pine tips appeared blurred and top-heavy. Hogan studied it carefully; then he depressed the safety button on the shotgun, cradled the weapon, and put the flashlight beam dead-center on that blur. In a moment, he felt the familiar mental irritation as the blur began to flow down through the branches toward him. Remembering that Greenface didn't mind a long drop to the ground, he switched off the light and watched it take shape among the shadows, and then begin a slow retreat toward the treetops and the moon.

Hogan took a deep breath and raised the gun.

The five reports came one on top of the other in a rolling roar, while the pine top jerked and splintered and flew. Greenface was plainly visible now, still clinging, twisting and lashing in spasms like a broken snake. Big branches, torn loose in those furious convulsions, crashed ponderously down toward Hogan. He backed off hurriedly, flicked in five new shells and raised the gun again.

And again.

And again . . .

Greenface and what seemed to be the whole top of the tree came down together. Dropping the gun, Hogan covered his head with his arms. He heard the sodden, splashy thump with which Greenface landed on the forest mold half a dozen yards away. Then something hard and solid slammed down across his shoulders and the back of his skull.

There was a brief sensation of diving headlong through a fire-streaked darkness. For many hours thereafter, no sort of sensation reached Hogan's mind at all.

❖   ❖   ❖

"Haven't seen you around in a long time!" bellowed Pete Jeffries across the fifty feet of water between his boat and Hogan's. He pulled a flapping whitefish out of the illegal gill net he was emptying, plunked it down on the pile before him. "What you do with yourself— sleep up in the woods?"

"Times I do," Hogan admitted.

"Used to myself, your age. Out with a gun alla time!" Pete's face drew itself into mournful folds. "Not much fun now any more . . . not since them damn game wardens got Old Battler."

Hogan shivered imperceptibly, remembering the ghastly thing he'd buried that July morning six weeks back, when he awoke, thinking his skull was caved in, and found Greenface had dragged itself away, with what should have been enough shot in it to lay out half a township. At least, it had felt sick enough to disgorge what was left of Old Battler, and to refrain from harming Hogan. And perhaps it had died later of its injuries. But he didn't really believe it was dead. . . .

"Think the storm will hit before evening?" he asked out of his thoughts, not caring particularly whether it stormed or not. But Pete was sitting there, looking at him, and it was something to say.

"Hit the lake in half an hour," Pete replied matter-of-factly. "I know two guys who are going to get awful wet."

"Yeah?"

Pete jerked his head over his shoulder. "That little bay back where the Indian outfit used to live. Two of the drunkest mugs I seen on Thursday Lake this summer—fishing from off a little duck boat. . . . They come from across the lake somewhere."

"Maybe we should warn them."

"Not me!" Jeffries said emphatically. "They made some smart cracks at me when I passed there. Like to have rammed them!" He grunted, studied Hogan with an air of puzzled reflection. "Seems there was something I was going to tell you . . . well, guess it was a lie." He sighed. "How's the walleyes hitting?"

"Pretty good." Hogan had picked up a stringerful trolling along the lake bars.

"Got it now!" Pete exclaimed. "Whitey told me last night. Julia got herself engaged with a guy in the city-place she's working at. Getting married next month."

Hogan bent over the side of his boat and began to unknot the fish stringer. He hadn't seen Julia since the night he last met Greenface. A week or so later he heard she'd left town and taken a job in the city.

"Seemed to me I ought to tell you," Pete continued with remorseless neighborliness. "Didn't you and she used to go around some?"

"Yeah, some," Hogan agreed. He held up the wall-eyes. "Want to take these home for the missis, Pete? I was just fishing for the fun of it."

"Sure will!" Pete was delighted. "Nothing beats walleyes for eating, 'less it's whitefish. But I'm going to smoke these. Say, how about me bringing you a ham of buck, smoked, for the walleyes? Fair enough?"

"Fair enough," Hogan smiled.

"Can't be immediate. I went shooting the north side of the lake three nights back, and there wasn't a deer around. Something's scared 'em all out over there."

"Okay," Hogan said, not listening at all. He got the motor going, and cut away from Pete with a wave of his hand. "Be seeing you, Pete!"

Two miles down the lake, he got his mind off Julia long enough to find a possible significance in Pete's last words.

He cut the motor to idling speed, and then shut it off entirely, trying to get his thoughts into some kind of order. Since that chunk of pine slugged him in the head and robbed him of his chance of finishing off Greenface, he'd seen no more of the thing and heard nothing to justify his suspicion that it was still alive somewhere, perhaps still growing. But from Thursday Lake northward to the border of Canada stretched two hundred miles of bush-trees and water, with only the barest scattering of farms and tiny towns. Hogan sometimes pictured Greenface prowling about back there, safe from human detection, and a ghastly new enemy for the harried small life of the bush, while it nourished its hatred for the man who had so nearly killed it.

It wasn't a pretty picture. It made him take the signs indicating Masters Fishing Camp from the roads, and made him turn away the occasional would-be guest who still found his way to the camp in spite of Whitey Allison's unrelenting vigilance in town. It also made it impossible for him even to try to get in touch with Julia and explain what couldn't have been explained, anyway.

A rumbling of thunder broke through his thoughts. The sky in the east hung black with clouds now; and the boat was drifting in steadily toward shore with the wind and waves behind it. Hogan started the motor and came around in a curve to take a direct line toward camp. As he did so, a pale object rose sluggishly on the waves not a hundred yards ahead of him. With a start, he realized it was the upturned bottom of a small boat, and remembered the two fishermen he'd intended warning against the approach of the storm.

The little bay Pete Jeffries had mentioned lay half a mile behind; in his preoccupation he'd passed it without becoming conscious of the fact. There was no immediate reason to assume the drunks had met with an accident; more likely they'd landed and neglected to draw the boat high enough out of the water, so that it drifted off into the lake again on the first eddy of wind. Circling the derelict to make sure it was what it appeared to be, Hogan turned back to pick up the stranded sportsmen and take them to his camp until the storm was over.

When he reached the relatively smooth water of the tree-ringed bay, he throttled the motor and moved in slowly because the bay was shallow and choked with pickerel grass and reeds. There was surprisingly little breeze here; the air seemed almost oppressively hot and still after the free race of wind across the lake. Hogan realized it was darkening rapidly.

He stood up in the boat and stared along the shoreline over the tops of the reeds, wondering where the two had gone—and whether they mightn't have been in their boat anyway when it overturned.

"Anyone around?" he yelled uncertainly.

His voice echoed back out of the creaking shore pines. From somewhere near the end of the bay sounded a series of splashes—probably a big fish flopping about in the reeds. When that stopped, the stillness turned almost tangible; and Hogan drew a quick, deep breath, as if he found breathing difficult here.

Again the splashing in the shallows—closer now. Hogan faced the sound, frowning. The frown became a puzzled stare. That certainly was no fish, but some large animal—a deer, a bear, possibly a moose. The odd thing was that it should be coming *toward* him. . . . Craning his neck, he saw the reed tops bend and shake about a hundred yards away, as if a slow, heavy wave of air were passing through them in his direction. There was nothing else to be seen.

Then the truth flashed on him—a rush of horrified comprehension.

Hogan tumbled back into the stern and threw the motor on, full power. As the boat surged forwards, he swung it around to avoid an impenetrable wall of reeds ahead, and straightened out toward the mouth of the bay. Over the roar of the motor and the rush and hissing of water, he was aware of one other sensation: that shrilling vibration of the nerves, too high to be a sound, which had haunted him in memory all summer. Then there was a great splash behind the boat, shockingly close; another, a third. How near the thing actually came to catching him as he raced through the weedy traps of the bay, he never knew. Only after he was past the first broad patch of open water, did he risk darting a glance back over his shoulder—

He heard someone screaming. Raw, hoarse yells of animal terror. Abruptly, he realized it was himself.

He was in no immediate danger at the time. Greenface had given up the pursuit. It stood, fully visible among the reeds, a hundred yards or so back. The smiling jade-green face was turned toward Hogan, lit up by strange reflections from the stormy sky, and mottled with red streaks and patches he didn't remember seeing there before. The glistening, flowing mass beneath it writhed like a cloak of translucent pythons. It towered in the bay, dwarfing even the trees behind it in its unearthly menace.

It *had* grown again. It stood all of thirty feet tall. . . .

The storm broke before Hogan reached camp and raged on through the night and throughout the next day. Since he would never be able to find the thing in that torrential downpour, he didn't have to decide whether he must try to hunt Greenface down or not. In any case, he told himself, staring out of the lodge windows at the tormented chaos of water and wind, he wouldn't have to go looking for it. It had come back for him, and presently it was going to find its way to the familiar neighborhood of the camp.

There seemed to be a certain justice in that. He'd been the nemesis of the monster as much as it had been his. It had become time finally for the matter to end in one way or another.

Someone had told him—now he thought of it, it must have been Pete Jeffries, plodding up faithfully through the continuing storm one morning with supplies for Hogan—that the two lost sportsmen were considered drowned. Their boat had been discovered; and as soon as the weather made it possible, a search would be made for their bodies. Hogan nodded, saying nothing. Pete studied him as he talked, his broad face growing increasingly worried.

"You shouldn't drink so much, Hogan!" he blurted out suddenly. "It ain't doing you no good! The missis told me you were really keen on Julia. I should've kept my trap shut . . . but you'd have found out, anyhow."

"Sure I would," Hogan said promptly. It hadn't occurred to him that Pete believed he'd shut himself up here to mourn for his lost Julia.

"Me, I didn't marry the girl I was after, neither," Pete told him confidentially. "Course the missis don't know that. Hit me just about like it's hit you. You just gotta snap outta it, see?"

Something moved, off in the grass back of the machine shed. Hogan watched it from the corner of his eye through the window until he was sure it was only a big bush shaking itself in the sleety wind.

"Eh?" he said. "Oh, sure! I'll snap out of it, Pete. Don't you worry."

"Okay." Pete sounded hearty but not quite convinced. "And drive over and see us one of these evenings. It don't do a guy no good to be sitting off here by himself all the time."

Hogan gave his promise. He might, in fact, have been thinking about Julia a good deal. But mostly his mind remained preoccupied with Greenface—and he wasn't touching his store of whiskey these nights. The crisis might come at any time; when it did, he intended to be as ready for it as he could be. Shotgun and deer rifle were loaded and close at hand. The road to town was swamped and impassable now, but as soon as he could use it again, he was going to lay in a stock of dynamite.

Meanwhile, the storm continued day and night, with only occasional brief lulls. Hogan couldn't quite remember finally how long it had been going on; he slept fitfully at night, and a growing bone-deep fatigue gradually blurred the days. But it certainly was as long and bad a wet blow as he'd ever got stuck in. The lake water rolled over the main dock with every wave, and the small dock down near the end cabins had been taken clean away. Trees were down within the confines of the camp, and the ground everywhere was littered with branches.

While this lasted, he didn't expect Greenface to put in an appearance. It, too, was weathering the storm, concealed somewhere in the dense forests along the lake front, in as much shelter as a thing of that size could find, its great head nodding and pulsing slowly as it waited.

By the eighth morning, the storm was ebbing out. In mid-afternoon the wind veered around to the south; shortly before sunset the cloud banks began to dissolve while mists steamed from the lake surface. A few hours earlier, Hogan had worked the car out on the road to see if he could make it to town. After a quarter of a mile, he turned back. The farther stretches of the road were a morass of mud, barricaded here and there by fallen trees. It would be days before anyone could get through.

Near sunset, he went out with an ax and hauled in
a number of dead birches from a windfall over the hill
to the south of the lodge. He felt chilled and heavy
all through, unwilling to exert himself; but his firewood
was running low and had to be replenished. As he came
back to the lodge dragging the last of the birches, he
was startled into a burst of sweat by a pale, featureless face that stared at him out of the evening sky
between the trees. The moon had grown nearly full
in the week it was hidden from sight; and Hogan
remembered then that Greenface was able to walk in
the light of the full moon.

He cast an anxious look overhead. The clouds were
melting toward the horizon in every direction; it probably would be an exceptionally clear night. He stacked
the birch logs to dry in the cellar and piled the wood
he had on hand beside the fireplace in the lodge's
main room. Then he brewed up the last of his coffee and drank it black. A degree of alertness returned
to him.

Afterwards he went about, closing the shutters over
every window except those facing the south meadow.
The tall cottonwoods on the other three sides of the
house should afford a protective screen, but the
meadow would be flooded with moonlight. He tried
to calculate the time the moon should set, and decided
it didn't matter—he'd watch till it had set and then
sleep.

He pulled an armchair up to an open window, from
where, across the sill, he controlled the whole expanse
of open ground over which Greenface could approach.
The rifle lay on the table beside him; the shotgun, in
which he had more faith, lay across his knees. Open
shell boxes and the flashlight were within reach on the
table.

❖   ❖   ❖

With the coming of night, all but the brightest of stars were dimmed in the gray gleaming sky. The moon itself stood out of Hogan's sight above the lodge roof, but he could look across the meadow as far as the machine shed and the icehouse.

He got up twice to replenish the fire which made a warm, reassuring glow on his left side. The second time, he considered replacing the armchair with something less comfortable. The effect of the coffee had begun to wear off; he was becoming thoroughly drowsy. Occasionally, a ripple of apprehension brought him bolt upright, pulses hammering; but the meadow always appeared quiet and unchanged and the night alive only with familiar, heartening sounds: the crickets, a single whippoorwill, and now and then the dark wail of a loon from the outer lake.

Each time, fear wore itself out again; and then, even thinking of Julia, it was hard to stay awake. She was in his mind tonight with almost physical vividness, sitting opposite him at the kitchen table, raking back her unruly hair while she leafed through the mail-order catalogues; or diving off the float he'd anchored beyond the dock, a bathing cap tight around her head and the chin strap framing her beautiful stubborn little face like a picture.

Beautiful but terribly stubborn, Hogan thought, nodding drowsily. Like one evening, when they'd quarreled again and she hid among the empty cabins at the north end of the camp. She wouldn't answer when Hogan began looking for her, and by the time he discovered her, he was worried and angry. So he came walking through the half-dark toward her without a word; and that was one time Julia got a little scared of him. "Now wait, Hogan!" she cried breathlessly. "Listen, Hogan—"

He sat up with a jerky start, her voice still ringing in his mind.

The empty moonlit meadow lay like a great silver carpet before him, infinitely peaceful; even the shrilling of the tireless crickets was withdrawn in the distance. He must have slept for some while, for the shadow of the house formed an inky black square on the ground immediately below the window. The moon was sinking.

Hogan sighed, shifted the gun on his knees, and immediately grew still again. There'd been something . . . and then he heard it clearly: a faint scratching on the outside of the bolted door behind him, and afterwards a long, breathless whimper like the gasp of a creature that has no strength to cry out.

Hogan moistened his lips and sat very quiet. In the next instant, the hair at the back of his neck rose hideously of its own accord.

"Hogan . . . Hogan . . . oh, please! Hogan!"

The toneless cry might have come out of the shadowy room behind him, or over miles of space, but there was no mistaking that voice. Hogan tried to say something, and his lips wouldn't move. His hands lay cold and paralyzed on the shotgun.

"Hogan . . . *please!* Hogan!"

He heard the chair go over with a dim crash behind him. He was moving toward the door in a blundering, dreamlike rush, and then struggling with numb fingers against the stubborn resistance of the bolt.

"That awful thing! That awful thing! Standing there in the meadow! I thought it was a . . . *tree!* I'm not crazy, am I, Hogan?"

The jerky, panicky whispering went on and on, until he stopped it with his mouth on hers and felt her relax in his arms. He'd bolted the door behind them, picked Julia up and carried her to the fireplace couch. But when he tried to put her on it, she clung to him hard, and he settled down with her, instead.

"Easy! Easy!" He murmured the words. "You're not crazy . . . and we'd better not make much noise. How'd you get here? The road's—"

"By boat. I had to find out." Her voice was steadier. She stared up at his face, eyes huge and dark, jerked her head very slightly in the direction of the door. "Was that what—"

"Yes, the same thing. It's a lot bigger now." Greenface must be standing somewhere near the edge of the cottonwoods if she'd seen it in the meadow as she came up from the dock. He went on talking quickly, quietly, explaining it all. Now Julia was here, there was no question of trying to stop the thing with buckshot or rifle slugs. That idea had been some kind of suicidal craziness. But they could get away from it, if they were careful to keep to the shadows.

The look of nightmare grew again in Julia's eyes as she listened, fingers digging painfully into his shoulder. "Hogan," she interrupted, "it's so big—big as the trees, a lot of them!"

He frowned at her uncomprehendingly a moment. Then, as she watched him, Julia's expression changed. He knew it mirrored the change in his own face.

She whispered: "It could come right through the trees!"

Hogan swallowed.

"It could be right outside the house!" Julia's voice wasn't a whisper any more; and he put his hand over her mouth.

"Don't you smell it?" he murmured close to her ear.

It was Greenface, all right; the familiar oily odor was seeping into the air they breathed, growing stronger moment by moment, until it became the smell of some foul tropical swamp, a wet, rank rottenness. Hogan eased Julia off his knees.

"The cellar," he whispered. "Dark—completely dark. No moonlight; nothing. Understand? Get going, but quietly!"

"What are you—"

"I'm putting the fire out first."

"I'll help you!" All Julia's stubbornness seemed concentrated in the three words, and Hogan clenched his teeth against an impulse to slap her face hard. Like a magnified echo of that impulse was the vast soggy blow which smashed at the outer lodge wall above the entrance door.

They stared, motionless. The whole house had shaken. The log walls were strong, but a prolonged tinkling of glass announced that each of the shuttered windows on that side had broken simultaneously. The damn thing, Hogan thought. It's really come for me! If it hits the door—

The ability to move returned to them together. They left the couch in a clumsy, frenzied scramble and reached the head of the cellar stairs not a step apart. A second shattering crash—the telephone leaped from its stand beside Hogan. He checked, hand on the stair railing, looking back.

He couldn't see the entry door from there. The fire roared and danced in the hearth, as if it enjoyed being shaken up so roughly. The head of the eight-point buck had bounced from the wall and lay beside the fire, glass eyes fixed in a red baleful glare on Hogan. Nothing else seemed changed.

"Hogan!" Julia cried from the darkness at the bottom of the stone stairs. He heard her start up again, turned to tell her to wait there.

Then Greenface hit the door.

Wood, glass, metal flew inward together with an indescribable explosive sound. Minor noises followed; then there was stillness again. Hogan heard Julia's choked breathing from the foot of the stairs. Nothing else seemed to stir.

But a cool draft of air was flowing past his face. And now there came heavy scraping noises, a renewed shattering of glass.

"Hogan!" Julia sobbed. "Come down! It'll get in!"

"It can't!" Hogan breathed.

As if in answer, the lodge's foundation seemed to tremble beneath him. Wood splintered ponderously; there was the screech of parting timbers. The shaking continued and spread through the entire building. Just beyond the corner of the wall which shut off Hogan's view of the entry door, something smacked heavily and wetly against the floor. Laboriously, like a floundering whale, Greenface was coming into the lodge.

At the bottom of the stairs, Hogan caught his foot in a roll of wires, and nearly went headlong over Julia. She clung to him, shaking.

"Did you see it?"

"Just a glimpse of its head!" Hogan was steering her by the arm along the dark cellar passage, then around a corner. "Stay there. . . ." He began fumbling with the lock of the cellar exit.

"What will we do?" she asked.

Timbers creaked and groaned overhead, cutting off his reply. For seconds, they stared up through the dark in frozen expectation, each sensing the other's thoughts. Then Julia gave a low, nervous giggle.

"Good thing the floor's double strength!"

"That's the fireplace right above us," Hogan said. I wonder—" He opened the door an inch or two, peered out. "Look over there!"

The dim, shifting light of the fireplace outlined the torn front of the lodge. As they stared, a shadow, huge and formless, blotted out the light. They shrank back.

"Oh, Hogan! It's horrible!"

"All of that," he agreed, with dry lips. "You feel something funny?"

"Feel what?"

He put his fingertips to her temples. "Up there! Sort of buzzing? Like something you can almost hear."

"Oh! Yes, I do! What is it?"

"Something the thing does. But the feeling's usually stronger. It's been out in the cold and rain all week. No sun at all. I should have remembered. It *likes* that fire up there. And it's getting livelier now—that's why we feel the buzz."

"Let's run for it, Hogan! I'm scared to death here! We can make it to the boat."

"We might," Hogan said. "But it won't let us get far. If it hears the outboard start, it can cut us off easily before we're out of the bay."

"Oh, no!" she said, shocked. She hesitated. "But then what can we *do*?"

Hogan said, "Right now it's busy soaking up heat. That gives us a little time. I have an idea. Julia, will you promise that—just once—you'll stay here, keep quiet, and not call after me or do anything else you shouldn't?"

"Why? Where are you going?"

"I won't leave the cellar," Hogan said soothingly. "Look, darling, there's no time to argue. That thing upstairs may decide at any moment to start looking around for us—and going by what it did to the front wall, it can pull the whole lodge apart. . . . Do you promise, or do I lay you out cold?"

"I promise," she said, after a sort of frosty gasp.

Hogan remained busy in the central areas of the cellar for several minutes. When he returned, Julia was still standing beside the exit door where he'd left her, looking out cautiously.

"The thing hasn't moved much," she reported, her tone somewhat subdued. She looked at him in the gloom. "What were you doing?"

"Letting out the kerosene tank—spreading it around."

"I smelled the kerosene." She was silent a moment. "Where are *we* going to be?"

Hogan opened the door a trifle wider, indicated the cabin immediately behind the cottonwood stand. "Over there. If the thing can tell we're around, and I think it can, we should be able to go that far without starting it after us."

Julia didn't answer; and he moved off into the dark again. Presently she saw a pale flare light up the chalked brick wall at the end of the passage, and realized Hogan was holding a match to papers. Kerosene fumes went off with a dim BOO-ROOM! and a glare of yellow light. Other muffled explosions followed in quick succession in various sections of the cellar. Then Hogan stepped out of a door on the passage, closed the door and turned toward her.

"Going up like pine shavings!" he said. "I guess we'd better leave quietly. . . ."

"It looks almost like a man in there, doesn't it, Hogan? Like a huge, sick, horrible old man!"

Julia's whisper was thin and shaky, and Hogan tightened his arms reassuringly about her shoulders. The buzzing sensation in his brain was stronger, rising and falling, as if the energies of the thing that produced it were gathering and ebbing in waves. From the corner of the cabin window, past the trees, they could see the front of the lodge. The frame of the big entry door had been ripped out and timbers above twisted aside, so that a good part of the main room was visible in the dim glow of the fireplace. Greenface filled almost all of that space, a great hunched dark bulk, big head bending and nodding slowly at the fire. In that attitude, there was in fact something vaguely human about it, a nightmarish caricature.

But most of Hogan's attention was fixed on the two cellar windows of the lodge which he could see. Both were alight with the flickering glare of the fires he had set; and smoke curled up beyond the cottonwoods, rising from the far side of the lodge, where he had opened other windows to give draft to the flames. The fire had a voice, a soft growing roar, mingled in his mind with the soundless rasping that told of Greenface's returning vitality.

It was like a race between the two: whether the fire, so carefully placed beneath the supporting sections of the lodge floor, would trap the thing before the heat kindled by the fire increased its alertness to the point where it sensed the danger and escaped. If it did escape—

It happened then, with blinding suddenness.

The thing swung its head around from the fireplace and lunged hugely backward. In a flash, it turned nearly transparent. Julia gave a choked cry. Hogan had told her about that disconcerting ability; but seeing it was another matter.

And as Greenface blurred, the flooring of the main lodge room sagged, splintered, and broke through into the cellar, and the released flames leaped bellowing upwards. For seconds, the vibration in Hogan's mind became a ragged, piercing shriek—became pain, brief and intolerable.

They were out of the cabin by that time, running and stumbling down toward the lake.

❖   ❖   ❖

A boat from the ranger station at the south end of Thursday Lake chugged into the bay forty minutes later, with fire-fighting equipment. Pete Jeffries, tramping through the muddy woods on foot, arrived at about the same time to find out what was happening at Hogan's camp. However, there wasn't really much to be done. The lodge was a raging bonfire, beyond salvage. Hogan pointed out that it wasn't insured, and that he'd intended to have it pulled down and replaced in the near future, anyway. Everything else in the vicinity of the camp was too sodden after a week of rain to be in the least endangered by flying sparks. The fire fighters stood about until the flames settled down to a sullen glow. Then they smothered the glow, and the boat and Pete left. Hogan and Julia had been unable to explain how the fire got started; but, under the circumstances, it hardly seemed to matter. If anybody had been surprised to find Julia Allison here, they didn't mention it. However, there undoubtedly would be a good many comments made in town.

"Your Pa isn't going to like it," Hogan observed, as the sounds of the boat engine faded away on the lake.

"Pa will have to learn to like it!" Julia replied, perhaps a trifle grimly. She studied Hogan a moment. "I thought I was through with you, Hogan!" she said. "But then I had to come back to find out."

"Find out whether I was batty? Can't blame you. There were times these weeks when I wondered myself."

Julia shook her head.

"Whether you were batty or not didn't seem the most important point," she said.

"Then what was?"

She smiled, moved into his arms, snuggled close. There was a lengthy pause.

"What about your engagement in the city?" Hogan asked finally.

Julia looked up at him. "I broke it when I knew I was coming back."

It was still about an hour before dawn. They walked back to the blackened, twisted mess that had been the lodge building, and stood staring at it in silence. Greenface's funeral pyre had been worthy of a Titan.

"Think there might be anything left of it?" Julia asked, in a low voice.

"After that? I doubt it. Anyway, we won't build again till spring. By then, there'll be nothing around we might have to explain, that's for sure. We can winter in town, if you like."

"One of the cabins here will do fine."

Hogan grinned. "Suits me!" He looked at the ruin again. "There was nothing very solid about it, you know. Just a big poisonous mass of jelly from the tropics. Winter would have killed it, anyway. Those red spots I saw on it—it was already beginning to rot. It never really had a chance here."

She glanced at him. "You aren't feeling sorry for the thing?"

"Well, in a way." Hogan kicked a cindered two-by-four apart, and stood there frowning. "It was just a big crazy freak, shooting up all alone in a world where it didn't fit in, and where it could only blunder around and do a lot of damage and die. I wonder how smart it really was and whether it ever understood the fix it was in."

"Quit worrying about it!" Julia ordered.

Hogan grinned down at her. "Okay," he said.

"And kiss me," said Julia.

Rogue Psi

❧

Shortly after noon, a small side door in the faculty restaurant of Cleaver University opened and a man and a woman stepped out into the sunlight of the wide, empty court between the building and the massive white wall opposite it which bordered Cleaver Spaceport. They came unhurriedly across the court towards a transparent gate sealing a tunnel passage in the wall.

As they reached the center of the court, a scanning device in the wall fastened its attention on them, simultaneously checking through a large store of previously registered human images and data associated with these. The image approaching it on the left was that of a slender girl above medium height, age twenty-six, with a burnished pile of hair which varied from chestnut-brown to copper in the sun, eyes which appeared to vary between blue and gray, and an air of composed self-reliance. Her name, the scanner noted among other details, was Arlene Marguerite Rolf. Her occupation: micromachinist. Her status: MAY PASS.

Miss Rolf's companion was in his mid-thirties, big, rawboned and red-haired, with a formidably bulging forehead, eyes set deep under rusty beetle-brows, and a slight but apparently habitual scowl. His name was also on record: Dr. Frank Dean Harding. Occupation: marine geologist. Status—

At that point, there was an odd momentary hesitancy or blurring in the scanner's reactions, though not quite pronounced enough to alert its check-mechanisms. Then it decided: MAY NOT PASS. A large sign appeared promptly in brilliant red light on the glassy surface of the wall door.

WARNING—SOMATIC BARRIERS!
Passage Permitted to Listed Persons Only

The man looked at the sign, remarked dourly, "The welcome mat's out again! Wonder if the monitor in there can identify me as an individual."

"It probably can," Arlene said. "You've been here twice before—"

"Three times," Frank Harding corrected her. "The first occasion was just after I learned you'd taken the veil. Almost two years now, isn't it?" he asked.

"Very nearly. Anyway, you're registered in the university files, and that's the first place that would be checked for an unlisted person who showed up in this court."

Harding glanced over at her. "They're as careful as all that about Lowry's project?"

"You bet they are," Arlene said. "If you weren't in my company, a guard would have showed up by now to inform you you're approaching a restricted area and ask you very politely what your business here was."

Harding grunted. "Big deal. Is someone assigned to follow you around when you get off the project?"

She shrugged. "I doubt it. Why should they bother? I never leave the university grounds, and any secrets should be safe with me here. I'm not exactly the gabby type, and the people who know me seem to be careful not to ask me questions about Ben Lowry or myself anyway." She looked reflective. "You know, I do believe it's been almost six months since anyone has so much as mentioned diex energy in my presence!"

"Isn't the job beginning to look a little old after all this time?" Harding asked.

"Well," Arlene said, "working with Doctor Ben never gets to be boring, but it *is* a rather restrictive situation, of course. It'll come to an end by and by."

Harding glanced at his watch, said, "Drop me a line when that happens, Arlene. By that time, I might be able to afford an expert micromachinist myself."

"In a dome at the bottom of some ocean basin?" Arlene laughed. "Sounds cozy—but that wouldn't be much of an improvement on Cleaver Spaceport, would it? Will you start back to the coast today?"

"If I can still make the afternoon flight." He took her arm. "Come on. I'll see you through the somatic barrier first."

"Why? Do you think it might make a mistake about me and clamp down?"

"It's been known to happen," Harding said gloomily. "And from what I hear, it's one of the less pleasant ways to get killed."

Arlene said comfortably, "There hasn't been an accident of that kind in at least three or four years. The bugs have been very thoroughly worked out of the things. I go in and out here several times a week." She took a small key from her purse, fitted it into a lock at the side of the transparent door, twisted it and withdrew it. The door slid sideways for a distance of three feet and stopped. Arlene Rolf stepped through the opening and turned to face Harding.

"There you are!" she said. "Barely a tingle! If it didn't want to pass me, I'd be lying on the ground knotted up with cramps right now. 'Bye, Frank! See you again in two or three months, maybe?"

Harding nodded. "Sooner if I can arrange it. Goodbye, Arlene."

He stood watching the trim figure walk up the passage beyond the door. As she came to its end, the door slid silently shut again. Arlene looked back and waved at him, then disappeared around the corner.

Dr. Frank Harding thrust his hands into his pockets and started back across the court, scowling absently at nothing.

The living room of the quarters assigned to Dr. Benjamin B. Lowry on Cleaver Spaceport's security island was large and almost luxuriously furnished. In pronounced contrast to the adjoining office and workrooms, it was also as a rule in a state of comfortable disorder. An affinity appeared to exist between the complex and the man who had occupied it for the past two years. Dr. Lowry, leading authority in the rather new field of diex energy, was a large man of careless and comfortable, if not downright slovenly personal habits, while a fiendish precisionist at work.

He was slumped now in an armchair on the end of his spine, fingering his lower lip and staring moodily at the viewphone field which formed a pale-yellow rectangle across the living room's entire south wall, projecting a few inches out into the room. Now and then, his gaze shifted to a narrow, three-foot-long case of polished hardwood on the table beside him. When the phone field turned clear white, Dr. Lowry shoved a pair of rimless glasses back over his nose and sat up expectantly. Then he frowned.

"Now look here, Weldon—!" he began.

Colors had played for an instant over the luminous rectangle of the phone field, resolving themselves into a view of another room. A short, sturdily built man sat at a desk there, wearing a neat business suit. He smiled pleasantly out of the field at Dr. Lowry, said in a casual voice, "Relax, Ben! As far as I'm concerned, this is a command performance. Mr. Green just instructed me to let you know I'd be sitting in when he took your call."

"Mr. Green did *what*?"

The man in the business suit said quickly, "He's coming in now, Ben!" His hand moved on the desk, and he and the room about him faded to a pale, colorless outline in the field. Superimposed on it appeared a third room, from which a man who wore dark glasses looked out at Dr. Lowry.

He nodded, said in a briskly amiable manner, "Dr. Lowry, I received your message just a minute ago. As Colonel Weldon undoubtedly has informed you, I asked him to be present during this discussion. There are certain things to be told you, and the arrangement will save time all around.

"Now, doctor, as I understand it, the situation is this. Your work on the project has advanced satisfactorily up to what has been designated as the Fourth Stage. That is correct, isn't it?"

Dr. Lowry said stiffly, "That is correct, sir. Without the use of a trained telepath it is unlikely that further significant advances can be made. Colonel Weldon, however, has seen fit now to introduce certain new and astonishing conditions. I find these completely unacceptable as they stand and . . ."

"You're entirely justified, Dr. Lowry, in protesting

against an apparently arbitrary act of interference with the work you've carried out so devotedly at the request of your government." One of Mr. Green's better-known characteristics was his ability to interrupt without leaving the impression of having done it. "Now, would it satisfy you to know that Colonel Weldon has been acting throughout as my personal deputy in connection with the project—and that I was aware of the conditions you mention before they were made?"

Dr. Lowry hesitated, said, "I'm afraid not. As a matter of fact, I do know Weldon well enough to take it for granted he wasn't simply being arbitrary. I . . ."

"You feel," said Mr. Green, "that there are certain extraneous considerations involved of which you should have been told?"

Lowry looked at him for a moment. "If the President of the United States," he said drily, "already has made a final decision in the matter, I shall have to accept it."

The image in the phone field said, "I haven't."

"Then," Lowry said, "I feel it would be desirable to let me judge personally whether any such considerations are quite as extraneous as they might appear to be to . . ."

"To anybody who didn't himself plan the diex thought projector, supervise its construction in every detail, and carry out an extensive series of preliminary experiments with it," Mr. Green concluded for him. "Well, yes—you may be right about that, doctor. You are necessarily more aware of the instrument's final potentialities than anyone else could be at present." The image's mouth quirked in the slightest of smiles. "In any event, we want to retain your ungrudging cooperation, so Colonel Weldon is authorized herewith to tell you in as much detail as you feel is necessary what the situation is. And he will do it before any other steps are taken. Perhaps I should warn you that what you learn may not add to your peace of mind. Now, does that settle the matter to your satisfaction, Dr. Lowry?"

Lowry nodded. "Yes, sir, it does. Except for one detail."

"Yes, I see. Weldon, will you kindly cut yourself out of this circuit. I'll call you back in a moment."

Colonel Weldon's room vanished from the phone field. Mr. Green went over to a wall safe, opened it with his back to Dr. Lowry, closed it again and turned holding up a small, brightly polished metal disk.

"I should appreciate it, incidentally," he remarked, "if you would find it convenient to supply me with several more of these devices."

"I'll be very glad to do it, sir," Dr. Lowry told him, "after I've been released from my present assignment."

"Yes . . . you take no more chances than we do." Mr. Green raised his right hand, held the disk facing the phone field. After a moment, the light in Dr. Lowry's living room darkened, turned to a rich, deep purple, gradually lightened again.

Mr. Green took his hand down. "Are you convinced I'm the person I appear to be?"

Lowry nodded. "Yes, sir, I am. To the best of my knowledge, there is no way of duplicating that particular diex effect—as yet."

Arlene Rolf walked rapidly along the passage between the thick inner and outer walls enclosing Cleaver Spaceport. There was no one in sight, and the staccato clicking of her high heels on the light-green marblite paving was the only sound. The area had the overall appearance of a sun-baked, deserted fortress. She reached a double flight of shallow stairs, went up and came out on a wide, bare platform, level with the top of the inner wall.

Cleaver Spaceport lay on her left, a twenty-mile rectangle of softly gleaming marblite absolutely empty except for the narrow white spire of a control tower near the far side. The spaceport's construction had been begun the year Arlene was born, as part of the interplanetary colonization program which a rash of disasters and chronically insufficient funds meanwhile had brought to an almost complete standstill. Cleaver Spaceport remained unfinished; no spaceship had yet lifted from its surface or settled down to it.

Ahead and to Arlene's right, a mile and a half of green lawn stretched away below the platform. Automatic tenders moved slowly across it, about half of them haloed by the rhythmically circling rainbow sprays of their sprinklers. In the two years since Arlene had first seen the lawn, no human being had set foot there. At its far end was a cluster of low, functional buildings. There were people in those buildings ... but not very many people. It was the security island where Dr. Lowry had built the diex projector.

Arlene crossed the platform, passed through the doorless entry of the building beyond it, feeling the tingle of another somatic barrier as she stepped into its shadow. At the end of the short hallway was a narrow door with the words NONSPACE CONDUIT above it. Behind the door was a small, dimly lit cube of a room. Miss Rolf went inside and sat down on one of the six chairs spaced along the walls. After a moment, the door slid quietly shut and the room went dark.

For a period of perhaps a dozen seconds, in complete blackness, Arlene Rolf appeared to herself to have become an awareness so entirely detached from her body that it could experience no physical sensation. Then light reappeared in the room and sensation returned. She stood up, smoothing down her skirt, and discovered, smiling, that she had been holding her breath again. It happened each time she went through the conduit, and no previous degree of determination to breathe normally had any effect at all on that automatic reaction. The door opened and she picked up her purse and went out into a hall which was large, well-lit and quite different in every respect from the one by which she had entered.

In the wall screen across the hall, the image of a uniformed man smiled at her and said, "Dr. Lowry has asked that you go directly to the laboratory on your return, Miss Rolf."

"Thank you, Max," she said. She had never seen Max or one of the other project guards in person, though they must be somewhere in the building. The screen went blank, and she went on down the long, windowless hall, the sound of her steps on the thick carpeting again the only break in the quiet. Now, she thought, it was a little like being in an immaculately clean, well-tended but utterly vacant hotel.

Arlene pressed the buzzer beside the door to Dr. Lowry's quarters and stood waiting. When the door opened, she started forward, then stopped in surprise.

"Why, hello, Colonel Weldon," she said. "I didn't realize you would be on the project today." Her gaze went questioningly past him to Dr. Lowry, who stood in the center of the room, hands shoved deep into his trousers pockets.

Lowry said wryly, "Come in, Arlene. This has been a surprise to me, too, and not a pleasant one. On the basis of orders coming directly from the top—which I have just confirmed, by the way—our schedule here is to be subjected to drastic rearrangements. They include among other matters our suspension as the actual operators of the projector."

"But why that?" she asked startled.

Dr. Lowry shrugged. "Ask Ferris. He just arrived by his personal conduit. He's supposed to explain the matter to us."

Ferris Weldon, locking the door behind Arlene, said smilingly, "And please do give me a chance to do just that now, both of you! Let's sit down as a start. Naturally you're angry ... no one can blame you for it. But I promise to show you the absolute necessity behind this move."

He waited until they were seated, then added, "One reason—though not the only reason—for interrupting your work at this point is to avoid exposing both of you to serious personal danger."

Dr. Lowry stared at him. "And what's that supposed to mean?"

"Ben," Ferris Weldon asked, "what was the stated goal of this project when you undertook it?"

Lowry said stiffly, "To develop a diex-powered instrument which would provide a means of reliable mental communication with any specific individual on Earth."

Weldon shook his head. "No, it wasn't."

Arlene Rolf laughed shortly. "He's right, Ben." She looked at Weldon. "The hypothetical goal of the project was an instrument which would enable your department telepaths to make positive identification of a hypothetical Public Enemy Number One ... the same being described as a 'rogue telepath' with assorted additional qualifications."

Weldon said, "That's a little different, isn't it? Do you recall the other qualifications?"

"Is that important at the moment?" Miss Rolf asked. "Oh, well ... this man is also a dangerous and improbably gifted hypnotist. Disturb him with an ordinary telepathic probe or get physically within a mile or so of him, and he can turn you mentally upside down, and will do it in a flash if it suits his purpose. He's quite ruthless, is supposed to have committed any number of murders. He might as easily be some unknown as a man constantly in the public eye who is keeping his abilities concealed. . . . He impersonates people. . . . He is largely responsible for the fact that in a quarter of a century the interplanetary colonization program literally hasn't got off the ground. . . ."

She added, "That's as much as I remember. There will be further details in the files. Should I dig them out?"

"No," Ferris Weldon said. "You've covered most of it."

Dr. Lowry interrupted irritably, "What's the point of this rigmarole, Weldon? You aren't assuming that either of us has taken your rogue telepath seriously. . . ."

"Why not?"

Lowry shrugged. "Because he is, of course, one of the government's blandly obvious fictions. I've no objection to such fictions when they serve to describe the essential nature of a problem without revealing in so many words what the problem actually is. In this case, the secrecy surrounding the project could have arisen largely from a concern about the reaction in various quarters to an instrument which might be turned into a thought-control device."

Weldon asked, "Do you believe that is the purpose of your projector?"

"If I'd believed it, I would have had nothing to do with it. I happen to have considerable confidence in the essential integrity of our government, if not always in its good sense. But not everyone shares that feeling."

Ferris Weldon lit a cigarette, flicked out the match, said after a moment, "But you didn't buy the fiction?"

"Of course not."

Weldon glanced at Miss Rolf. "You, Arlene?"

She looked uneasy. "I hadn't bought it, no. Perhaps I'm not so sure now—you must have some reason for bringing up the matter here. But several things wouldn't make sense. If . . ."

Dr. Lowry interrupted again. "Here's one question, Weldon. If there did happen to be a rogue telepath around, what interest would he have in sabotaging the colonization program?"

Weldon blew two perfect smoke rings, regarded their ascent with an air of judicious approval. "After you've heard a little more you should be able to answer that question yourself," he said. "It was precisely the problems connected with the program that put us on the rogue's trail. We didn't realize it at the time. Fourteen years ago . . . Have you had occasion to work with DEDCOM, Ben?"

Lowry made a snorting sound. "I've had a number of occasions . . . and made a point of passing them up! If the government is now basing its conclusions on the fantastically unrealistic mishmash of suggestions it's likely to get from a deducting computer . . ."

"Well," Ferris Weldon said deprecatingly, "the government doesn't trust DEDCOM too far, of course. Still, the fact that it is strictly logical, encyclopedically informed and not hampered by common sense has produced surprisingly useful results from time to time.

"Now don't get indignant again, Ben! I assure you I'm not being facetious. The fact is that sixteen years ago the charge that interplanetary colonization was being sabotaged was frequently enough raised. It had that appearance from the outside. Whatever could go wrong had gone wrong. There'd been an unbelievable amount of blundering.

"Nevertheless, all the available evidence indicated that no organized sabotage was involved. There was plenty of voluble opposition to the program, sometimes selfish, sometimes sincere. There were multiple incidents of forgetfulness, bad timing, simple stupidity. After years of false starts, the thing still appeared bogged down in a nightmare of—in the main— honest errors. But expensive ones. The month-by-month cost of continuing reached ridiculous proportions. Then came disasters which wiped out lives by the hundreds. The program's staunchest supporters began to get dubious, to change their minds.

"I couldn't say at the moment which genius in the Department of Special Activities had the notion to feed the colonization problem to DEDCOM. Anyway, it was done, and DEDCOM, after due checking and rumination, not only stated decisively that it *was* a matter of sabotage after all, it further provided us with a remarkably detailed description of the saboteur. . . ."

Arlene Rolf interrupted. "There had been only one saboteur?"

"Only one who knew what he was doing, yes."

"The rogue telepath?" Dr. Lowry asked.

"Who else?"

"Then if the department has had his description . . ."

"Why is he still at large?" Ferris Weldon asked, with a suggestion of grim amusement. "Wait till you hear what it sounded like at the time, Ben! I'll give it to you from memory.

"Arlene has mentioned some of the points. The saboteur, DEDCOM informed us, was, first, a hypnotizing telepath. He could work on his victims from a distance, force them into the decisions and actions he wanted, leave them unaware that their minds had been tampered with, or that anything at all was wrong.

"Next, he was an impersonator, to an extent beyond any ordinary meaning of the word. DEDCOM concluded he must be able to match another human being's appearance so closely that it would deceive his model's most intimate associates. And with the use of these two talents our saboteur had, in ten years, virtually wrecked the colonization program.

"Without any further embellishments, DEDCOM's report of this malevolent superman at loose in our society would have raised official eyebrows everywhere. . . ."

"In particular," Miss Rolf asked, "in the Department of Special Activities?"

"In particular there," Weldon agreed. "The department's experience made the emergence of any human super-talents worth worrying about seem highly improbable. In any event, DEDCOM crowded its luck. It didn't stop at that point. The problems besetting the colonization program were, it stated, by no means the earliest evidence of a rogue telepath in our midst. It listed a string of apparently somewhat comparable situations stretching back through the past three hundred years, and declared unequivocally that in each case the responsible agent had been the same—our present saboteur."

Weldon paused, watched their expressions changing. A sardonic smile touched the corners of his mouth.

"All right," Dr. Lowry said sourly after a moment, "to make the thing even more unlikely, you're saying now that the rogue is immortal."

Weldon shook his head. "I didn't say it . . . and neither, you notice, did DEDCOM. The question of the rogue's actual life span, whatever it may be, was no part of the matter it had been given to investigate. It said only that in various ways he had been interfering with mankind's progress for at least three centuries. But added to the rest of it, that statement was quite enough."

"To accomplish what?"

"What do you think?" Weldon asked. "The report passed eventually through the proper hands, was properly initialed, then filed with DEDCOM's earlier abortions and forgotten. Special Activities continued, by its more realistic standard investigative procedures, to attempt to find out what had bogged down the colonization program. As you're aware, the department didn't make much headway. And neither has the program."

"The last is very apparent," Lowry said, looking puzzled.

"But the fact that you've failed to solve the problem seems a very poor reason to go back now to the theory of a rogue telepath."

Weldon blew out a puff of smoke, said thoughtfully, "That wouldn't have been too logical of us, I agree. But our failure wasn't the reason for reviving DEDCOM's theory."

"Then what was your reason?" Irritation edged Lowry's voice again.

"The unexpected death, five years ago, of one of the world's better-known political figures," Weldon said. "You would recognize the name immediately if I mentioned it. But you will not recognize the circumstances surrounding his death which I am about to relate to you, because the report published at the time was a complete falsehood and omitted everything which might have seemed out of the ordinary. The man actually was the victim of murder. His corpse was found floating in the Atlantic. That it should have been noticed at all was an unlikely coincidence, but the body was fished out and identified. At that point the matter acquired some very improbable aspects because it was well known that this man was still alive and in the best of health at his home in New York.

"It could have been a case of mistaken identification,

but it wasn't. The corpse was the real thing. While this was being definitely established, the man in New York quietly disappeared . . . and now a number of people began to take a different view of DEDCOM's long-buried report of a hypnotizing telepath who could assume the identity of another person convincingly enough to fool even close friends. It was not conclusive evidence, but it did justify a serious inquiry which was promptly attempted."

"Attempted?" Arlene Rolf asked. "What happened?"

"What happened," Weldon said, "was that the rogue declared war on us. A limited war on the human race. A quiet, undercover war for a specific purpose. And that was to choke off any kind of investigation that might endanger him or hamper his activities. The rogue knew he had betrayed himself; and if he hadn't known of it earlier, he learned now about the report DEDCOM had made. Those were matters he couldn't undo. But he could make it very clear that he wanted to be left undisturbed, and that he had methods to enforce his wishes."

Dr. Lowry blinked. "What could one . . ."

"Ben," Ferris Weldon said, "if you'll look back, you'll recall that a little less than five years ago we had . . . packed into the space of a few months . . . a series of the grimmest public disasters on record. These were not due to natural forces—to hurricanes, earthquakes, floods or the like. No, each and every one of them involved, or might have involved, a human agency. They were not inexplicable. Individually, each could be explained only too well by human incompetence, human lunacy or criminal purpose. But—a giant hotel exploded, a city's water supply was poisoned, a liner . . . yes, you remember.

"Now, notice that the rogue did not strike directly at our investigators. He did that on a later occasion and under different circumstances, but not at the time. It indicated that in spite of his immense natural advantages he did not regard himself as invulnerable. And, of course, he had no need to assume personal risks. By the public nonspace and air systems, he would move anywhere on earth within hours; and wherever he went, any human being within the range of his mind became a potential tool. He could order death at will and be at a safe distance when the order was executed. Within ten weeks, he had Special Activities on the ropes. The attempts to identify him were called off. And the abnormal series of disasters promptly ended. The rogue had made his point."

Arlene said soberly, "You say he attacked some of your investigators later on. What was that about?"

"That was a year later," Weldon said. "A kind of stalemate had developed. As you're aware, the few operating telepaths in the government's employment are a daintily handled property. They're never regarded as expendable. It was clear they weren't in the rogue's class, so no immediate attempt was made to use them against him. But meanwhile we'd assembled—almost entirely by inference—a much more detailed picture of this opponent of mankind than DEDCOM had been able to provide. He was a freak in every way. His ability to read other minds and to affect them—an apparent blend of telepathy and irresistible hypnosis—obviously was a much more powerful and definite tool than the unreliable gropings of any ordinary telepath. But there was the curious point that he appeared to be limited— very sharply limited—simply by distance, which to most of our trained telepaths is a meaningless factor, at least this side of interplanetary space. If one stayed beyond his range, the rogue was personally harmless. And if he could be identified from beyond his range, he also could be—and by that time almost immediately would have been—destroyed by mechanical means, without regard for any last-moment havoc he might cause.

"So the first security island was established, guarded against the rogue's approach by atmospheric blocks and sophisticated somatic barriers. Two government telepaths were brought to it and induced to locate him mentally.

"It turned out to be another mistake. If our unfortunate prodigies gained any information about the rogue, they didn't live long enough to tell us what it was. Both committed suicide within seconds of each other."

"The rogue had compelled them to do it?" Arlene asked.

"Of course."

"And was this followed," Dr. Lowry asked, "by another public disaster?"

"No," Weldon said. "The rogue may have considered that unnecessary. After all, he'd made his point again. Sending the best of our game telepaths after him was like setting spaniels on a tiger. Ordinarily, he could reach a telepath's mind only within his own range, like that of any other person. But if they were obliging enough to make contact with him, they would be instantly at his mercy, wherever he might be. We took the hint; the attempt wasn't repeated. Our other telepaths have remained in the seclusion of security islands, and so far the rogue has showed no interest in getting at them there."

Weldon stubbed his cigarette out carefully in the ashtray beside him, added, "You see now, I think, why we feel it is necessary to take extreme precautions in the further handling of your diex projector."

There was silence for some seconds. Then Dr. Lowry said, "Yes, that much has become obvious." He paused, pursing his lips doubtfully, his eyes absent. "All right," he went on. "This has been rather disturbing information, Ferris. But let's look at the thing now.

"We've found that diex energy can be employed to augment the effects of the class of processes commonly referred to as telepathic. The projector operates on that theory. By using it, ordinary mortals like Arlene and myself can duplicate some of the results reportedly achieved by the best-trained telepaths. However, we are restricted in several ways by our personal limitations. We need the location devices to direct the supporting energy to the points of the globe where the experiments are to be carried out. And so far we have not been able to 'read the mind'—to use that very general term—of anyone with whom we are not at least casually acquainted."

Weldon nodded. "I'm aware of that."

"Very well," Lowry said. "The other advantage of the projector over unaided natural telepathy is its dependability. It works as well today as it did yesterday or last week. Until a natural telepath actually has been tested on these instruments, we can't be certain that the diex field will be equally useful to him. But let's assume that it is and that he employs the projector to locate the rogue. It should be very easy for him to do that. But won't that simply—in your phrasing—put him at the rogue's mercy again?"

Weldon hesitated, said, "We think not, Ben. A specialist in these matters could tell you in a good deal more detail about the functional organization in the mind of a natural telepath. But essentially they all retain unconscious safeguards and resistances which limit their telepathic ability but serve to protect them against negative effects. The difference between them and ourselves on that point appears to be mainly one of degree."

Lowry said, "I think I see. The theory is that such

protective processes would be correspondingly strengthened by employing the diex field. . . ."

"That's it," Weldon said. "To carry the analogue I was using a little farther, we might again be sending a spaniel against a tiger. But the spaniel—backed up by the projector—would now be approximately tiger size . . . and tiger-strong. We must assume that the rogue would be far more skilled and deadly in an actual mental struggle, but there should be no struggle. Our telepath's business would be simply to locate his man, identify him, and break away again. During the very few seconds required for that, the diex field should permit him to hold off the rogue's assault."

Dr. Lowry shook his head. "You can't be sure of it, Ferris!" he said. "You can't be sure of it at all."

Weldon smiled. "No, we can't. We don't really know what would happen. But neither, you see, does the rogue."

Lowry said hesitantly, "I'm afraid I don't follow you."

"Ben," Weldon said, "we don't expect your diex projector will ever be put to the use we've been discussing just now. That isn't its purpose."

Lowry looked dumfounded. "Then what is its purpose?"

Arlene Rolf's face had gone pale. "Doctor Ben," she said, "I believe Colonel Weldon is implying that the rogue already knows about the diex projector and what might be attempted with it."

Weldon nodded. "Of course, he knows about it. How many secrets do you think can be kept from a creature who can tap the minds of anybody he encounters? You can take it for granted that he's maintained information sources in every department of the government since the day we became aware of his existence. He knows we're out to get him. And he isn't stupid enough to allow things here to develop to the point where one of our telepaths is actually placed in front of that projector. He can't be sure of what the outcome would be. After all, it might . . . very easily . . . be fatal to him."

Lowry began, "Then I don't . . ." He checked himself, gave Arlene Rolf a bewildered look. "Are *you* still with this madman, Arlene?"

Her smile was twisted. "I'm afraid so! If I am, I don't like the situation at all. Colonel Weldon, have you people planned to use the diex projector as a trap for the rogue?"

"As bait for a trap," Weldon said. "Ben, put yourself in the rogue's place. He regards this entire planet as his property. But now the livestock is aware of him and is restless. On the technological side it is also becoming more clever by the decade—dangerously clever. He can still keep us in our place here, and so far he's succeeded in blocking a major exodus into the solar system where his power would vanish. But can he continue indefinitely? And can he find any enjoyment in being the lord of all Earth when he has to be constantly on guard now against our efforts to get rid of him? He's blocked our first thrusts and showed us that he can make it a very costly business to harass him too seriously. But the situation is as unsatisfactory to him as to us. He needs much more effective methods of control than were required in the past to bring us back to heel."

Lowry said, "And the diex projector . . ."

Weldon nodded. "Of course! The diex projector is the perfect solution to the rogue's problems. The security islands which so far have been our principal form of defense would become meaningless. He could reach any human mind on Earth directly and immediately. Future plots to overthrow him would stand no chance of success.

"The rogue has shown no scientific ability of his own,

and the handful of other men who might be capable at present of constructing a similar instrument have been placed beyond his reach. So he has permitted the development of the projector to continue here, though he could, of course, have put an abrupt stop to it in a number of ways. But you may be sure that he intends to bring the diex projector into his possession before it actually can be used against him."

Arlene said, "And he's assumed to know that the projector is now operational, aside from any faults that might still show up in the tests?"

"Yes," Weldon said.

She went on, "Does the fact that I was allowed to leave the project several times a week—actually whenever I felt like it—have something to do with that?"

Weldon said, "We believe that the rogue has taken advantage rather regularly of that arrangement. After all, there was no more dependable way of informing himself of the exact state of affairs on the project than . . ."

"Than by picking my mind?"

Weldon hesitated, said, "There's no denying that we have placed you both in danger, Arlene. Under the circumstances, we can offer no apology for that. It was a matter of simple necessity."

"I wasn't expecting an apology, Colonel Weldon." Her face was white. "But I'm wondering what the rogue is supposed to attempt now."

"To get possession of the projector?" Weldon hesitated again. "We don't know that exactly. We believe we have considered every possible approach, and whichever he selects, we're prepared to trap him in the process of carrying it out."

Dr. Lowry said, "But he must suspect that you intend to trap him!"

Weldon nodded. "He does, naturally. But he's under

a parallel disadvantage there—he can't be certain what the traps are. You don't realize yet how elaborate our precautionary measures have been." Weldon indicated the small door in the wall beyond Dr. Lowry. "The reason I use only that private conduit to come here is that I haven't stepped off a security island for almost three years! The same has been true of anyone else who had information we had to keep from the rogue . . . including incidentally Mr. Green, whose occasional 'public appearances' during this critical period have been elaborately staged fakes. We communicate only by viewphone; in fact, none of us even knows just where the others are. There is almost no chance that he can do more than guess at the exact nature of our plans."

"And with all that," Lowry said slowly, "you expect he will still go ahead and make a bid for the projector?"

"He will because he must!" Weldon said. "His only alternative would be to destroy this security island with everything on it at the last moment. And that is very unlikely. The rogue's actions show that in spite of his current troubles with us he has a vast contempt for ordinary human beings. Without that feeling, he would never have permitted the diex projector to be completed. So he will come for it—very warily, taking every precaution, but confident of outmaneuvering us at the end."

Arlene asked, "And isn't it possible that he will do just that?"

There was a barely perceptible pause before Weldon replied. "Yes," he said then, "it's possible. It's a small chance—perhaps only a theoretical one. But we're not omniscient, and we may not know quite as much about him as we think. It remains possible."

"Then why take even that risk?" Arlene asked.

"Wouldn't it be better to destroy the projector now—to leave things as they are—rather than offer him a weapon which would reduce us all to helpless chattels again?"

Weldon shook his head. "Arlene, we can't leave things as they are! Neither can the rogue. You know that really—even though you refuse to admit it to yourself at the moment."

"I . . . what do you mean?"

"This year," Weldon said patiently, "we have the diex projector. What will we have five years from now when diex energy has been more fully explored? When the other fields of knowledge that have been opened in recent years begin to expand? We could, perhaps, slow down those processes. We can't stop them. And, at any point, other unpredictable weapons may emerge . . . weapons we might use against the rogue, or that he might use against us.

"No, for both sides the time to act is now, unless we're willing to leave the future to chance. We aren't; and the rogue isn't. We've challenged him to determine whether he or mankind will control this planet, and he's accepted the challenge. It amounts to that. And it's very likely that the outcome will have become apparent not many hours from now."

Arlene shook her head but said nothing. Dr. Lowry asked, "Ferris, exactly what is *our* role in this situation supposed to be?"

"For the next few hours," Weldon said, "you'll be instructing me in the practical details of operating the projector. I've studied your reports very carefully, of course, and I could handle it after a fashion without such help. But that isn't good enough. Because—as the rogue knows very well—we aren't bluffing in the least in this. We're forcing him to take action. If he doesn't"—Weldon nodded at the polished hardwood box on the table before Dr. Lowry—"one of our telepaths presently will be placed before that instrument of yours, and the rogue will face the possibility of being flushed into view. And there is no point on the globe at this moment which is more than a few minutes' flight away from one of our strike groups.

"So he'll take action . . . at the latest as soon as the order is given to move our telepath to the Cleaver Project. But you two won't be here when it happens. You're not needed for that part, and while we've been talking, the main project conduit has been shunted from our university exit here to a security island outside the area. You'll move there directly from the project as soon as you finish checking me out, and you will remain there until Operation Rogue is concluded.

"And now let's get busy! I think it would be best, Ben, if I assumed Arlene's usual role for a start . . . secondary operator . . . and let you go through the regular pattern of contacts while I look on. What do you say?"

Arlene Rolf had taken a chair well back from the table where the two men sat before the diex projector. She realized it had been an attempt to dissociate herself—emotionally as well as physically—from what was being done there, and that the attempt hadn't been at all successful. Her usual composure, based on the awareness of being able to adjust herself efficiently to the necessities of any emergency, was simply gone. The story of the rogue had been sprung on them too abruptly at this last moment. Her mind accepted the concept but hadn't really assimilated it yet. Listening to what Weldon had said, wanting to remain judiciously skeptical but finding herself increasingly unable to disbelieve him—that had been like a slow, continuous shock. She wasn't yet over it. Her thoughts wouldn't follow the lines she set them on but veered off almost incoherently every minute or two. For the first time in her adult life she was badly frightened—made stupid with fear—and finding it something she seemed unable to control at will.

Her gaze shifted back helplessly to the table and to the dull-blue concave viewplate which was the diex projector's central section. Unfolded from its case, the projector was a beautiful machine of spider web angularities lifting from the flat silver slab of its generator to the plate. The blurred shiftings of color and light in the center of the plate were next to meaningless without the diex goggles Dr. Lowry and Weldon had fitted over their heads; but Arlene was familiar enough with the routine test patterns to follow their progress without listening closely to what was said. . . .

She wanted the testing to stop. She felt it was dangerous. Hadn't Weldon said they still couldn't be sure of the actual extent of the rogue's abilities? And mightn't the projector be luring their minds out now into the enemy's territory, drawing his attention to what was being done in this room? There had been seconds when an uncanny certainty had come to her that she could sense the rogue's presence, that he already was cynically aware of what they were attempting, and only biding his time before he interfered. That might be—almost certainly was—superstitious imagining, but the conviction had been strong. Strong enough to leave her trembling.

But there was, of course, exactly nothing she could do or say now to keep them from going on. She remained silent.

So far it had been routine. A standard warm-up. They'd touched Vanderlin in Melbourne, Marie Faber in Seattle. The wash of colors in the viewplate was the reflection of individual sensory impressions riding the diex field. There had been no verbalizing or conscious response from the contacted subjects. That would come later. Dr. Lowry's face was turned momentarily sideways to her, the conical grey lenses of the goggles protruding from beneath his forehead like staring insect eyes.

She realized he must have said something to Weldon just now which she hadn't heard. Weldon's head was nodding in agreement. Dr. Lowry shifted back to the table, said, "Botucato, Brazil—an untried location. How the pinpointing of these random samplings is brought about is of course . . ." His voice dropped to an indistinct murmur as he reached out to the projector again.

Arlene roused herself with an effort partly out of her foggy fears. It was almost like trying to awake from a heavy, uncomfortable sleep. But now there was also some feeling of relief—and angry self-contempt—because obviously while she had been giving in to her emotional reactions, nothing disastrous had in fact occurred! At the table, they'd moved on several steps in the standard testing procedure. She hadn't even been aware of it. She was behaving like a fool!

The sensory color patterns were gone from the viewplate, and now as she looked, the green-patterned white field of the projector's location map appeared there instead. She watched Dr. Lowry's practiced fingers spin the coordinating dials, and layer after layer of the map came surging into view, each a magnified section of the preceding one. There was a faint click. Lowry released the dials, murmured something again, ended more audibly, " . . . twenty-mile radius." The viewplate had gone blank, but Arlene continued to watch it.

The projector was directed now towards a twenty-mile circle at ground level somewhere in Brazil. None of their established contacts were in that area. Nevertheless, something quite definite was occurring. Dr. Lowry had not expected to learn much more about this particular process until a disciplined telepathic mind was operating through the instrument—and perhaps not too much more then. But in some manner the diex energy was now probing the area, and presently it would touch a human mind—sometimes a succession of them, sometimes only one. It was always the lightest of contacts. The subjects remained patently unaware of any unusual experience, and the only thing reflected from them was the familiar generalized flux of sensory impressions.

Arlene Rolf realized she was standing just inside the open records vault of Dr. Lowry's office, with a bundle of files in her arms. On the floor about her was a tumbled disorder of other files, of scattered papers, tapes. She dropped the bundle on the litter, turned back to the door. And only then, with a churning rush of hot terror, came the thought, *What am I doing here? What happened?*

She saw Dr. Lowry appear in the vault door with another pile of papers. He tossed them in carelessly, turned back into the office without glancing in her direction. Arlene found herself walking out after him, her legs carrying her along in dreamlike independence of her will. Lowry was now upending the contents of a drawer to the top of his desk. She tried to scream his name. There was no sound. She saw his face for an instant. He looked thoughtful, absorbed in what he was doing, nothing else. . . .

Then she was walking through the living room, carrying something—the next instant, it seemed, she'd reentered Lowry's office. Nightmarishly, it continued. Blank lapses of awareness followed moments in which her mind swayed in wild terrors while her body moved about, machinelike and competent, piling material from workshop and file cabinets helter-skelter into the records vault. It might have been going on for only three or four minutes or for an hour; her memory was enclosed in splinters of time and reality. But there were moments, too, when her thoughts became lucid and memory returned. . . . Colonel Weldon's broad back as he disappeared through the narrow door in the living room wall into the private conduit entry, the strap of the diex projector case in his right hand; then the door closing behind him. Before that had been an instant when something blazed red in the projector's viewplate on the table, and she'd wondered why neither of the two men sitting before it made any comment—

Then suddenly, in one of the lucid moments, there was time for the stunned thought to form: *So the rogue caught us all!* Weldon's self-confidence and courage, Dr. Lowry's dedicated skill, her own reluctance to be committed to this matter . . . nothing had made the slightest difference. In his own time, the rogue had come quietly through every defense and seized their minds. Weldon was on his way to him now, carrying the diex projector.

And she and Dr. Lowry? They'd been ordered by the rogue to dispose of every scrap of information dealing with the projector's construction, of course! They were doing it. And after they had finished—then what?

Arlene thought she knew when she saw Dr. Lowry close the vault, and unlock and plunge the destruct button beside the door. Everything in there would be annihilated now in ravening white fire. But the two minds which knew the secrets of the projector—

❖   ❖   ❖

She must have made a violent effort to escape, almost overriding the rogue's compulsions. For she found herself in the living room, not ten feet from the door that opened into the outer halls where help might still have been found. But it was as far as she could go; she was already turning away from the door, starting back across the room with the quick, graceful automaton stride over which she had no control. And terror surged up in her again.

As she approached the far wall, she saw Dr. Lowry come out of the passage from the office, smiling absently, blinking at the floor through his glasses. He turned without looking up and walked behind her towards the closed narrow door before Colonel Weldon's nonspace conduit entry.

So it wasn't to be death, Arlene thought, but personal slavery. The rogue still had use for them. They were to follow where Weldon had gone. . . .

Her hand tugged at the door. It wouldn't open.

She wrenched at it violently, savagely, formless panic pounding through her. After a moment, Dr. Lowry began to mutter uneasily, then reached out to help her.

The room seemed suddenly to explode; and for an instant Arlene Rolf felt her mind disintegrating in raging torrents of white light.

She had been looking drowsily for some moments at the lanky, red-headed man who stood, faced away, half across the room before any sort of conscious understanding returned. Then, immediately, everything was there. She went stiff with shock.

Dr. Lowry's living room . . . she in this chair and Dr. Lowry stretched out on the couch. He'd seemed asleep. And standing above him, looking down at him, the familiar rawboned, big figure of Frank Harding. Dr. Frank Harding who had walked up to the Cleaver

Spaceport entry with her today, told her he'd be flying back to the coast.

Frank Harding, the . . .

Arlene slipped quietly out of the chair, moved across the room behind Harding's back, watching him. When he began to turn, she darted off towards the open hall entry.

She heard him make a startled exclamation, come pounding after her. He caught her at the entry, swung her around, holding her wrists. He stared down at her from under the bristling red brows. "What the devil did you think you were doing?"

"You . . . !" Arlene gasped frantically. "You—" What checked her was first the surprise, then the dawning understanding in his face. She stammered, almost dizzy with relief, "I . . . I thought you must be . . ."

Harding shook his head, relaxed his grip on her wrists.

"But I'm not, of course," he said quietly.

"No . . . you're not! You wouldn't have had to . . . chase me if you were, would you?" Her eyes went round in renewed dismay. "But I don't . . . he has the diex projector now!"

Harding shook his head again and took her arm. "No, he doesn't! Now just try to relax a bit, Arlene. We did trap him, you know. It cost quite a few more lives at the end, but we did. So let's go over and sit down. I brought some whisky along . . . figured you two should be able to use a little after everything you've been through."

Arlene sat on the edge of a chair, watching him pour out a glass. A reaction had set in; she felt very weak and shaky now, and she seemed unable to comprehend entirely that the rogue had been caught.

She said, "So you were in on this operation too?"

He glanced around. "Uh-huh . . . Dome at the

bottom of an ocean basin wasn't at all a bad headquarters under the circumstances. What put you and Dr. Ben to sleep was light-shock." He handed her the glass.

"Light-shock?" Arlene repeated.

"Something new," Harding said. "Developed—in another security island project—for the specific purpose of resolving hypnotic compulsions, including the very heavy type implanted by the rogue. He doesn't seem to have been aware of that project, or else he regarded it as one of our less important efforts which he could afford to ignore for the present. Anyway, light-shock does do the job, and very cleanly, though it knocks the patient out for a while in the process. That side effect isn't too desirable, but so far it's been impossible to avoid."

"I see," Arlene said. She took a cautious swallow of the whisky and set the glass down as her eyes began to water.

Frank Harding leaned back against the table and folded his arms. He scowled thoughtfully down at her.

"We managed to get two persons who were suspected of being the rogue's unconscious stooges to the island," he said, "and tried light-shock out on them. It worked and didn't harm them, so we decided to use it here. Lowry will wake up in another hour at the latest and be none the worse. Of course, neither of you will remember what happened while the rogue had you under control, but . . ."

"You're quite wrong about that," Arlene told him. "I don't remember all of it, but I'm still very much aware of perhaps half of what happened—though I'm not sure I wouldn't prefer to forget it. It was like an extremely unpleasant nightmare."

Harding looked surprised. "That's very curious! The other cases reported complete amnesia. Perhaps you . . ."

"You've been under a heavy strain yourself, haven't you, Frank?" she asked.

He hesitated. "I? What makes you think so?"

"You're being rather gabby. It isn't like you."

Harding grunted. "I suppose you're right. This thing's been tense enough. *He* may have enjoyed it—except naturally at the very end. Playing cat and mouse with the whole human race! Well, the mice turned out to be a little too much for him, after all. But of course nothing was certain until that last moment."

"Because none of you could be sure of anyone else?"

"That was it mainly. This was one operation where actually nobody *could* be in charge completely or completely trusted. There were overlaps for everything, and no one knew what all of them were. When Weldon came here today, he turned on a pocket transmitter so that everything that went on while he was being instructed in the use of the diex projector would be monitored outside.

"Outside was also a globescanner which duplicated the activities of the one attached to the projector. We could tell at any moment to which section of Earth the projector's diex field had been directed. That was one of the overlapping precautions. It sounded like a standard check run. There was a little more conversation between Lowry and Weldon than was normal when you were the assistant operator, but that could be expected. There were pauses while the projector was shut down and preparations for the next experiment were made. Normal again. Then, during one of the pauses, we got the signal that someone had just entered Weldon's private nonspace conduit over there from this end. That was *not* normal, and the conduit was immediately sealed off at both exits. One more overlapping precaution, you see . . . and that just happened to be the one that paid off!"

Arlene frowned. "But what did . . ."

"Well," Harding said, "there were still a number of questions to be answered, of course. They had to be answered fast and correctly or the game could be lost. Nobody expected the rogue to show up in person at the Cleaver Project. The whole security island could have been destroyed in an instant; we knew he was aware of that. But he'd obviously made a move of some kind—and we had to assume that the diex projector was now suspended in the conduit.

"But who, or what, was in there with it? The project guards had been withdrawn. There'd been only the three of you on the island. The rogue could have had access to all three at some time or other; and his compulsions—until we found a way to treat them—were good for a lifetime. Any of you might have carried that projector into the conduit to deliver it to him. Or all three might be involved, acting together. If that was the case, the conduit would have to be reopened because the game had to continue. It was the rogue we wanted, not his tools. . . .

"And there *was* the other possibility. You and Dr. Ben are among the rather few human beings on Earth we could be sure were not the rogue, not one of his impersonations. If he'd been capable of building a diex projector, he wouldn't have had to steal one. Colonel Weldon had been with Special Activities for a long time. But he could be an impersonation. In other words, the rogue."

Arlene felt her face go white. "He was!" she said.

"Eh? How do you know?"

"I didn't realize it, but . . . no, go ahead. I'd rather tell you later. "

"What didn't you realize?" Harding persisted.

Arlene said, "I experienced some of his feelings . . . after he was inside the conduit. He knew he'd been trapped!" Her hands were shaking. "I thought they were my own . . . that I . . ." Her voice began to falter.

"Let it go," Harding said, watching her. "It can't have been pleasant."

She shook her head. "I assure you it wasn't!"

"So he could reach you from nonspace!" Harding said. "That was something we didn't know. We suspected we still didn't have the whole picture about the rogue. But he didn't know everything either. He thought his escape route from the project and away through the conduit system was clear. It was a very bold move. If he'd reached any point on Earth where we weren't waiting to destroy him from a distance, he would have needed only a minute or two with the projector to win all the way. Well, that failed. And a very short time later, we knew we had the rogue in the conduit."

"How did you find that out?"

Harding said, "The duplicate global scanner I told you about. After all, the rogue *could* have been Weldon. Aside from you two, he could have been almost anyone involved in the operation. He might have been masquerading as one of our own telepaths! Every location point the diex field turned to during that 'test run' came under instant investigation. We were looking for occurrences which might indicate the rogue had been handling the diex projector.

"The first reports didn't start to come in until after the Weldon imitation had taken the projector into the conduit. But then, in a few minutes, we had plenty! They showed the rogue had tested the projector, knew he could handle it, knew he'd reestablished himself as king of the world—and this time for good! And then he walked off into the conduit with his wonderful stolen weapon. . . ."

Arlene said, "He was trying to get Dr. Ben and me

to open the project exit for him again. We couldn't of course. I never imagined anyone could experience the terror he felt."

"There was some reason for it," Harding said. "Physical action is impossible in nonspace, so he couldn't use the projector. He was helpless while he was in the conduit. And he knew we couldn't compromise when we let him out.

"We switched the conduit exit to a point eight hundred feet above the surface of Cleaver Interplanetary Spaceport—the project he's kept us from completing for the past twenty-odd years—and opened it there. We still weren't completely certain, you know, that the rogue mightn't turn out to be a genuine superman who would whisk himself away and out of our reach just before he hit the marblite paving.

"But he wasn't. . . ."